An Eye for Justice

by Mark Young

Published by Funky Ink Press

ISBN 978-0-9955676-3-4

Prologue

April 9th 1943 – Eastern Poland

The half-starved girl stood on the ramp as the sky above her cried and roiled with dark rolling thunder clouds. She peered around dazedly, her tired eyes moving slowly, searching for her grandfather's familiar face. Her mother and father lay dead in the cattle truck behind her. In her arms she held her baby sister, Helena, who slept on peacefully.

Strands of mist hung in the air as grey shapes flitted amongst those still living from the transport. As her gaze moved out she saw scattered uniformed figures with guns and dogs, and then further out, what looked like the edge of a forest, but then she could see it was just branches threaded through fencing; then there were barracks and a watchtower over a square.

It had seemed silent before, no sound permeating her consciousness, but then it all came rushing in: guttural commands, shouts, whimpers and screams, the thud of a rifle butt against bone. Then they were in the square and she couldn't remember moving, and she clung ever tighter to Helena in her arms who miraculously slept on. And now Grandpa was there as well, stooped over but mentally unbowed, his eyes clear. He handed her his small bundle of possessions and said: 'live, child, live.' Then he began to whisper the prayer for the dead.

A uniformed figure loomed out of the mist screaming at her in a foreign tongue, gesturing that she relinquish the child. She clung tighter to Helena, and as she saw the rifle butt swinging at her she turned her shoulder to protect her sister, and then she was down on the ground, still clinging to the sleeping child. Now another figure was there, tall with epaulets on his shoulders, black aviator goggles and a peaked cap with deaths head insignia. He pulled her up, smiled and spoke in German. He pointed to a building at the side of the square and led them to it; it had a sign on the front saying it was the infirmary.

But inside it was bare apart from a huge pit from which belched smoke and flame. The smell was indescribable. The tall soldier took Grandpa's bundle and opened it. First he removed a rolled up canvas which he unfurled and studied closely. Then he took out the other item, a gold, diamond encrusted pendant. He ran his fingers over it lovingly, admiring the skill of the goldsmith and the beauty of the flashing diamonds.

He seemed to nod to himself and straighten up his posture, his smile still affable. He turned to grandpa and made a small bow and as grandpa smiled in acknowledgement the soldier drew a pistol from his side holster and leisurely shot grandpa in the head, gently pushing him back into the pit of fire. And now the girl could see through the flickering flames that the pit was filled with silent corpses; mostly old men, women and babies, all smoking and burning. She teetered on the edge, ready to fall, but the warm helpless bundle in her arms held her rooted to the spot.

She could see blood had sprayed onto the soldiers aviator goggles. He pulled them off and slowly began to clean them with a handkerchief, quietly humming to himself. Then she saw his eyes and it was the most beautiful thing she had ever seen.

He put the goggles back on, walked over and placed the barrel of the gun to the sleeping child's head. Then he smiled again and fired. She felt the impact and then she was falling back into the abyss.

Chapter One

I still didn't quite know how I'd got myself into it but I wasn't about to complain, not when I'm sitting on a BA flight quaffing Scotch heading for New York City. I was going there on the off chance that a multi-billion dollar corporation was gonna take a meeting with me. Nothing strange in that you might think until you had a look at my credentials, or lack of them. You see these days my legal chops weren't exactly smoking hot, and I was about as far removed from what you might call a big-hitter attorney as you could get. I was plain Jonas Calver, a pretty average criminal lawyer from East London with a law practice that nobody'd ever heard of.

Yeah we had a case, or so they told me, but even to me it sounded pretty thin stuff - an 87 year old client who apparently couldn't remember a damn thing - nada, nothing. And maybe that should have worried me a bit more than it did, or maybe I was just slipping.

And the way we got the case? Flukesville: the client's niece worked for me.

Emma'd tried to run it herself for a while - she was studying to be an attorney at night school - but then when it had got complicated she'd roped me in. And then when it got real complicated she'd said I had to go to New York to meet the defendants, even though we didn't know if they'd take the meeting. And then she played her ace card: if I didn't go she'd look for another job. That was basically code for she would pull the plug on my law firm, because she was the string and glue that bound it all together, and without her, well……

And so here I was, reluctantly eyeing up a three inch thick file of papers she'd handed me about five minutes before departure. It was hard to summon up real enthusiasm but the complimentary scotch helped. I slipped it down the hatch and hunkered down to read.

Three hours later I snapped the file shut and sat for a while staring out of the window at the fluffy white clouds as they zipped by below. Later as we began our descent I looked down and noticed the short note Emma had appended to the back of the file. It reminded me that our client's daughter, Helena, would be arriving in New York to meet me, imminently - she would text me - and finally the note confirmed that Emma would notify me if the defendants were going to take the meeting.

On the 58th floor of the K building on Water Street in the financial district of New York City, Charles Browder IV, general counsel for the Kurrilick Corporation, looked up at the founders son, 45 year old David Milken, and said, 'this is bullshit, yes?'

Browder tossed the letter he had been reading onto the massive oaken desk top and drew the bifocals off the end of his nose, then looked down at the letter again. It was from Jonas Calver Associates

LLP, a small obscure London law firm, and the letter was signed by a paralegal called Emma Calthorp.

Milken shrugged, unconcerned. 'We thought it was done, Charlie, but maybe it ain't. New kids on the block. Meet the new boss, same as the old boss,' he purred. Milken was fond of quoting lines from old rock songs whenever he could.

'So what do you want to do about it, boss?' Browder asked, moving to place the letter back in his folder.

'Nothing, yet,' Milken said, turning to look out of the grand bank of office windows at the skyscrapers that surrounded them. 'Let 'em sweat it while we do some digging. Schmidt's on it. Then maybe we'll take the meeting.'

Browder looked surprised for a millisecond, then his inscrutable lawyer look shuttered back down over his face like the drop hatch coming down on a rabbit hutch.

After a sleepless night in a midtown hotel I got a text that my clients daughter, Helena was on her way, so I said I'd meet her in the hotel bar mid-morning. As I waited, sipping orange juice, my mind drifted back, fastening onto a subject that lately I couldn't seem to let go of: Carmen, my wife.

She'd said the separation would be temporary, so I could get my head together, but I knew she wouldn't be coming back any time soon. But then I guess waking up with my hands around her throat wasn't the best way to make a marriage work. I'd started to black-out and that throttling incident really broke the camels back. She'd called the cops, but we'd managed to smooth things over for a while, but I think I had scared her, and that first small fissure soon turned into a crack. And now I couldn't stop thinking about her, going over it all in my head, again and again.

Emma'd told me get my act together or I could kiss Carmen goodbye for good. Pretty sound advice I suppose but not much help to me stuck thousands of miles away in America. I checked my watch again whilst mulling on the vicissitudes of romantic longing, but also thanking the fates that had endowed me withe one valuable skill that hadn't deserted me: the ability to compartmentalise. So that's what I tried to do. Shove my problems with Carmen into a box marked 'later', and then start trying to think about Helena Palmer.

I ran through what I knew about her, which wasn't much. She was the 49 year old daughter of our client, Hannah Palmer, née Cohen, who was 87. As I happened to glance up I saw the bartender whispering to a rather attractive looking woman and pointing over at me, and a few moments later she stood at my table, looking down at me with a shy smile.

She took a seat and then there was a pause whilst we waited for the waiter to bring her coffee. I cast a look at her; pretty, milky skin with freckles, grey eyes and copper coloured hair, maybe looking younger than her 49 years; maybe not; who knew these days.

After a few stilted pleasantries she tapped her smart phone off and turned it face down on the table, and said, 'so tell me, Mr Calver, what d'you make of mums case? 'Cause frankly, what I know about the law you could print on the head of a pin.'

She sounded slightly nervous, and maybe she was still grieving.

'I was sorry to hear about your brother,' I said, subtly trying to divert the conversation away from case detail. 'Were you close?'

She snorted and almost laughed. 'God, no. Not for years. We may have been twins but we were strangers,' she said, sipping some coffee and looking pensive. 'They're hinting it was suicide, which is bullshit. Can't get my head around it.'

She looked like she wanted to talk, so I decided not to interrupt. I sat back and waited.

'I guess you probably know that brother John had been handling the case for mum with the US attorneys, and I basically had nothing to do with it. Then John died, and that's when mum turned to me and cousin Emma to sort it out. John was the one who started it all, and then pushed it. I don't think mum was ever very keen, mostly because she couldn't really remember anything, and from what I gathered, didn't really want to. I didn't speak to John because of our estrangement and only heard odd snippets about the case, which I think had been going on for around three years and not really getting anywhere. But then a few months ago they got the offer of $2.5 million to settle it with no admissions of liability, and mum said take it - she'd had enough, and even her US attorneys said settle as they were adamant she couldn't prove ownership.'

I watched her for a beat. Her eyes were turned inwards and she was biting her lip. 'But,' I chipped in, guessing it had got to the stage where she needed a nudge.

'But, John didn't want to settle. He said they'd go to US$5 million. I think just before he died he spoke to the defendant's lawyer, Browder I think his name was, over the phone, probably trying to be clever, hinting a deal could be done at a higher price and he would persuade mum to accept it. But I don't think it came to anything because he died. It all seems a bit up in the air, and maybe they're as confused as we are, so I guess thats why we're here, to clarify it. Do I have that about right?' she said, looking at me with a wan smile.

'On the nail, and you're doing beautifully. Say, maybe you should come work for me,' I quipped, but she didn't smile. 'The thing is, Helena, you're right,' I said, turning serious again. 'There was an offer on the table of US$ 2.5 million, and we thought it was simple. Did Hannah want to accept it, or not, but then they went quiet, John died, and now we don't know what's happening. They don't respond to any approaches and for all we know, the offers off the table. Hence Emma suggesting a meeting which we're still waiting on. Oh, and those US attorneys she was using seem useless. I can't get a response from them either. You call, they say they'll get back to you, but they never do?'

Helena frowned. 'It's funny. Mum was so clear she wanted to settle, but then with John, I don't know. She said we should decide what to do, and she will go with it. I know that's not much help.'

'What do you think, Helena?'

'I think losing John crushed her. If we go on with the case she'll have to dig up stuff that's probably better staying buried. But,' she said with a quick smile and glance at me, 'what d'you think – you're the lawyer.'

As I pondered that one, the one that no lawyer ever really wants to answer, I got a reprieve, my cellphone vibrating on the table with an incoming text from Emma. 'Saved by the bell,' I murmured as I looked down and read it. 'Whatever I think, Helena,' I said, tapping the screen, 'K Corp want the meeting.' I handed her the phone so she could read the text, and then I added, 'you've come all this way, so lets go see them, see what we can shake loose. Then we can decide. After all, you've got nothing to lose.'

As it turned out, I couldn't have been more wrong.

Chapter Two

As our cab approached K Tower the traffic was snarled up, engines idling, vehicles crawling, making the city feel like a growling beast. I didn't think it would do our credibility much good to turn up late so we got out the cab and walked the last bit down the sidewalk, trying not to sniff the engine fumes.

Then we were in the supercharged lift, gliding up the slick sleek building. Even the elevator looked like it was fitted out in gold leaf. I felt shaky and I needed a drink. I took a peek at Helena; she looked apprehensive, maybe wondering what the hell she was doing coming into a place like this with just a guy like me.

In another part of the building, in a hidden observation hub, John Schmidt, K Corp's head of security stood and watched the banks of flat screens as they flickered around him. They showed interior views from all over the building, including the restrooms. He listened as information came in through his earpiece, his eyes lazily traversing the imagery.

Schmidt wasn't tall but you'd never call him small either. He was built like a bulldog with a face to go with it, all swarthy harsh planes riven over with pockmarks from old acne scars. Growing up in Saudi Arabia with a native mother and a sadistic German father hadn't been kind to Schmidt, but it had given him certain skills; an uncommon low cunning and a penchant for explosive violence.

Now he turned and glanced over at the man sitting to his right in a high-tech wheelchair. The man was clearly old and yet still seemed to exude a sense of authority. He had fine, short blonde hair cut in a military style and his one grey eye gleamed with intelligence and vigour. He sat ramrod straight, the black patch covering his other eye giving him a rakish look.

At the back of the hub, David Milken stood leaning against the wall sipping his coffee and listening to soft rock through an elaborate audio head rig.

Schmidt tilted his head to a crackling sound from his earpiece, listened and grunted. He nodded at the old man, then picked up a remote control and pointed it at a large central screen affixed to the wall at shoulder height. He pressed a button and an empty conference room materialised on the screen and then the door opened into it.

As we took our seats around a large mahogany table I studied Charles Browder. In house counsel are a strange breed of lawyer; usually fuck-ups who can't cut it in private practice, so they become kept men with one client they don't have to bust a gut to keep. Browder had that kind of washed out pseudo distinguished look that every lawyer on Wall

Street seemed to have. Cadaver like craggy face with a shock of spiky grey hair sprouting out the top of his head, but his suit looked cheap.

He noticed me looking at a camera that was perched up in the corner of the room. 'Hope you don't mind,' he said. 'A precautionary safeguard, for both sides.'

'Not at all. We've got nothing to hide,' I said.

'Good. So lets cut to the chase shall we?' he said. 'We thought we had a deal. $2.5 million. We were expecting to receive heads of agreement for signature from you, but we got nothing. So, Mr Calver, simple question: why exactly are we here? We appreciate that you and Miss Palmer are new to the case and are perhaps feeling your way in, after the sad and tragic death of John Palmer, but what exactly has changed?'

He paused to watch me, assessing the effect of his words. Maybe he was shrewder than he looked. He didn't know it, but like always, I was trying to wing it, feel things out without doing too much work; laziness I guess you'd call it, and maybe he'd sussed me out already. Maybe he'd even divined that I hadn't wanted the case in the first place because I was so consumed with sadness over Carmen that it was hard to care about anything else, and I was only there because Emma had press-ganged me into it. I was already floundering, struggling to come up with something to say, to move it forward, and he seemed to have sensed it.

As the silence stretched out he seemed to nod to himself with satisfaction as if my lack of response confirmed his view. He said, 'perhaps if I were to elucidate on where we are right now, given that you don't seem to know, it might help, yes?'

He didn't wait for an answer, which was fine with me.

'Some three years ago, in a premature and wholly misconceived action, your client, Hannah Palmer, issued a claim in the Southern District Court here in New York City, against K Corp, its chairman Angel Milken, its CEO David Milken and his wife Kendra. Palmer's action alleges ownership and return of a distinctive gold and diamond pendant with matching broach, which she alleges went missing, probably in Poland sometime in 1943. Apparently other things went missing as well, but it is the pendant and broach that she seeks return of - or damages in lieu of their return. She says the jewellery holds huge sentimental significance for her, because of its history.'

As Browder paused to take a sip from a glass of water, I glanced sideways at Helena - she looked okay now, more relaxed, listening carefully. Browder continued. 'But now it gets a bit tricky, because we're getting into the realms of evidence, and your client, Mr Calver. No offence,' he said, nodding at Helena, 'doesn't seem to have any. Or none that would stand up in court. In her depositions Hannah Palmer tells us that three years ago she happened to be watching a US episode of the popular TV series, *Lives of the Rich and Famous*, when she alleges she positively identified the missing pendant and broach. During a 59 second segment of the program, Kendra Milken, wife of the current CEO of K Corp, can be seen wearing the missing jewellery. In response to an admiring query from the presenter, Kendra says, "yes, they are an original matching set, gold with inlaid diamonds, very old and currently worth around 5 million dollars,"' Browder said, reading the quote from notes on a tablet he was scrolling through as he spoke.

He looked up. 'How am I doing so far, Mr Calver?' he asked, cocky as hell.

I just looked at him. He smiled, and continued. 'Now, when we served interrogatories on your client. Those are formal written questions, Ms Palmer,' he said with a nod at Helena. 'The court allows us to serve them on the plaintiff and she is required to answer them, and answer them she did. One of her quite extraordinary replies was that she currently had no memory of the circumstances of how or even where this jewellery allegedly went missing. She suggests that she and her family were deported from Holland by the Nazi's in 1943, and that's it, that's the extent of her memory. She thinks they probably ended up in Poland, but can't be sure. To repeat - and I guess you'll know how well this goes down in a court room,' he said looking at me with a meaningful smile - 'she can't remember.'

He glanced at each of us in turn, enjoying my frown and Helena's look of dismay. 'Now,' he continued, 'if all that wasn't enough, here's the rub: we say she can't even prove ownership of the jewellery, and that's fatal in the state of New York. Hell, its fatal in every common law jurisdiction on the planet. You want it back, you gotta prove you own it; and we say she can't. And if you want more, we can give you more; we can prove that Angel Milken, founder of K Corp, legitimately purchased the jewellery from a licensed dealer in Munich in 1953.'

Now Browder sat back, satisfied. Even with my sketchy knowledge of our case I knew he'd just delivered a devastating critique, and what made it worse was that he hadn't needed to exaggerate. Now he sat there watching us, supremely confident, waiting for my comeback, but I didn't have one; essentially I mostly agreed with him. I could feel Helena's eyes on me, and I sensed her confidence starting to drain away as she waited in vain for me to say something that suggested I had the slightest grip on the case.

'So tell me, Browder,' I finally said. '*If* everything is as you say, why are you so desperate to settle?' Then I sat back too, to study my fingernails.

The room went quiet. Browder sat, no change in his expression apart from the involuntary flicking of his eyes up at the camera perched above us. I guessed there was an audience out there somewhere.

'Okay, Mr Calver, we're both lawyers, so I'll humour you,' Browder said, leaning forward in his chair, smirk gone. 'You know the score, its cheaper for us to settle now than go to trial even though we know we'd win. Yeah, there's an offer on the table, 2.5 million US, but all it signifies is the economic reality of the situation; it says nothing to the strength of your client's case, which, without wishing to labour the point, is hopeless. But get this, the offer is strictly time limited now. You got about 8 hours left to accept, failing which we're withdrawing it, and then we'll go to trial, and we'll bury you. And by the way, Calver, I'm sure you have exhaustively gone over the downside of this case with your client, but it might be worth reminding her: if she loses at trial, and she will, we'll get our costs, which are huge, and that, my friend, will bankrupt her, because we will go after every cent. Incidentally, you seen this?' he said, sliding a document across the table.

It was a notification from Hannah's US attorneys filing notice they were no longer acting for her and terminating their retainer. Without thinking, I slid it across to Helena, trying not to show anything on my face.

'What's this?' she asked.

Browder smiled, picking up on the fact we hadn't known about it. 'That, my dear, is your US attorneys throwing in the towel.'

'What does it mean?' she asked.

'We'll talk about it later,' I said, trying to shut her down.

But Browder was enjoying himself now. He said, 'what it means, my dear, is that even your own US attorneys have lost confidence in your case, but don't worry, you still have Mr Calver's expertise to protect you.'

I could feel my face flushing as Browder's heavy sarcasm, on top of his forensic dismantling of our case, finally began to get to me. Time to fly a kite, and if I needed to make stuff up to get it soaring away, no worries. 'I'll tell you what, Browder,' I said, straightening up in my chair and looking him in the eye. 'How about we forget about your pathetic offer, which by the way works out at about 50% of fair value, and instead, we'll play a game. Its a game called, what if?'

Browder sighed theatrically. 'What if what, Mr Calver? This is getting tedious and I'm sure your client has better things to do,' he said dismissively.

'What if—' I started to say, but was interrupted by the door opening.

I recognised the guy coming through immediately, his face was all over the business pages, and sometimes the society columns as well.

'I'm David Milken, Mr Calver,' he said, holding his hand out to me, but focusing his attention on Helena. He looked like every other fortune five hundred CEO I'd ever seen; wannabe alpha male with an expensive suit and a fake tan, but this guys eyes had a kind of unnerving blandness about them. As we shook he surprised me by not trying to cripple my hand, then he took a seat beside Browder. He leaned forward and locked his eyes on mine. 'Sorry to interrupt, but I've been watching the feed, and I want to play Mr Calver's game too,' he said, blank, dead smile. 'What if what, Mr Calver?

It was my turn to smile, my kite was about to soar. 'What if Hannah Palmer has started to remember,' I said slowly, letting my smile hang there for a beat, then pushing it some more. 'What if its…. how can I describe it? Imagine a dam,' I said, leaning back in my chair and sketching something out in the air with my hands. 'A dam with a tiny hole in it, but each day a few pebbles, a few small pieces of concrete wash away. Eventually, if nothing is done, we all know what happens. We get a raging torrent. In this case, a raging torrent of memories, and I'm guessing you guys are not going to want to go anywhere near where that might take us.'

Milken turned to Helena, ignoring me. 'Miss Palmer,' he said. 'We've extended every courtesy to you by agreeing to meet, and we've answered your questions, but apparently that's not enough for Mr Calver here, although I get the impression you are more sympathetic. You know,' Milken said, his voice softening and his face taking on a sympathetic sheen, 'maybe it would help if I could talk to your mother face to face, in person and persuade her she's mistaken. I mean,' he said, upping the wattage of his smile, shooting for sincerity, 'where is she now? We can set up a meet real quick and sort this?'

Helena smiled. 'She's in—'

I gripped her leg sharply under the table. 'Hannah is being well looked after – we'll let you know if she wants to talk,' I said.

I watched Milken struggle to keep his anger under wraps. I guessed he was a guy who didn't do rejection well. He stood up. 'We're done here, Charlie,' he said glancing at Browder, words clipped.

Browder was standing now as well, collecting up his papers. He said, 'offer of 2.5 Mill. expires at midnight. Last chance. If we hear nothing back from you, I hope you've got your ducks lined up for Monday morning…'

'Monday morning……?' I said. 'What d'you mean?'

'I guess you haven't studied the court papers too closely, right? That's when this case is listed to start,' he said, turning to smile at Helena. 'You really want to go to trial with this clown? He doesn't even know your mothers case is due to start in 3 days time.'

I said, 'we've had no notice of trial dates.'

'Well you wouldn't,' Browder said patiently, as if speaking to a child. 'This was agreed with John months ago at the last pre-trial hearing, to give time for settlement talks. Judge insisted we actually list the trial start date, to concentrate our minds on settlement, and stop us dicking around. Mind you, when we agreed it, no one thought you would be reckless enough to take it to trial, but its your funeral.'

'Yeah, its your funeral,' Milken echoed him, looking hard at

Helena and adding, 'and so soon after your brothers. How about that?'

No one answered. Then we left.

Later after we got back to the hotel I ordered up some room service, simple steaks. They came up good and bloody, like only the Americans seem to know how to do. Then we sat around and talked. Helena sipped red wine as I took occasional shots from a bottle of spring water. My first impression had been that she was pretty buttoned up, but now she was hanging loose, probably a combination of wine, different time zone and pent up emotion. As I listened to her I couldn't help my eyes sliding unerringly to the half full glass in her hand.

'Boy, have you got it bad,' she said. 'Why don't you have one?'

'Better not,' I said, then, 'Anyway, you got a decision to make. What about their offer?'

She giggled, the wine starting to kick in. 'We got till midnight,' she said, taking another sip. Then, sombre, 'that Milken guy is one scary character. You see his face when you were winding him up about mum remembering? Boy, what a crock that was, but he looked like he'd seen a ghost.'

'Yeah, I did see, so the real question becomes: why? Why would they worry? And what Browder said about settling for economic reasons is true. Big corporations get rid of low level litigation like this all the time, even when they hold all the cards, because it works out cheaper. So the offer doesn't really mean shit.'

'2.5 million dollars is low level?'

'It is to them; its peanuts, small change. K Corp, on current stock prices on the Dow, is worth around sixteen billion dollars.'

Helena whistled. I reached over and topped her glass up. There were things going on in this case, under the surface, that I really couldn't get a handle on. So I needed to try change that, and I guessed a good place to start would be the person at the centre of it all. 'Tell me a a bit about Hannah,' I said. 'Back in the day, she must have been quite a woman.'

A shadow crossed her face. 'She was, is….'

'But?'

'But, nothing. She's my mother, and I love her, of course – but she can be difficult, you know, hard, unyielding'

'I guess you'd have to be to endure what she did.' I said, thinking back over the story, albeit sketchy, I had read in Emma's briefing notes. 'How did she actually get away from all the chaos of the war, and then to Britain,' I asked.

'You know, for years, I knew nothing about mums history, where she came from, all that,' Helena said, a kind of puzzled look on her face. 'Its taken a long time to get even the little we now have. Partly I guess because she'd either blocked it out or wouldn't or couldn't remember. Then she saw that ridiculous TV program with what she certainly genuinely believed to be the long lost family heirloom, and it kind of opened the door of memory, just ajar, and I don't know whether that's been a good or a bad thing. Since then little bits and pieces have been coming back to her, and maybe one day we'll get it all. So far we've got her family deported from Holland, and then nothing. She can't remember anything else. Nothing until she's liberated, living in the forrest with Partisans in 1945 from where she finally makes her way to Britain, marries, and me and John turn up.'

She looked away towards the window and the lights from the city below were reflected onto her face. She looked sad and her eyes seemed to have lost their lustre.

'What?' I asked.

'Oh, I was just thinking about John,' she said.

I sighed.'Why don't you tell me what happened?'

She looked down into her glass, eyes hooded, then she started to speak in a kind of dull, matter of fact monotone. 'They say he drove his car into the harbour. Take your pick; accidental death or suicide. It was a five year old Lincoln, and the brakes were patchy, but not enough to fail unless you were doing a hundred and twenty, and they reckon he was doing about forty. There were no marks on the body apart from a bump on the forehead from the steering wheel, and there was no airbag until it hit the water, so no earlier impact. His clothing, as well as water, had traces of whiskey in it and there was a large broken bottle on the floor of the car. There was alcohol in his blood stream, and barbiturates.'

She had delivered her words in a flat unemotional tone, and her face looked troubled, as if she was trying to understand something, grasping for something, but it wouldn't quite come.

'But something doesn't sit right with you?'

'Yeah,' she said slowly. 'John didn't drink.'

I felt a far away alarm bell start to ring in my head, but only fools jump to hasty conclusions. 'Well, maybe he'd started to drink, or he did drink, just for this. It happens with suicides, for courage, or whatever, to deaden the pain.'

'No, not John,' she said firmly. 'He got drunk once when he was ten years old, broke into dads drinks cabinet. I think they had to pump his stomach, and he was so sick, he never touched alcohol after that, never. Drugs, yeah, maybe, recreational, occasionally; nothing heavy.'

Our eyes met and held for a moment. Then she looked down at the table top, looking like she was in a trance, eyes unseeing. I was still unnerved by her comments about John's death. We both sat for a while, silent, but it was a comfortable, companionable kind of silence. It seemed natural when I lifted the bottle and poured a generous shot of red wine into my glass and took a long, deep pull. Helena watched me, eyes smoky, distant, non-judgemental.

'What about the offer?' I finally jogged her, pulling her back to the now. I knocked back another slug, feeling more relaxed with each mouthful, but Helena just looked more mournful.

After a moment she murmured, 'fuckem.' Then repeated it louder, and then she burped. She turned to me and our eyes met, and she said, 'lets take them to trial, Jonas, for John, and for mum. I don't care if we do lose.' Then she stood up unsteadily and started towards the door. 'Look I……. I better go…… back to my room and get some sleep,' she said. I got up and followed her to the door.

Close up she seemed preoccupied, conflicted, a sad smile playing on her lips. I felt light headed. I stumbled a bit as I leant up to kiss her goodnight. She looked into my eyes; all I could see was loneliness and vulnerability. I put my arms around her and she turned her lips up to mine, and it just seemed natural, a long lingering kiss.

24

Chapter Three

At first I thought it was a dream, loud banging and buzzing sounds echoing around inside my head, then insistent calling, coming from a long way off. Then I opened my eyes. At first I couldn't remember anything, then it started to come back, and then it turned into a torrent of flashing images: Helena talking, sad, then happy, and then making love, arching her body against mine, then later, whispering softly and then leaving, going back to her room to sleep.

I looked around; some of my clothing was strewn across the floor, and on the sideboard were three empty wine bottles standing like sentinels, judging me. As my eyes slowly traversed the room, I felt uneasy; something was missing but I couldn't put my finger on it. Then something else registered; someone was getting pretty pissed outside, banging and pressing on the buzzer. I got up gingerly and went over, pulled the door open and stood dumbly trying to rub the sleep from my eyes.

'NYPD. Detective Daly,' the guy standing there said, flicking a badge at me. He was big, athletic and the suit looked good, but the eyes were cold and suspicious. He came into the room leaving the door open, a patrolman standing outside. 'Better wake up, buddy,' he said. 'You Jonas Calver?'

'Yeah. What time is it?

'Its gone eleven. D'you know a Helena Palmer, guest here, room 202?'

'Yeah. I do. She's my client,' I said, still trying to gather myself together. Then, more calmly, 'look what's this about? I mean, I spent the evening with her?'

'Yeah, we know,' Daly said, looking me over some more, his eyes narrowing as he took in my state - bleary eyes, unshaven, coming out of a drunk. Then he said, 'about an hour and a half ago, Helena Palmer's body was found, strangled.'

He kept his eyes on me, steady and unmoving, watching me carefully for a reaction. I didn't give him one, just stopping myself from swaying with a superhuman effort, just standing there looking back at him, my face blank.

'Any comment? You seem calm,' he said, still watching.

I looked back at him and years of experience told me he had something, so I waited. Never show your hand, and there would be no point doing the histrionics bit, because Daly looked ice cold.

I watched his eyes change subtly as he got the fact I wasn't going to bite. He continued, 'we've been looking at the Hotels CCTV while you've been sleeping it off. Know what it shows?'

'Nope,' I said.

'You. That's what it shows. You and only you, going in and out of her room at the time she was murdered. No one else.'

I finally found my voice. 'You're kidding me, right? This is a joke? A set up.'

'You think so?' he said with a grim smile, turning his face full on me. He looked at me as if weighing me up some more, but I knew he'd already decided. He said, 'I'm arresting you on suspicion of the murder of Helena Palmer. You have the right to remain silent. Anything you say can and will be used against you in a court……………'

I stopped listening; it was the Miranda warning, equivalent to the UK caution given on arrest. My mind was reeling, and a delayed reaction was setting in. 'I didn't kill her,' I said, but my voice sounded weak and unconvincing, and the cops weren't listening anymore.

'……you have the right to an attorney. If you cannot afford an attorney, one will be appointed for you,' Daly concluded. He nodded to the patrolman who had now joined us in the room. 'Cuff him.'

After they got me down to the street I sat in the back of a squad car. My mind was sluggish from the booze and I couldn't seem to concentrate. Daly didn't seem like he wanted to talk. I guessed he had a problem with drunks, but then he probably didn't like killers much either. But then he leaned back over the seat and said casually, 'you happen to own a green silk tie by Drake's of London?'

In my banging head the question seemed surreal. I thought about my clothing strewn across the floor of the hotel room. Maybe there was a cat burglar doing the rounds, stealing guests clothing? I felt like laughing. 'You're kidding, right? Yeah, I do. So what?'

'It was found pulled tight around the vic's neck,' he said. He turned back to stare out the window, and I knew he was smiling.

As I tried to get my head around that, it suddenly dawned on me what had been missing from the room. Before Helena and I had ordered up room service, I had put all Hannah's case notes, statements, tapes and depositions on a side table. I rebooted in my mind images of the room from when I'd woken up, then panned around, over the clothing strewn floor, the bed, table and chairs - nothing. The stuff was gone.

At the precinct house they processed me and didn't bother using kid gloves, but by then I was in a kind of lockdown trance, so I went with the flow, head down and mouth shut, except to give them the basics. Until I could figure out what the hell had happened, that seemed like the best option. I knew US cops were trigger happy and aggressive, but it was still a culture shock to get pushed around like that. They took all my stuff, wallet and cell phone then rough-housed me through a body search, fingerprinting and mug shot.

Then they sat me down in a bare room, kind of interrogation cell, and left me to stew. I stared at the walls, trying not to scream and tear my hair out. Twenty minutes later Daly was back. He sat and kind of sprawled in the chair across from me, and said, 'so, you want to tell me what happened in there?'

He watched me with a kind of lazy look, eyes half-lidded, as if he wasn't too bothered whether I spoke to him or not. I waited.

'Look, Calver,' he finally said, 'you'll be arraigned shortly and the judge'll want to talk bail. I hear you're a lawyer back in the UK so you'll know the score. Talk now and maybe we can work something out.'

Never make it easy for them, and never swallow the line they're going to help you if you talk to them, because its bullshit. My take: Daly wasn't going to listen anyway, because he'd already decided on my guilt. And that was the worst of the worst because it meant that any inconvenient evidence that didn't fit their hypothesis would either get binned or be massaged to fit their pet theory.

I could see Daly's patience was beginning to run out, but he managed to come up with a smile of sorts, like he really wanted to help. 'Look, Calver,' he said, leaning closer across the table as if that would give his words more sincerity. 'Maybe it was a sex game gone bad. That would be a good start. Hell, maybe she asked you to do it. I hear some woman like that kind of shit. Talk to me, man, 'cause I'll tell you this: a rich white lawyer boy like you? Down in the Tombs, which is where you'll be going, you won't last ten seconds '

The thought of being remanded to a US jail scared the shit out of me. But my brain, unrealistically, just kept saying go on denying, something'll turn up. I licked my lips, and said, 'you seem like a regular guy, Daly, so I'm going to give you the heads up before I close up the shop and make my phone call.

'I didn't kill her,' I said, enunciating each word carefully, in case he didn't get it. 'I did have sex with her, consensually, in my room, so you're gonna find a shed load of my DNA, which'll prove nothing. But if you're smart,' I said, eyeing him up with a challenge, 'there's one question you'll be asking yourself: if I'm such a hotshot lawyer, why the fuck would I set the crime scene up to guarantee my own murder conviction?'

'You're a lush, Calver,' he replied, watching me, eyes unforgiving. 'And evidence says you did it, so if you're not going to explain what happened, we're going to nail you down for murder one. And in case you don't know it, counsellor, that's life without parole.'

We glared at each other. I said, 'I'm done talking. I want my phone call.'

In London I knew people would just be waking up. I called Emma at home, wondering, for about a millisecond, if NYPD would bitch about the international call charges, then she was picking up, voice fuzzy with sleep.

'Jesus, Jonas. Couldn't this wait till I—'

'Sorry, Em. I'm in trouble,' I said, cutting in and wondering how I was going to tell her that her cousin was dead. I looked around the bare room, then over at Daly leaning against the door, just out of earshot. He held his wrist up and tapped his watch, intent on hustling me.

'Look, I don't have time to dress this up, soften the blow, or whatever. Helena is dead, and…….and, they think I did it, but it's not true. We had a drink and..' My voice tailed off, and I instantly knew I'd made a mistake. I shouldn't have mentioned the drink. There was silence. I blustered. 'Em, I need you to get me—

'What the hell happened, Jonas? What did you do?' she said, her voice accusatory, but distant and far away. She continued slowly, each word uttered as she processed it. 'I mean, she's my cousin. How can she be dead? My God, and *still* you drink, even with this.'

'I *didn't* kill her, for christsakes. We had a drink. She went to her room. They found her strangled, with my......With my tie round her neck. And now they're holding me and I'll be up before the judge soon.'

'Just like Carmen,' she whispered.

'What? What do you mean?' I said, but I knew exactly what she meant. I'd told her about my blackout and the incident with Carmen when I'd put my hands around her throat.

'It's not like that. I—'

'I'm sorry, Jonas. I can't deal with this right now,' she said.

I heard a click as she replaced the receiver. I just looked at the phone, disbelieving.

Daly sauntered over, smiling. He'd been watching and I guess my face said it all. He grabbed my arm roughly. Let's go,' he said.

Then it was another blur as I drifted through the nightmare. They took me to central booking and processed me some more. As they moved me through the system I was listless, like I was sleep walking.

After an hour or so Daly came back. Maybe I should have been alerted by the fact that he'd spruced himself up, changed his suit and was now wearing shades. As he led me out the door onto the street, my handcuffs prominently displayed in front of me, there was a small group of media, including TV, waiting for us. Then I got it: they'd set me up for the fabled perp walk. It was a pantomime performance designed for the media, highly prejudicial, and calculated to influence opinion, especially amongst future potential jurors. Look, honey, the guys in chains, must be guilty.

I was taken by surprise, unable to do anything to hide the dumb, stupid and scared look on my face. The camera's snapped and ran, and the comments rained down on me as I was led to the car.

'Did you kill her, Jonas?'

'What would you like to say to your friends back in the UK?'

I just managed to mouth the words, 'I'm innocent,' before Daly bundled me into the car, but I don't think anyone was listening.

Courtney Pascal sat in the almost empty pub, at the bar, sipping a bloody Mary. It was mid morning. She felt restless. She turned on her stool to watch the grey swirling waters of the Thames flow by as she re-ran the conversation she had just had with the guys at MI5. Looked like finally a green light. She was going back in, but this time she had choices, maybe even a spell at 6, overseas.

She smiled at the young Polish girl behind the bar, admiring the girls clean lines and sparkling eyes. She was about to say something playful to the girl when her attention was grabbed by images on the TV screen over the bar. She immediately recognised the face.

'Turn it up,' she said, nodding at the screen.

As the girl pressed a button on the remote the Sky News reporters words filtered in…….'the UK lawyer was arrested this morning in Manhattan in connection with the murder of Helena Palmer, who is believed to be his client. He is now on his way to court to be arraigned, and seasoned court watchers suggest he is unlikely to get bail,' the reporter finished breathlessly. The clip accompanying the reporters words showed Jonas Calver, looking deathly pale, being led handcuffed out to a car, surrounded by NYPD and media.

For a long time Pascal sat looking out at the Thames, then she picked up her smart phone, got up and made for the door. The Polish girl watched her go with a pang of regret. The strange looking customer hadn't said much, but she sure as hell left an impression, but when the girl thought about it, she couldn't exactly work out why.

As a couple of burly police officers hustled me through the surging cathedral like halls of the New York State Criminal Court I gazed around trying to get my bearings and figure out what the hell I was doing there. The place was overflowing with people; a constant flow of lawyers, court officials, family members, witnesses and victims, all yapping at each other at the same time.

My guys left me sitting on a bench at the side of the court, still handcuffed and watched by a deputy. As I waited for my case to be called on I settled down to watch. At first blush it looked like organised chaos, but there was a familiar rhythm to it. The docket number was called, the defendant with his attorney shuffled up in front of the presiding judge, a verbal exchange took place and two minutes later the next case came on, with generally the defendant not having uttered a single word. In a way, it was just like being back home.

I felt a tap on my shoulder. I looked up into the face of an earnest young woman with a dark bouffant of wavy hair and thick black glasses.

'Joanna Rodriguez, Public Defender,' she said, holding out her hand. 'We met earlier, with the forms, but maybe you weren't paying too much attention,' she said with an uncertain smile.

I vaguely remembered her approaching me and taking some details as they'd hustled me in about twenty minutes earlier when I was still in a kind of idiot trance. Now I sized her up. She looked like a law student. Some cavalry I thought. I nodded, gesturing at my cuffed hands. She smiled perfunctorily. She sat down next to me with pen poised over her yellow legal pad. 'We don't have much time. You'll get called on any minute now as there's media here, and they like to get those ones out the way quick. Let me do all the talking. The only thing at issue here is bail, and I don't think you're going to get it,' she said, drawing breath for the first time.

I studied her closely. She looked nervous, talking too fast. ' How long you been doing this, Joanna?' I asked her.

'Three months,' she said, turning to look at the back of the court as we caught the rising inflection of chatter. Someone was making an entrance. A group of men moved in led by a tall well dressed guy with a Hollywood smile; he nodded and grabbed a hand here and there as he made his way into the well of the court.

'That's assistant district attorney Owen Stahl,' she said, with something like awe in her voice. 'Come to bury you,' she added, helpfully.

Before I had a chance to respond to that the usher standing at the side of the court was intoning, 'People against Jonas Calver.'

I noticed a slight pall in the noise and the press corp perking up and starting to take notice. I was no celebrity, but I knew the case would be garnering media attention outside, partly because of my nationality and profession but also because of the specifics; they were saying I'd killed my own client in a posh Midtown hotel.

Joanna pulled me up and we shuffled in front of the judge. The sign on the desk said he was the Honourable Cyrus J. Timmins. I hadn't really taken much notice of him until now. He looked gnomic, jowly, with a cherubic smile that seemed to be permanently in place, but he moved his courtroom along at a fair lick.

The Court officer asked Joanna if she was going to waive the reading. She nodded assent and that's when my survival instincts started to kick in. I knew this was about whether or not there was a formal reading of the accusations against me, and that it was generally dispensed with. But as I still didn't know what the hell was going on, I didn't think it was a good idea to stand mute just because it was a convention in New York City, and might piss the court off if I spoke up.

'Whoa there,' I said loudly. 'Wait a minute.'

Joanna tried to shush me and I noticed the assistant DA regarding me with an expression that was pretty close to a smirk. The judge raised his eyes and looked at me for the first time. 'Is there a problem here, Ms Rodriguez?' he said, flicking his gaze onto Joanna. 'We can't have you both speaking at the same time.'

I whispered to Joanna, 'sorry,' and she nodded, thinking I was apologising for interrupting. I turned back to the Judge. 'Your honour, I'm grateful to the New York City authorities for providing me with the services of the public defender, and good as Ms Rodriguez's skills undoubtedly are, I'm afraid I have just sacked her and hereon in I will be representing myself.'

Cyrus J briefly glanced at Joanna's crestfallen face, then back to me, his eyes intermittently flicking down at the papers in front of him.

'I understand you're a UK attorney, Mr Calver, but as I'm sure you're aware, our court procedures are very different to yours and these are very serious charges. My advice is stay with Ms Rodriguez, and let her help you. She's a very fine attorney.'

'Well that's just it your honour, what are these very serious charges? I've yet to find out. And incidentally, your honour, I did pass the New York bar last year so I think I can manage on my own.'

'Mr Stahl?' the judge said looking over at the DA.

'No problem your honour, as long as he's clear about the risks,' Stahl replied. Then he added, 'and he should know that any subsequent appeals he might want to raise based on incompetent counsel aint gonna fly.'

Judge Timmins nodded with approval then glanced at his watch. 'Lets move this along, people. Mr Stahl, bail? I'm sure you'll be sketching out the allegations here sufficient for Mr Calver so we can forego a formal reading.'

'Thank you your honour. We'd like you to remand Mr Calver to custody pending trial. He's clearly a flight risk being resident in the UK, and he has means. More importantly, I would highlight the obvious seriousness of these allegations. Helena Palmer was essentially garrotted in her hotel bedroom with a distinctive green silk tie belonging to Mr Calver. He admits earlier in the evening having what he calls consensual sex with her. However, early forensic indications are that Ms Palmer was brutally raped, anally, prior to death.'

That got my attention.

'In addition we are getting information that this defendant may have been involved in similar conduct to that alleged here today on at least one other occasion, that took place outside the US and that is being followed up as we speak.'

What the fuck was he talking about? Then a cold chill began to seep through my guts. They'd listened in to my call to Emma from the precinct house, and she had mentioned the incident with Carmen. She hadn't spelled it out but it wouldn't have taken them long to run it down.

'To sum up your honour, all the preliminary indications, CCTV, forensics and eye witness evidence leading up to the offence, powerfully point to this defendant as being the perpetrator. He's a dangerous man and a flight risk and we say no bail.'

Timmins looked over at me. 'Mr Calver.'

I took a deep breath. 'I didn't kill Helena Palmer and I sure as hell didn't rape her. She was my client for christsakes. You know, the one who's going to pay my bill. Why the hell would I kill her? What possible motive could I have?' I said, and I could feel my voice about to break with emotion.

I looked around the court, seeking a sympathetic face, but there were none, then Timmins was pushing again. 'Mr Calver, we're not here to try the case today, just deal with bail, if you could address that.'

'Your honour, I would be happy to surrender my passport, wear a tag, reside anywhere the court directs or report to a police or court official on a regular basis if it will get me bail. I need to be out to clear my name. If I don't make bail, I can't fight the charges.'

'Sorry, Mr Calver,' Timmins said. 'The evidence against you is compelling, you have no discernible ties to the community here and you're clearly a flight risk. I won't deny bail but I will set it at one million dollars cash and bond.'

I stood in a daze, barely listening. Even if I had access to my funds in the UK I couldn't raise that kind of money – nowhere near, even for a bond. I half listened to Timmins as he finished up, thinking it couldn't get any worse, but then it did. He mentioned the name of a place I had heard of. I was to be remanded to Rikers, the notorious island prison. All I could think about was a movie I'd recently watched on cable called the Shawshank Redemption.

Chapter Four

Courtney Pascal walked down Dalston High Street, East London, past the junction and on until she reached the offices of Jonas Calver Associates. They looked even more forlorn than usual she thought as she pushed her way in through the street door and into the small reception area.

Emma, typing away, looked up, a brief shadow crossing her face when she saw who it was. They didn't get on too well; she thought Pascal was weird and rude, and Pascal thought she was condescending and patronising. On the few occasions when they did speak, usually when Pascal was carrying out investigative work for Calver, they tended to be stilted and formal with each other, neither ready to let their guard down. But this time Pascal had brought a peace offering along; a large blue Café Nero takeout cup of coffee. She placed it down on the desk in front of Emma. 'Thought you could use some,' she said. 'Seeing as you're on your lonesome.'

Emma looked up, ready to push her away with a sarcastic quip, but this time she didn't seem to have the energy. She carefully took the lid off the coffee, and took a sip. For a long moment she just looked dazed, looking at nothing, then she murmured, so quiet Pascal almost didn't hear, 'Helena's dead. I can't believe it.' She looked up at Pascal, an expression of desolation on her face. 'And what's going to happen to all this?' she whispered, gesturing round the office. She looked down, fighting back tears.

Pascal sighed, then slid into the seat opposite and said, gently, 'I saw the news, Emma. Calver on his way to the clink, and I know its scary, but we're going to sort it out, trust me. So, tell me what's happened – everything.'

Emma sniffed and took another sip of the coffee. That seemed to convince her. She nodded, and then slowly began to talk.

Rikers jail sits on a tear drop shaped island of over 400 acres in the East river between the New York city boroughs of Queens and the Bronx, a stones throw away from the runways of La Guardia. It holds around 11,000 inmates, sometimes considerably more in peak times, either awaiting trial or serving sentences of less than a year.

As our bus crossed the bridge from Queens I watched the huge penal colony materialise out of the ether to dominate the horizon, in the background aeroplanes took off and landed and barges and boats meandered up and down the east river from Long Island sound.

I sat trussed up like a Christmas turkey; hands, ankles and waist chained and then attached to another inmate who constantly fidgeted and shook like he was having a fit. As we approached the complex I could feel the fear in the pit of my stomach threatening to overwhelm me the closer we got.

What the hell do you do when you're faced with something so outside your own sphere of experience, that you have no frame of reference for it? I guess you panic, and you run scared. But I knew if I did that I wouldn't last a day. I wanted to vomit, but my stomach was empty. I knew one thing though - to show fear would be fatal.

It's the unknown that really scares us. I knew I had to get through that first day unscathed. I guessed we'd be given a load of written rules, but it was those other, unwritten ones that would be critical. The key would be to try and quickly work out what they were.

Then we were moving, like a snake, all chained together, led down the steps onto the tarmac, then into a building, all around noise, commotion, clanging doors and shouts.

In the end it was tedium interspersed with bouts of extreme fear; waiting and waiting and waiting, then slowly being dragged through their bureaucratic process. I had my picture taken again, height and weight measured then a urine sample taken; I declined the optional AIDS test. The worst was the search. Strip, turn your back and squat.

And then it was over. I was handed a thin grey blanket, two small white sheets, a small towel, a bar of prison-manufactured soap, a floppy plastic toothbrush, and some toilet paper. Then they led me to a single cell, which was a relief, pushed me in and shut the door. In twenty four hours I had gone from being a moderately successful lawyer with a life and a future to being a jailed con facing a murder charge. In the end, despite it all, the fear and despair, and the constant shouting and screaming outside my cell, I was so dog tired that I fell into a deep dreamless sleep.

Solly sat in the anonymous looking black hire car parked across the street from the offices of Jonas Calver Associates. He'd been watching the building, bathed in light from the street lamp, for nearly an hour, his eyes crawling over every brick, doorway, window aperture and drain pipe. Now the preternaturally wiry looking ex-ranger checked his watch again; just about 3 a m, the witching hour, and time to move. It took the ex-pat freelance cat burglar all of 3 minutes to gain entry, scaling the side of the building, moving up the drainpipe like a monkey, then in through a skylight, dropping down silently onto the office floor, clad all in black, flashlight held between his teeth.

First to filing cabinets; three lined up in what he assumed was Calver's office, then a thick blue file marked "Hannah Cohen". He pulled it out, rifling through, thin circle of light flickering over the pages.

A minute later he had it: Sunnybrook Nursing Home, Barking, East London. He took his phone out and texted the address to Schmidt who was currently inbound to Heathrow, then he began to laboriously copy each page of the file.

I woke to night sounds, a low-level layer of noise, muffled shouts, moans in the dark. As my eyes opened that familiar wearying corrosive fear returned, sitting like a brick of ice in my gut. I looked around in the half light; the cell was tiny, about 8 foot by 11, with bed and toilet, and it stank.

I lay for a moment, my mind floating, unconsciously searching for something positive to think about, to give me a lift. I thought about trying to contact Carmen, but how the hell could she help? Then I realised I didn't even know whether I could make phone calls out of Rikers. I didn't have her number anyway, nor access to any funds. I had to get out, or get someone on the outside to help me find out what had happened.

Then I thought about Pascal. We hadn't talked in ages, but I knew she fit the bill, if I could get a hold of her. It was a long shot. I thought some and realised I could remember her UK landline number, if she hadn't moved or changed it.

As I pulled her number up from memory, I realised above the noise outside that someone was trying to talk to me, from the cell next door. 'You dead in there? Talk to me, man. You the English guy, right? Lawyer. Clipped your client?'

My first thought was keep my mouth shut, but then I thought that was crazy, and dissing somebody was probably not a good move.

'News travels fast,' I said cautiously.

'Believe it. I'm Jared,' he said.

I guessed he was black, and he sounded awful young. 'Jonas,' I said.

'Cool.'

'Say, Jared. How do I make a phone call out of here?'

'You got funds in commissary?'

'Nope.'

'Call collect. Phones at the corner of the cell block but you'll have to queue, and watch out. Don't get in any beefs.'

'Thanks, man. When can I call?'

'After breakfast.'

Breakfast was pretty disgusting; brown bread with red jelly on it, carton of milk and some gritty cereal, but I was hungry and wolfed it down, barely tasting it.

Then I was out queuing for the phone. I was nervous, but stayed calm, eyes down, constantly moving. What I saw when I infrequently looked up was mainly black and Hispanic guys moving around, with a few whites mingled in.

I joined the queue and waited. I recognised the guy in front of me as the head-case I had been shackled to on the bus. He looked even worse now, muttering to himself and still shaking. I nodded but he seemed not see me, off in a world of his own - in a way I envied him. When it was his turn, instead of taking the phone, he just wandered off. I watched him for a moment before the guy behind me pushed me hard in the back with his knuckle.

I turned to say something, but had to look up as the guy towered over me. He had obviously pushed in because he hadn't been there before. He was Hispanic, heavily muscled with strikingly vivid tattoos covering every inch of his bare arms, and with some black inking around his eyes like tear drops. The eyes themselves were black and flat, and there was a thin knowing smile on his face, because he knew I was scared. I'd guess everybody he ever met was scared.

'Sorry—' I began. The usual timid ingrained reaction of the middle class Englishman abroad, but now suddenly there was a female corrections officer there as well who I hadn't notice before. But now I did as she was incongruously pretty; curvaceous body just discernible under her black uniform, dirty blonde hair compressed under her cap and strikingly blue eyes.

'Back off, Delgado,' she said mildly. 'Let the man make his phone call.'

'Of course, officer McClellan' he said with exaggerated courtesy. He stepped back, turning his attention to me. 'Don't worry, Chiquita, we'll have plenty of time to get to know each other later,' he said, running his tongue suggestively around his lips.

A couple of guys behind him sniggered; I shivered inside. In a kind of panic I grabbed the phone, but then I couldn't remember the number. I had to get a grip. I took a couple of deep breaths, very conscious of Delgado, a few steps away watching me. Then the phone number slowly materialised from memory.

When I connected, her familiar voice came through loud and clear. 'What the fuck have you got yourself into this time, Calver?' She said, and the sense of relief I felt almost made my knees buckle. I was choking up, unable to utter a word.

'You there, Calver?'

'Yeah,' I managed to croak.

'Look, I've talked to Emma and she's told me every—'

'Stop!' I said, waking up quick. I wasn't going to get fucked over again. 'Walls have ears.'

'Understood,' she said, immediately.

Then there was silence. Now I had her on the phone, I couldn't think of what to say, and time was running. One thing was clear: our client Hannah had to be in danger.

'You remember that place of safety order we got, couple of years back for the elderly aunt?' I said, hoping she'd pick it up that there hadn't been any such case.

'Yeah,' she said, slowly, dragging the word out, as her mind worked on it. I knew she'd get it as she was bright as hell.

'Well, you need to get another one of those place of safety orders, *right now*.'

There was a pause whilst she digested what I was saying.

'Got it.'

'Good. Now, next bits important. Hannah's court claim has gotta somehow be linked to what is happening to me. Now, due to a procedural fuck up I didn't know about, her case is starting here Monday morning. If no one turns up at court from our side, they'll chuck it out, dismiss it with costs, and we can't allow that to happen,' I said, voice cracking with tension.

'Easy,' Pascal murmured.

'Sorry,' I said, swallowing hard. 'We need to try and sort something out for that, but also all our statements and other evidence was stolen from my room, night of the murder. Thats not critical but can you, and Emma, if she is still on side, try and get Hannah to do another statement - see if she's remembered anything more that might help.'

I looked over at the clock and guessed my time was just about up. 'And Pascal, I need you to start digging into her past - there's something there. Got to be, maybe way back, when it all started, 1942/43. And when you're done in London, get on a plane and get the fuck over here, 'cause I really don't know if I can make it,' I said, my voice catching on the last word and tailing off to nothing.

There was silence over the line as I tried to collect myself together. Then Pascal said, 'stay strong, Calver. I'm coming.'

Those last few simple words gave me huge boost, because now I knew she'd come, but then Delgado was jabbing my shoulder. Time to go. 'I'll try and call again at 4.30 pm your time,' I said quickly.

As the phone clicked thousands of miles away across the Atlantic I turned back to Delgado. The smile was gone and now there was a kind of calculating look on his face that in a way was worse. I turned on my heel and walked away towards my cell and I could feel his eyes boring into my back. Then a slight young black guy was lightly punching me on the shoulder.

'Jared,' he said. It was the guy from the cell next door. I was still a little shook up and preoccupied from my run in at the phones, but I nodded and looked him over. He seemed friendly, with an open, guileless face.

He said, 'I don't want to worry you, man, but that guy, Delgado. He a captain in the Bloods, you know what I'm saying. You don't wanna be messin with him, not if you want ta git outta here alive.'

An hour later I was sat on a bunk bed. I'd been assessed low risk and they'd moved me into general population, so now I was housed in one of the 60 bed dorms. I looked up.

'You got a visitor,' the guard said.

'Who?'

'Search me, fella.'

I followed him off the landing, down some stairs, along a corridor, up some more stairs and into the attorney visiting area where they stuck me in a room to wait. It was one of those chicken hutch interview rooms, one door, bare walls, single table riveted to the floor with a chair each side. A few minutes later a young woman came in; she didn't speak, just slid into the seat opposite and studied me with a kind of playful half smile on her face.

I'd had a long and frightening introduction to Rikers and my patience and manners were just about all used up. I glared at her. 'So who the fuck are you?' I said. 'The prison diversity officer?'

My comment seemed to amuse her. She flashed a quick smile. There was something strangely familiar about her face but I couldn't place it.

'Not quite. I'm Morganna. Morganna Fedler. Brad's little sister. Thought you could do with some help,' she said.

Brad was a London based US attorney I had got friendly with a couple of years back when we had co-defended in an insider trading case. It was him who had persuaded me to take the New York bar exams, which I had passed the year before. Now I could see the resemblance. I studied her wordlessly; she calmly returned my gaze. She was compact and self contained, I guessed 23 or 24 years old, pretty with dark brown hair like Brad, but hers was worn long in a cascade over an elegant shoulder encased in a crisp white blouse.

'Morganna,' I said, trying out the name. 'Le Morte D'Arthur; Morgan Le Fay, sometimes known as Morganna?'

'Very good, Mr Calver, but Brad tells me your more into Alice in Wonderland than the Tales of King Arthur. Useful in here I'd guess, when you need to retreat into fantasy,' she said, looking around.

'Yeah, well, if memory serves, wasn't Morganna the wicked sister?'

'It's only a legend, Mr Calver.'

I liked the warmth I could see in her eyes, something she shared with her brother. 'Call me Jonas,' I said, 'and thanks for coming. Sorry to be short but as you can imagine, I'm not in a good place, in more ways than one. You mentioned help. How?'

'I'm an attorney too, just got my plate, but,' she said with another quick smile, 'I only do civil law, no crime, so far.'

I dug back in my memory, thinking about what Brad had told me about his family background. Although he now worked for one of the big international law firms in London, he'd told me his father ran a small law firm out in Queens. He'd worked there when he was a teenager, every summer holiday, but he'd never mentioned a sister, but then we'd never been that close.

'And,' she added, looking sheepish. 'Brad doesn't know I'm here.'

I watched her, trying to work out whether that was good or bad - it didn't sound good.

She continued, talking rapidly, 'you see, Brad spoke about you and the bar exams last time he was back from London, and when I saw you on the news last night, I phoned him and said we should help, but he told me not to get involved. He said we couldn't know. You might be guilty.'

'Maybe he's right,' I said. 'You don't know me at all.'

'I don't believe you did it. C'mon,' she said, like she was joshing me, merriment in her eyes. But then she was serious again, 'but even if you did, you're still entitled to a defense - every attorney knows that.'

The idealism of the newly qualified lawyer - you couldn't beat it. I looked at the clock. I needed to use whatever time we had left to get things moving on the outside, before I got swallowed back up in the hell waiting for me on the block.

I studied the girl carefully, assessing and wondering if she could handle it - end of the day, there was no one else. I said, 'How d'you fancy being lead counsel on a major international lawsuit against K Corp, starting Monday morning in the Southern District Court?'

I watched a look of disappointment spread across her face. 'Don't make fun of me,' she said. 'If you don't want my help just say so.'

'Hey. I've never been more serious in my life,' I said. 'The person I'm accused of murdering is of the daughter of our client in this civil case. And I'm pretty sure that I'm in here because of that, so its absolutely critical we keep those proceedings alive, even if that means concentrating on that and leaving me kicking my heels in here a bit longer. I can handle it for now,' I said, knowing that that was bullshit but needing to say it to persuade the girl to take the case.

She looked at me for a long moment, eyes searching my face, then she slowly nodded. 'Okay, so tell me about this claim,' she said.

I sighed with relief. Fifteen minutes later she finished scribbling notes in her neat hand across a yellow legal pad. She'd listened attentively, only asking the odd question, and the ones she did ask were bang on the money. I took a sheet of paper and her pen and quickly scribbled a note to Emma and signed it. Then I set out Emma and Pascal's contact details. 'Can you scan this note to Emma and then speak to her on the phone and establish a link.'

She nodded, absorbed, excitement starting to rise. I needed to bring her down a bit, so I paused, eyes locked on hers and said, 'and Morganna.'

'Yeah.'

'Please be careful. These people are dangerous.'

She held my eyes, serious. 'I understand.'

I hoped to God she did. 'Good. One last question. How long

have you been practicing at actually being an attorney?'

She smiled. 'Three weeks, but hey, don't worry. I'm very, very good.'

Despite everything, I had to laugh. She had that kind of effervescence that only the very young seem to have, and there was a kind of mirth in her personality bubbling away just beneath the surface. She stood up as the CO came in to take me back to the block. I nodded to her and then she was walking away and I wished to Christ I was going with her. But then the screw was roughly pushing my shoulder and telling me to get moving, bringing me crashing back down to hell on earth.

Chapter Five

Pascal manoeuvred her beat up old Volkswagen Golf down the winding drive way, past the hanging sign that read "Sunnybrook Nursing Home", and on into the large shingled car park area in front of the home. She came to a halt, then leaned over and studied the paperwork lying on the passenger seat; release forms signed by Emma as well as a letter of authority directing the care home authorities to release Hannah into Pascal's custody.

It was gone six in the evening and it took an hour to straighten out the staff with the paperwork, and then Pascal was being ushered into a bedroom and announced to Hannah Cohen by Candy, her care worker.

Hannah was sitting in an armchair, wearing headphones, eyes closed. Candy gently touched her shoulder, and her eyes slowly came open to blink and look around. She was small and birdlike with close cropped grey hair and barely a line on her face, other than around her eyes and mouth, which crinkled when she smiled at her visitors.

'This is, Courtney, Hannah. She's a friend of your niece, Emma,' Candy said, and then quietly left.

Pascal was glad that Emma had phoned Hannah earlier and broken the news of Helena's death, so she didn't have to do it. She would not have known what to say, and even now she was struggling to know how to act. In the end she just said, quietly, 'I'm so sorry.'

Hannah nodded, then passed Pascal a framed photograph she had been holding in her lap. 'That's Helena,' she said with a sad smile.

Pascal said, ' she's a beautiful girl.'

The old lady's bright eyes searched Pascal's face. Most people found Pascal cold and soulless, but Hannah obviously divined something human there, perhaps a heart that had known suffering as well, and she seemed comforted by what she saw in Pascal's face. Hannah looked away for a moment, and seemed to wipe away a tear. When she turned back her face had a sad and wounded look. All she said, was, 'no more.' And that was all.

After settling Hannah into the car with her immediate belongings – they'd come back later for the main stuff – Pascal walked back to sign the release form and say goodbye to the staff. At the door she turned back to watch a large black Mercedes drew up outside in the parking lot. She swept her eyes over the car and the sole occupant, then carried on into the reception area.

As she walked she felt that familiar jangling of her nerves. Her antenna, developed over time in the field, had picked up on something about the big car and its occupant, something that wasn't quite right.

It was gone seven now and only Candy was still on duty at the desk, doing paperwork; she looked up and smiled as Pascal approached. She slid the release form across for her to sign, and Pascal leaned down to scribble her signature and slid it back across the desk, almost instantly

realising she'd made a stupid mistake. She had given her true address in

St John's Wood London. Too late to change it now. As she said

goodbye to Candy, the outer door opened and the driver of the Mercedes

entered and approached the desk, Pascal standing to one side.

The guy was built like a brick house, solid and swarthy,

sweating, in a tight, ill-fitting suit, the buttons of which looked like they

were about to burst off at any moment. He seemed to give off an

extraordinary aura of menace, even though he was doing a good job of

trying to cover it with a phoney superficial smile.

He ignored Pascal and said to Candy, 'Miss, I'm hoping to talk

to a resident you have here, a Hannah Cohen.' The guy was clearly

American, the voice clipped and authoritative.

Before Candy could reply, Pascal said, as if she was a member of

staff, 'let me handle this, Candy.

The girl nodded gratefully, clearly intimidated by the guy.

Pascal turned to him. 'I'm sorry, Mr?'

'Eh, Smith. Mr Smith,' he said quickly, his eyes suspicious.

Probably not hired muscle, Pascal thought. The false name was

shit, but didn't really matter. She could see the wheels turning as he

assessed the situation.

'I'm afraid you're too late, Mr Smith. Hannah was removed from

this home earlier today.'

'Oh that's too bad. I was so hoping to talk with her. Its about a

relative of hers, information she'll be desperate to hear. If you can give

me an address, I'll skedaddle out of here,' he said, false smile in place, eyes flat and lethal.

'I'm afraid that won't be possible, Mr Smith. Client confidentiality and data protection rules, we could lose our licence.'

Candy was answering a phone call, so Pascal made a play of riffling through papers on the desk, picking one up and studying it. She knew the guy wasn't going to leave without an address, and she knew Candy would give it, probably unwillingly, under threat of violence, if Pascal left.

'But, I will make an exception, since its urgent information she needs to hear, so long as you don't tell.'

'Honey, my lips are sealed,' he said, a little more relaxed now he thought he was going to get what he wanted.

'She's gone to stay with her cousin, at,' Pascal said, pretending to read off the form, and reeling off a fake address in Great Yarmouth.

The guy nodded and tapped the address into his phone. Then as he turned to go Hannah poked her head around the door, and said, 'when are we going, Courtney? I'm getting very cold waiting out here.'

'Right now,' Pascal said, moving towards the door and nodding at Smith, who was watching like a hawk, suspicion rising every second. She put her arm around Hannah and part led, part frog marched her back to the car. As they moved down the drive, Pascal looked in the rear view mirror and could see Smith standing just outside the doors of the home, watching them. She knew he was taking down her plate number.

As Pascal drove through the darkening streets, Hannah wrapped up and sleeping peacefully beside her, she worked through what she knew so far, and what she could guess. All she really had to go on was Emma's rather emotional re-telling of Hannah's story, which had more holes in it than a swiss cheese, and it wasn't really a story at all. Young girl with her family and possessions deported to probably somewhere in eastern Poland in 1943, but she wasn't even sure about the date. Family disappear along with an heirloom but no one seems to know the details of what actually happened, but the girl survives. Fast forward seventy plus years to Calver's trip out to New York with Hannah's daughter, Helena and a meeting with the K Corp. He intimates the lawsuit over the missing heirlooms is maybe not over, and more - maybe Hannah has started remembering what happened. Right after that meeting, Hanna's daughter, Helena ends up dead, and Calver's charged with the murder, neutralised, and now sitting on Rikers Island. Calver asks her to protect Hannah. Events show Calver's on the money; if she'd come an hour later, Hannah would probably be dead by now.

She looked over at the sleeping woman, and couldn't help smiling. Someone up there was watching over Hannah – so far. Then her smile faded. The guy Smith was a pro, but there was something else she'd sensed about him, even on such a short run-in. Smith was what she termed a force of nature. They were the kind who never gave up, and kept on coming whatever the odds or the risks, usually impervious to pain and completely unbound by any kind of moral notions of right or wrong. They were the worst; usually the only way to stop them, was to kill them.

But her first job was to arrange a hidden safe haven for Hannah, then she would have to get to New York. One thing was sure, Smith would track down her house in St John's Wood in about five seconds flat so she would have to think of somewhere else. Christoff Wisliceny was an old colleague from her MI5 days, possibly the only male figure, other than her father, she'd ever been emotionally close to. She phoned ahead and he was waiting when they arrived at his flat in Southwark, south London.

Hannah Cohen v Kurrilick Corporation and Milken

Southern District Court

Day 1

Charles Browder IV drummed his fingers on the defense table and quietly hummed to himself in anticipation. He checked his watch again and looked up at the bench expectantly.

Judge William T. Friedman scanned the sparsely populated courtroom and the Plaintiff's empty chair. Friedman had a rather bookish look about him; thick wedge of dark hair, flecked with grey, swept across his head, and heavy black-rimmed glasses that made his eyes look like small goldfish swimming in a bowl. 'I'm inclined to agree with you, Mr Browder,' he said. 'Plaintiffs US attorneys have removed themselves from the court record, and if its a no show from the Plaintiff herself, I'm going to dismiss the action with costs, so—'

He was interrupted mid-sentence by the crashing open of the courtroom doors. He looked up as Morganna Fedler hustled in looking frazzled, weighed down by her heavy attache case. She struggled to the Plaintiff's table, dropped the case, and looked up at the judge. She stammered, 'I'm so sorry your honour, for my lateness. Morganna Fedler, attorney for the Plaintiff, Hannah Cohen.'

For a moment Browder just looked on open mouthed, then his jaws clamped shut and he was rising to his feet, but judge Friedland waived him back down, and turned to Morganna with a half smile. 'Well, Miss Fedler. Just in the nick of time. I was about to dismiss your clients action. What have you got to say for yourself?' he asked.

'Your honour, we seek a brief adjournment. I, I…have only just received the sketchiest of instructions. All plaintiff's papers have been stolen and—

'That's not going to happen, Miss Fedler,' he said, not unkindly. 'This case has been dragging on for three years, but more importantly, we have jurors waiting here to be empanelled and to hear this case. You wouldn't want to keep them - or me - waiting now would you?'

Morganna studied the judge's face and knew, despite the folksy tone, he was not going to listen to argument. She swallowed, and said, 'thank you your honour,' and then she sat down.

The judge nodded. 'Good. Incidentally, where is the Plaintiff? Is she going to put in an appearance?' he asked.

Browder's ears pricked up at the defense table and he looked over at Morganna.

'I believe she is on her way your honour, although I am not

exactly sure of her current whereabouts,' Morganna said, looking down at her blank legal pad, and wishing she was somewhere else.

The judge nodded again. 'Well, no sense waiting around,' he said. 'Lets get ourselves a jury.'

Pascal woke early, on the couch - Hannah had taken Christoff's spare room. She got up and stretched then made for the kitchen. She found the coffee machine and set it up to percolate with a full tank of water. Then she took a heavy bottomed, blackened with use frying pan off the wall, stuck it on the hob, dial half way round, then to the fridge for butter, eggs, bacon and tomatoes, all into the pan.

She put on the wall TV and flicked through the news stations, settling on RT, sound down low so as not to wake her compadre's. As Christoff came into the kitchen wearing a dressing gown, Pascal handed him a cup of coffee and sipped one herself. She went over to the hob, picked up the frying pan and carried it back to the table and began to lay out her breakfast on a plate. Christoff politely declined, hiding his horror at the grease laden food – he was strictly a fruit and nut man.

'Guess what? Five want me back,' she said as she examined a fried tomato on the end of her fork, popped it in her mouth and started to munch and speak around it. 'Went for a chat, few days ago, and they're pretty relaxed about how I come in. You know, maybe part time stringer to start, or something more permanent, serious. Even suggested secondment to Six overseas for a spell. What do you think?'

He smiled. 'I think you're incorrigible, Courtney. And the fact that going to six might include a free trip to New York and a cushy berth at the Consulate never crossed your mind, right?'

'As if, Christoff?' she replied, deadpan.

As they sipped their coffee Hannah wandered in and Christoff made her a cup too. A few moments later she said, suddenly, 'how will you get Jonas out of prison?'

'Well, we have a bit of problem there,' Pascal said, turning to her. 'I'm no expert but I think the only way we're going to get him out is by posting a big pile of cash for bail, and so far we can't access his accounts, and even if we could, I get the impression from Emma, the cupboard's bare.'

'Well, perhaps I can help,' Hannah said 'I have money.'

Pascal looked puzzled. 'So why were you stuck in a care home?'

Hannah sipped her coffee. 'It's a long story. When you get old its……..there didn't seem to be any purpose or reason for going on and with Helena working so hard and away all the time, and John gone, I got to feeling lonely and alone. The care home seemed like a good idea at the time, to be surrounded by people again, you know, but with all this..' she said looking around. 'I don't know anymore….' she said, her voice tailing off.

Pascal said. 'We can talk about bail money later, right now we need to set up a little conundrum for our friend Mr. Smith.'

She reached for the phone and dialled British Airways.

Southern District Court

Morganna watched as Browder stood and questioned another juror. She had to admit, he was pretty good on his feet; smooth and confident; everything she wasn't. They'd been going at it for around two hours and she still didn't really know what she was doing. Browder had already bumped a juror off the panel, arguing that their answers to his questions suggested they could not be fair and impartial, although Morganna thought they seemed perfectly reasonable. She was trying to remember principles from law school about peremptory challenges and challenges for cause, but it was a blank. She was beginning to feel out of her depth and Browder was picking up on it, looking more and more confident by the minute as he realised he had a real rookie for an adversary.

She looked at her watch willing on the lunch break so she could get out and make some phone calls. Her old law professor and mentor, who was a civil trial lawyer in his spare time, was always there for her; she knew he was sweet on her, which helped. She'd give him a call and pick his brains, long as he didn't ask for a date, although maybe that wouldn't be such a bad idea.

Day three and lunch was brown bread sandwich, bologna, and side dish of cold, wet pasta salad with pickle relish and some cold beans. But I was ravenous, so I shoveled it down the hatch. And I was learning fast too - little things; I'd noticed you had to eat real quick as they moved people in in groups, and then hustled you out after about 6, 7 minutes to let the next group in, whether you'd finished or not.

'Man, you's hungry,' Jared said, watching me from across the table, his food untouched.

'If you don't want yours?' I said, eyeing up his plate. He slid it across. 'Tell me about Delgado,' I said, scooping up some salad.

'He Blood,' he said, dragging the word out, as if mentioning the name of the notorious street gang was enough in itself.

'Any reason why he'd pick on me, like that? I mean, I'm nothing to him, and I was minding my own business?'

'Yeah, and you sure ain't no ass candy,' he said, brow furrowed.

I let that one pass. 'So why?' I said, again.

Jared studied me, thinking. He looked around at the eating men and the few corrections officers standing watching, then looked back at me. 'You do have a point, my man. Hadn't thought about it, but you's right. I's watchin'. Know what I'm sayin'. He comes over. Positions his self behind you in the queue, then starts hittin' on you.'

'What does it mean?'

'Probly means the fix is in. Someone outside pulling some strings, as Delgado's got no personal beef with you.'

I held his eyes, then looked down at my empty plate. There was no hiding place in Rikers. I had to get out.

The guy stood on the concourse at JFK and watched as the passengers from the London flight disembarked and filtered through passport control. He looked down at his phone screen, switching between pictures of Pascal and Hannah.

And he almost missed Pascal. She was about last out and was wearing a woolly bobble hat pulled well down, and shades. He kept one eye on her as she moved away and the other on the gate, but there didn't seem to be anyone else coming through. As Hannah was old you'd expect them to be together so Pascal could help her, but Pascal seemed to be going solo and was now moving away fast and would be gone soon. Goddammit, he should have brought a partner along; Schmidt would tear him a new one if he fouled up.

The old lady wasn't on the flight, he was pretty sure of that, and if he didn't get moving soon he'd lose Pascal. He turned and quickly followed, checking his phone screen for flight times. Schmidt would be in the air by now following, so nothing to do but tail Pascal and find out where she was staying. Looked like Hannah's plane ticket was a good old fashioned diversion - she'd stayed in the UK.

Pascal settled back in the yellow cab as it moved off from the crush of the airport. She told the driver to take her to Calver's old Mid-town hotel. She'd stay there, check out the murder scene, nose around, maybe talk to some staff.

She didn't bother checking behind. She'd clocked the spotter guy on the concourse; couldn't miss him really. Man, where did they get them from these days? He'd be following, probably in the car behind, but that was fine.

Southern District Court

Morganna was back at the Plaintiff's table. Lunch had been a wash-out, a half-eaten sandwich and then Joel, her professor mentor, had been unavailable, teaching a class apparently, so she'd had to leave a message. Now Browder was questioning another juror, a stout looking lady with a blue rinse.

'Now, you said your parents came to America in the 1930's, from Germany, fleeing the Nazi's?' Browder suggested.

The woman nodded, and said, 'that's right,' although her expression suggested she wanted to add a couple more words on the end of her reply, like, "so what?"

Browder kept the friendly enquiring look on his face. 'So I guess you're probably not particularly sympathetic to anybody who may have been in the German armed forces during the war, right?'

Morganna wondered what the hell Browder was up to. The line of questioning of the juror seemed surreal and to have no possible relevance to the claim being made. She wondered whether she should object but wasn't sure how to, but the juror was already responding.

'Brother, you can say that again,' the woman answered, looking around the court, as if it was so obvious it hardly needed saying.

'So in all conscience, might you not find it hard to be be fair and impartial in judging a defendant if it was alleged he had such a background?'

The juror was trapped and she knew it, but disappointed as well. 'I guess,' she finally said.

'Strike for cause,' Browder said.

Judge Friedman nodded. 'That's the last of your challenges, I think, Mr Browder, and Ms Fedler,' he said, turning to look at Morganna with a quizzical expression. 'You've exercised none?'

'That, that's right, your honour,' Morganna mumbled, half rising. 'I am happy with this panel of jurors,' she said quickly and unconvincingly. Truth was she didn't know if she was happy with the panel or not. She'd thought her case was simple; the return of a family heirloom or damages, but it was starting to look as if there was a hell of a lot more going on here than met the eye. And if she didn't know the parameters of her case, how the hell was she supposed to challenge jurors for bias? Bias in favour of, or against, what? She didn't know, and she guessed Calver didn't either.

She looked over at the panel of six jurors and two alternates. They looked okay; three black, two Hispanic and three whites; four men, four woman. Then she looked over at Browder; he was watching her with a calm, confident look, half smile on his face. Then judge Friedman was saying, 'I will adjourn now for the day, and we'll start tomorrow with opening speeches.'

Morganna grabbed her case and was moving before the Judge had finished rising. Cell phone in her other hand, she speed-dialled Joel as she manoeuvred her way through the door, praying that this time he'd pick up.

Chapter Six

Pascal climbed out of the cab in front of the hotel, sweeping the street with her eyes as she tipped the driver. Her tail was parked a hundred metres back, sticking out like an unwanted piece of ice in a glass of brandy. At the desk, after some strange looks, she was able to swop and take Helena's old room. Apparently things were slow.

In the room she moved around, unpacking her meagre luggage. She didn't expect to find anything; the room would have been steam-cleaned and swept after forensics had finished and then occupied by other guests. She went to the large windows across one wall and looked out over New York. Then she went to the mini bar where she dug out a bottle of Bud and cracked the cap off with her teeth, then the phone buzzed. Someone downstairs to see her – a gentlemen.

She peeped through the eye hole. The guy had to be Six. She let him in. He looked way too young. 'Rob Galloway,' he said, aristocratic tone, but the smile seemed genuine. 'I'm the welcoming party. We only got your flight details from London an hour ago.'

'That why they sent the office boy? You want a beer?'

'No, thank you.'

'I insist,' she said, handing him another uncapped Bud, watching him.

He smiled. 'They warned me about you,' he said, taking the bottle and lifting it to his lips for a long drag.

'What did they say?'

He didn't hesitate. 'They said you could be difficult.'

She just looked at him, nodded, half smile, then clinked her bottle against his.

'I was just sent down to welcome you really and be your point of contact,' he said.

She said, 'where you based?'

'We're attached to the consulate on Third avenue, which is where you'll come in for your briefing in a couple of days.'

'If I wanted access to old second world war records and maybe some immigration as well from the 1940's, would it be available?' she asked.

Rob, taken aback by the sudden change of subject, said, 'I don't know. I guess you'd need authority from pretty high up to access it.

'What about US records?'

'You're kidding, right?

'No, I'm not.'

'I really don't know, but I doubt it. Look why don't you ask, when you come in.'

'I will. Thanks for coming, Rob,' she said, as she ushered him towards the door, yawning. She'd take a quick nap and then get moving.

I stood at the bank of phones again, receiver to my ear, listening to the ringing sound, hoping she would pick up. Then she was there, saying, 'Morganna Fedler,' sounding slick and lawyerly.

'Calver,' I said, no time for pleasantries. 'How'd it go?'

Deep sigh, then, 'not too well, I guess,' she said, sounding down. 'Look, Jonas, maybe I'm not cut-out for this hotshot lawyer routine. I'm out of my depth, and that Browder guy's eating me alive. He bumped four jurors today, and I bumped zilch. I don't know what I'm doing and I need some help.'

She'd gone from suave lawyer to little girl lost in about five seconds flat. I looked up and there was my nemesis, Delgado, this time with two other big guys who always seemed to be hanging around him. All three were watching me. I tried to block them out and concentrate, but it was damn near impossible. Here I was trying to lift Morganna and give her some confidence but I'm standing in a phone queue in Rikers scared out of my fucking wits. I felt like hanging up and walking over to Delgado and begging him to tell me what I could do to make him like me. And what I would give for a drink right now....

But I had to keep going. I took a deep breath. 'Forget jury selection. Case like this, it doesn't matter,' I lied. 'You're doing great, Morganna, because you're keeping the claim alive, and that's all we need right now. By the time the important testimony comes around we'll be ready.'

'But I've got to make an opening speech tomorrow morning, Jonas. What the hell am I going to say?' she wailed.

I gritted my teeth and counted to ten. I looked over again at

Delgado. Big mistake; all three were watching me and one of them was grotesquely rubbing his crotch whilst running his tongue around his lips, eyes locked on mine. I just saw red then and flipped. Whatever I did, they were going to come for me, whether I rolled over and begged for mercy, or whether I gave them the finger, so why roll over. I held my hand up and gave them what I think is a particularly English gesture of insult; the crude universal hand-job motion of masturbating. I didn't wait for a reaction, but I heard a couple of guys in the queue behind me stifle some laughs. I tried to blank it all out again and said, 'opening speech is a doddle, Morganna. You'll walk it. Just introduce yourself and don't do detail. Bare bones, then simply say your client, Hannah is going to talk to them and tell them her story, and leave it at that.'

'I don't know Jonas I—'

'*Hey*, I need you strong, and I'm struggling in here,' I said, and I could't keep the desperation out of my voice. 'You got no idea what it's like in……….'

'I'm sorry, Jonas,' she said immediately. Voice strong again, and I could hear her brother in there somewhere, a kind of toughness. 'I'll do it. Oh,' she suddenly exclaimed. 'I should have said. Pascal's here, just arrived. She left a message for me. Tell me what you need?'

That lifted me like nothing else could. 'Good. No time left so I'll be short,' I said. 'Grand jury have handed down the murder indictment and I'm in Supreme Court tomorrow morning for arraignment. Talk to Pascal and tell her to be there, and remind her about keeping Hannah safe and lining her up for when she will be needed to testify for you. Lastly can you rough me out a couple of motions I need to make tomorrow, and email them to Pascal to bring to court?'

I gave her brief details. Then I hung up and turned around to face whatever Delgado might have for me, but he'd gone, along with his buddies. I let out a long sigh of relief, but I knew it would only be temporary. I slowly walked back to the block.

In the end Pascal couldn't sleep. Time zone clash and jet lag ganging up on her. She got out of bed and walked around, beer in hand, trying to work off the excess energy. Then her cell was buzzing. Ten minutes later she clicked the phone off and finished her beer.

Morganna Fedler had sounded inexperienced but enthusiastic. Pascal heard a pinging sound on her laptop which stood open on the coffee table, as an email came in. She guessed it was the court motions from Morganna she needed to take to court for Calver in the morning.

She moved to the windows to look out on the city. She thought about earlier in the day when she'd gone walkabout. She'd taken the lift to the top of the building and then walked down, checking out each floor; fire escapes, CCTV, maid stations, cupboards and storage rooms. It looked like a slick well run hotel, mid-range, comfortable, not ostentatious. She hadn't yet managed to check out the kitchen, office and back room operation, but she'd get to them soon enough.

Back in the day during those long hot summers when she'd been a student she'd worked casual in hotels, and one thing she'd learned was that it was almost impossible for stuff to happen that the staff didn't know about. Deconstructing Calver's murder charge, and assuming it was a frame, her first conclusion was that it would have been impossible to carry it out undetected without inside help. The reports she had seen suggested the cops had CCTV security camera footage showing only Calver entering and leaving Helena's room at the time the murder was committed. Just to get around the CCTV covering the corridor and showing the entrance to both Calver and Helena's rooms, would have been hugely difficult, and impossible without inside help.

Pascal finished her beer and tossed the empty into a waste bin with a loud crash. She knew she wouldn't sleep if she went back to bed, so she grabbed her tablet and left the room, heading for the lifts.

She walked through the lobby and into the hotel bar. It was a small, dark and intimate place, palm fronds overflowing from giant tan coloured tubs, low kaleidoscope style lighting, tinkling piano in the background, and it was empty apart from a couple of lovers cooing to each other in the corner. Pascal climbed onto a high stool at the bar and ordered a Jack Daniels. She set her tablet down and began to scroll through and read local news reports covering the murder.

She tried her drink. Out of the corner of her eye she watched the waitress; she was leaning on the bar just up from her, arms crossed, chewing gum, looking mournfully into the distance. Pascal signalled for a re-fill, edging her tablet around so the girl would see the screen when she came over; it showed a headline from a web news channel reporting on the murder story.

'Quiet night, huh?' Pascal said, as the girl placed the drink down on the bar, her eyes flicking down over the screen.

She looked at Pascal, expression less friendly. 'If you're a journo looking for something on that,' she said nodding down at the screen, 'I wouldn't let O'Leary find you in here.'

'D'you talk to all your guests like that?' Pascal asked, wide-eyed.

The girl looked at her again, sizing her up some more. 'Sorry. Guess I didn't pick up on the accent. We've had some characters coming in here, nosing around, you know how it is?'

'Sure. No harm done. You join me in a drink?' Pascal asked. Then, 'who's O'Leary, anyway?'

The girl smiled. She was young, early twenties, rather mousy, with short hair and glasses. She made herself a Jack Daniels and topped Pascal's up. 'John O'Leary's head of security here,' she said, and left it at that. Despite the smile, Pascal could tell the girl was still wary.

'I'm Courtney, by the way,' Pascal said, extending her hand over the bar.

The girl shook and said, 'Lorraine.' She took a sip of her drink, then she was looking up, over Pascal's shoulder and nodding. She said, 'evening John.'

Pascal half turned on her stool to look at the guy as he moved in to the bar beside her. She swore under her breath; her tablet still showed the murder story headline.

The guy was average height and build, pale complexion with reddish brown hair. 'Everything all right, Lorraine?' he asked, his eyes taking in the tablet screen.

'Sure thing boss, quiet as a tomb,' Lorraine said.

'And Miss Pascal,' he said turning to her. 'I hope you're enjoying your stay with us?'

His eyes were unreadable, but there was something of the lizard about the guy, a kind of slow languid air of insolence in the way that he looked at her. 'And I hope you enjoyed your little tour of the building earlier today as well,' he said, letting her know she was already a mark. He continued, same slow cadence. 'I understand you specifically asked for the room in which the murder took place. But alas, if you're looking for ghoulish kick's,' he said, with a thin smile at Lorraine, 'you'll find no traces, as the room was re-decorated as soon as the police tape came down. And at the hotel we don't encourage discussion about such macabre and unfortunate events, and I hope you'll respect that. The hotels reputation is of course paramount. I'm sure you understand.'

'Of course. No problem,' Pascal said, knowing she'd completely blown it. Maybe it was jet lag, but she couldn't keep blaming that. Fact is she might as well have worn a big sign saying she'd come to dig up stuff about the murder. She'd have to find another way in. But now she needed to make her exit as it was clear O'Leary wasn't going to leave until she did.

She signed the bar chit with her room number and dropped five bucks on the tray with a wink at Lorraine. Then she picked up her tablet, nodded to both and moved off her stool. She could feel their eyes on her back as she made her way to the door, a busted flush. But she had picked up one thing: O'Leary had a cocaine habit, maybe quite a heavy one if he could come out on duty with tiny amounts of white powder still showing on the tip of his nose. Might be nothing; lots of hotel workers imbibed, but in her experience it was usually lower level staff, less so older guys in the more responsible positions, but it might be something. She'd sleep on it, if she could, then she'd better hitch a ride out to see Calver at court.

Pascal woke early, then sat on the bed chewing a bagel as her mini printer spewed out the court motions Morganna had emailed over the night before. As she munched away she idly watched the maid bustling around her doing the dusting. She had invited her in to do her work rather than putting her off until she was out the room. Pascal checked her watch; she'd have to leave for court soon.

She watched the maid some more, then smiled at her and gestured at the coffee pot on the table. The maid graciously declined the offer with a shake of her head and a shy smile. She was middle aged with a mahogany coloured face with few lines, and dark somnolent eyes. Pascal watched her for a moment longer, and then said, '*perdon, habla usted Ingles?*'

'Of course,' the maid replied with a mild look of reproach.

'Please forgive my rudeness. Why wouldn't you speak English?' Pascal said, rolling her eyes at her own stupidity. 'Come, lay down your duster, take a moment and join me for a coffee - please.'

The maid checked her watch. 'Okay, but only for a moment. We are not supposed to, but on the other hand, we must not be rude to guests. Thank you,' she said.

Pascal poured the still hot coffee into a cup and passed it to the woman, saying, 'I'm Courtney.'

'Dolores,' she replied, nodding solemnly.

Pascal said, 'look, I wonder if you can help me, Dolores?'

'I try.'

'Your head of security, Mr…….O'Leary, I think,' Pascal said, feigning uncertainty.

A faint shadow seemed to drop across Dolores's face, a slight tightening of her features. She finished the coffee and placed the cup back on the table.

'You see,' Pascal continued, 'he's been so helpful settling me in here - problems with lost luggage and other things - that I just wanted to give him a small present, a token of my gratitude. Any ideas? What's he like?'

Dolores picked up her duster, and said, 'he is not a man for presents, I think. Save your money, or give to the church, it will be better used there.'

'Is he not a family man, Dolores? Maybe I just get him a bunch of flowers for his wife?' Pascal persisted, trying to shake something loose, anything.

'I believe he does have a wife and a daughter, but he also keeps a room here - on the top floor - and seems to spend many hours there, sometimes not alone, ' she said, eyes veiled, unreadable.

A small nugget of intel that could lead anywhere. Not the time to press too hard now; retreat gracefully with scope to develop the connection later if she needed to. 'You have children, Dolores?'

Her smile was as wide as the Sierras as she reached for her pocket. 'And grandchildren too,' she said, holding out a small cheap phone with the face of a smiling child on the screen.

Pascal spent a few moments admiring the images of the children and then went to her wallet and took out twenty dollars. Dolores started to shake her head in the negative. Pascal took Dolores's hand and rolled her fingers around the note squeezing them closed, murmuring, 'for the children. I insist.'

'Thank you,' she said.

'No problem. Dolores, say I wanted to go up and see O'Leary, give him the flowers,' Pascal persisted.

Dolores smiled. 'Room 495, but he sure don't like unexpected visitors. I'd stay away from there if I were you.'

There wasn't much chance of that, but Pascal'd make damn sure he wasn't around when she went up there.

Southern District Court

Morganna sat at the Plaintiff's table, girding herself for the opening speech she was going to have to make in a little while. She watched Friedman as he went through the swearing in process for the jurors and the lengthy pep talk that went along with it. All the do's and don'ts and what they should expect from jury service.

She still didn't know what she was going to say in her opening. Her old tutor Joel had been no help; seems he'd got himself a new squeeze from the latest intake of idealistic and naive young students, and he hadn't had any words of wisdom for her. Apart from the brief advice Calver had given her she was on her own, but maybe that was a good thing. Sink or swim, that's what her father and Brad were always telling her. She began to idly rough out some bullet points on her yellow legal pad; she knew Friedman was likely to be some time.

Chapter Seven

The Supreme Court at 100 Centre Street, Manhattan was instantly recognisable. It must have been in just about every US cop and lawyer show I'd ever seen. As you approached from the front it looked like a modern cathedral, but I came in through the back way, hustled in quick like a convicted felon, then down into holding. The journey over had been a blur, me trussed up like a chicken, but tripping out on freedom, snatching glimpses of the city through the dirty windows of the beat up old corrections bus.

They shoved me in a hard chair in the holding cage and my jailer unbuckled my handcuffs and chains. I rubbed my wrists to get the circulation going, then sighed as he put the cuffs back on, but he left the leg irons off. He stepped back and nodded. 'I'll be watching you, Calver,' he said, not unkindly. They knew I was an unlikely candidate for a jail break.

'Hey, Hector, how 'bout some coffee, man?' I said. 'I gotta consult with my attorneys and I can barely speak my throat's so parched.'

'Don't push it, Calver,' he said, shovelling my court papers and well thumbed copy of Criminal Procedure Law of the State of New York, onto the desk in front of me. I started to sort the papers but then a corrections officer was telling me it was time to see the judge, so I bundled the stuff up, two handed and followed him out. The courtroom was busy but there was no judge yet; looked like I was first up. Then Pascal was there at the court doorway talking animatedly to an usher and a security guy, then she was being lead over and seated next to me.

'How d'you manage that?' I asked, emotion threatening to wash me away, and me trying to stay cool.

'It's how you tell 'em,' she said with a wink.

As we waited for the judge I studied her. I hadn't seen her for ages, and she never seemed to change. She had to be over thirty now but still looked like a geeky student. Her hair was still orange, but now it was tightly curled on her scalp, and she still had that incredibly direct look in her eyes suggesting she knew all your secrets. I knew she ate like a horse whilst somehow still managing to remain preternaturally thin, but at least today, for court, she had made an effort with her dress. I didn't know if she had any Scottish blood but today she was wearing a short green and black tartan kilt that looked surprisingly smart, although the punk leather jacket she wore on top did a good job of spoiling the effect.

'How you bin, Calver, if it's not a stupid question?' she asked.

'How d'ya think?' I replied, smiling, stupidly. I knew she hated shows of affection, so I kept on trying to keep a lid on it.

I had first met her years before when I'd defended her against a murder charge. She'd been accused of killing her step-father. At the time she had been working for British Intelligence and they'd dropped her like a stone. In the end she'd done time, but when she came out she had started doing investigative work for me, and our kind of strange, spiky relationship had grown up from there.

'Morganna Fedler asked me to give you these,' she said, sliding a couple of sheets of paper across the desk. 'She sounds way too young, Calver, and not too clued up either. Asked if I wanted to come stay with her in her brothers loft apartment, here in Manhattan. What is she, a millionaire?'

'She's all right. Take her up on her offer. Better if we're all together while we try and fight this.'

'Maybe I will. I'm still at your old hotel, digging.'

Our eyes met. I didn't ask. Let her get on with it. She'd tell me when she had something.

'Hannah can stand you bail you know, Calver. She has money and wants to help. But,' she added before I got carried away. 'It's not in place yet. She's given instructions to sell some assets, shares I think, so you'll just have to sit tight for the moment,' she said, dashing my hopes for an early release.

'Okay,' I said, mentally shaking myself. 'First order of business, protect Hannah. I don't want to know how you're doing it, but we need to keep her under wraps and then produce her when her testimonies due in the district court, so you'll have to liaise with Morganna on that.'

'Check,' she said.

'Thanks, Pascal— ' I started to say, but then the usher was announcing, 'all rise,' and the judge swept in and took a seat.

In the end the hearing was a bit of an anticlimax, but the judge did order the removal of my handcuffs, which was something. I was given the murder one indictment, and I pled not guilty. Stahl, in an even more expensive suit, handed over some discovery, and the judge talked motions and timescales. I only had a couple of points I wanted to make. As I stood up to speak, I briefly scanned the two motions Pascal had handed me.

Under the constitution I was entitled to a speedy trial, but I knew most murder trials took six months to a year to come on. I could not afford to stay in the States for any length of time, as if I couldn't get back to the UK soon, my practice would go down the pan and I would lose everything. On the other hand, insisting on going to trial straightaway, without ammunition - hard evidence showing I did not rape and kill Helena Palmer - could be the dumbest move I'd ever make.

Then the judge was looking at me. 'Mr Calver?' he prompted me.

I stood and regarded him for the first time. He was a small asian american guy, almost bald, but with bushy eyebrows and a bustling quick style. I dug in my pocket and pulled out a nickel I had picked up off the floor earlier. I'd always been a gambler. I rubbed it as I pondered on the vicissitudes of fate, then I tossed it and slapped it down on the table. Heads!

'Your honour, under the constitution I'm entitled to a speedy trial, so lets have one. I am ready, subject to a couple of minor pre-trial motions,' I said, handing them over to the clerk for copying and distribution.

'Your honour, we want access to the original CCTV digital file or tape, the prosecution say shows only me entering and leaving the victims room during the night of the murder. And we also want access to the green tie, allegedly used by me to murder my client,' I said.

I glanced at Stahl, and he was no longer smiling. Then there was some furious whispering going on between him and the team behind him, which included detective Daly. I guessed I was about to find out what the problem was.

'Your honour, we welcome a speedy trial,' Stahl said, voice clipped and tight. He continued, 'on the motions we have no objection, but we do have a temporary problem in that we cannot currently locate the original CCTV digital file showing this defendant entering and leaving the victims room. I am assured we will locate it shortly and in the meantime we have copies available for Mr Calver, and if necessary we shall rely on these at trial and the testimony of those investigators who viewed the original tape.'

I was already on my feet. 'Your honour, thats a crock, and the DA knows it. I know I didn't kill Helena Palmer, so I'm guessing someone else did. Someone else entered her room and raped and killed her, and that is no doubt why this vital original evidence has conveniently gone missing. If the assistant district Attorney fails to provide the tape I will be making a motion to suppress it.'

The judge quelled Stahl with a hand as he rose to speak. 'Ignoring for the moment Mr Calver's inference about your integrity and honesty, Mr Stahl,' the judge said looking at him but then turning his gaze on me, 'Mr Calver does have a point. I will expect the original film to be produced for the defendant and or his experts within 48 hours or I will entertain a motion to suppress it.'

So I'd got something out of it, but if we didn't get the tape and discredit it, or we failed in our motion to suppress, I would still be toast.

We were asked to return in 48 hours to resolve the tape issue and try to agree trial dates, and then I was being led out to holding.

Southern District Court

Day 2

Morganna sat at the Plaintiff's table still doodling on her yellow legal pad, nervously waiting to make her speech. Although she hadn't got anything out of her old law tutor, she had managed to speak to the expert who had been lined up by Hannah's original US attorneys, before they resigned. Professor Efraim Borkowski had managed to fill in a few of the gaping holes in Hannah's backstory, and Morganna had used some of this new information to help craft some points for her opening speech that she would shortly have to make. As she turned these thoughts over in her mind, Judge Friedman arrived, and then she was back on her feet.

'May it please the court. My name is Morganna Fedler and I represent the plaintiff,' she said. And all the time she was trying to keep in mind the mass of mostly conflicting advice she had received from other attorneys about trial advocacy. "Be natural, move around, it will relax you. Don't read your speech, use it as an outline only, and make eye contact. You have to make the jury like you." Blah, blah, blah. Easier said then done, she thought. She looked down at her handwritten bullet points on the desk in front of her, hoping it would give her some inspiration. Nothing doing.

Friedman coughed, reminding her they were all still waiting for her to get on with it, and if she didn't start soon, the jury would think she was weird. Time to fly, if she could. She stepped away from the plaintiffs table and moved into the well of the court to stand directly in front of the jury.

'In early 1943, when Hannah Cohen arrived, aged just fourteen years old, in eastern Poland at the Nazi cam—'

'Objection, your honour,' Browder barked as he rose to his feet. 'Appreciate plaintiff counsel is inexperienced but this is ridiculous. To hint at a connection between my clients and those events is both false and highly prejudicial, but more than that, the circumstances alluded to, even if true, are completely irrelevant to the issue being tried before the court, and therefore inadmissible.'

'Miss Fedler?' judge Friedman nodded at Morganna.

Morganna winging it, trying to remember the rules of evidence, said, 'Your honour, surely Mr Browder's objection is premature.'

'How so?' Friedman asked, amused expression.

'Because you can't be asked to rule on such matters until trial and the evidence itself is to be introduced.'

'That's right, you know, Mr Browder,' he said, nodding at him. 'But, Miss Fedler, I think you should still stick to the relevant facts in your opening. This is after all a case about the alleged loss and possible restitution of a family heirloom, nothing more. Objection overruled. Please proceed, Miss Fedler.'

Morganna swallowed, relieved. She'd got it in, even though it was highly speculative and based purely on the brief discussions she had had with the expert, Borkowski, the night before. She swallowed again and looked down at her notes. So far so good.

Pascal, back from seeing Calver at court, sat in the little cubby-hole MI6 had found for her down near the basement at the UK Consulate. It was almost as if they didn't know what to do with her. She looked around. The room was only just big enough for two desks, hers and Rob's. He was out now, running an errand, so she was alone, which was fine with her.

Looking around the threadbare room it was like the inside of a second world war Quonset hut. Drab green walls, uncarpeted hard crimson coloured flooring, old style grey filing cabinets and wall units, and light brown coloured, varnished desks like something out of a 1970's class room. Opposite Rob's desk was the noticeboard, festooned with office rules and regulations and fire escape procedures that looked to be at least thirty years old.

She tapped on to the old fashioned desk top they had said was hers. First problem, it asked for a password that she didn't have. Great. She looked over at Rob's desk which was much bigger than hers. It was stacked with papers and reports which he'd said she was welcome to look through. He seemed to spend much of his time trawling through paper reports and online trying to pick up snippets of information that might be of interest to Her Majesties Government. Other than that he didn't seem to be required to do anything else, certainly no field work.

She looked back at her computer screen debating whether to try and hack her way in, but then there was a knock on the half open door, and a mans face appeared around the edge. 'Hi. Rob around?' he asked in an american accent, as he edged into the room. Pascal looked him over. He was short, plump and balding with a mass of curly black hair on each side of his head, and seemed to be sweating a great deal; he wore no jacket and there were huge damp patches spreading under his arms.

'He's not here right now. Can I help?' she asked, hoping he'd go away so she could get on with hacking the computer.

'Say, you must be Courtney Pascal, right?' he said, big smile splitting across his face. 'Heard a lot about you, Courtney. By the way, I'm Bob Jeffreys, Homeland Security,' he said holding his hand out.

Ten minutes later, after a short walk in the Manhattan sunshine, they sat in a Starbucks, on stools at the front window drinking coffee and watching the crowds. Jeffreys seemed to want to talk a lot and Pascal was happy to let him do it. 'So there's lots of informal contacts between us every day, you being our closest ally and all,' he said.

'Apart from Israel, of course,' she said, just to say something. Before he could respond she said, 'what d'you know about the Kurrilick Corporation?'

'K Corp?' he said, puzzled. 'What about them? They're a major blue chip US company, close to the government in some areas, and a major contributor to the GOP. What's your governments interest?'

'Oh no, this isn't work. I'm just helping a friend out on something.'

'Against K Corp? Your friend must have big cojones, or he's stupid.'

'So they're protected?'

'No they're not protected. It don't work like that over here,' he said, impatient with a subject he clearly didn't want to talk about. 'So, what's the Brit government got you on? Reading the funny pages, looking for tips? We thought that kind of intelligence gathering went out with invisible ink. Anyway, we thought you were one of their star gurus. De-radicalisation expert on islamists, and just about a rock star after that Buckingham Palace gig where you saved the Queen. What happened to all that?'

He was very good, Jeffreys. Subtle and slick, they way he dug a bit, and flattered, and then did it again. His appearance helped; he looked a bit liked Danny De Vito which made you think he was like a cuddly, friendly clown, but Pascal could sense a keen intelligence at work underneath the facade. She'd have to watch the guy.

'So, Bob. I'm guessing nothing ever changes in this game. You dig, I dig, but in the end, we're only ever going to talk to each other if there's something to trade - it was ever thus, right?'

'So cynical already, Courtney, and you've only just arrived. Look, I'm a good contact for you here. You've got a rep for finding stuff, and I've got a nose that tells me you can be valuable, that's all. Keep in contact with me. If you want to talk, here's my card,' he said, cod sincerity glistening in his eyes.

'Cool,' she said, just to be irritating. 'So, what's your field, Bob?'

'You need to ask? We're all in the same boat now, honey. Islamic terrorism. Camel Jockey towel heads, baby. Name of the game.'

Southern District Court

As Morganna moved falteringly into her speech she happened to look up at old Glory on the flag pole, and then at the embossed seal of the eagle on the wall behind Friedman's chair. She felt a tiny frisson of excitement ripple through her as she experienced the moment. For christsakes she thought, isn't this where she had always wanted to be? Out here showing the two men in her family and all the other lawyers out there that she was just as good as they were. Hell, that she was better? She looked back at the jurors and mentally squared her shoulders. She looked down at the notes for her speech, and then she walked away from them, starting to speak as she moved.

'Hannah Cohen, as she then was, was just fourteen years old when the events you are about to hear about took place,' she said, voice firm and clear. 'They revolve around a priceless family heirloom. A beautiful gold and diamond encrusted pendant with matching brooch. It went missing in 1943 in circumstances that will probably form the basis of the main dispute you will hear over the coming days. Hannah did not see these family jewels again until about three years ago, when they were identified as being in the possession of the Kurrilick Corporation and its founding family, the defendants in this case.

'They will say many things to convince you that they acquired these jewels fairly and legally and that they are the rightful owners. They will say that Hannah never owned them, that she is too late to claim them, and that K Corp founder, Angel Milken legally purchased them from a reputable dealer in Munich in 1953.

'Well, ladies and gentlemen of the jury, that's going to be for you to decide. That's your job. All I'll ask of you is that you listen carefully to Hannah - its an extraordinary story - and then you decide. Thank you.'

As Morganna sat down and looked at her watch she wondered where the day had gone? Then Friedman was adjourning overnight.

Browder had to bust a gut getting from the courtroom to the 58th floor of the K building, so he was sweating buckets by the time he arrived. David Milken was waiting for him in the penthouse, drink in hand, soft rock playing quietly in the background.

'How d't go, Charlie?' Milken asked, voice low key, but with an undercurrent.

'Pretty good, boss,' Browder said, taking a handkerchief out and mopping his brow. He moved into the room and subsided into a deep leather chair. 'Plaintiff attorney's a rookie from Queens, for Christ sake. What can I tell you? I don't anticipate any problems.'

'Yeah? Well, you said there'd be no court case, and what have we got? I don't like the odds, Charlie. Tell me this is going to go away.'

'Its going to go away, boss, but it may take a bit longer than we planned.'

'But now we've got a trial, Charlie, and that's a trial that's open to the public and the media. Why don't we just offer them more money? You know what I've got riding on this.'

'Boss the next mayoral race is three years away. Even if we have a trial it will be finished long before you would even have to declare. As to offering them more money, that's no longer an option. Seems the death of her daughter, Helena, has hardened the plaintiff's position. I'm told there has to be an apology as part of any settlement. And that's non negotiable.'

As Lynyrd Syknyrd's southern anthem, "Sweet Home Alabama" came on the audio, Milken upped the volume, and then he was on his feet, air guitar in hand as he went through some moves. Browder, face expressionless, rose and walked to the drinks cabinet and mixed himself a large scotch, and then stood for a moment, looking anywhere but at Milken. After a few moments Milken smiled and moved back to his chair and lowered the volume. 'Its been kid gloves so far, Charlie,' Milken said. 'I've held Dad and Schmidt back and let you make the running, but maybe its time to get tough?'

Browder watched Milken, marvelling at the mans characterisation of the death of Helena and imprisonment of Jonas

Calver for her murder as somehow being the result of handling it with kid gloves. He was only guessing of course, given the lengths they went to to keep him, as their legal counsel, out of the loop, cocooned and quarantined from anything remotely unsavoury, but he still had a pretty good idea about what had been going on.

'Boss, why not wait until she takes the stand; see what happens? This woman's eighty seven years old with a bad memory. Let me rip her apart on my cross, discredit her on the stand, and it'll be game over.' Browder said.

Milken watched him. 'We can do that, Charlie, but its always good to have an edge, an insurance policy, right? Calver's pulling strings, still, even in Rikers, and thats with a murder trial hanging over his head. And then what happens if he gets bail? We can't have that, Charlie. If I'm going to make a run for the biggest prize the city's got to offer, then nothing is going to get in my way. So all this, this *bullshit*, needs to disappear, right?'

Browder watched Milken, so like his father in many ways, especially the messianic zeal with which he approached the big projects.

'Sure boss, sure,' Browder said, rising to his feet, picking up his case and making for the door.

Chapter Eight

Hannah and Christoff stood at the rail of the mighty vessel, looking down, watching the dirty grey green waters swirl and boil against the wall of the dock as the massive container ship slowly edged its way out of Southampton harbour. They had been lucky to bag the last shared cabin on the freighter bound for New York. It was a less well known form of transport used by the more adventurous traveller, a trip across the Atlantic on a cargo vessel, especially good if you wanted to avoid prying eyes that might be watching the airports.

It would result in Hannah arriving in New York just in time to testify in the trial for the return of her family heirloom. Meantime she could travel safely ensconced in the bowels of the mighty ship as it slowly made its way across the Atlantic.

Christoff had already noticed an uptick in Hannah's mood. Some of her grief for Helena seemed to have passed, and her eyes looked bright and clear. Now as she turned from the rail into the wind and her hair blew up violently off her head, she grasped Christoff's hands and let out a whoop of joy. He smiled indulgently, then cupped his hands to her ear and shouted above the wind that it might be a good idea to get inside and have some hot coffee, or something stronger. She nodded, but he guessed she would far rather stay out in the wind and watch the sights. He shouted he would go and make some drinks and left her standing at the rail watching the boats bobbing on the waves and the steadily receding shoreline.

Later she came in and sat with him in the cabin. It was surprisingly luxurious, but then it should be, given the prices they had been charged. But then price wasn't the selling point; the selling point for these journeys was romance and adventure.

Pascal sat in the coffee bar opposite the hotel. She was sipping an espresso. It was gone 8.30 pm and she'd been there over an hour watching, but nothing was happening. Time to go. She checked her phone screen one last time, then looked up and stiffened. O'Leary was coming out of the hotel, looking harassed and moving fast. She chucked a bill on the counter and followed. She kept her eyes on his back someway up ahead as he forged his way through the early evening crowds. After a couple of minutes he turned into a smart looking bar set back off the pavement.

She stood across the street looking in at the well lit interior. The place was busy, probably mostly office workers taking a drink before the commute home. O'Leary was sat in a booth on his own. Pascal checked her reflection in the shop window; she was wearing shades and a beanie hat, and not much of her face was visible. With the crowd in there, there was no way O'Leary would recognise her.

She crossed the street and slipped inside, head down moving

smoothly, then up onto a stool at the bar diagonally across from O'Leary's booth. She ordered a Jack Daniels and hunched over, elbows on the counter, watching him in the mirror reflecting back at her over the bar.

He seemed pensive, maybe worried, staring down into a double scotch. Then his phone lit up on the table; he grabbed it up and clamped it to his ear. Looked like he was waiting for the call, then it was a lot of nodding, like he was talking to someone in authority. The call finished and he immediately sunk his drink and signalled the waiter for another; he checked his watch.

Pascal sipped her drink, intermittently scanning the crowd in the mirror and then coming back to O'Leary. As the minutes stretched out her eyes on the mirror scanned up the bar at the other punters sitting on stools either side of her, and about half way up she met the eyes of a man who immediately looked away. She'd clocked him as he had come in about a minute after her, and thought nothing of it, but now she felt that intuitive flicker, an alarm bell ringing. He was clean cut and well dressed and she smelt cop, but that couldn't be right.

But then her attention was caught by the door opening behind her. She looked up in the mirror into the eyes of John Schmidt, K Corp head of security, or Mr Smith, as he'd called himself at the Sunnybrook Care Home, when they'd last met. He was accompanied by the spotter guy from JFK, looking like back up muscle. Pascal was glad she'd kept her shades on, shielding her eyes from Schmidt's searching glance. She hunkered down low on the bar making herself look as small as possible. Schmidt made straight for O'Leary's booth where he took a seat opposite, the other guy sliding into the seat alongside O'Leary, his eyes constantly scanning the bar.

To start with the conversation in the booth looked like some old friends having a drink, smiles all round, but then it changed, subtly at first, with O'Leary starting to shake his head in the negative. Then he seemed to listen a bit, and then it got darker, like he was pleading, his body language all supplication, and then finally a resigned kind of slow nodding of his head. Then he just sat silent, looking like a spaced out refugee from a war zone. As Schmidt spoke Pascal could feel the malevolence of the guy radiating out all the way up to the bar. Now Schmidt was leaning forward talking fast, his huge out of proportion hands making quick slashing motions as he emphasised each point. Then O'Leary was getting up out of the booth, looking spooked, moving quickly away, almost stumbling in his anxiety to get out of the bar.

Pascal leaned back on her stool and stretched, eyes staying on Schmidt who was now talking on he phone. Then there was another guy coming in, looking around, then approaching Schmidt's booth - she guessed the bar must be some kind of secret meeting place for Schmidt. The new guy looked middle eastern, tall with a finely sculpted goatee on his chin, dressed in expensive suit and silk tie. He looked vaguely familiar, but she couldn't place him right now.

This time the meet seemed more positive with a reasonable level of mutual trust going on, but an edgy wariness as well. A moment later, yet another entrant to the party; this time a stunning blonde in evening dress, Pascal tagged as a high class hooker. There was some bawdy style laughter as Schmidt made some introductions and then he and his back-up muscle got up and left, leaving the Arab guy canoodling with the hooker.

Pascal watched for a bit but guessed they would soon decamp to a bedroom somewhere. She got up off her stool and turned to leave, but her way was blocked by the guy who had been watching her. He flashed a badge and said, 'Detective Daly, NYPD. You going somewhere, Pascal?'

How the fuck did he know her name she wondered. She covered her surprise with a bland expression whilst she studied him, recognition slowly dawning. He'd been sitting behind the prosecutor at Calver's hearing. Instant assessment: he was a hard-ass pin up boy in love with the power of the badge. Now he was trying to crowd her, edging into her space, but she stood her ground, watching and waiting, the punters around them jabbering and drinking, unaware of the stand-off.

He said, 'interfering in a police investigation is a crime. So is operating as a private investigator without a licence.'

'Sorry, I can't help you, officer. I'm a tourist having a quiet drink in a bar.'

'Wrong answer. John O'Leary's a state witness in the murder trial of Jonas Calver, who you work for. You followed O'Leary in here and you watched him until he left. In my book that's interference with a state witness.'

She knew she better row back, because if this got out of hand it could hurt Calver. 'I'm not operating as a private investigator,' she said. 'I have not questioned Mr O'Leary about anything. And the best of luck if you want to try and prove otherwise.'

They watched each other warily; checkmate. Pascal continued to study him, assessing and calculating, an idea slowly forming. 'Look, Daly, if you've been sent down here to warn me off, fine, message received. But now you're here, how about doing some real detective work?'

He said nothing, just watched her with those slaty cops eyes. So she ploughed on. 'You questioned Calver, so you'll know who he's been pointing the finger at. And I'm damn sure you also know who that rather unpleasant guy with O'Leary was just now. You know, the squat guy with the aura you could launch a space rocket off. So K Corp's enforcer is meeting with the head of security of the hotel where the murder took place. That looks like conspiracy to me. So how about joining up the dots, detective?'

Daly's hard-ass expression didn't change. 'You've been warned, Pascal,' he said. You step out of line, a millimetre, I'll be there, and I'll bury you.' He kept his eyes on her, cold and hard. Then he said, 'have a nice evening,' as he moved off.

She watched him go, wondering; had she just planted a seed, or made another enemy.

Half an hour later she sat in her cubby hole at the consulate staring at her desk-top screen, ploughing through watch lists. Dead end. Then onto the database of foreign persons of interest. She knew she'd seen the Arab guy somewhere before.

She got up and walked around the pokey office, stretching and yawning. She went out and got a coffee from the vending machine, and wandered back, enjoying the quietness and being on her own. There were still lots of people working in the building, but down here you wouldn't know it.

She sat down in Rob's chair and idly glanced at the pile of papers and reports scattered over his desk. Then she looked at his desk top computer. She tapped the keyboard and the screen came alive. Looked like Rob was in the middle of drafting a weekly digest of intel from the last seven days. It was pretty comprehensive already, stretching over 70 pages. Just to pass the time she started to scroll through; it contained all sorts of snippets of information lifted from myriad sources; mainstream newspapers, TV channels, trade journals, blogs, extremist feeds and more. And it was all skilfully melded together into a taught, sharp narrative. It was hard to do that kind of unglamorous intelligence work well, but Rob clearly had a knack for it.

She sipped her coffee, slowly scrolling away, and then on page 58 of the report there he was, the guy from the bar. She almost missed him because he was in a group. It was a small story with a photograph about the visit of General Khalid bin Ali bin Abdullah al-Faisal, from Saudi Arabia, arriving with a small entourage. The general was billed as a senior director in the defence procurement department, but Pascal knew from her work in London he was in fact director general of their security service, Al Mukhabarat Al A'amah. The man from the bar was in a group of four standing behind the general, all dressed down and inconspicuous. She leaned back and closed her eyes. She'd seen him before about three years earlier at a meeting, a kind of security conference about intelligence sharing, at the Saudi embassy in London, and he had been standing at the back of the room watching. She'd immediately tagged him as being the only real intelligence guy in the room. The rest of it was just high class window dressing for the media, desperate for a story showing there really was intelligence sharing between allies.

She read Rob's brief narrative which tagged the guy as a low level diplomat, the usual euphemism for an intelligence guy. Rob drew no conclusions from the general's visit which appeared to be entirely routine. The Saudi press release merely said he was there for some high level meetings with his US counterparts, and that was it. Pascal wondered. She sat for a long time staring into space, then she reached in her pocket and took out the card Bob Jeffreys had given her. She tapped it against her teeth, mulling, then she reached for her phone.

Bob was on a hot date - hard to imagine - but he'd see her for a coffee, same place, Starbucks, at noon next day.

I was back in the attorney visiting area, in the chicken hutch, waiting, stomach making unpleasant gurgling noises from the breakfast I'd just wolfed down. I knew it was pointless asking who my visitor was. Maybe it was Morganna with some good news. It wasn't. It was Assistant DA Stahl and Detective Daly.

Stahl was wearing an expensive suit to go with his even more expensive dental work. Daly was in a cheap blue job with a natty striped tie.

'Since you're the attorney of record, Calver, I gotta speak to you, so here we are,' Stahl said, looking around distastefully.

'Well I must be important, Stahl, to get you out here – or maybe its your boss cracking the whip? Media coverage is not always good, is it? And he's told you to handle it, right?'

I watched Stahl. Not much of a flicker, but it was there, and Daly was smiling. Stahl hadn't wanted to come, but Daly had.

'Okay, guys, lets make things easy, shall we?' I said. 'What do you want?'

Stahl looked at Daly.

'And hey, how about some coffee? Or even tea. Us English, we always work better on a nice cuppa.'

'Tea's for faggots,' Daly said. 'So I'm guessing you're having a ball in here, right, Calver?'

Stahl watched me for a second, gauging things, then nodded at Daly. 'See what you can rustle up, detective.'

'Yeah, Daly, and make mine Earl Grey, two sugars, easy on the milk.'

'Fuck you, Calver,' Daly said, but he did Stahl's bidding, banging the door as he went out.

'Okay, Calver. Two things: first, we've managed to locate the CCTV file and it will be made available to you along with the tie,' he said. That stumped me. Way too easy.

Stahl watched, looking for the faintest reaction. He didn't get it.

He continued, 'secondly, its incumbent on us – and you – to explore whether there's scope for an early disposition of this case. See if we can avoid a trial and save the tax payer a ton of money.'

'You want a deal?' I said.

'No. But we are prepared to let you plead to lesser charges in exchange for a guilty plea.'

They wanted a deal. This was one of the parts of the US system I didn't like; the plea bargain. We had something similar in the UK but it was nothing like as unfair. US justice fostered a system that frequently forced completely innocent defendants to plead guilty to crimes they had not committed, because the risk of rolling the dice, going to trial, and losing, was simply too great. It was blatantly unfair and disproportionately affected the poor who couldn't afford expensive lawyers to fight their cases.

But I wasn't going to play the game as there was no way I was going to plead to anything. But I needed to gauge how bad they wanted a deal, because that might hint at some vulnerability in their case. Then again the sudden and miraculous appearance of the missing CCTV militated against that, but what did I know.

'So what are you offering me,' I said, looking up as Daly banged his way back in carrying three coffees. He slapped mine down, spilling half of it.

'Sex game gone bad, second degree murder, fifteen years to life. You'll be out sooner than you can write your memoirs. Hell, we'll even look to getting you repatriated to a UK jail if you want,' Stahl said, taking a tentative sip of his coffee.

Then again, maybe they just wanted to get shot of me. You couldn't blame them really. Bit of media pressure; victim and alleged perp both British citizens, so why not ship the whole mess back to the UK and let them sort it out, and pay the freight. But just maybe it meant there was a weakness in the case. 'So where would I do my time?' I said, probing, seeing if I could shake anything loose.

Stahl looked at Daly, thinking they were getting somewhere. 'I'm sure we can work something out. A nice federal facility in upstate New York with the gentlest of regimes, and all kitted out for nice white folks like you, Calver. How about that? What d'you think, Daly?' Stahl said, with a wink at his underling.

'Be just like Sunday school, boss,' Daly chipped in, but I got the impression he was gritting his teeth. I guessed he'd far rather go for murder one and a big trial.

'So what's it to be, Calver?

I adopted a meditative expression as if considering his offer carefully and then said slowly, enunciating each word carefully, 'no fucking way.'

'You sure about that, Calver?' Stahl said.

'Damn tootin' right I am.'

'Okay,' he said. 'But it'll be your funeral.'

Stahl got up, buttoning his jacket. 'You change your mind, Calver, here's my card,' he said, placing it on the table. Then, as if as an afterthought, 'Oh, and by the way. We're ready for trial as well, so we can agree a start date for Monday morning. The court have okayed it so we don't have to go back to see the judge tomorrow.'

That got me. If they were saying they were ready for trial and they had given up the CCTV so easily, maybe I'd completely misread them. After all, the prosecution routinely offered to take a plea to lesser charges to save the people the costs of a trial so why did it have to mean anything? This seemed to be borne out by the fact that Stahl didn't push it. They knew I was done talking and I knew they hadn't tried very hard to make me talk, just enough to satisfy protocol. Stahl gave me a brief, barren look, then knocked on the door and called the guard to take me back to my cell. Then they both nodded to me and left. Maybe Stahl was a lot cleverer than I was. I guess we'd find out at trial.

Chapter Nine

Southern District Court

Day 3

'Your honour, the defense reserve their opening statement until the start of their case,' Browder said. Then he sat down with a half smile on his face, turning slightly in his chair so he could watch Morganna. He knew she would have been expecting him to take up some time with his speech, but now he'd thrown her on the back foot again, hustling her, forcing her to call her first witness before she was ready.

She cursed under her breath, pondering. Why was Browder reserving, foregoing the advantage of making a speech straight after her opening? The ploy left her feeling insecure again, questioning whether she had missed something. She tapped her ballpoint pen against her teeth, thinking hard. Then she half guessed it. Browder still didn't really know what Hannah was going to say, if she ever turned up, so he was playing it safe. When he found out, then he'd make his speech.

She sensed Friedman fidgeting. As she looked up, he said, 'Miss Fedler?'

'Yes your honour. Call Doctor Efraim Borkowski,' she said. She heard the usher echo her call outside and then the court doors were opening. She watched Borkowski move across the courtroom and into the witness box. He was a small man with thick black hair, a bushy beard and glasses. He wore a kind of grey green, tweed three piece suit, and stretched across his waistcoat was a gold watch chain. Other than the one longish evening phone call, Morganna had not spoken to him face to face.

'Doctor Borkowski, could you state your full name for the record and then detail your qualifications and experience for the court, please?' Morganna asked, smiling politely at her witness.

He didn't smile back. He didn't look at Morganna, but turned to the jury and said, 'my name is Efraim Borkowski and I am visiting emeritus professor of Jewish European history at New York University. I have worked with the Justice Departments office of Special Investigations, now known as the Human Rights and Special Prosecutions Section, and I have also worked at the US Holocaust Memorial Museum and the Berlin Documents Centre, and I am currently also serving as a director of the Museum of Jewish heritage here in New York City.'

'That's quite a resume doctor—'

'Professor, please,' he interrupted her.

'Professor. Now, have you had occasion to speak with the plaintiff in this case, Hannah Cohen?'

'Yes I have, extensively, as well as via email.'

'I'm sorry, your honour,' Browder interjected lazily from his chair. 'This is a claim for restitution of some jewellery, nothing more. Now I'm sure professor Borkowski could keep us all spellbound for hours with his historical knowledge, but what possible relevance could it have to this case?'

'I'm inclined to agree, Mr Browder,' Friedman said, turning to look at Morganna.

'Your honour, please give us some leeway. Plaintiff is currently on her way here and the jury will hear from her extensively. But, she is eighty seven years old and with the best will in the world cannot remember all the background and context, and she will find testifying here extremely trying. We have called professor Borkowski here, essentially to fill in the historical gaps, to give the jury the backstory if you like, without which they may struggle to understand the environment in which these events took place,' Morganna said, pausing to draw breath. She knew she was gabbling, her mouth running away with it through nerves.

She took another breath. 'Furthermore, your honour,' she said, slower, more measured, 'we shall be asking professor Borkowski to authenticate or cast a professional opinion on certain artefacts or articles of historical evidence we intend to adduce.'

Morganna held her breath as she watched Friedman cogitating; if he blew them out, she'd lose half her case. He pursed his lips. 'I'll allow it,' he said grudgingly, 'for now, but if I feel your straying into anything that is not within the narrow parameters of this case, I'll call a halt, is that understood, Miss Fedler?'

'Absolutely, your honour,' Morganna said, offering up a little prayer to the God of trial lawyers. She was learning, but it was hard and slow.

'So what you got for me?' Bob Jeffreys said, sipping black coffee and focusing all his attention on his cellphone. They were sat back in the window seats in Starbucks, midday sun streaming down, Pascal watching the teeming Manhattan streets, wondering how to play it with Jeffreys.

Look, Bob,' she said, 'I been thinking, maybe you could help me out with some information I need. Low level run of the mill stuff you'd have easy access to. And some of it's old, going way back. In exchange we could trade, and I could do some freelancing for you.'

Bob didn't say anything, almost as if he hadn't heard her, or maybe he was just playing stupid, hard to get. She'd try another way. She held her phone out with a picture of the guy from the bar. Jeffreys glanced, poker faced. 'Yeah, who is he?' he said.

'Names Saad Al-Masrahi. Of Al Mukhabarat Al A'amah fame.'

'And?

'Saw him last night, here in the city.'

'So?' Jeffreys said, still concentrating on his phone screen, but adding, 'we know that crew came in with General Khalid from Saudi Arabia. All cleared and squeaky clean.'

'Yeah, but he's got some interesting friends…..,' she said, and left it hanging there, hoping he would bite.

'Yeah? And who might they be?' he said, still studying his phone screen.

Pascal lcaned over and took a surreptitious glance. Looked like a steamy exchange of sexual banter with someone. 'Bob,' she said, 'are you listening to me?'

He looked up from his phone screen, face flushed red. 'So what have you got?' he said again, as if he hadn't heard a word she'd said.

Pascal held her temper in check and ploughed on. 'This Al-Masrahi guy met the head of security for the Kurrilick Corporation, guy called John Schmidt. Deep discussion ensued, then a high class hooker appeared. Looked like Schmidt was pimping for him, providing a special gift for the end of the evening.'

'You gotta picture of her?' Jeffries said, licking his lips.

'No, Bob, I don't have a picture of her,' Pascal said, patience finally exhausted. 'Look, if I'm keeping you from something, maybe we can do this another time. You know, like when you're not trying to have phone sex?'

Jeffreys watched her for a moment, slowly divining that she wasn't kidding. He sighed and put his phone down. 'Sorry,' he said. 'Just letting off steam. We all need to do that sometimes. That's my way.'

'Hey, no problem.' Pascal said. 'I've been there. Fact I know a guy who builds model aeroplanes for the same reason. It takes all sorts, Bob. Don't worry about it.' She sipped more coffee, glancing sideways at him, hoping she hadn't embarrassed him, but he looked fine. She ploughed on, 'so why would a Saudi secret service guy be hobnobbing with K Corp's head of security, who by the way, is one awesomely frightening looking motherfucker?'

'K Corp, eh?' Jeffrey's mused. 'Never come across them in an intelligence context. CEO, what's his name?'

'David Milken.'

'Yeah, that's the guy. They say he's going to run for mayor, so I doubt they're gonna do anything to screw that up,' Jeffreys said. 'I'll have a look, can't hurt. But, hey, no promises.'

'Well, look, Bob, if you're taking a look at K Corp, maybe you can have a look at the founder, Angel Milken, David's father, as well?' she said, hoping he wasn't going to think she was being too pushy, trying to work too much out of the connection before she'd brought anything to the table. But then again, if she didn't ask?

'I'd be particularly interested in anything from the war years and how he entered the USA. The British have no record of him anywhere?'

'This for your guy Calver, is it, Courtney? He must be some tough monkey, roughing it out on Rikers,' Jeffreys said.

'Calver's fine – in the courtroom,' she said, before adding, quietly, 'anywhere else he's a fucking disaster.'

'I should get him outta there kiddo - and quick,' Jeffreys said, getting up to go. 'And I'll get back to you on the other stuff.'

'Good enough. I'll be waiting,' she said.

Southern District Court

'Now, professor Borkowski,' Morganna said, handing him a document, 'can you tell the court what this is?'

'I surely can,' Borkowski said. 'Its an extract from *De Telegraaf,* a dutch newspaper, dated June 20th 1938, with a certified english translation.'

'Yes it is, and I'm introducing this as Exhibit HC1, your honour,' Morganna said as the usher distributed copies to the jury and judge. 'Professor, tell the court, in essence about the little story depicted in the extract.'

'Yes,' Borkowski said, perching some bifocals on the end of his nose. 'Its what nowadays we might call a human interest story, and it concerns the Cohen family, then living in an area of Amsterdam called *Jodenhoek*, or the Jewish quarter. The story tells of a local girl, Hannah Cohen, saving the life of a five year old boy, by grabbing him and pulling him out of the canal. The child's mother, a member of a prominent diamond dealing family, as a mark of her undying gratitude for saving the life of her son, gave to Hannah Cohen's parents, for Hannah, a magnificent gold and diamond encrusted pendant with matching brooch. And there in the article is a picture of little Hannah, holding the pendant and brooch.'

'Thats's right, professor,' Morganna said. 'Now, we shall be hearing from another expert about the jewellery shown in the picture, but in the meantime, professor, perhaps you might put this story into its historical context for the jury - what does it tell us?'

Morganna could sense both Browder and Friedman getting impatient with the generalised testimony and she knew it wouldn't be long before one of them objected. 'As briefly as you can please, professor,' Morganna added with a smile at Friedman.

Borkowski took the bifocals off the end of his nose and leaned back in his chair. 'Prior to the war more than half of Hollands 140,000 registered Jews lived in Amsterdam, and *Jodenhoek* was the epicentre of that, until the Nazi's marched in, in May 1940. By the end of the war virtually all of *Jodenhoek's* Jews had gone.

'From the article we see that the Cohen's appear to have been a normal lower middle class Jewish family who were art conservators, the father, David working at one of the local museums, having taken over that job from his father, Isaac. They also appear to have done some art dealing.'

'Thank you professor. Now we shall hear from Hannah, that the family were deported from their home in April 1943, although unfortunately at this stage it is unclear what happened to them after that. Again looking at historical context, can you tell us what happened to the majority of Jews who were deported at that time from *Jodenhoek*?'

'Yes. There is a clear historical record. Almost all Jews from there were moved first to Westerbork, a transit camp in North east Holland. From there commencing in July 1942 we know that there were some 93 transports mostly to Auschwitz and Sobibor death camps.'

'Your honour,' Browder said, rising to his feet. 'Again, might I ask, what is the relevance of any of this to the simple issue facing the court?'

Friedman looked about ready to concur. He said, 'unless you've got an answer to that, Miss Fedler, I'm—'

'Thank you your honour,' Morganna said, breaking in, light smile covering her gritted teeth as she tried to think of a way to keep Borkowski on the stand. She would have to go for a half way house.

'Your honour, I am in some difficulty in the absence of my client, and without clear instructions, so perhaps I will finish here with professor Borkowski for now, on the proviso - I understand he intends to remain here to observe proceedings - that I may recall him later if necessary.'

Friedman smiled at her meek acquiescence. 'By all means, Miss Fedler. Mr Browder, cross examination?'

'Yes, thank you your honour', Browder said, rising to his feet to start his cross examination. 'Professor Borkowski. As far as you are aware, does Hannah Cohen have a tattooed number anywhere on her body? As I am sure you know, that was the traditional identification method used by the concentration camp authorities for inmates.'

'No she does not, but—'

'Thank you, professor,' Browder said, cutting him off. 'In the historical record is there any mention of a fourteen year child named Hannah Cohen escaping from the two concentration camps mentioned by you?'

'Again, no, but—'

'Thank you professor,' Browder said, brutally chopping him off again. He turned to the judge, 'I have no more questions your honour,' he said.

Morganna sat for a moment, wondering whether she should re-examine Borkowski, give him a chance to flesh out the answers Browder had just chopped the ends off. But then again, maybe better to leave off now. She looked up at the clock, 3.50 p m. 'Your honour, I have no more questions for this witness right now, but as mentioned before, I may wish to recall him at a later date.'

'Thank you, Miss Fedler,' Friedman said. 'Given the time, we'll adjourn now for the weekend, back here Monday morning at 10 am, folks,' he said looking at the jury. 'I take it,' he said, turning back to Morganna, 'you will be ready to call your next witness then?'

'Yes, your honour,' Morganna said, fingers crossed behind her back.

'And who might that be, if I might ask?' Friedman said.

'Hannah Palmer, nee Cohen,' she replied, hoping to hell she could rely on Pascal's garbled phone message that Hannah was on her way, whatever that might mean. If Hannah arrived maybe her money would too and they could get Calver out on bail. Then he could give her some help, 'cause boy did she need it.

Hannah came into the cabin, cheeks red from the wind outside, eyes alive and dancing. Their room was spacious with a small dining area to the side with a table in the centre of it and chairs each side, set on blue vinyl flooring. Then there was a larger living and sleeping area alongside, with bunk beds against the wall and a old battered leather settee in the middle, and at shoulder height, a couple of smallish portholes out of which all you could see was the grey green sea stretching away for miles.

As Hannah sat down on the settee, Christoff pushed his way in through the cabin door carrying a tray. 'Dinner is served, madame,' he said laying the tray on the table with a flourish. 'Its a bit early I know, but its the best time to get the good stuff from the galley.'

On the tray were a couple of plates containing sausages in onion sauce, mashed potatoes and carrots. There was also a small bottle of vodka, two glasses containing crushed ice and a cardboard container of orange juice.

Hannah clapped her hands together with delight. She moved to the table looking at the food and smelling the aroma. 'You know,' she said with wonder, 'I'm famished.'

'Good. Lets eat,' Christoff said, holding out her chair

Later they sat on the couch making small inroads into the vodka, the movement of the giant freighter virtually undetectable, only the distant rumble of the engines reminding them of where they were. Hannah's upbeat mood seemed to have passed, and now she seemed sombre, as if she were wrestling with some internal conflict. 'Wisliceny?' she finally said. 'Your surname. It has a history.'

Christoff grimaced. 'Indeed it does. Alas, we cannot escape our past.'

'Dieter Wisliceny,' Hannah said, as if trying the name out and finding it distasteful. 'He was a Captain in the SS and an associate of Eichmann's. Heavily involved in the deportation of Jews from Greece, Hungary and Slovakia. Hanged by the Czechs for war crimes in 1948.' Hannah glanced at him quickly. 'Don't tell me you're related?'

'Distantly. Father was a cousin, maybe once removed. I wish permanently removed.'

Hannah smiled. 'That's a trap you mustn't fall into, Christoff. Guilt by association. I only know what I know about such things because John insisted I read some Holocaust history. He thought it might jog my memory, help with the pendant claim and what happened. It didn't. It just horrified and depressed me.'

Christoff watched her, examining her face as if for clues. 'Just how much do you remember, Hannah, really?'

She looked down into her glass, then took a small sip of vodka, eyes smoky and distant. 'Fragments,' she said. 'And even then I sometimes think its memory or dreams mingled and playing tricks on me.'

Christoff finished his drink and leaned his head onto the back of the settee. For a while, neither spoke. Then Christoff said, 'years ago, as part of our training in the security services, I was involved in testing some interrogation techniques, and one of those techniques was hypnotherapy.' He laughed nervously. 'It was canned long ago as being dangerous, and worse, possibly unreliable, so they dropped it. But I've never forgotten the techniques, and from time to time, in the past when I was out in the field, I did have cause to improvise if you like, and revisit those techniques. Never officially of course.'

Hannah turned to him, fascination and fear in her eyes. 'D'you suppose…….. It might…..' She said, her words tailing off.

'It is or can be dangerous, unlocking parts of your mind that your subconscious has closed off to protect your sanity. And it can take you to places you may not wish to go,' Christoff said slowly, his words also tailing off as he thought about it. 'And' he said, continuing almost as if he were talking to himself, trying to convince himself, 'lawyers hate it. Any hint that you've even thought about hypnotherapy to help with your memory, you'll get destroyed and laughed out of court, but……'

'But, it might get me back my memory, so we actually know what happened,' Hannah said, voice firming up with conviction. 'I mean, to be honest, I don't care about the pendant. What I mean is, if it wasn't stolen and was purchased legitimately, then they can keep it. But I do want to know what happened to my family.'

Half an hour later, after Hannah had insisted she had only had one sip of Vodka, and there was no way it would affect her mind, she lay stretched out on the couch. Christoff sat in a chair pulled up to her side. For a while he spoke to Hannah in a slow and soothing voice, talking with her calmly about early and happy childhood experiences. Later he asked her to visualise walking slowly down a country lane, then as his voice got slower he began to count down from 10 to 1. When he reached 3, Hannah was deeply under, eyes closed, breathing regular and slow.

As Christoff continued to speak to her, softly and calmly, he looked down at the trial notes, and Hannah's last statement. 'Hannah, you are fourteen years old. It is April 1943 and you are standing in the square in Amsterdam with your parents, baby sister Helena and your grandfather. You each, apart from Helena, are carrying a small bag or valise,' Christoff said, trying to keep the anxiety out of his voice so that it remained calm and peaceful.

For a moment Hannah remained calm, body limp, then Christoff could see rapid movements under her eyelids. Hannah began to moan quietly, and her body began to shiver, tremors passing through her like an electric current. Then she screamed abruptly in a child's voice so loud that Christoff drew back in his chair, 'Mama, *no.*'

Frightened by her reaction, Christoff quickly, desperately, drew her back, counting up from 1 to 10. Then she was waking, seemingly from a gentle sleep.

Christoff watched her, concern deepening the lines on his face. She smiled uncertainly, her eyes haunted. She said, 'what happened?'

He said, eyes bleak, 'we need to talk.'

As I walked away from breakfast Sunday morning, still hurriedly chewing on the granular crud they called cereal, they told me my bail was coming through. I thought they were kidding, trying to raise a cheap laugh, but it was solid, and a couple of hours later I signed the paperwork and I was out.

Morganna came to meet me in her little blue Subaru car. As we crossed the bridge there were tremors in my hands and I felt shaky, like I was coming out of a long drunk. Getting out of Rikers was great, of course it was, but tomorrow morning at 10 a m I would be going on trial for my life, and if we didn't have anything to counter the prosecution evidence, we might as well turn the car around and go straight back.

I tried to relax, tried to enjoy the sunshine and the people, but as I listened to Morganna chatter away about nothing it was beginning to dawn on me that it had been a very bad idea to insist on a quick trial. I wondered if we could row back from it now. I turned and looked at Morganna, basking in the glow of getting me out and getting the trial listed so quick, and decided I didn't want to break her mood. She said she was taking me to Brad's loft apartment in Manhattan where she was staying whilst he was in London. She said she would be making dinner that evening and Pascal was coming. I leaned my head back on the rest and closed my eyes. It felt good to be out, but I was filled with trepidation for the future. Did I even have a future. I wondered about praying.

Chapter Ten

People v Calver - Manhattan Supreme Court

Day 1

The 13th floor courtroom had a kind of faded majesty about it. Faux oak panels, flags, embossed seals and tired looking court officials who I'm sure had seen it all before. I was sat at the defense table alone because I didn't want anyone else there with me on that first day - I don't know why. Perhaps I was ashamed of being in the dock on trial for murder. Who knows.

Most of life is a gamble and I'd taken a calculated risk on insisting on a quick trial and now it looked like I'd blown it. I had assumed that with Pascal onboard we'd easily be able to discredit the hotels CCTV camera footage that stood at the heart of the prosecution case, but we hadn't even got close. If things stayed as they were, I was going back to jail.

I watched Stahl as he rose to make his opening speech. He looked serious. Gone was the glib Hollywood smile and the rather stagey hand movements. Today he looked sombre, dark suit with a crisp white shirt, simple and effective. He turned to the jury. 'Jonas Calver was a washed up UK attorney with a drink problem and a dirty little secret, and that secret was that he got off on strangling women,' he told them.

And there we had it. Their whole case encapsulated into a pithy little statement that the jury were unlikely to forget. And then Stahl was moving on, fast and efficient, laying out the witnesses he would be calling and what they would say. 'You will hear from witnesses and see on the hotels CCTV that during the time that the murder took place, only one other person besides the victim was ever in that hotel room, and that person was Jonas Calver, this defendant,' he said, stretching his arm out in my direction. I kept my face expressionless and my head stationary. Defendants who shake their head and scowl every time something negative is said pretty soon end up alienating a jury.

Stahl talked about the sexual assault, then cause and time of death and lastly about my green silk tie, giving a masterly overview of what was to come. Then he hit his peroration: 'This case couldn't be simpler,' he said. 'It's not a "whodunnit" style murder with multiple suspects. There is only one person who could have committed this crime, and that person is Jonas Calver.'

As Stahl retook his seat I glanced over at the jury. They looked determined and resolute; a group of ordinary New Yorkers doing their civic duty, but they'd only heard one side of the story, and now it was my turn. I had a choice; I could make a speech now putting my side - essentially that I didn't do it - or I could reserve my statement and make it just before I called my own witnesses. The former option was almost always right but in this case I was going for the latter.

I looked over at the Judge, Millicent "Milli" Gonzalez. She'd walked both sides of the aisle, prosecuting and defending, so she knew the score. She was small and bird like, with large owlish eyes behind faintly ostentatious bright blue rimmed eyeglasses. Her hair was tawny brown and cut short, and her voice was strong and authoritative. She looked over at me now. 'Mr Calver?' she said.

I half rose from my seat, saying, 'your honour I will reserve my statement.'

She nodded and turned to the prosecutor. 'Call your first witness, Mr Stahl.'

Southern District Court

Day 4

Across Manhattan, in the Southern District Court, Morganna stood and watched, along with the jury, as Hannah Palmer made her way slowly across the courtroom to the witness box. Hannah was smartly dressed in a simple blue skirt and matching top with white blouse underneath, and her grey-streaked hair was pulled up into an old fashioned bun on the back of her head. Her face looked healthily weatherbeaten and brown from the sun and wind that had come off the north Atlantic on the crossing. She looked refreshed, calm and resolute, if a little tired.

The giant freighter had docked the night before and she and Christoff had gone straight to the loft apartment, eaten and gone to bed. There had been no time to talk, and Morganna and Calver had been closeted away, focused entirely on Calver's murder trial.

As Hannah settled herself into the witness box Morganna looked around the sparsely populated courtroom. Civil trials were generally dry and staid affairs. They didn't tend to pull in the crowds of popcorn chewing courtroom junkies like criminal trials did, and that suited Morganna fine. She glanced at Browder sitting at the defense table on his own. Today he wore a coal black three-piece suit, his spiky grey hair acting as a counterpoint, giving him the look of lawyer as cliche, the embodiment of slick, empty superficiality. Hey, easy on the cynicism, she told herself

She flicked her eyes over judge Friedman; he was hunched over reading some last minute notes, scribbling some annotations in the margin, then he manoeuvred his bottom around in his seat, trying to get comfortable, preparing to call everyone to order and get the ball rolling. Lastly Morganna checked the jury. They looked refreshed after the weekend, ready to go. Now they had the main character in their drama, in front of them, ready to tell her story, there was an expectancy in their eyes. They wanted to hear her, hear what she had to say.

Friedman nodded at Morganna, 'Miss Fedler,' he prompted her.

'Thank you your honour,' Morganna said, rising to her feet. She turned to Hannah, nodded with brief smile and then she began, her voice calm and steady. 'Please tell the court your full name?'

'My name is Hannah Palmer, which is my married name, but I was born Hannah Cohen,' she said. Her voice had a low musical quality and still carried a faint european lilt.

'And when and where were you born?'

'I was born on 12th February 1929 in Amsterdam, Holland,' she said. Morganna paused a moment as she sensed some surprised smiles passing between jurors. They were finding it hard to believe the witness was 87 years old.

'Whereabouts in Amsterdam were you born?'

'I was born in the Jewish quarter, known as *Jodenhoek*.'

'Earlier the jury were shown this newspaper,' Morganna said, passing her a copy of *Der Telegraaf*. 'In the story it tells us of a little girl called Hannah Cohen saving a boy from drowning in the canal.'

'Yes.'

'Was that you?'

'Yes it was.'

'Tell the jury what happened?' Morganna said.

Hannah seemed surprised by the question. Maybe she had never been asked it before. She looked at Morganna, perhaps not sure what her lawyer wanted from her. Then her eyes seemed to turn inwards, her mind running back, delving across time.

'We were just kids,' Hannah said. 'Three of us. Tommy Van Der Valk, Greta and me, walking home from school by the canal. We were horsing around with a ball like kids do, but then Tommy tripped when reaching for a catch and he went over. But he hit his head on the wall going into the water.

'All I did was jump in and get him out. A man gave him mouth to mouth and he was okay in the end,' Hannah said.

Morganna was learning that witnesses didn't always say what you wanted them to. She tried to keep the frustration out of her voice. 'Well the newspaper story suggests it was a little more than that. They talk of your heroism, that the boy was knocked unconscious and couldn't swim, and that a child had already drowned in that stretch of the canal a year earlier. And the boys mother clearly believed you saved his life?'

Hannah nodded, perhaps realising what Morganna wanted from her. 'Yes I suppose I did save him, and he would have drowned if I hadn't jumped in and swam back with him to the bank,' she said, almost grudgingly.

'Tell us about the pendant and how you acquired it?' Morganna asked.

'Well a few days later, Mrs. Van Der Valk came around to our house to thank me for saving Tommy. I remember she was very emotional and said more than once that Tommy was the light of her life as he was their only child. She called me an Angel. Then she took out of her bag a large black rectangular wooden box which she put on the table. Inside was the gold pendant, and beside it in the box, the matching brooch. We were not rich and we had never seen anything so valuable or so beautiful. Mama tried to refuse but Mrs Van Der Valk wouldn't hear of it, so we accepted the gift and thanked her.

'Then a few days later a reporter turned up with a photographer and the story appeared in the next days edition of *Der Telegraaf*. That's the extract you now have here, all those years later.

'In fact at the time my father was so proud, he had the story framed and hung on our dining room wall,' Hannah said, smiling gently as she remembered.

Morganna breathed a sigh of relief that she'd got that first piece in, but there was a long way to go. She looked up at the clock then moved on to her next question.

People v Calver - Manhattan Supreme Court

Stahl's first witness was the dispatcher who had taken O'Leary's call at 9.45 am just after he had discovered Helena's body in her room. I wasn't sure why Stahl called this witness since I didn't dispute her evidence. He then went back in time and called the bellhop who had served us in my room prior to the murder. His name was Ramon, and I remembered him for his easy smile and natural charm. Stahl stuck to eliciting the basic facts that Ramon had been called to my room twice that evening, firstly at around 8.30 pm when he had brought up our dinner of steaks and a bottle of red wine, and secondly, later at around 9.50 pm, when he'd brought up two more bottles of wine. Then Stahl turned him over to me for cross examination.

'Just a couple of questions, Ramon?' I said. 'When you brought up the steaks and bottle of wine at eight thirty, how did I seem?'

'Pretty good,' he said. 'You looked like you was having a good time. I didn't see the lady then, as I guess she was in the bathroom.'

'That's right,' I said. 'And what about the second time, later, when you came up with the two bottles of wine?'

'Same thing. Lady was there as well that time, and you was both smiling and kiddin' around that maybe I should join you.'

'Did I look like someone who a couple of hours later was going to rape and murder her?' I asked, letting the jury see the faint curl of my lip. I expected an objection from Stahl, but it never came.

'No way, man. You was chillin' and fine.'

I sat down, strangely pleased with myself, a small victory, but then Stahl was up on his feet for re-direct.

'I guess Mr Calver tipped you each time, right? How much, can you remember?'

'I don't forget that. It was a five spot, each way, man,' he said, smiling at the memory.

'That's pretty generous, Ramon. I guess it might make you want to help Mr Calver out if he was in a tight spot, right?'

'I guess,' he said, before he picked up on the inference in the question, his expression turning indignant. 'I's tellin' what I saw,' he added.

'No further questions,' Stahl said.

He'd just neutralised my cross - even steven's again. Then Judge Gonzalez called a halt; it was time for lunch.

It was Pascal's last day at the hotel and she wanted one last crack at finding something that might help Calver. Dolores the maid had told her that the hotel manager, O'Leary had, as well as his room, a small office in the back area where the CCTV surveillance monitors were kept. She said O'Leary had feeds running off them direct to his laptop and smartphone, so essentially he had eyes everywhere, running 24/7, and when he wasn't viewing this he was out prowling the floors. But there were some blind spots: the service elevators and fire escape and, apparently most of the back area.

Pascal had been studying the CCTV systems used in the hotel, reading up on the dry technical specs. She had also lifted Dolores passkey and got Rob Galloway at MI6 to make a copy, before slipping the original back into Dolores bag.

She stood in the lobby reception area completing the check-out procedure. She glanced at the clock on the wall behind the desk and surreptitiously pressed the stop watch starter button on her wrist. Then she slapped her hand against her forehead. 'Hot damn. Forgot my shoes. I know I left them under the bed. Mind of I just run back up and get them?' she asked the girl.

'Sure,' the girl said handing her entry card back.

In her old room she opened her bag, took out some clothing and quickly dressed in black jeans, tee shirt and beanie hat. She also put on some disposable rubber gloves. Then she moved out into the corridor with her small carry bag, and into the fire escape. Two floors up she came on a large utility store room she'd scouted earlier. It contained maintenance and cleaning paraphernalia, industrial sized vacuum cleaners, mops, brushes, bleach and other cleaning fluids. In the corner was a pile of sheets used for covering furniture. She moved over to them, crouched down and opened her bag again, and took out a cigarette and disposable lighter.

During her stay she'd watched O'Leary whenever she could, trying to get a handle on the guy. He was an inveterate smoker who seemed to take a puff whenever he could get away with it. A corollary of that was his habit of taking his disposable lighter, or more usually, an unlighted cigarette out of his pocket, and toying with them whilst speaking to staff or talking on the phone. So when he'd done just that, whilst on the phone in the bar, and then suddenly got up and left, leaving the cigarette in a cup on the table, she'd grabbed it.

Now she lit that very cigarette, holding her gloved fingers over her lips so none of her DNA would get onto it, and drew on it until the tip burned bright. Then she opened the lighter and poured the contents onto the pile of sheets, knelt down and held the cigarette to the moist area until it started to burn.

She stood up, checked her stopwatch and scanned the smoke detectors above the growing embers and small licking flames. Then she dropped the plastic lighter and ground it into splinters with her boot heel, then the cigarette as well, and then she moved to the door. If there was a major investigation they'd find the cigarette, and might get O'Leary's DNA. It was just a precaution as far as she was concerned.

She watched the smoke build and curl up under the alarm, then as it started to shriek, she was moving into the stairwell, then up towards O'Leary's room. She knew he wouldn't be around that day as he was due to be giving evidence at Calver's murder trial. She peeped around the fire door and watched for a moment as some guests exited their rooms and ran for the lifts. She checked her watch; seven minutes down, and now she could hear fire sirens in the distance and there was a tannoy announcement telling all guests to exit immediately.

She dug her dummy door card out and approached the room, and then she was in. It looked like a tramp lived there, dirty as hell with unwashed clothing lying around as well as plates with half eaten meals congealing on them. There was a laptop sitting open on the desk, running. She looked at the screen and was startled to see herself - it must be monitoring the room. If it was feeding to O'Leary he could be watching her right now, but then he wouldn't be allowed to use his phone in court so maybe she'd be okay for now.

She quickly tossed the room - nothing. The only personal thing in the room seemed to be the picture of a young girl on the desk, no doubt his daughter. She went back to the laptop, ignoring her image on the screen. It would be password protected, and she didn't have time to crack it. She made a quick decision. She powered it down, put it in her bag and left. If it had a tracking device, she reckoned Rob would be able to disable it.

In the corridor a few last stragglers were moving to the lifts even though the tannoy was saying don't use them. Pascal ran to the service elevator and pressed for ground floor. She checked her watch again; twelve minutes gone. On the ground floor as the doors opened in the back service area, it was empty. She peeped around the corner looking into the lobby as a group of fireman came running in towards the elevators and stairs.

She turned back and moved into the small office and looked at the monitors, then she sat down at the console. She had gone over the hotels CCTV system theoretically with Christoff when trying to work out how Calver had been framed, and also as preparation for this little jaunt, but it was a different ballgame trying to operate it in the real world. She checked into the central operating system and looked for the delete and overwrite monitor and controls. She knew they would quickly be able to discover that the CCTV covering the period of the fire had been deleted and overridden, but she didn't care about that, so long as they didn't discover the identity of their arsonist.

She couldn't find the controls and was starting to sweat and curse. Any second now she would be found out, maybe a fireman or more likely a staff member. She stopped, counted to five, took a deep breath and started again. After a tense few seconds the system control page materialised. She checked her watch again; fourteen and a half minutes gone. She clicked on the command to delete and overwrite the last sixteen minutes of cctv recording, and then adjusted the timing and clock. That was the best she could do right now. She took a last look around, grabbed her bag and moved out of the office and peeked around the corner, awaiting the right moment. Then as three burly fire guys ran past her towards the entrance she pulled her beanie hat down over her head and coughing and covering her face as if suffering from smoke inhalation, she veered out from the side so it would look on the monitors that she was coming from the lifts, and then she followed them out onto the street.

Chapter Eleven

People v Calver - Manhattan Supreme Court

I studied O'Leary as he answered Stahl's initial questions about who he was and what he did at the hotel. With that name, pale complexion and reddish hair, an Irish ancestry was a pretty safe bet, but the blarney seemed to have been removed from O'Leary at birth. His answers were short, sharp and monosyllabic - a prosecutors dream. Stahl appeared to have him under tight control; after each question there was a very slight pause as he considered his answer, before he opened his mouth.

'And when did you first come across the defendant?'

Pause, then, 'It was early hours of the morning of the murder, about 1.45 am, in the hotel bar.'

'Tell us about that?'

O'Leary paused for a bit longer this time. 'I was on my rounds and had stopped off in the bar. Mr Calver was there on his own. He invited me to join him for an Irish Coffee, which I declined. But I chatted with him for a few minutes, which is all part of the job,' he said.

'And how did this chat end?'

'A message came through that Helena Palmer had called down and asked that Mr Calver should go up to her room.'

There was a rustling sound of movement coming from the jury

box. I had known that answer was coming because it was in the discovery provided by the prosecution, but the jury didn't. I looked at O'Leary, lying through his teeth, and there wasn't a flicker.

'What happened?'

'He finished his drink, and left, I assume to go to Helena Palmer's room.'

'What time did he leave?'

'Around about fifteen, twenty minutes after two.'

'And how did he seem?'

Longer pause than usual, then O'Leary said, 'I'd say he was used to drink, but he'd had a lot, and his speech was slightly slurred, eyes were glassy and bloodshot, and when he walked to the lifts, it wasn't exactly in a straight line.'

'How was he dressed?'

'Blue suit, pale pink shirt and distinctive green silk tie.'

'What happened next?'

'Much later I got a call from housekeeping about 9.35 in the morning that they couldn't get a response from Helena Palmers's room. Seems she had been insistent she get a wake up call for 9 am, which they'd tried then sent someone up at 9.30 and he couldn't get a response so I was called up there.'

'What did you do?'

'I used my passkey and gained entry to the room at 9.40 am.'

'What did you find?'

'Helena Palmer naked on the bed, dead, with a green silk tie around her neck. The room was neat and tidy, with no signs of disarray.'

'What did you do?'

'I called 911 at 9.45 am and NYPD were there within ten minutes.'

'Thank you Mr O'Leary. I have no further questions.'

I rose without waiting for the judge. This was a witness I had to shake, because he had to be lying; trouble was I didn't know what had really happened, so I was fishing blind, and that could be dangerous. 'You ran a nice little scam, back in the day, didn't you, O'Leary?' I said, gloves off, looking down at a copy of an extract from a newspaper from around five years earlier.

Stahl was already on his feet, bristling. 'What is this your honour?'

'You opened the door, Stahl. He's a top notch hotel security specialist with fifteen years experience, according to you. Well, lets have a look at some of that experience, shall we? Jury need to know.'

'Enough,' Judge Gonzalez said, eyeing both of us.

I handed copies of the newspaper extract to the usher for distribution. I knew I was on firm ground; I watched the judge as she scanned it and nodded. 'I'll allow it,' she said.

I watched O'Leary as he briefly read the same extract; again, not a flicker. The guy seemed to have ice water running through his veins.

'Tell us about the blackmail scam,' I said.

No pause this time, maybe he was getting angry; good. 'There was no blackmail scam, counsellor,' he answered, emphasising the last word with a hint of sarcastic contempt. 'You know how many people a year make false claims against the hotel for money? How many times we pay up, because its mostly easier and cheaper, given we can't take bad reputational publicity? This was just another example.'

'Fine. So tell us about it. We've got the time,' I said, allowing myself a half smile at the jury.

If O'Leary could squirm, he was doing it now. 'A rich, bored housewife got found out cheating on her husband at the hotel, and said the staff were running a scam and she had been offered silence and the tape for money. It was all bullsh—. It was all baloney,' he said, biting off the epithet and correcting himself.

'But NYPD were called in?'

'Initially, yes, but they soon dropped the investigation and no charges were brought.'

'You paid her off?'

'The hotel made a small *ex-gratia* payment to make it go away, yes.'

'The allegation was that the victim was identified as a mark by a member of the hotel staff and surveillance equipment - you can buy it for nickels and dimes these days - was set up prior to the tryst. The sexed up couple were then filmed *in flagrante* and the squeeze applied. But this couple didn't play ball, did they? Seems your boys miscalculated. The husband loved his wife, indeed knew about the assignation.'

'Not true, and they weren't "my boys", as you put it. And do you really believe I would still be working for the hotel if there was anything in these allegations?'

'Maybe you've got something on your boss as well,' I said with a smile, before quickly adding, 'I'll withdraw that,' as Stahl started to rise to his feet. Then, before he could utter an objection, I switched direction. 'Tell me about the message. The call down allegedly made by Helena Palmer at around two fifteen in the morning, that I should go up to her room.?'

'Nothing to tell. It was just that, she called down to the bar and said to ask you to go up to her room. That was it.'

'Okay, but who took the message.'

'You don't remember, then?' O'Leary said slowly, a taunting smile playing on his lips. Then, perhaps emboldened by my silence, he continued in the same vein, 'Drink can do terrible things to a persons memory, right, counsellor?'

I could feel my face start to redden and the jurors eyes on me, waiting for a response. O'Leary had turned the tables and now I was the one squirming. I couldn't seem to think of a suitably cutting response, so settled on. 'Just answer the question, Mr O'Leary. My memory is not the issue here, but your reliability is.'

'The call was taken by Lorraine, who was behind the bar. She passed the message to me and I told you. That's it,' he answered.

'One last thing. How did Helena Palmer know I was down in the bar? I never told her, and by then she'd been back in her room for an age?'

O'Leary shrugged. 'I have no idea,' he said. Then with a quick smile, 'but she knew you were a booze hound, so maybe it was just a lucky guess.'

I felt like slugging the guy, but I kept my cool. 'Thank you. I have no further questions,' I said.

Pascal sipped from a bottle of spring water as she made her way down to the basement at the consulate. Rob was already there, working away online and speaking on a telephone wedged between the crook of his neck and his chin, his hands hovering over his keyboard. She lifted O'Leary's laptop out of her bag and placed it on Rob's desk just as he straightened up in his chair and replaced the phone back in its cradle.

'They've finally got some work for you to do,' he said, then noticing the laptop, added, 'what's this?'

'Little rush job I've got for you,' she said, opening up the laptop and powering it on. 'I need this baby password cracked, decrypted, copied and then returned to its place of origin, all within the hour.'

'You don't want much, do you?' Rob said, tapping a random key and watching the screen shimmer into a scene that looked like a Belfast street after an IRA car bomb, circa early seventies. 'Happy bunny, isn't he?' he said, and then, 'where d'you get it?' He was looking up at her and then his eyes widened. 'Fire engines, sirens, Mid-Town hotel going up in smoke. Let me guess.'

'We don't have time for that. With any luck the owner of this laptop is still in court giving evidence, so we need to get it back to the hotel before he comes out and starts monitoring his feeds. Take it back and covertly offload it somewhere prominent like a toilet or trash can were they'll find it quick. If we're lucky they'll buy it as a looter getting caught short inside, maybe seeing a cop and dumping it.'

Rob nodded. 'I'm on it, boss,' he said, fingers descending onto the keyboard.

She was beginning to like Rob because he just got on with it. No stupid questions - her kind of guy. She checked her watch and started to move towards the door, but then stopped short, looking back. 'You said they've got some work for me?'

He looked up irritated at the interruption. 'Oh, yeah. Seems Bob Jeffreys, Homeland security's been pressing us for intel on what he calls, London Jihadi's. Essentially anyone we've ID'd in London, but who subsequently turns up in New York. And guess what? Because of your background and experience, you've been nominated. Your brief: to look into it and report to him.'

'Great,' she said unenthusiastically.

'Thought you'd like it,' Rob said with a smile, then, 'We're in,' as he punched another key, keenly watching the screen, but Pascal had already gone.

She made her way out of the building and began to walk down third avenue, deep in thought, unaware of the people bustling past either side, but then she did became aware of someone beside her. 'Detective Daly,' she said, out of the corner of her mouth. 'What a nice surprise. What can I do for you?'

'You can start by telling me about the fire today at the hotel where your boy Calver murdered Helena Palmer,' he said. Maybe she was imagining it, but she thought she detected a faint hint of humour in his words.

They carried on walking side by side but then both stopped at the same time, and she turned to face him, middle of the wide pavement, pedestrians still walking by either side. He looked calm and in no hurry to hustle her. He was dressed down in dark chinos, pale blue shirt and casual jacket. Maybe he was off duty.

'You stalking me, detective?' she said, eyebrow raised, beginnings of a smile. She checked her watch again, thinking quickly. 'Tell you what. Why don't you take me somewhere down and dirty in this great city of yours, and buy me drink? We can get drunk together, swop tall stories about what great fearless seekers after truth and justice we are.'

'That sounds cool,' he said, smiling and raising his arm to hail a cab. 'And then maybe you can start being straight with me as well.'

They were silent for a while as the cab moved off from the curb. Later she saw a sign, 'Canal Street', which she knew meant Chinatown. Couple of minutes later the cab dropped them off in front of a large building and Daly led her inside. It looked like some kind of sports bar, big and roomy with flags and pendants, football jerseys, and balls of all shapes hung around and draped over everything. And along the walls were mounted giant TV screens showing ball games, and the place seemed to be full of jocks, and no women.

'Thanks, Daly. This isn't exactly what I had in mind,' Pascal said, lifting a Coors beer off the waitresses tray as she walked by. 'But, hey, the beers good, right?'

'The beer's great, and the scotch is even better,' he said sipping from a large tumbler of amber coloured liquid. He checked his phone for messages, and said, quiet, as he scrolled down his screen, 'I checked you out after we spoke. That was quite something you did in London. Taking down a terrorist, saving the monarch, almost getting blown up, and turning down a medal.'

She smiled. 'I did get blown up, but he wasn't really a terrorist in the sense that you mean,' she said, taking another drag on her bottle. 'And I'm way too young for a medal.'

Daly watched her, then reached over and clinked his tumbler against her bottle and took another sip, grimacing. Then he said, 'Calver's guilty as hell, and even you know it.'

She didn't say anything because she knew from his tone that there was a question mark floating around in there somewhere. She'd let him torture it out, see if he could articulate it.

'That Schmidt guy in the bar. So he's capable of murder, I'll buy that, but so what? He wasn't there, Calver was, with the Vic, in her room, raping and strangling her with that poncy green silk tie.'

Pascal grabbed another bottle from the harassed waitress as she went by on her rounds, then she looked up and noticed three guys at the next table, a few metres away. They were looking at her, talking and smirking. They looked like redneck gym bunnies, probably steroid poppers. They wore designer jeans and tight singlet's showing off lots of bulging, oiled, inked up bicep. Daly clocked them as well, looking down, smiling to himself.

'You know about John Palmer, Daly?' she said, dismissing the sports jocks with a toss of her head.

'Who?'

'Helena Palmer's brother.'

'What about him?'

'You don't know, do you, Daly?'

'Don't know what?' he said, irritation creeping into his voice.

'He drove into the harbour here few months ago. Coroners tagging it suicide. Toxicology says blood alcohol level was off the graph.'

'So?'

'Just before Helena was murdered, she told Calver, John wasn't a suicide. Never, nada, no chance.'

'You know I do remember reading something about that, but never tied it to our Vic. Never needed to, because this was always a slam-dunk. Anyway, she's family and they never admit a relative might be dumb enough to commit suicide.'

'Yeah. Well get this, Daly. John Palmer never drank alcohol, never. Apparently got sick drunk as a kid and wouldn't touch it after that.' She had Daly's full attention now. 'So how's about you dig out that police report and let me have a copy?'

It was then that one of the trio of sports jocks chose to hassle Pascal. She hadn't seen him come over, but now he was standing in front of her, swaying slightly on his feet, intermittently looking back at his two buddies who were sat there with goading smirks on their faces. 'Me and my buddies was wondering what you was doing in here, cause this is a mans bar, and we don't like no feminazi in here. Specially not bull dikes,' he said, giggling, looking back at his buddies. Daly was trying not to smile, leaning back on his stool, watching and waiting. He wasn't going to intervene, he was enjoying it too much.

Pascal regarded the guy. 'Well I'm truly sorry you don't like girls,' she said, solicitously. 'That's too bad. Especially if maybe someday you wanted to start a family. But never mind. How's about you go back to your buddies and I'll buy you all a drink?'

He seemed disappointed by her response and his face dropped, then a red flush of anger appeared, followed by a sly, calculating look. He slowly reached over to her blouse and took hold of her nipple - she wore no bra - and began to squeeze it, watching her face all the time. His buddies giggled some more, then whooped. For a second Pascal did nothing, just watched him, then she reached over and took Daly's tumbler, recently replenished with Scotch, and slowly tipped the contents over the guys head.

For a moment he stood there looking shocked and stupid, face dripping with scotch, while Pascal watched him, thin enigmatic smile on her lips. She casually stepped away, edging back towards the jocks table, watching for the tell. It came with a subtle downward shift of his eyes and then he was coming. As he reached her, Pascal stepped inside, grabbing his arm, stooping and turning, letting the guys momentum work for her. Then she pulled him into a swing up and over her shoulder, and then swung him down so that he landed across the centre of the jocks table with a huge crash. His two shocked buddies scuttled out of the way as his body rolled and then slid off the table top onto the floor amongst the broken bottles and spilt drink.

Pascal turned to the two other guys, eyebrow raised, and said calmly, 'you want some?' They backed away, eyes scared, then they knelt down and lifted the other guy, throwing some notes on the table, whilst apologising to the waitress who was now stood there with the manager.

Daly watched chuckling as the manager mentioned compensation for damage, until he saw Daly's NYPD badge. Daly said, 'I saw it all. These hillbillies were trying to throw a scare into this little lady, and she just about kicked the shit out of them. They'll be paying,' he said, looking at them ominously. They nodded and quickly anted up some more notes and then left in a hurry.

As Pascal and Daly stood on the sidewalk outside, as her cab pulled up, he said, 'its been interesting.' As he watched her there was a new look of respect in his eyes. He looked down at his shoes, perhaps embarrassed. 'Look, maybe I should have leant a hand in there, but frankly you didn't look like you needed it. So, maybe I've got some penance to do to make up for that. Listen, I'll take a look at that police report, no harm in it. You enjoy the rest of your day now,' he said. Then something else seemed to occur to him. 'Man, and I didn't even ask you about the fire,' he said, shaking his head with that slow smile. Then he leaned down and slammed the car door.

Pascal relaxed as the cab pulled away, reflecting that perhaps Daly wasn't such an asshole after all.

Chapter Twelve

Southern District Court

Hannah paused in her testimony to take a sip of water. Morganna had asked her to tell the jury about life in *Jodenhoek*, and any particular incidents that stuck out in her mind from that time. Browder had objected as she'd known he would, and she hadn't held out much hope of getting it in, but Friedman had surprised her. Maybe he'd taken a liking to Hannah, because he seemed somehow less abrasive in his dealings with her. He had looked over at her sitting quietly in the witness box, and then he'd nodded and said he'd allow it. He explained that a certain leeway was permissible in cases involving testimony covering events from so long ago where a jury might need some context to assist with their deliberations.

Morganna, now glowing inside, turned back to Hannah sitting calmly in the witness box and said, 'earlier you were telling us about the arrival of your cousin Rudi from Germany?'

'Yes, it was late summer of 1939 and I only mention it because it is the first time that I became aware of Nazism, but also because Rudi brought with him a painting which later also disappeared, along with the gold pendant, which I guess makes it relevant,' she said looking up pointedly at Friedman.'

'Go on,' Morganna said.

'Well at supper that first night after he arrived, he shocked us with talk about how bad life was for Jews in Germany and how he had had to leave his job at the art museum in Magdeburg. He said it was getting worse by the day, and he'd only managed to get out of the country by forging exit papers.

'Then he talked about the art exhibitions the Nazi's were running all over Germany, trying to run down Jewish impressionist and abstract art, labelling it degenerate. And I couldn't believe it when he told us that at the end of each exhibition they would take all those beautiful paintings out and burn them.

'But what really intrigued me was what he told us that night,' Hannah said, pausing again for another sip of water.

Morganna smiled to herself. She didn't think there was much she could teach the old lady about creating dramatic suspense. 'What did he tell you?' she said.

'Well, he said that he'd taken the best picture in the Magdeburg gallery where he worked, during the exhibition, and replaced it with a beautiful copy in his own fair hand, and he said, "the dumb Nazi's never even noticed."'

'He forged it?' Morganna said.

'That's what he said. And then later they took the forged work out with all the others and burned it.'

'What was the work and who was it by? Morganna asked.

'Well, that's just it. That's the mystery. He wouldn't tell me at the time, and he didn't have it with him. He couldn't have taken it out of the country with him for fear of being searched by border guards, so he arranged for it to be sent out later by a close friend, with a consignment of export goods.

'He treated it all as a kind of mysterious joke to tease me with, always asking me whether I had guessed who the picture was by. And even when the picture arrived he would never show it to me or identify the artist. He was just kidding around and I am sure he would have revealed all eventually, but he never got the chance because of what happened later, after the Nazi's invaded Holland and occupied the country.'

'We'll come to that later, Hannah, but you said earlier that this painting, whatever it was, also disappeared along with the golden pendant and brooch, that are the subject matter of these proceedings. Is that correct?'

'Yes it is.'

'Thank you.'

'Miss Fedler,' Judge Friedman said, looking at the clock. 'Might this be a good time to adjourn for the day.'

'Yes indeed your honour,' Morganna said, relieved, but also quietly pleased with how things had gone. She was still learning and there was a long way to go. She bundled up her books and waited for Hannah

Brad Fedler's Tribeca loft apartment was on the fifth floor of a large building off Hudson Street, not far from Broadway, and I was finding it hard to get used to the place. Maybe it was a bit too luxurious for me, especially after Rikers. I kept worrying I was going to break something or soil the bed.

That night we were all there eating Chinese takeout and having a drink. Morganna had been talking about Hannah's trial, worrying about what raking over such painful old history might be doing to her, but Hannah seemed strangely unmoved by those sentiments. She said, 'maybe I've been waiting all my life to talk about these things. When I'm in that witness box strange things happen to me. I don't know what I am going to say until I am sitting there, and then it just seems to pop out.'

'But you're having nightmares, aren't you?' Pascal said, chewing on a fortune cookie. 'I know, because you're shouting and moaning in your sleep, and you wake up soaked in sweat with the sheets all twisted around you.'

'It's nothing,' Hannah said, dismissively, looking around the table at all of us. 'And really, I have to do this. And you must help me.'

We all nodded and mumbled assent to that, the mood around the table muted and subdued.

I turned and watched Pascal for a beat as I sipped a single brandy, all I would allow myself these days. I could feel the alcohol starting to affect me, a slight edge of unreasonable resentment at Pascal rising up in my throat. She might as well have been on holiday for all the good she seemed to be doing me I thought, awash with maudlin self pity. 'So you got anything for me?' I blurted out, not worrying too much about the tone of my voice.

Instead of answering she flicked something across the table at Christoff who snatched it out of the air and turned it over in his palm. It was a memory stick. 'Take a look at that will you, Christoff,' she said. 'See what you can find.'

'What is it?' I asked.

'Its a copy of everything on John O'Leary's laptop, but maybe its best you don't know that, right?' she said, acid tone.

I smiled. Maybe she hadn't just been sitting on her ass twiddling her thumbs after all. I noticed Morganna's questioning look, but we needed to be careful. Morganna had a future at the local bar, so we had to avoid compromising that, so we needed to keep her out of the loop.

'We'll talk about it later.' I said. 'O'Leary's finished testifying, but we can recall him if we need to. I reckon Detective Daly will be up next.'

'You know, Calver,' Pascal said. 'I've got a hunch about Daly. I think he could turn out to be an ally, if handled right. So you might want to go easy when you cross examine him.'

I'd have to think about that; it was my ass on the line. Then Pascal was abruptly getting up and excusing herself, saying she had some errands to run. I checked my watch. Where the hell could she be going this time of night?

Outside on the street corner, Mayberry Wilkins looked up at the lighted windows of the fifth floor apartment and wondered what the hell he was doing out there. What was the point of standing outside and watching the joint? They knew the crew were all inside, so why the fuck did he have to stand outside watching the place? But the swarthy fuck, Schmidt, had insisted, so here he was.

Ever since Wilkins had set eyes on Pascal at JFK when she'd arrived in the country, Schmidt had been on his case, wanting reports 24/7, and frankly, he had better things to do. His mind started to wander as he thought about his best friends girl who he'd just started fucking. Boy was she hot, and betraying his friend like that gave him that extra jolt he seemed to need these days.

'Anything?' a voice suddenly said from the darkness, so near he almost jumped out of his skin. Jesus! The fucking freak had come up from nowhere and he hadn't heard a damn thing. He turned as Schmidt stepped out of the shadows.

'Nothing, boss,' he said, quickly, subserviently. Schmidt had that look in his eyes, as if he knew exactly what Wilkins was thinking.

'I want you to observe the old lady specifically, yes?' Schmidt said, lazy brutal eyes scanning the frightened man. 'I want to know her routine and her movements so that if it becomes necessary. If, for example, her testimony were to become dangerous, uncomfortable or even mildly inconvenient for us, you will be in a position to liquidate her immediately, yes?'

'No problem, boss. I'm on it,' Wilkins said.

'I hope so,' Schmidt said.

When Wilkins looked back Schmidt had gone, just as silently as he had arrived. Wilkins let out a relieved sigh. Jesus! The guy was the only person who had ever managed to frighten him. As he flicked his cigarette butt into the gutter he noticed light glint off the main door as it opened and Pascal came out, dressed in black, head to foot. He quickly stepped back into the shadows. For a moment he wondered whether to follow her, then remembered Schmidt's orders to concentrate on the old lady.

Pascal sipped black Turkish coffee, trying to clear her head. She didn't really know where she was, had just given the address to the cab driver. She looked around. It was a dingy bar with twenty or so people in ones and twos, the sound of their conversation muffled and understated as if they didn't wish to be overheard. She had been watching the door, but Bob Jeffreys came out the back rolling down his shirt-sleeves and fastening his cuffs.

'Hey, you found me then?' he said

'Apparently. What are we doing here?'

'Poker game, and I did pretty good as it happens,' he said, sliding into the seat opposite and transferring a wad of notes to his wallet. 'You said you wanted to see the city. Well here it is, the bit the tourists don't see.'

'Yeah, I can see why. So, what have you got?'

'Hey, not so fast. Good news, what, old girl, as I guess they might say in limey land. You're on the team, hunting down ex-London

Jihadi's who may be holidaying in New York. Let's drink to that,' he said, raising his hand and signalling the waiter. A moment later a tray arrived with two scotches on board.

Pascal grimaced. 'Boy, is my liver getting a pounding,' she murmured, putting the glass to her lips and took a drag.

Bob nodded appreciatively. 'Hey, maybe its not glamourous stuff, but its important. It gives you something to do, and, you help me, I'll help you. And I got a little taster for you. Some bits and pieces I picked up, to foster our little arrangement.'

'What have you got, Bob?' she said, interest starting to kindle.

'Okay. Angel Milken, founder of K Corp, first shows up in our records in August 1945 in a displaced persons, or DP camp in Seedorf. There he was known as Franz Bauer, or to give him his full title, Major, or *Sturmbannfuhrer*, Franz Bauer of the Waffen SS. And before you leap to any hasty conclusions, this was the military branch of the SS, elite combat troops, not concentration camp guards. This guy had been at Stalingrad, in Manstein's relief column that never got through, and then he'd been at Kursk, biggest tank battle in history and then in the defence of Berlin, which is where he was picked up. OSS or Office of Strategic Services, forerunner of the CIA, liked the look of him, apparently, and he was co-opted for a time. Could speak perfect English, so they used him initially in the DP camp, and picked his brains for a time. Then he seems to go off the grid, before being picked up again, entering the US, perfectly legally, in August 1947 as a legitimate immigrant with a visa. Soon after he is naturalised and changes his name to Angel Milken.'

Bob looked up from his tablet. Pascal was staring into space, deep in thought. Then she said, 'there were no SS divisions at Stalingrad. And what's with the name, Angel? Seems an odd choice.'

'He seems to have been peripatetic and moved around, attached to various divisions, bit of a troubleshooter you might say, so my guess is he was seconded to a Wehrmacht unit. As for the name, who knows. Could be a nickname of a loved one.'

Pascal finished her drink. 'Is that all?' she said.

'No, its not all. You've got a job to do here as well remember? There's some mug-shots on this tablet which you can take away with you, and have a look at. See if you recognise any from your days in London?'

'No problem,' she said. 'I'm grateful, Bob.'

'Good,' he said, rolling his sleeves back down. 'I think we'll work well together, Courtney. Incidentally, I've got one other tidbit for you. Its all on the tablet. Its about Angel's early life in New York, and a couple of run-ins he had with the law that, shall we say, never got any publicity, if you know what I mean,' he said, with an exaggerated wink.

'Now I've got to resume my poker game and win some more money,' he added, getting up, finishing his scotch and placing the glass back on the table. 'I'll be seeing you,' he said, walking away with that jaunty step. Pascal was beginning to like Bob, even though he could be highly irritating.

Chapter Thirteen

People v Calver - Manhattan Supreme Court

Day 2

I watched Detective Daly as he settled himself into the witness box. Clean shaven, nice dark suit, solid and dependable, the perfect image for the jury. Stahl took him through the call out and first attendance at the crime scene. 'And what did you find there?'

'I found the victim on the bed, lying on her back, dead. The green silk tie was like a ligature around her neck. Her body was quite cold so I guessed she had been there for a while. The room was neat and tidy with no evidence of a disturbance,' Daly said, calm and professional. He was an impressive witness and I could tell the jury liked him.

'And what did that signify?' Stahl asked. 'The lack of disturbance.'

'That she knew and trusted whoever killed her.'

'What did you do?'

'We secured the room, and got the CSI's in to do their work. Then we fanned out and started taking statements from witnesses in adjoining rooms. I went with the Manager O'Leary to look at the CCTV. He told me that the defendant was associated with the victim, that they had spent the evening together and about the call down from the victims room.'

'Did you view the CCTV then?'

'Yes I did. In fact, O'Leary had already pulled the tape. He showed me Calver going into the victims room at around 2.20 am, and coming out around 25 minutes later at 2.45 am. No one else visits the room, other than Calver.'

'What did you do?'

'I spoke on the phone to the captain and the DA's office, and was told to question Calver immediately, arrest him and bring him in.'

'You spoke to Calver?'

'Yes I did. When he answered the door he seemed disoriented and had clearly been drinking. He volunteered that he had spent the evening with the victim and admitted he owned a green silk tie made by Drake's of London, so I read him his rights and arrested him.'

'Now, the jury will see the defendants taped interview, but in essence, what did he tell you when questioned?'

'He denied murder, said he had no motive, but was at a loss to explain who else could have done it, then he essentially clammed up.'

Stahl paused for a moment, looking down at his papers. I gazed around the courtroom, still full. Interest in the trial did not seem to have diminished. I scanned the jury. They still looked alert and engaged, but I noticed that they rarely looked at me. They were focused on Daly who sat calmly awaiting Stahl's next question.

'Now, detective, you obviously carried out background checks against the defendant?'

'Yes, that's right. He's not a resident here, he's a citizen of the UK, so we contacted our counterparts over there.'

'And what did you find?'

Time to remind everyone I was still around. I rose to my feet. 'Your honour, I apprehend that the District Attorney is about to call some inadmissible evidence.'

Judge Gonzalez regarded me balefully. 'Sidebar,' she said. Stahl and I approached the bench as the judge muffled her mike so the jury wouldn't hear our exchange. 'What is it Mr Calver?'

I knew they were going to try and get in the incident with Carmen when I had put my hands around her neck, on the basis that it showed a propensity on my part to this kind of behaviour. I needed to keep it out because of the tendency of juries to say, oh he's done it before, therefore he's guilty of this crime. I knew they had federal rules on such evidence which most state courts adopted in various guises, saying you couldn't call evidence of a defendants convictions and bad acts unless it came within an exception. 'Your honour, the DA is about to call evidence about a load of unsubstantiated crap involving my wife and I in the UK. Its an alleged incident where I was never charged, the *modus operandi* is different, and quite clearly, the prejudicial effect of such evidence completely outweighs its probative value.'

'Mr Stahl?'

'Your honour, around three months ago Mr Calver attempted to strangle his wife and she called the police. The case is documented and only did not go ahead because he persuaded her not to proceed and— '

'Bullshit, she voluntarily withdrew the charges,' I said

'Mr Calver,' the judge said, icily. 'I will not tolerate that kind of language in my courtroom. If I hear it again, you're in contempt.'

I knew I'd gone too far. Stahl's Cheshire cat smile confirmed it. 'I'm very sorry your honour. I'm on trial for my life, and that slipped out in the heat of the moment. Won't happen again.'

'Good. See that it doesn't. I'm going to allow it. I'm satisfied this evidence will be valuable to the jury and that far outweighs any possible prejudice Mr Calver is likely to suffer. Now, lets move along,' she said.

I walked slowly back to the defense table, despondent. I needed to get a grip because Stahl was slaughtering me. He skipped back to his table, ready to throw his next grenade.

'Detective, what did you discover about this defendant from your counterparts in the UK?'

Pascal poked her head above the covers and checked the clock - it was nearly eleven. Then she noticed the cup sitting next to her on the bedside table, steam slowly rising from the rim. Someone had woken her bringing it in.

She looked around. Hannah was long gone, presumably back on the witness stand in the Southern District Court, facing her demons. Pascal debated running for a shower but then noticed on the table next to her, the tablet Jeffreys had given her the previous evening. She picked her coffee up and took a sip, mind running over what Jeffreys had said during the brief interval in his poker game.

She plumped her pillow up and switched the tablet on. It sprang to life with the appearance of the American flag, then a hand of poker cards, followed by a rendition of the Star Spangled Banner, presumably Bob's little joke. Then she was presented with two files on the desk top; one entitled "London/New York Faces", and the other "Angel Titbits". She clicked the latter, work could wait.

There wasn't much there. Some old press cuttings from the early 70's detailing suspicious fires at rundown properties mostly owned by Angel Milken, with a lot of borderline libellous scuttlebutt about who was responsible. But there was also a formal report about an alleged rape. Pascal already knew about the fires. It was an open secret that in rundown 1970's New York City, that was how Angel had built up what became K Corp's property portfolio.

But the alleged rape was something else. The report was just a few pages long but didn't say who had prepared it or for what purpose. The prose was indicative of law enforcement, although which particular branch was a mystery.

Essentially it was a succinct retelling of a rape allegation. In the early hours of August 8th 1988, Chantelle Bouvier had appeared at a Manhattan Police precinct in a disoriented and distressed state alleging that she had been drugged and raped by her employer, Angel Milken. Bouvier had been employed for five years in the penthouse suite at the top of the K Building in Water Street as a domestic maid. She alleged her employer had come to her live-in quarters late at night. She had offered him coffee because he seemed upset about something. She made the point he had never come there before, and unusually his wife was away visiting family on the west coast on that particular evening. He had declined coffee but had brought a part drunk bottle of wine with him which he had begged her to share with him. She didn't really drink but felt under pressure to join him as she needed the job, and he seemed so down and out of character that she accepted a glass, but only had a few sips.

She then alleged that during the night she woke up and he was raping her, but when pressed she couldn't categorically say it wasn't just a bad dream. During questioning she kept breaking down in tears and was incoherent and inconsistent in her testimony. She also alleged sodomy and oral rape and pointed to physical soreness, and a swollen lip.

The officers listened but never suggested a medical examination. This was before the real advent of DNA although the first conviction based upon it in the US had happened the previous year. It would however be a long time before it became a widely used forensic tool.

Pascal stopped reading and took another sip of coffee. Back in the day police forces in the western world were extremely primitive when it came to sexual assault against women. It was before the touchy feely days of rape suites at police stations, rape counsellors and victim liaison officers, so perhaps the reaction of New York's finest wasn't so surprising.

She read on. Essentially the police didn't believe Bouvier, or said they didn't believe her. However, they were duty bound to file a report, and so a patrolman and detective were dispatched to K Tower.

There they interviewed Angel Milken, who perhaps surprisingly already had his lawyer, Charles Browder III, presumably the father of his current lawyer, in attendance. Milken denied any sexual contact but admitted visiting the maids room to ask her about something, he forgot what. Milken and lawyer didn't demur when the officers suggested looking over the maids room, they confirming they had her prior authority. On a perfunctory search they found no evidence of disarray or struggle, but they did find a large bag of heroin conveniently hidden in the pillowcase. The bag, on checking, had only Chantelle Bouvier's fingerprints on it.

Bob had appended a short coda to the report suggesting no charges were ever brought for the sexual assault, but Bouvier was charged with conspiracy to supply heroin, convicted and imprisoned.

Pascal finished her coffee, hardly surprised by the outcome of the little story. Poor underprivileged employee takes on immensely wealthy and powerful employer and gets royally shafted, the story of life itself and certainly of modern America. She looked down at the tablet screen as a kind of little podcast materialised of Bob's smiling face, saying, 'good titbit, eh, Courtney? And that's not all. I'm going to give you Bouvier's current name and address in Brooklyn, on the off chance you might just want to speak to her,' he said. 'But, big but, I want you to start looking at the other file on the tablet, tout suit, as they say in France, capiche?'

Pascal couldn't help cracking a smile at Bob's antics. She owed him. So she would have to help him out and have a look at the photos in the other file. But first, as Bob reeled off the info, she scribbled down

Bouvier's current name - Chantelle Lattifah - and her address in Brooklyn. Then the screen went blank.

People v Calver - Manhattan Supreme Court

I looked over at the jury; they were completely engaged now and anxious to hear what Daly was going to say about me. He looked down at his notes and then addressed them. 'The Metropolitan Police in London told us that around three months ago, Carmen, that's the defendants wife, made a complaint against her husband. The complaint was that he assaulted her, specifically, he placed his hands around her neck and attempted to strangle her.'

'And detective, did they provide you with a copy of the recording of her call to the emergency services?' Stahl asked, innocently.

I hadn't known about this. I rose to my feet. 'Your honour, I've had no notice of this tape, and its admission is highly—'

'Sit down, Mr Calver, I've already ruled,' she said, barely acknowledging me.

Stahl pressed play on his laptop. At first there was a faint sound of harsh, heavy breathing, then some snuffled sobs, then the dispatchers voice breaking in, saying, 'what is your emergency please, caller?' Then a pause, then Carmen's frightened voice. 'Please, help me, you have to come. My husband's gone mad, he's trying to kill me, strangle me.' Then another brief pause before the dispatcher asked for her location, which Carmen gave her. Another pause, then Carmen again, pleading this time, almost whimpering, saying, 'no, Jonas, please, no.' Then she shouted '*No,*' followed by a frightened scream.

I wanted to kill Stahl for playing the tape. There was no hiding place for me there in that courtroom and I felt naked and demeaned. I'd never heard the tape before, couldn't remember anything about it or even being there, but I still felt a burning hot shame rippling through me and I knew that the jury couldn't fail to see it.

Stahl prolonged my torture by allowing the tape to play on even though it was just background noise, then the caller telling Carmen to hold on, the police would be there within minutes, then the tape ended.

Stahl turned back to Daly. 'What did Carmen tell the police had happened that night?'

Daly checked his notes again. 'The defendant had been drinking heavily, and apparently that wasn't unusual. They had gone to bed in the usual way. Later Carmen said the defendant had put his hands around her neck and started to squeeze. He seemed to be in a trance. She had violently struggled and screamed at him, and she almost passed out before he suddenly seemed to break out of the trance and pull his hands away. She had run down to the kitchen and called emergency. He followed her and, as we've heard, engaged with her again, grappling with her and taking the phone from her. Luckily by then the emergency services were already on their way. Apparently he then settled down and went and sat in a chair to await the police.'

'Now, we know, for whatever reasons, in the end, the defendant wasn't charged or prosecuted for this, but when he was questioned about the incident, what did he say?' Stahl asked.

'He didn't expressly deny the allegation. He said he couldn't remember anything.'

'He didn't expressly deny it,' Stahl repeated slowly, so the jury would get the message.

'That's right.'

Judge Gonzalez looked up at the clock, it was quarter to one. 'Perhaps now might be a good time to break for lunch, back here in one hour,' she said.

I didn't feel like eating.

Southern District Court

Day 5

Morganna was thinking that if Browder would keep his mouth shut and Friedman would continue with a light touch, they could finish the early background stuff off quick and then get onto the real issues in the case.

Lunch was over and Hannah was back in the witness box describing the arrival of the Nazi's, her voice low and matter of fact but the jury could feel the tension in her as she recalled events.

'The Germans arrived 16th May 1940 and of course it sticks in my mind. Rudi and I watched them enter the city at *Merwedeplein*. They came in an endless stream of trucks, tanks, horses and infantry, and from then on my life became hell, steadily worsening as each month went by.

'I won't bore the jury with day to day incidents, because as the judge says, they're not really relevant, but a significant event that did take place was the riot that took place in *Waterloo-Plein*, which was the central part of *Jodenhoek*, when drunken out of control racist thugs from the Dutch Nazi party had arrived in the square with rifles. Rudi had got involved in the fighting and was injured, just a crack to his head but it bled terribly.

'Next day, using the unrest as a pretext, the trucks and soldiers as well as Dutch Police had arrived in *Jodenhoek* and fences and barbed wire had gone up, and the bridges over the canals had been raised, cutting us off entirely from the rest of the city. Then the signs "*Judenviertal*" and "*Joodsche Wijk*" went up as well, sealing us in to what had just become a ghetto.

'It was also at about this time that the first massive round-ups began and soon after, around February 1941 I believe, they arrived at our door with loud knocking and sounds of vehicles, shouts and dogs barking. We wouldn't let them in so they broke the door down and immediately arrested Rudi, not for the fighting, but because he was on their list. A German Jew who had fled the Fatherland illegally, and all such persons were subject to arrest. I never saw him again, and I still hadn't seen the mystery painting he'd smuggled out.'

Hannah stopped abruptly there, looking dazed, as if she were waking from a dream. She shook her head as if to clear it. Morganna frowned, looking down at her notes, wondering how to phrase her next question.

165

Chapter Fourteen

People v Calver - Manhattan Supreme Court

I could feel the half digested ham sandwich lying in the pit of my stomach as the Stahl Daly double act turned its attention to the hotel's CCTV. This was the footage from the corridor outside Helena's hotel room on the night of the murder, and it was the centre of their case. We, being me, Pascal, Christoff and Morganna, had watched the tape over and over but were still coming up empty. We had no idea how they had done it.

There was a strange kind of fascination in watching the pictures, as if they were of someone else, a phantom figure, which in some ways they were. First we saw Helena returning to her room, after leaving mine, at around 1 am, and it was clear that this was genuine un-doctored tape showing what had actually taken place.

Later on as the tape rolled, Stahl got Daly to provide a running commentary to accompany the pictures.

'This is the defendant in the bar at around 1.40 am, as described by Mr O'Leary when he gave evidence earlier,' Daly said, at Stahl's prompting. 'You will notice the distinctive green tie he is wearing, and that he is perhaps slightly the worse for wear,' Daly added.

I watched myself at the bar, bright green silk tie indelibly marking me out for the jury, my body swaying lightly to and fro, and if you looked very closely you could just about discern my glassy eyed stare and the goofy grin on my face. Then O'Leary is seen saying something to me, presumably the alleged call down from Helena, asking that I go up to her room.

A few moments later I am seen making my way out of the bar to the lifts. CCTV then tracks my movements, via different cameras all the way to Helena's room, where I can be seen pressing her buzzer. It seems to take around two minutes before Helena's door opens and I enter. The time on the CCTV ticker tape says it is 2.20 am.

Daly picks up the story again. 'There is no further activity in the corridor for some 25 minutes.' Daly pauses a beat whilst Stahl fiddles with the laptop to compress this period of time before continuing with the tape. 'Until we see the defendant leave Helena Palmer's room at 2.45 am.'

The tape shows the door opening and me leaving the room. I have my head down and jacket buttoned, so it is difficult to see my expression, and impossible to see whether I am still wearing the green tie. My movements do not appear to be hesitant, or furtive and my gait is stable now, as if the alcohol might be wearing off. I move quickly away from the room down the corridor.

'There is no further activity concerning Helena's room until a staff member appears at around 9.30 am in the morning when the body is found,' Daly said as the tape ended and the lights went up.

'So let me get this straight, detective,' Stahl said. 'After the defendant leaves her room at 2.45 am, no other person enters that room until the body is found?'

'That's right,' Daly said, just about sealing my fate.

'Thank you, detective,' Stahl said, turning to the judge. 'I have no further questions.'

Judge Gonzalez looked at the clock. 'It's 3.50 pm, Mr Calver . Can I suggest you start your cross examination, assuming you have questions for this witness, 10 am sharp tomorrow morning?'

'Fine, your honour, and yes I certainly do have questions for this witness,' I said, grimly.

Pascal grimaced. She'd been there so long her coffee had gone cold. She was sitting in her basement cave at the consulate laboriously slogging through the 'London/New York faces' file on the tablet Bob Jeffreys had given her. There was a lot of them, around three hundred. She got up, yawned and stretched. Rob was out again doing God knows what.

She flexed her fingers and got back to work. Earlier she had called Chantelle Latifah. She was listed in the phone book, but she'd hung up as soon as Pascal had mentioned the name Angel Milken. So she would have to go out to the East Bronx and knock on the door and see what happened.

Something delayed, tripped in her mind, and she pulled back a mug shot she'd just looked at, and stared intently at it. She had seen the face before in London, she was pretty sure. She dug back in her memory, but couldn't quite grab a hold of it. It was a modern photo staring back at her, and the image she was grasping for dated from a while ago. She looked harder at the picture and pulled up the associated bio. The individual was tagged as Zaid Hamdani, which rung no bells, suggesting if she had known him it was under a different name.

Then just as she was minutely examining the image again, Bob Jeffreys was poking his head around the door, then sauntering into the cave, his eyes raking across the screen mug shot in one sweep. 'Anything?' he asked innocently.

'Sorry, Bob. Nothing,' she said, nonchalantly moving onto the next mug shot.

Jeffreys watched her, eyes narrowing. He'd seen something and it looked like recognition, but he'd leave it for now. He guessed she'd fess up when she was ready. He'd heard the rumours about her, that you couldn't push her.

'Oh,' he said. 'We had a look at the Saudi General's boy, Al-Misrahi, and he's clean as a whistle. And John Schmidt, the K Corp guy is half Saudi as well, so maybe they're just buddies having a meet? Far as I can see, there's nothing in it.'

Pascal just nodded. It was their country, and if that was their assessment, she'd leave them to it. She went back to her scrolling, Jeffrey's watching over her shoulder, uncertain smile playing on his lips.

'Okay, Courtney, I'll leave you to it then,' he said, still hovering, as if he wanted her to ask him to stay a while. She didn't, so after a moment he edged away towards the door, saying he'd catch up with her later, then he was gone.

She let out a sigh and leaned back in her chair, yawning again.

Later she sat back in the yellow cab, early evening, on her way to Chantelle Latifah's home. Her cabbie had turned his nose up when she had hailed him in Manhattan and given the address, somewhere called Crotona Park out in East Bronx. 'What you going out there for, lady?' he'd asked, looking her up and down, and tagging her as an eccentric British tourist. 'That's low income housing. You don't want to be walking around there at night, especially if you aint familiar with the area.'

Pascal had muttered that she could look after herself but had thanked him for his concern. Then she had sat back and relaxed to watch the New York scenery fly by, and then they were there. She looked around as she got out of the cab. They were parked in front of a large imposing red brick coloured high rise block with a white stripe down the middle where she guessed the staircase and elevators were. She looked around some more as the cab driver got her change, and she tipped him a five spot. He thanked her and told her to take care. She checked her phone for the full address as the cab pulled away, and then she walked up the path to the building, attracting some curious stares from people coming out. Inside a large entry area there was an array of numbered apartment buzzers and names, which she carefully scrutinised.

She found C Latifah under apartment 111 and pressed the buzzer and waited. Nothing happened so she tried again. Still nothing. Looked like the buzzer was broken. Pascal watched for a moment as a few people came and went; she pretended she was talking to someone on her phone, hunched over. When the next couple with a baby came in she tagged on behind them and followed them through the security entry door as if she was a tenant, still talking to her imaginary caller. Then she took the stairs as it looked like Chantelle's place was on the first floor. She moved down the corridor checking the numbers until she came to 111.

She put her ear to the door. She could hear voices inside, raised, over the sound of a TV. She pressed the bell and waited. Inside the voices stopped but the TV sound of canned laughter continued. The door was flung open and an angry black man stood there glaring at her. 'What d'you want?' he snapped. He was mid-twenties, big, around 6, 2, skinny but muscular, with red eyes and an amazing afro. It was a haircut Pascal had always liked but had thought was long gone, along with all those blaxploitation movies and black and white minstrels. But maybe she was wrong.

The guy was looking at her with a hostile and suspicious look maybe just starting to register the fact that she was probably not a Jehovah's Witness out collecting contributions. A moment later a large black woman with a frightened face and questioning eyes appeared behind the man, peering around his shoulder at her.

Pascal's initial thought was that the guy was maybe an angry son, but there was no resemblance and the body language between the two looked all wrong. One thing was sure, the woman was petrified of the guy. Pascal's mind processed the scene. With a guy like that there was only one way in: full on and take no prisoners.

'Hello, Chantelle. We spoke on the phone earlier and here I am. Pleased to meet you,' Pascal said loudly, pushing roughly past the black guy and into the apartment. He was so shocked for a moment that he actually moved aside to let her pass, but then he was re-grouping and grabbing her arm.

'Hey, bitch. No one invited you in, so git,' he spat, pushing her back towards the door.

She let herself go limp as if ready to be led back to the door, then gripped the guys wrist, pulling it down, around and up behind his back all in one fluid movement. Then she slammed him up against the wall in an explosive demonstration of power that was extraordinary for someone of such a slight build. She held his wrist pushed far up behind his back so that the more he struggled the further she pushed the arm, the more it hurt him. His face was contorted with rage and crushed sideways against the wall. He winced, breathing deeply, his struggles starting to subside.

'You's dead, bitch. You have no idea who you're dealing with,' he said.

Pascal, ignoring the words, patted him down with her other hand. She dug out a Beretta Cougar automatic pistol, looked like .357, from his baggy pants pocket, and handed it to Chantelle. She gingerly took the weapon, looking at it with horror as if she didn't want to touch it.

'Tough guy, aren't you?' Pascal murmured, pushing him further into the wall as she sensed the guy tensing to take another crack at her. He relaxed again. Pascal said, 'now, you're leaving. I am going to walk you to the door where you can have your pop gun back, less the clip.

And just so you know, I'm a PI and I am working with a detective Daly out of NYPD in Manhattan, and if you want to fuck with me, I will call him up now and get him down here with a squad of patrolmen.'

Pascal held her cell up with her other hand, scrolling through until she got to speed dial for Daly, then she said, 'Your call. What's it to be, headbanger?'

She loosened her grip slightly so he could raise his head off the wall. 'I'll be back for the money, Chantelle. This dike can't protect you, not round here. Cops or not,' he said.

Pascal pulled him roughly away from the wall then slammed him back again, case he forgot who was in charge, all the time keeping him under tight control. Then she shuffled him to the door, keeping his arm pushed up his back, and pushed him out. She handed him the Beretta less the clip and slammed the door shut in his face, cutting off the stream of abuse.

She turned to find the large black woman staring back at her. There seemed to be relief in her face and even the glimmerings of a faint smile. Her skin was very black, almost purple, and her face handsome and lived in. It told you of pain but also laughter, and her eyes were inquisitive, but there was also reserve. Finally she spoke. 'I told you I had nothing to say to you on the phone. Why d'you come? And don't think I'm grateful for what you just did. He'll be back, when your gone, and it will be much worse for me.'

'Who is he?' Pascal asked.

'What does it matter?'

'I might be able to help you.'

'Forget it. This not your world. You're not even American, with that accent.'

'Fine. If you wont talk to me, I can't make you, but I've trekked all the way out here to see you, so how about a quick coffee before I have to go all the way back. Where's all that legendary American hospitality I've heard so much about?'

Chantelle held her eyes, considering her words. Pascal held her breath. 'I guess I can spring to that,' Chantelle finally said, gruffly. 'Come on in. One coffee and then your gone.'

'Fine. Thank you,' Pascal said and followed her through into a small, neat and tidy living room. Chantelle bustled out to the kitchen while Pascal looked around. There were some photo's on a side writing table. Looked like smiling adult daughter graduating, and then a much younger and slimmer looking Chantelle with a serious looking guy in military uniform. Probably a husband, but both pictures looked quite old. The room and flat itself had the feel of a single occupant. On the writing table she noticed a pile of bills with handwritten calculations on them.

Chantelle returned with a mug of coffee and thrust it into Pascal's hand almost spilling some. There was no hint of a smile on her face now, just an expression suggesting she would like Pascal to finish her drink quickly and then leave. Pascal studied her, wondering how the hell she could break through the barrier that seemed to surround the woman.

Pascal sipped. 'Good coffee,' she said.

Chantelle continued to watch her, and Pascal could see the big lady was curious, but was biting her lip, determined not to ask any questions. But then as Pascal remained silent that curiosity seemed to get the better of her. 'Where d'you learn that?' she finally asked. 'To take on a guy like Montell, and whup his ass, when you is so small, like a child, and he is such a big ugly motherfucker?'

Pascal couldn't help bursting out with pent-up laughter at her words, but Chantelle got the wrong idea, a sharp look of anger flickering across her face. But then she saw that Pascal's laughter was genuine, that she wasn't laughing at her, and she began to smile.

Then their laughter stopped abruptly, and there was silence. Pascal finished her coffee and gave Chantelle a last questioning look. She knew she'd just about run out of time, and needed to go. Chantelle seemed to hesitate, eyes fearful again, then she said, 'it was nearly thirty years ago, you know, and I can't talk about it. About Angel Milken, the penthouse and K Corp. I'm sorry, because you seem like a real nice person, and I'd like to help you but I can't.'

'Why?' Pascal asked.

'I can't talk about that either.'

Pascal's mind worked on that. Maybe there was a deal done, a payoff for her silence, but then why did she have to go to prison for the drug bust, if there was a deal? Or maybe she was just still too scared to talk. That would make more sense. 'Look, Chantelle,,' she said. 'I can tell you're a good person too, and if you feel you can't talk to me, I understand that and I wont press you. But, give me ten minutes of your time now, so I can tell you why I am here. Then I will give you my number and I will leave. Later, if you wanted to talk, great. If you don't, that's fine as well, and I won't contact you again.'

Chantelle hesitated again, conflicted, then she seemed to nod to herself. 'You better sit down,' she said, maybe resignedly, but also maybe relieved as well. 'I'll get us a proper drink.'

The proper drink turned out to be sherry which was fine. Then Pascal sat and told her about Hannah's claim and some of Angel Milken's suspected history, which Chantelle listened quietly to without reaction. Then Pascal moved on to Calver's linked murder trial and the problems they were having in raising any kind of viable defence. It was only a bare bones generalised re-telling, and Pascal kept detail to a minimum.

'So you see, Chantelle, we're trying to fill in the gaps.'

'You mean you want dirt on Milken?' she said.

'I want to know what happened, Chantelle. That Heroin wasn't yours, was it? Wouldn't you like your daughter to know the truth about you?' Pascal said, looking over at the photo on the writing desk.

Chantelle stood up abruptly, expression suddenly closed again. 'My daughter's dead, and you need to leave, now,' she said.

Pascal sighed. Looked like she'd blown it. Shouldn't have mentioned the daughter, as it seemed to have hit a nerve. She shrugged and got up, scribbled her contact details on a piece of paper and handed it to Chantelle.

At the door they regarded each other. Chantelle eyes were still hot and hostile, but as she looked Pascal up and down, they softened slightly, and she said, 'don't hang around outside. Its dangerous here. Turn left and walk straight up to the main drag, about half a mile and you can hail a cab there. Be careful.'

'Last question,' Pascal said. 'What's Montell's surname?'

Chantelle sighed. 'Castro. Now git,' she said, half smile.

Pascal opened the door and then surprised the big lady by quickly turning back and kissing her on the cheek. 'Take care, Chantelle,' she said before turning and making her way down the corridor.

Chapter Fifteen

I was sat at the kitchen table ostensibly doing some prep work for my cross examination of Daly, due to start in the morning, but actually concentrating on sipping some good Bourbon I'd found salted away in the back of a kitchen cupboard. Pascal came in and dumped her stuff on the table, and said, 'gimme me one of those will you, Calver?'

I poured her a large one as well. As we clinked glasses Christoff poked his head round the door and said, 'nothing doing on O'Leary's computer stick, Courtney.'

When he saw the drinks he came in and I got him a glass and poured him one as well. He continued, 'there's actually some kiddie porn hidden away on there, which these days unfortunately seems almost de rigueur. I didn't really look at it as its clearly not relevant for our purposes. Oh, and there's a couple of old clips - from maybe six, seven years ago - of couples *in flagrante* in the hotel bedrooms, but that's it. Nothing, Nada on the murder or the CCTV'

'You sure?' Pascal asked, deep frustration in her voice.

'Positive. Been over it, scraped and peeled it every which way, and its clean. If he's got anything incriminating to do with Jonas' trial, its somewhere else.'

Pascal grimaced. She should have searched O'Leary's room

properly when she had the chance. All that effort with the fire for nothing.

'Sorry,' Christoff said.

Then Pascal seemed to remember I was there. She looked up, meeting my eyes, and said, 'I'm still digging, Calver, but nothing you can use as yet.'

It didn't sound encouraging and she saw my look. 'I'm trying, Calver, believe me, but I need more time.'

'Yeah, and that's just what I don't have,' I said, getting up and heading for my bed, leaving her sitting there sipping her bourbon.

People v Calver - Manhattan Supreme Court

Day 3

'Detective Daly, you said earlier in your testimony,' I said, looking down at my notes, 'that because Helena Palmer's room was not disturbed, she must have known and trusted her killer, yes?'

We were back in court, two minutes after 10 and I was trying to pick Daly open, get some points on the board, because boy did I need some.

Daly thought for a moment, pretending to genuinely consider the question. 'If an intruder had say knocked and then burst in when she answered the door, you would certainly expect to see some evidence of disturbance. A turned over table, maybe stuff spilled on the floor. Something. In the absence of that, I think its reasonable to assume that she knew and trusted her killer. That's just my professional opinion of course,' he added.

'But if the crime scene was *staged*, detective, as the defense will argue,' I said, 'surely even the most incompetent of killers could smooth out and tidy the room, if there was disarray after the killing. Straighten up the odd chair, pick up any spilled items from the floor, to make it look like she knew her killer. Wouldn't take much, would it, detective?'

Daly had a half smile on his face as he considered my latest desperate ploy. 'That would be fine and dandy, counsellor, if we had any evidence that anyone other than you had been in the room at the time of the killing. The CCTV is frankly—'

'Thank you detective,' I said, quickly cutting him off. 'Now, earlier you played the tape of my wife's call to the emergency services where its alleged I assaulted her. Have you attempted to speak to her about the incident?'

'No.'

'Why not?'

'Your honour,' Stahl broke in. 'The resources of NYPD and the DA's office are limited, and bringing over a peripheral at best, witness, from the UK to testify can't be justified. Defendant is free to call his wife if he so wishes.'

'He's right Mr Calver,' Judge Gonzalez predictably intoned. 'Move along.'

I was getting nowhere, and running out of ideas. Querying the CCTV when we had no evidence to challenge its validity was pointless, so I couldn't venture into that area either, so I was left with a few pitiful scraps to argue about.

'Detective Daly, you're of course aware that in the UK I am an experienced criminal lawyer?'

'So they tell me,' Daly said, half smile still in place.

'If, as was the case, I had spent the evening and part of the night with the victim, and then strangled her with my green silk tie. As an experienced trial attorney, does it make any sense for me to leave the crime scene in that state and admit to my ownership of the tie used to strangle her?'

'You were drunk, counsellor, just like when you tried to strangle your wife. When I buzzed you up the morning the body was found, you didn't know where you were, let alone what you had done. You had consumed virtually all of the three bottles of red wine found in your room, over a short period of around three hours. And that's a lot of booze for anyone, even a heavy drinker like you, Calver.'

Time to call a halt. If I went on digging I'd end up in Australia. 'I have no further questions,' I said, and sat down heavily. I could feel it all slipping away from me. We had to come up with something to fight back with, but Pascal was giving me nothing. All I could see to do was to try and drag things out as long as I could in the hope that she might come up with something to save my bacon. It was no strategy but it was all I had.

Pascal considered Daly over the rim of her beer bottle. When he had texted her suggesting they meet in the bar where she'd had her bust-up, she'd thought he was kidding, but he wasn't, so here they were again, sitting at the same table. Daly had just come from court so he looked a deal smarter than last time; blue suit, and a shirt and tie.

'Your guy's dying, you know,' he finally said in his slow drawl. There was no triumphalism in his voice, it was just a statement of fact.

Pascal carried on looking at him over her beer. 'Thanks, Daly,' she said. 'If you've got any more helpful comments like that, do me a favour. Keep them to yourself, yeah?'

He smiled. 'Calver may be great shakes in an English courtroom full of faggots in wigs, but in the good ol' US of A, he just aint cutting it. Maybe he should hire himself a big hitter US attorney. Or he should cut a deal with Stahl, but if he leaves it any longer, Stahl won't give him shit. Why would he need to? He's got a nailed on conviction.'

'Look, Daly. Can we talk about something else?' Pascal said. 'You're beginning to depress me.'

'Sure. What do you want to talk about?'

'Hey, you texted me, so I'm guessing you wanted to tell me something, right? Like John Palmer was murdered, and you're going to give me a copy of the deeply flawed autopsy report, if there was one.'

'Oh, there was one alright, but its going down as accidental death at the moment. I've been too busy with the murder trial to have a closer look, but what you said about him not touching alcohol was kind of arresting. Stopped me in my tracks a little bit, if you like. Its something we need to have a look at. What's your proof, anyway?'

'Calver was told by Palmer's sister, the murder victim, but I'm sure her mother, Hannah, will confirm it for you.'

'Okay, I'll do some more digging, and I'll call you.'

Pascal was disappointed that was all he seemed to have for her - nothing - but she kept it to herself. Daly was under no obligation to help her, and giving out confidential information from NYPD was no doubt a pretty serious infraction of their rules, so she would just need to stay patient for now. She nodded when he hailed the barman for another round of beers, wondering just why he seemed to be so keen on meeting her again. Maybe he was lonely and wanted a date she thought, but then another idea struck her from left field, and she jumped straight in. 'I was out the other night, Daly, chasing down a lead for Calver. Not of course acting as a PI, cause that would be illegal, right?' she said.

'Glad you're keeping you're nose clean. What of it?'

'Well, I was out in some burg called, Crotona Park, in the East Bronx.'

Daly raised his eyebrows. 'Boy, you sure get around. You should be careful out there on the street, can be dangerous.'

'Yeah, I know. I found that out. But a couple of things. I've got a name, that maybe you can run down for me. And I've got a serial number for a Beretta 8000, .357 calibre semi-automatic, associated with that name. Interested?'

Daly's eyes showed nothing, but she could tell there was a faint gleam of interest there, just under the surface. 'Maybe,' he said. 'Talk to me.'

Pascal gave him a highly edited and partial version of why she had wanted to meet with Chantelle Latifah, and where the lead had originated from. Then she described the scene she had encountered when Chantelle's door had opened, sticking pretty much to the truth.

'Big black guy answered the door, name of Montell Castro. Tall, skinny, about 28, tats all over, but I'm not familiar with what they mean. Looked like a gang-banger and he was definitely putting the squeeze on her - she was scared. I'd guess loan sharking, or maybe drugs, although she didn't seem like a junkie.'

'What happened, and where does the Beretta Cougar come in?'

'He threatened me and tried to throw me out, so I kicked his ass.'

Daly laughed. 'Get outta here,' he said, appraising her with a keen look.

'He tried to hustle me out, so I disabled him, frisked him and thats when I found the Beretta. I kicked him out and gave him the gun back, less the clip, but I clocked the serial number and memorised it when I gave it back.'

'So, I guess this Latifah chick, she was pleased, right?' Daly said.

'Not exactly. In fact, she wasn't. She said I'd just made it a whole lot worse and he'd be back. And then she refused to talk to me'

Daly looked at Pascal speculatively. 'So you want a way to get into her good books, and maybe getting this Castro guy off the street will do it?'

Pascal returned Daly's look, expressionless. Then she took a drag from her bottle, and he took a sip from his Bud, still watching at her, weighing things. Then he said, 'don't get your hopes up, but its odd he has a gun with a serial number on it. These gang-bangers almost always file them off.'

Pascal scrolled her smart phone and then read Daly the serial number she had noted down out in the East Bronx. Before leaving, all Daly would say was that he would take a look, and get back to her, on both things. Maybe next time they could have dinner?

Pascal didn't say anything, then they left. She hoped she'd planted a couple of seeds that might bear fruit, that might edge Daly a little closer to trusting her, and maybe even coming on board and helping Calver. Daly never said why he had asked to meet.

Chapter Sixteen

People v Calver - Manhattan Supreme Court

Day 4

Stahl was up and running again as we ground into the morning session. He told the judge he would be calling a couple of heavyweight experts; the Medical Examiner and then a surveillance expert. Just in case, he said, with a virtual wink to the jury, the defendant was going to be foolish enough to challenge the hotel CCTV evidence.

So first up we got Dr. Oskar Reitman the ME who had carried out the autopsy. He was a big bear of a man with a large halo of frizzy brown hair streaked with grey, and as you would expect, he was a more than competent witness. His testimony was given in short bite sized pieces, for easy digestion by the jury, and they ate it up like nobody's business.

Essentially he told them that Helena had died from Asphyxia caused by the ligature, my green silk tie, around her neck, which caused *cerebral hypoxia*. That is, low levels of oxygen in the brain, contributed to by the constricted blood flow caused by the pressure on both carotid arteries in the neck. And here he livened things up by showing the jury - over my futile objections Gonzalez rejected out of hand - horror inducing blow-up crime scene photographs of the body. In particular a photograph showing Helena's neck with the green tie almost lost from view because it had sunk so far into her flesh. And then another with the tie removed showing the awful bloody tracks it had left, followed by a wholly gratuitous photograph of her face with bulging eyes.

He then moved on briefly to time of death, where he was able to isolate a window of sometime between 2.30 and 9 am when she was likely to have expired. Here he also mentioned the steaks consumed by myself and Helena at around 8.30 pm in the early evening preceding the murder. The evidence of her stomach contents - the steak had been partly digested and moved into the small intestine, a process that usually takes between 4 − 6 hours - essentially corroborated his time of death assessment.

He then moved on to the sexual aspects of the case. If the jury were expecting anything juicy here they were to be disappointed. In the end what they got was a lot of dry medical testimony, and I could see their eyes begin to glaze over - a good sign for me. Essentially what Reitman told them was that he found evidence of sperm in the vagina, and DNA testing confirmed it was mine, something of course I would have freely admitted they would find. There was no evidence of bruising or abrasions around the vagina or labia minora suggestive of force or assault; conclusion: this particular sex was almost certainly consensual. However, there was significant bruising and abrasions evident around the victims anus and also lacerations, but no spermatozoa present there. Reitman's conclusion here: non-consensual, indeed violent, anal sex had been perpetrated upon the victim.

As Reitman concluded his examination in chief I could see the jury looking at me in a different way, as if maybe they had lost a bit of warmth towards me, which I guess was not surprising given what they had just heard.

Judge Gonzalez, nodded at me. 'Cross examination, Mr Calver?'

'Yes indeed your honour,' I said, rising to my feet, still trying to work out how to come at the estimable Dr. Reitman, the big fuzzy-haired hit-man. I regarded the guy for a couple of beats, mulling my approach. He stared back owlishly, calm and collected.

'Doctor Reitman, you testified there were, apart from the ligature, some significant scratch marks and abrasions, possibly from fingernails, at the front of the victims neck, beneath her chin, yes?'

'Correct.'

'But none at the back of her neck?'

'Correct again.'

'Now doctor, I guess we all know, and the Kama Sutra certainly tells us so, that there are many ways and positions for having consensual sex, not all of which involve the conventional face to face missionary position,' I said. 'But those neck scratch marks presumably could only have been inflicted upon the victim by a perpetrator positioned behind her?'

I could see some puzzlement on the faces of the jurors as to where I was going with this, but Reitman nodded affirmatively, and said, 'yes I would say that is probably so.'

'So taking that a step further, doctor. Given the violence of the alleged anal assault - the bruising and lacerations - and the fact that this was almost certainly accomplished by a perpetrator from behind the victim, wouldn't you say its likely that these neck injuries were also inflicted during the alleged anal rape?'

'Again, all I can say is that that is a probability. So What?'

'I'll get to that,' I muttered. Then, 'so, okay, doctor, so let me summarise so far, and for the moment we're not considering the ligature or the strangulation. We have consensual vaginal sex with evidence of semen and no bruising, then we have violent non consensual anal sex accompanied by scratch and fingernail marks to the front of the neck, and, *crucially*, no semen?'

'Are we going somewhere with this, your honour?' Stahl interjected lazily from his seat, trying to break up my flow.

'Your honour—' I began, but she stilled me with her hand.

'No. I am interested in where Mr Calver is going with this, and I think the jury are too. So I am going to give him a little leeway here,' she said, surprising me for once. 'Proceed.'

Reitman looked slightly flustered for the first time, not understanding where I was going either. 'You have made a statement of fact, Mr Calver with which I wouldn't disagree,' he answered, rather convolutedly, but in the way I wanted.

'So, given the distinct differences between the two sexual approaches, if you didn't know better from other extraneous sources of evidence, could you categorically assert that these two distinctly different sexual behaviours had *not* been carried out by two different people?' I asked. Then added, 'forget the CCTV, witness statements and the green tie for a moment and consider just the medical evidence produced by your autopsy.'

'Of course, Mr Calver, its a hypothetical, and on that basis, I would clearly not be able to categorically assert that two people were not involved, particularly in the absence of spermatozoa, and therefore DNA, from the anal rape.'

'And isn't there another difference, doctor, in that the consensual sex took place in my hotel room, and the assault in her room. So the two incidents have yet another differentiating factor?'

'We don't know that for a fact, although its a probability, yes.'

'And just out of interest, doctor, have you ever heard of a case, where you have a couple having wonderful consensual sex, and then, shortly after, that same guy brutally rapes and murders his erstwhile partner?'

'It is highly unusual I'll grant you, but not unheard of. I have had the odd case where sex has taken place and then something has happened, one party becomes aware of an affair, for example, and murder follows, although sexual assault then, is unusual.'

'But that couldn't be the case, here, doctor, discovery of an affair, because I'd only just met her?'

Reitman merely shrugged. I flicked a glance across the jury box. There was certainly interest there, they were starting to think about and question the scenario I was trying to sketch out with my questions.

I moved on. 'Did you or any of your colleagues examine and take scrapings from under my fingernails?'

'Yes we did.'

'And what did you find?'

'Nothing, apart from traces of red wine and grease from the

steaks.'

'So no scrapings of the victims skin or DNA were found under my fingernails despite the clear evidence of scratches, abrasions and lacerations to the victims neck?'

'That is so.'

'How do you account for that?'

'I can't, really, and you are asking me to speculate. Maybe you just cleaned up,' he said with a wry smile.

'But not the steak and the wine,' I said as a contemptuous throwaway, then ploughed on. 'Now, given the ferocity of this assault, and now I am including the strangulation in our discussion, wouldn't you have expected the victim to have fought like crazy to try and save her life, and wouldn't you further expect that the perpetrator would at the least have suffered some cuts, bruises and maybe scratches from the victim?'

'Not necessarily, if the perpetrator wore protective clothing or immobilised the victim before the rape.'

'Was there any evidence of that, doctor?'

'No,' he replied, slightly less sure of himself.

'Did you examine the victims fingernails as well, given that she may have tried to fight off her assailant?'

'Yes we did.'

'And what did you find?'

'Nothing.'

'What, no broken nails; no trace evidence; no reside under the fingernails?'

'No.'

'Didn't you find that odd?'

'No. I believe someone may have cleaned under her nails post mortem.'

I thought I'd gone about as far as I could with Reitman, which wasn't very far at all. So I finished off my questioning and sat down. Stahl immediately re-examined his witness neutralising all the small gains I had made. He essentially got Reitman to reiterate his autopsy findings and then brought the elephant back into the room, the CCTV tape evidence, and asked Reitman whether he thought any other perpetrator could have done it. And there was only one answer to that. Bottom line: that CCTV was everything to the prosecution; it was unassailable and unanswerable - so far. If we couldn't find a way to challenge it, I was dead. And with that depressing thought, judge Gonzalez adjourned for lunch.

Southern District Court

Day 6

Morganna took up the questioning again. 'And around this time I believe your sister was born?'

'That's right. Helena was born on April 30th 1942,' Hannah replied, smiling briefly at the memory, then looking sombre again. 'It should have been a joyous occasion of course, but things were so bad by then that I think my mother might have preferred if Helena hadn't been born at all. There was so little food and we had to barter for everything. We sold most of our possessions, but we refused to sell the golden pendant and brooch.'

Hannah turned to the jury. 'You see,' she said, voice intense with emotion. 'The pendant had become a kind of symbol to me, like a talisman. I wanted it to be like a testament to my family's refusal to kowtow to the Nazis. It wasn't a religious cross, but I, in my naive adolescence, kind of wanted it to have the same kind of effect, of giving my family succour and empowering us to fight the Nazi's and never give in.

'But all the while around us the round-ups and the deportations continued, and we were so frightened of what would become of us. Helena was so small and helpless, and the world seemed so cruel. We tried not to despair, hoping salvation would come,' Hannah said, looking down at her hands, her eyes hooded and intensely sad.

Friedman coughed lightly, clearly concerned for Hannah's wellbeing. 'I think we could all do with a short fifteen minute break here,' he said. His words broke the spell on the courtroom and there was noise again as people made a break for the coffee machine.

People v Calver - Manhattan Supreme Court

Scott C. Ziegler was the prosecutions CCTV expert and I thought his resume was never going to end. It was hard to believe anyone could rack up that many stellar accomplishments in just one lifetime, but this guy seemed to have it all. He told the jury he was a Nevada licensed, board certified independent security consultant specialising in hospitality, gaming and retail security environments. He had over 30 years of practical hands on experience in security and surveillance operations including being Security Director for various resorts and hotels. He was also a member of ASIS International, holding the designation of Certified Protection Professional and was currently a member of the International Association of Certified Surveillance Professionals holding the designation of Certified Surveillance Professional as well as being a member of the International Association of Professional Security Consultants. If that wasn't enough, he was also a subject matter expert and Track Advisor for the American Gaming Association.

Now if this guy was going to tell us the hotel CCTV was kosher, I was in big trouble, and that's just about what he proceeded to do. There was a deal of technical jargon in what he said but essentially it boiled down to him telling the jury that the hotel had a state of the art CCTV system that was virtually impregnable to hacking or tampering. The surveillance system covering the hotel was comprehensive and comprised a number of different types of cameras, some rolling continuously, some based on motion sensors, covering all areas, including basement, parking lot and outside entrances. The only area not covered in some way or other were the guest rooms themselves and the security hub itself.

Footage was not monitored 24/7 but was stored digitally for 7 days. There were monitors showing CCTV footage at the front desk and also in the security hub in the hotel back office. Importantly for the purposes of this case, the hotel corridors leading to the rooms were covered by motion sensor cameras, whilst cameras in the lifts were monitoring continuously. So in the corridors, cameras would only be activated and film when there was detectable movement or motion taking place in front of those cameras.

After giving his masterclass on the hotels system, Ziegler turned his attention to Exhibit JC4, being the recovered CCTV footage of the corridors leading to Helena Palmer's room and to my room, on the evening and early morning of the murder. He reiterated that it was motion sensored, so in fact there was not a great deal to see. The part saved covered 8 hours real time, and boiled down to about 1 hour 10 minutes of filmed movement in the corridors. Ziegler had analysed and subjected the tape and the complete digital CCTV system itself to a plethora of tests, and he was absolutely adamant the tape had not been altered, doctored or falsified in any way whatsoever. It was one hundred per cent genuine. And if the jury didn't get that first time around, Stahl got him to repeat it, twice. Ziegler was happy to say on oath that in his professional opinion the tape was absolutely genuine and there was no room for doubt.

Then Stahl, with a smile, turned him over to me for cross. Where to start? We as yet had no expert of our own, so I was using Christoff. He was okay in his own way - ex-British intelligence encryption specialist after all - but I didn't think I could use him in court, as his resume couldn't compete with Ziegler's.

The problem was we could not see how they had done it, and it had got to the stage where I thought Christoff and Pascal were actually starting to doubt my honesty, because they could find absolutely nothing wrong with the tape, despite putting it through the grinder. Result: I had no idea how to attack Ziegler's testimony, but I had to try.

'Mr Ziegler,' I started, 'what's to stop someone just substituting a phoney, falsified tape for the real one?'

Ziegler smiled. He was a tall, thin, gangly man, mid-forties, with glasses and a beautifully trimmed beard, and you could tell he just loved to talk about surveillance systems. 'That's just about impossible with the Cyclops Surveillance system operated by the hotel,' he said, with deep satisfaction. 'And of course, we have clear chain of evidence testimony from NYPD confirming there has been no interference in that evidence between the hotel and the courtroom. You see,' he waxed lyrical, with an expansive sweep of his arm, 'the Cyclops system records everything that takes place on the system for every second of every 24 hour period. So it is not possible. Sorry, let me correct that. Yes it would be possible to falsify a tape, but as the system contains a complete record of all actions taking place on it, that falsification itself would be recorded on the system as well, and it is not possible to override that.'

'Right,' I said. ' But you said, "just about impossible", meaning, if we want to be precise, it is possible, although I accept, very difficult. How would you do it?'

I swept a veiled look over Stahl, and sensed a mild frown forming; good. But Ziegler was smiling. He clearly loved a challenge, and I could see the wheels turning. 'Well now, looky here,' he said. 'I hadn't thought about it, seeing as the system is of a really impregnable kind of a design, but I guess. I guess the only way we might be able to get in, would be to get into the original computer code of the system itself and maybe mess around with that. But again, its patented secret stuff, so I don't see how it could be done unless you had some kind of back door access or inside track, knowledge of the system or its original design.'

'So it is possible, after all?' I said, pausing, making sure it registered with the jury.

'Very, very difficult,' he replied. 'And as I say, we have carried out the most comprehensive testing imaginable and I stand by my assessment the tape is untampered with and genuine.'

'Okay, Mr Ziegler, but you have acknowledged that it is possible to tamper with the system,' I said, and then carried on quickly before he had a chance to jump back in and try and qualify what he had said. 'But I want to move on to the motion sensor issue. My understanding is that, the system allows you to alter the levels of motion that give rise to activation. So for example, if you have a camera trained outside and there are trees in the shot that move in the wind, you can set that up so the moving trees do not activate the camera, yes?'

'That's correct.'

'So what's to stop you just turning that feature off for a period, so for example, a person moving through the corridor doesn't activate the system?' I realised it was stupid question as soon as the words left my mouth.

'You're not listening, Mr Calver,' he rightly admonished me. 'If that had been done, the system would show it, and I can confirm to the jury, after extensive testing, that, the motion sensor control was on the manufacturers suggested level of 15 which would catch all human movement in the corridor. The tape is genuine.'

With that damp squib, I finished up and sat down, but we'd got something out of it - an acknowledgement that maybe it was possible to tamper with the tape, but it was probably too late to help. My real worry now was that the prosecution must be getting near ready to rest, meaning I would have to start putting on my defense - and I didn't have one, other than telling the jury I didn't do it, and that really wasn't going cut it.

Chapter Seventeen

O'Leary's laptop. The words bounced around in Pascal's head as she woke from a nap, her eyes snapping open and her head jerking up. She looked around; she was slumped over her computer keyboard, unaware where she was for a moment. Then her mind cleared and she clocked the familiar surroundings of the consular basement office.

O'Leary's Laptop. Christoff had said there was nothing on it. But he had also said that there *was* some low level kiddie porn on there that he hadn't really bothered to look at, because he didn't think it was relevant. At the time Pascal had let it go as well, tacitly agreeing with Christoff's analysis. The downloading of such material was often just a misdemeanor if prosecuted, and it happened all the time; guy takes his computer in for a fix and they notify law enforcement there's some questionable stuff on there.

So they had simply ignored it. But now she wondered. Calver's murder trial was turning into a slow motion car crash. Trying to discredit the CCTV footage had been a total wash-out, so they had to come at finding a hole in the prosecution case from a different angle, and once you broke it down there really was only one other logical way in: O'Leary. He had to be involved, and his meeting with Schmidt at the bar just about nailed that down. She guessed he also might be a weak link, a guy with a heavy coke habit.

Calver was going down the pan hard, in desperate straights, facing life in prison. So they had to find something right now. Any later and it would be too late. So maybe it was time to have another good look at the stuff on O'Leary's computer. If it was capable of being used as leverage, she would use it. Then maybe they could apply some serious pressure on Mr. John O'Leary, pressure that maybe wasn't exactly legal.

She picked up her phone and speed dialled Christoff. She needed to see what he had on the drive, and see if it was usable for what she had in mind.

Later, back at the apartment, Pascal sat at the kitchen table with her laptop and a cup of fresh coffee. She'd had to wait for Christoff to come out of the court where he was babysitting Hannah, to take her call. Following his instructions she'd located the flash drive in his bedside table and plugged it in to her laptop. Now she had a file on her desk top titled, "O'Leary - Secret Imagers I", which Christoff said contained the clips she needed to view. File II apparently contained the secretly filmed shots of hotel guests playing away, which she didn't need to see, at least not yet.

It felt slightly odd to be in the apartment during the day when everyone was out, but that's the way she wanted it, given the material she expected to be viewing in the next few minutes. She took a deep breath, double clicked on the file to open it, and then sat back on her stool to watch. Just as a face appeared on screen, her cell phone burst into life. She cursed and pressed stop on the laptop, and answered brusquely, 'yes?'

'Hey, Courtney, its Daly,' he said, no doubt expecting a squeal of joy.

What he got was a guarded, 'yeah, what?'

'Hey, don't be like that,' he said. 'I got some news on your guy, Castro. Thought you'd want to hear it.'

She briefly debated hanging up, but took a sip of coffee instead, and then said, 'what you got?'

He paused, disappointed she couldn't summon up a little more enthusiasm, but he let it pass, still eager to impress her. 'Following my tip-off, police in East Bronx arrested Montell Castro in a traffic stop, and found the gun. Get this: its linked to a shoot out with cops in LA, and there's an outstanding attempted murder warrant. I don't think Castro's linked, these guys pass guns coast to coast, but LAPD want to extradite him out there, so he's off the street for now.'

Pascal relented slightly. 'Hey, that's great, Daly. Look I'm in the middle of something right now. Maybe we can talk later.'

'That would be good, Courtney. I'll call you.'

'Do that,' she said, clicking her phone off and pressing play again on her laptop.

The same face re-materialised on screen, smiling at camera, then Pascal's cell exploded in sound again. She almost screamed. She pressed stop play again and grabbed the phone up, and thinking it was Daly again, said, '*What*?'

There was silence for a beat, and then a tentative female voice she didn't recognise, said quietly, 'is that Miss Courtney Pascal?'

'Yes, it is.'

'Well, this is Chantelle Latifah. Don't know if you remember me?' she said.

Pascal let out a deep sigh. She needed to calm down and get a grip. 'Of course I remember you. How you doing?' she said, then remembering how she had reacted. 'Yeah, look, sorry, you caught me on the hop.'

'I can call later if you're busy?'

'No, no, no,' Pascal said, anxious not to lose her again.

'Look, I heard Montell is gone, and maybe you had something to do with that. Don't want to know, even if you did. But I got to thinking, about the story you told me, and maybe its time I talked about my thing. What happened, and try and help you, and your client, if I can.'

'Really? That's. I don't know what to say, Chantelle, except, thank you.'

'Well why don't you come out here again, and we can have something to eat, and I'll just talk. How would that be?'

'That would be just fine, Chantelle. When?'

'How about tomorrow night, say seven?'

'Done. I will see you then,' Pascal said, smiling and feeling good. Then her face fell as she pressed play, bracing herself.

People v Calver - Manhattan Supreme Court

Day 5

I had been sitting for ten minutes with my yellow legal pad, desultorily doodling, trying to come up with the outlines of a speech. That's because Stahl was almost certainly about to rest the prosecution case, and as I hadn't made my speech at the start, I would have to make it now.

I looked around the half empty courtroom. We weren't due to start for another few minutes. In the past I'd always liked this time, that quiet period before the fury of judicial combat was renewed, when just the court clerk and a few ushers were quietly whispering to each other and there was just the faint sounds of rustling papers and the barely audible click of fingers skittering across keyboards. And it seemed to be the same in courtrooms the world over, but now I didn't like it at all. It felt threatening. Like the lull before the storm.

I looked up as Stahl breezed in with his retinue, followed a minute later by Judge Gonzalez and then the jury. Stahl rose to his feet and said, 'Your honour. The prosecution rest.'

My heart sank. I was back in it again, fighting for my life.

But then judge Gonzalez surprised us all. Looking up and addressing us, she said, 'Ladies and Gentlemen of the jury, I hate to do this, but something has come up in the judicial calendar that I must personally attend to, and this will necessitate a brief adjournment of today and tomorrow's proceedings.'

As I watched Stahl's face fall - just like me, he'd had no prior warning - I offered up a little prayer of thanks. As Pascal had said, all we needed was time, and now the judge had given us a little. Okay it was only a couple of days but every little bit helped. 'So,' Judge Gonzalez finished up. 'Take these couple of days. Have a holiday, forget the case and don't talk about it to anyone. Back here Thursday morning at ten sharp. Thank you.'

'*All rise,*' the Bailiff said, and we were out.

Pascal sat in Starbucks watching the hotel entrance, her stomach pulled tight into a series of taut knots. She had watched the hidden clips taken off O'Leary's laptop and they had sickened her. Images of him laughing and grinning as he had raped a female child of perhaps 8 years old. But it was possible there was something even worse going on. She'd seen a photograph of a child on O'Leary's desk when she'd taken the laptop, and although she wasn't certain, she thought it was the same girl.

Right on time a few minutes later she watched O'Leary some way off, making his way down the sidewalk towards the hotel entrance. From a distance he looked calm and collected. She watched him for a second, trying to quell the anger that was rising up within her. Then she got up and left, taking a line so she'd reach him about twenty metres from the entrance. As she closed on him she could see he was rubbing his nose and his eyes looked bloodshot, even from a distance, and then she was standing in front of him blocking his path.

He made to pass by her side, eyes vacant, but then there was a flash of recognition. She moved over into his path again. He stopped. 'You want something, lady?' he said.

'Yeah, as it happens, I do. I want to talk to you about a video clip I have of you raping a young girl, who I believe is your daughter.'

She watched fear crowding onto his face, flooding his eyes. His mouth worked. He said, 'what do you want?' in a tired, strangled voice. 'You know,' he added. 'I knew it wasn't looters who took the laptop.'

'Good for you. We can't talk out here. Lets go up to your room,' she said.

He nodded and walked away. She watched him for a moment then followed.

In the lobby Mayberry Wilkins sat on one of the settees pretending to read a newspaper. When he saw O'Leary he checked the wall clock. The guy was right on time. But then Wilkins started as he clocked Pascal following him. As they entered the lift and the doors closed, Wilkins lifted his cellphone and pressed call for Schmidt

In the lift O'Leary ignored Pascal, pretending to read messages on his phone, but she could tell he was thinking hard, weighing his options. As they entered the room Pascal studied the photograph on the desk. It was the same girl, no doubt about it.

She glanced around the room. The bed look pretty much the same, unused and covered in clothing and detritus. She noticed now though that the desk against the wall was not standard hotel furniture, it was large and executive style, and it had bundles of paperwork strewn across the surface. And there was also another non-standard addition to the room, a microwave oven, sitting on top of the minibar, and there was evidence of O'Leary's home cooking scattered around the room, mouldy remains of turkey burgers on dirty plates. Pascal guessed that the hotel maids did not have access to the room.

'You want a drink, check in the fridge,' O'Leary said as he flung himself into a chair.

Whilst Pascal looked around the unkempt room, O'Leary removed a small baggy of white powder from his pocket and carefully cut himself a line. A moment later he snorted loudly, hoovering up the white powder into his nostril off an old credit card. He grimaced, closed his eyes and leaned right back in the executive style leather chair, face peaceful.

Pascal walked over to the minibar and checked inside. Just a large bottle of vodka, almost full, lying on its side, and a cardboard carton of orange juice. She mixed herself a screwdriver, pouring herself two thirds of the glass full of Smirnoff, with just a dab of orange juice. And all the time O'Leary sat there unmoving with his eyes closed.

Then his eyes snapped open and he looked over at Pascal. 'So what d'you think you have, and what do you want?' he said, studying his fingernails. 'My daughter, Cara, loves me, but I wouldn't expect you to understand that. People like you just don't have the imagination to appreciate the purity of a relationship like ours.'

'Spare me the bullshit rationalisations, O'Leary. I've seen the clips, so I have no intention of debating with you. No, what I want is simple information. But get this, O'Leary. From this day forward, you'll be spending zero time with your daughter. That can be because you voluntarily agree to it and give me the information I want, or it can be because your sitting in gaol for life without parole - your choice. What's it to be, Michael?'

He laughed. 'That's no choice, and you know it. I talk, I'm dead. These people don't need to make threats. In fact it may already be too late. They've been watching me lately, and probably know you're here talking to me right now.'

'So they killed Helena and framed Calver? How'd they fix the CCTV?'

He laughed again, manic. 'You people have no idea who you're dealing with do you?'

'So tell me. Who they are. Schmidt?' she said.

'He's just the enforcer. Behind him you've got malevolence on a grand scale and billions of dollars. An unbeatable combination, as you will discover,' he said.

Pascal took another sip of vodka and slowly began to pace around. O'Leary leant forward over the desk and carefully separated out another line from the motherlode, and snorted again, throwing his head back this time as if that might get the cocaine into his blood stream quicker.

Pascal, watching him and trying to keep the contempt out of her voice, said, 'if we went to the District Attorneys office and you agreed to testify, it's a certainty you'd get immunity and witness protection. You're talking about bringing down a major US corporation and a reclusive billionaire, and what DA is going to turn that down?'

'You really don't get it, do you?' O'Leary said wearily. 'Things may work like that in your hopeless bankrupt little country, but it don't work like that over here. Big money rules the world here and always has done. Whatever I do, I'm dead. You coming in here, just about guaranteed that.'

'Spare me the melodramatics, O'Leary,' she said, tiring of his exaggeration. 'Just—'

'*Look*,' he said, his face a deadly serious mask - maybe a shard of reality had made it through. 'I'll give you what you want, but I want something.'

'You're in no position to bargain, O'Leary.'

'I want to see her, one last time,' he said. Then seeing Pascal's incredulity, he quickly added, 'to talk to her, and say goodbye. You have my word,' he said, looking Pascal full on, 'I will not lay a finger on her.'

Pascal held his gaze. She couldn't arrest or imprison him and even if she called the cops he could still get to his daughter before they could intervene. But fact is she believed him. He could perhaps see even through a drug induced haze that whatever he did, his old life was over.

'Also, I need to get something for you from home - proof,' he said.

'What?'

'Wait and see.'

She could tell he wasn't going to elaborate, but she needed to get something out of him now, just in case Schmidt got to him before they could meet again. 'Okay, O'Leary, I'm thinking about it, but I want something now.'

'I'll give you a name: John Fossey. You check it out. Then you come to my house at.' He looked at his watch - it was gone four already. '8 tonight.'

Pascal was seeing Chantelle at 7, and didn't want to blow that out. 'Make it midnight,' she said.

He smiled. He'd have a bit longer to say goodbye. 'Midnight it is.'

She watched him. 'And O'Leary….' she said

'Yeah, I know. Don't touch her.'

He looked solemn and wasn't smiling anymore. She'd have to trust him. She finished her drink and left, leaving him sitting at the desk staring into space.

Pascal wasn't answering, so I got a cab back to the loft apartment. I wanted to ask Christoff a couple of questions arising from my cross examination of Stahl's CCTV expert. But then my cell was buzzing again, and this time it was Pascal. 'You trying to get hold of me, Calver?' she said.

'Yeah. Got a couple of days adjournment from the judge, so I thought we should get together, see if there's anything I can do to help.'

'That's good, but right now I'm on the run, so we'll have to talk later. Meantime I have a name, but no information on how its connected. I want you and Christoff to have a look, see if you can come up with anything.'

'Shoot,' I said.

'Names, John Fossey,' she said, and then spelled it.

'I wont ask what you're doing, Pascal, but you better be damn careful,' I said as I hung up.

I gave Christoff the name and he said he'd see what he could dig up online. I went to Morganna's well stocked drinks cabinet and mixed myself a Scotch, then paced around the furniture sipping it and thinking hard. Then I went over to Morganna's communal desk top computer, sat down and typed into a google search: John Fossey. Might as well all pitch in together I thought. After all, it wasn't as if I had anything better to do.

Chapter Eighteen

It was half past seven when Pascal finally knocked on Chantelle Latifah's door. On the way over she'd stopped off to get a bottle of wine, and now she was sipping a glass of it in the kitchen while Chantelle cooked up what she said was her speciality - Goat Curry. Pascal watched the big woman as she leant over a large pot, slowly stirring the contents with a long wooden spoon.

When Pascal had last seen her, Chantelle had been wearing a big diaphanous gown, almost like a tent, and Pascal had assumed she was just very big lady, but now she could see that wasn't the case at all. This time she was wearing dark green coloured jeans that clung to her in all the right places, a black peasant blouse tied with a large sash at the waist, and on her feet comfortable looking soft black leather pumps. The word voluptuous sprang to Pascal's mind; the woman was seriously curvy. She caught Pascal's admiring looks and smiled demurely; but Pascal could sense a kind of shyness in her look.

Chantelle served up the food and they carried their plates and glasses through to the living room where they took their seats and tucked in. For a while no one spoke, then as Pascal was finishing up, she said, 'man, that was *good*! Where you learn to cook like that?'

'My Daddy was a chef in the US Navy,' Chantelle said. 'There wasn't nothing he couldn't cook good.' She wiped her lips with a napkin and took a sip of wine. 'A detective Daly called me about Montell, so I know it was you,' she said.

Pascal didn't say anything. She'd fouled up with Chantelle before by jumping in too quick about her daughter; this time she'd just let her talk. Chantelle hesitated a beat as if struggling with some internal conflict. Then she said, with a kind of anguished look on her face, 'Montell killed my little girl.

'Then he came to me to pay off her drug debts,' she said. She looked away, blinking as a tear snagged in her eyelash. 'Oh, he didn't kill her personally, I know that, but he supplied the poison that did. She OD'd seven months ago.'

'I'm so sorry, Chantelle. I didn't know.'

'How could you?'

'What was her name, Chantelle? I'd like to know.'

'Her name was Larissa,' she said with a proud smile.

'Its a lovely name.'

'Thank you.'

Then there was silence again, but it was an easy silence. They both sipped their wine, then Chantelle said, 'I thought a lot about the story you told me about your friend, Hannah. I've been turning it over in my mind ever since, but I don't see how I can help you. It all happened so long ago.'

Pascal took a deep breath, a little frisson of excitement starting to flutter in her gut. But she immediately tamped it down, determined this time not to get her hopes up. She'd just try and play it honest and straight.

'Hannah's story is a lot older than yours,' she said. 'And she's reliving it everyday in the Southern District Court, as we speak. And believe me, that's taken a lot of guts. She's taking on one of the most powerful corporations in the US - fearlessly,' Pascal said.

Then as a thought occurred to her, she added, 'you know, you could go down their, to the court, if you get some time, and listen to her testimony.'

Chantelle looked interested immediately. 'You think so,' she said. 'They'd let me in?'

'Of course they would. Its open to the public. Think about it.'

'I will,' she said, and Pascal knew she would.

'Look, Chantelle, we really don't know what we're looking for, so what I want you to do is just tell me about your time working for Angel Milken.'

Chantelle got up and walked over to a small writing desk set against the wall and picked up a large photograph - Pascal assumed it was of her daughter, Larissa - and carried it back to the couch where she sat down again. She held the picture in both hands, studying it intently. Then she began to speak.

'You know I loved that job, until….until that day. They treated me real well.'

'How did you get the job in the first place? I mean, I'm guessing Milken was a Nazi, and we all know their views on race, you being black and all..' Pascal said, running out of steam and then feeling embarrassed at the cack-handed way she had tried to raise the issue.

Chantelle didn't seem to notice though, her eyes veiled and turned inwards as she reminisced. 'It was his wife, I think who controlled the domestic household and did the hiring and firing,' she said. 'And he just went along with it. Also I think there were a lot of interviews for the role and each person they chose had a weeks try out. There were three before me, then I did my week, and they must have liked me because they offered it to me at the end of the trial period. That's another thing you need to understand. I had very little contact with Angel Milken, other than him giving me the odd order when his henchmen weren't around, like, "bring Coffee" or "clean my study" kind of thing. But he did give me a brief talking to when I started, saying everything that went on there was highly confidential, and any breach of that confidentiality would result in my immediate dismissal and a negative reference.'

Pascal watched her some more, wondering how to bring up the rape incident without inflicting further pain on her. But in the end, Chantelle raised it herself, sparing Pascal the trouble. 'As to the rape, it went down how I said it did,' she said, holding Pascal's eyes with what looked like a challenge to disagree if she dared. 'I know now he drugged me. It was before date rape drugs really took off, but my daughter investigated it when she was doing her law degree, at college. She said that one of K Corp's wholly owned subsidiaries was a pharmaceutical company, so it wouldn't have been difficult for him to get the drugs. And if he didn't get them there, then I'm sure his pet monster, Schmidt would have had no trouble sourcing them on the street.'

Pascal thought for a moment, and then said, 'why do you think it happened, and don't take that the wrong way. But this is a guy who has, from what I have seen, monumental self-control?'

'No, Courtney, I agree with you, and I've wondered over the years why it happened. He was actually incredibly good as an employer and there was never a hint of unpleasantness or, looks or inappropriate touching, before that. To be honest if someone had said he was attracted to me before it took place, I would have been shocked. That day, he had not seemed himself, and his wife was away, which was unusual, and he was drinking which was also unusual. I guess he got to feeling sorry for himself, and he came looking for me.'

'So then they framed you with the smack baggy in the pillowcase, yeah?' Pascal said.

'Yes. Believe it or not I've never ever taken drugs.'

'Oh, I believe you. Did you ever see or speak to any of them, after you were dismissed and went to prison?'

'Only Schmidt, once, and that was enough. Just after I got out.'

'What happened?'

'He turned up at my Mother's which is where I first stayed when I got out the joint. He turned up, out the blue, when I was there alone. He said they could do it all again, if I ever said anything to anybody. Then he said he would kill me, and I believed him, so I never spoke to anyone, and just tried to rebuild my life.'

'And now?' Pascal asked.

She smiled again but it was tinged with sadness. 'Larissa's gone, and I don't care anymore about me. If I can help your friend Hannah get something back, lets just do it.'

Pascal got up to get the half full bottle of wine and then she topped both their glasses up. As she moved, her mind was whirring away, processing everything Chantelle had told her. Problem was that there was no new information there that they could use. The rape was years ago, and statute barred, and there was nothing new there that would help Calver. As far as the world out there was concerned, Chantelle Latifah was a drug addict who had made false rape allegations against a pillar of the community and had gone to prison for it.

She tried another tack. 'What's the deal with Schmidt? What do you know about him, and did you ever witness anything, anything in the penthouse, that you considered illegal, criminal or odd, or……whatever?'

'That's just it, there was nothing other than that one incident. That was bad enough I know, but it was completely out of character for him and in relation to my overall experience working there. As for Schmidt, the guy is truly scary. I mean Montell scared me with like, what can I say, just normal kind of fear you get when someone threatens you, but Schmidt? I don't know. He never touched me physically, he didn't need to. Again though, you need to understand that I saw very little of him either, and that was mostly because Angel's wife flatly refused to have him in their living quarters unless it was an absolute emergency.'

Pascal frowned. Another blow-out. She already knew that Schmidt was a very bad guy capable of killing without hesitation, but that didn't really help either.

Chantelle could see Pascal's frustration in the stress lines on her face. 'I'm not much help am I, Courtney?'

'Hey. This is all good stuff, and I know Hannah will be grateful. But,' Pascal said, checking her watch, frustration creeping into her voice. 'Is there *anything* you can think of that struck you as odd. Something you may have seen that maybe didn't make sense or that you didn't understand?'

Chantelle closed her eyes tight, thinking hard. Then she laughed softly to herself.

'What?' Pascal said.

'Oh, its nothing. Silly.'

'Chantelle,' Pascal said, as if addressing a wayward child.

She took a sip of red wine, and was smiling. 'Well, he had a secret, concealed room. And I'm certain no one, not even his wife, knew about it. I caught a glimpse, I think. He never knew. But its concealed, with a secret doorway. I suppose it could be one of those secret bunkers for if criminals invaded the penthouse or a there was a nuclear war or something.'

'But you don't think so?'

'No. I think he kept things in there.'

This time Pascal felt a real frisson of excitement, at last, coursing through her veins. 'Tell me what you saw, or know, Chantelle,' Pascal said, looking at her watch again. She still had to see O'Leary at midnight. It was going to be a long night, but now she was excited. The adrenaline was kicking in.

'It was my day off, and I always went to my mothers in the mornings on those days, *always*, just not on that one particular day.

Mum had a doctors appointment I think. But Angel obviously thought he was alone in the penthouse. His wife was out, as she was most mornings. As you know I had my own self-contained living quarters, like a 3 room flat. It was as I was leaving to go out to see a friend, I had to pass through a common passage that runs through their living quarters to get to the lifts. Angels office study door was open and I could hear him on the phone. I hesitated outside the door, as usually if anyone was around I would just say Hi, and that I was leaving the building, so they'd know, as most of the time I was there round the clock 24/7.' She paused there for another sip of wine, smiling again as she registered how impatient Pascal was getting.

'Would you like another drink, Courtney?' she teased her

'Chantelle…..'

'Well,' she continued, 'I glanced through the office door, and was just going to wave, but he had his back to me. And the phone conversation had become heated. He was almost shouting and completely absorbed in the call, but its what I could see past him that shocked me. The far wall of his office was completely covered with bookshelves, but on that day, I could see they were like doors, and had slid open. And I could just see a large room the other side. All I could see was part of a picture on the wall near the door and that was all.

'Then I saw he was finishing his call and would be putting the phone down, so I ran, I don't know why, but I did. I ran on tip toes to the lift, and luckily it was there waiting and I jumped in and it went down.'

Pascal held her eyes, riveted. Then Chantelle added, 'later when

I was cleaning his study, and I did it a number of times, I tried to see a join, or a seam, or a lever or something, but I couldn't find *anything*. I even pulled some books off the shelves to look, and banged on it, but there was nothing. It was incredibly well concealed, but that's the only thing I ever saw, and only the once. I have no idea what it was for but I do know that he spent time in there. Or I assumed that's where he was, as when I was alone in the penthouse with him, he would disappear for periods when I couldn't find him, and later I guessed that's where he was at.'

Pascal's phone burst into life, but she ignored it. She was thinking hard. As her caller hung up and her ring tone stopped, she turned to Chantelle and said, 'last question, Chantelle. How do I get into the penthouse. And how do I get into the secret room?'

'Honey, you are stone crazy?' she said, eyes hot and bright. 'Breaking and entering? That's serious, man. Specially a rich folks place. And there is no way in there, seriously. I mean, even in my day, security was tight, but now? Give it up.'

'I'm not aiming to get caught, Chantelle. Look, I've got to go now. Will you just think about it. How it might be done?'

'You're crazy,' Chantelle said, but there was a mischievous smile on her face, and it looked like she might just be getting hooked into the action.

'And you know what,' Pascal said, soft and genuine smile on her face, 'I've really enjoyed this evening. It was like being back home for a while. Maybe we could do it again sometime?'

Chantelle didn't say anything but again there was that

incongruous shy smile on her face.

'So promise you'll call me, about how I get into the secret room, and don't wait too long,' Pascal said, rising to her feet, finishing the dregs of her wine and grabbing her bag. She needed to be at O'Leary's in around 30 minutes and that would be cutting it fine.

They hugged, and then Pascal was running for stairs.

Chapter Nineteen

Christoff looked bushed. "John Fossey" was proving intensely elusive. I'd given up looking soon after I'd started, but if Christoff was stumped, that was bad. We were back sitting in the huge living room again, and I'd just poured him a large Scotch to match mine. He still had his laptop open and was continuing to fiddle around with it.

'There are plenty of people around the world called John Fossey, apparently,' he said drolly, 'but I can't connect any of them to you or your case. And I have applied filters to my search, and qualified it, till its coming out of my head, but nothing's coming up.' His face looked tired; he took a shot of Scotch and looked up as Hannah came out of the bedroom.

'You boys drinking behind my back again?' she said. 'Get me one of those will you, Jonas, and make it large one, no ice.'

She seemed full of beans and had obviously had a good sleep. I got up and mixed her a scotch whilst Christoff explained to her what we had been doing and how we were getting a big fat zero in our search for the mysterious Mr Fossey. She listened as she took the cut glass tumbler full of scotch off me. She held it up and said, "cheers", before taking a huge gulp, giving only a slight cough as it hit the back of her throat. I had to say, she was one tough old bird. Then she sat down next to

Christoff, peeking at his laptop screen as he continued to fiddle with the keyboard.

As Christoff explained to her the various searches he had carried out, she slowly moved her head onto the back rest of the settee and closed her eyes. It was difficult to tell whether she was still listening or had gone back to sleep. Then she murmured, eyes still closed, 'you've tried K Corp and its subsidiaries, but have you looked at minority holdings?'

Christoff and I both stared at her, but she kept her eyes closed, and then she continued, 'you know, when my husband died, I got so down and low. Sometimes I thought I would just fade away if I didn't find something to occupy myself with. One of the things I did was to start looking at the shares we owned and I got quite interested in it. You know, looking at a company, analysing it, working out whether it might make a good investment. I even read books on security analysis by people like Benjamin Graham and I followed Buffet for a while until I saw what his world view was. Then I swiftly fell out of love with him, and stocks and shares generally. Thing is though, during that period I really did learn a lot, and one of the things I learned was always take a look at minority holdings. If you're thinking of investing in a company or a stock, you need to know what fingers they've got in what pies, before you puts your money down.'

I could hear the light patter of Christoff's fingers on the keyboard increase as he modified another search. Then he said, 'Bingo! Way out in Cincinnati, folks, is the head office of a little company that specialises in CCTV and security. It's called, Protecta. You just gotta love that name,' he said with a tired laugh. 'Their head of research is? Yeah, you've guessed it. Give the lady a prize - one John Fossey.

'K Corp currently hold 19% of the shares, worth today around 15 million dollars, so they're not exactly a big cap stock. I'm guessing K Corp are into them solely for the R & D and technology.'

Hannah opened her eyes and smiled. We three partially inebriated seekers after truth leaned in and clinked our glasses, each taking a shot, wondering what this latest revelation might mean, for me, but also for Hannah. Two cases running almost parallel, and with perhaps a common theme that was only just starting to make itself known. Time would tell.

Pascal paid the driver and climbed out the cab. In the lamplight and with a virtually full moon she could see a street of houses with cars parked outside. The neighbourhood was in a place called Battery Park City, and coming to it with an English sensibility, she found it kind of difficult to characterise. It looked sort of middle of the road suburban to her.

She calculated O'Leary's house was the third one down on the right at number 528; she looked the house over as she approached. It was a two storey grey looking family house with a drive-in garage built into the structure, alongside quite steep steps leading up to the front door. A large tree stood to the right of the property, partly shrouding it from the street, and there was a dim light showing in the large front curtained window next to the front door.

Pascal slowly climbed up the steps and pressed the white plastic doorbell. She listened as the chimes reverberated around inside the house. A few moments later a young girl opened the door on a chain and peeked out at Pascal. It was unmistakably Cara, O'Leary's daughter. She looked Pascal up and down carefully, and then said, 'if you're Courtney, show me ID.' The girl seemed kind of spooked but her voice was firm.

Pascal took out her wallet, slipped out her driving licence, and held it out to the girl who took it and scanned it. 'Its an English driving licence. Sorry, its all I have on me,' Pascal said.

The girl handed it back and pulled the chain off the hook saying, 'that's okay, come in, and go through.' She gestured with her hand, then closed the door behind Pascal, and followed her through into a living room off the hallway. They stood facing each other and Pascal studied the girl. She was wearing woolly white pyjamas patterned with brown coloured animals - rabbits, water rats and dormice - which made her look very young, but then the serious expression on her face worked against that. She was probably between eight or nine years old, of average height, but very thin with slightly angular features, long auburn hair with pale white, almost translucent skin and freckles that she had obviously inherited from her father. But her eyes were what drew you to her. They were huge and luminous, and dominated her face.

The girl seemed skittish and a little nervous. She half smiled and said, 'my name's Cara. Daddy told me you were coming and to give you a drink. There's lots on the table over there,' she said, pointing to a sideboard weighed down with bottles of spirits. 'Daddy's down in the garage doing something. Been there ages. Would you like something? I'll call him,' she said moving away towards the door.

Pascal said, 'thank you,' and made for the sideboard where she poured herself a glass of Jameson's irish whiskey. She could hear the girl calling out, sounding as if she was shouting down some stairs to the garage.

She came back, a worried frown on her face. 'I'm sure he'll come up in a minute,' she said doubtfully. 'I'm not allowed down there because its private,' she said, and then blushed.

'Where's your mother?' Pascal asked, to try to break the ice.

'Oh, she's gone,' she said matter-of-factly. 'A long time ago. Its just me and daddy now,' she said, wistfully.

As Pascal sipped her whiskey, she checked her watch - gone midnight. This was all wrong. Eight year old girl on her own, still up after midnight, parent nowhere in sight. She put her glass down. 'Come on, Cara,' she said. 'Lets go talk to your dad.'

It was as if she had been waiting for Pascal to take the lead, too scared to go alone where she was prohibited from going. She smiled, relieved, and those huge eyes lit up. 'Yeah, lets go and surprise Daddy,' she said, grabbing Pascal's hand and leading her to the door.

She guided Pascal down the hall to a door which she opened. Stairs then led down to what Pascal assumed must be the garage. She moved down the short flight of steps to another doorway which she tapped on. Then she pushed it open, saying, 'Mr O'Leary, its Courtney Pascal, for our midnight meet.' As the door swung open Pascal somehow instinctively intuited what she was going to see, and she was right, but she cursed anyway.

Bathed in the glow of a powerful arc light, O'Leary was hanging by a short rope from a beam running across the ceiling. Eyes bulging, and tongue lolling out of his mouth, he had obviously been there a while; couple of hours, Pascal guessed. Then she remembered the girl and quickly turned, starting to move to block the door, but it was too late.

Cara stood transfixed in the doorway, staring, face calm, almost serene. Pascal rushed at her, throwing her arms up and out to try and block the image, then around her in a kind of embrace as she bundled her out of the garage. Then she led the silent girl back up the steps to the living room, and sat her down on the couch.

She needed to calm the girl down, try and relax her, then go look at the body before the cops got there. Cara looked like she was going into mild shock, big eyes staring but unseeing. Pascal left her there and went to look around the house. In a medicine cabinet in the bathroom she found some sleeping tablets. She checked the instructions and took them downstairs, got a glass of water and went back in the living room. Cara looked at the pill, then mechanically placed it on her tongue and swallowed it with the water.

Pascal noticed a large teddy bear lying on one of the chairs. She retrieved it and handed it to Cara who immediately hugged it close to her chest. Pascal said, 'lie down with teddy for a sleep, and I'll come back in a minute.'

The girl nodded mechanically and lay down, eyelids already starting to droop. Pascal leant down and kissed her on the forehead, and as she drew back she was sure she saw the shadow of a ghostly smile slip across the girls face.

Pascal shook her head to clear it and then she was moving again, down the stairs into the garage. She dug her cell phone out and pressed speed dial as she began a minute examination of the crime scene.

'Daly?' she said gruffly, when he picked up.

'Jesus, Pascal, don't you limey's ever sleep?'

'You're prize witness, O'Leary, is dead. Looks like suicide, but then so did John Palmer. I'm at the house now. Interested?'

Daly was silent, digesting it. 'How'd he go?' he asked.

'Hanged. Not so easy to fake unless you're a pro, but O'Leary did have a good reason to kill himself. I'll enlighten you if you want to shift your ass down here. And it might go better if you do the 911 call? Oh, and I've got a very distraught, but currently sleeping, eight year old child here who is going to need looking after,' Pascal said.

'I'm on it,' Daly replied. 'And Pascal?'

'Yeah.'

'Don't foul up the crime scene, if it is a crime scene.'

She gave him the address and hung up. She knew she wouldn't have much time, so she got down on her hands and knees and began to crawl around the hanging body, looking for anything that might throw some light on what had happened. At the same time she was careful not to disturb anything. After a couple of minutes of finding nothing she sat back on her haunches to draw breath.

The garage was mostly empty, apart from an old desktop computer in the corner on a table. It was covered in dust and there was no mains plug so it probably hadn't been used this century. Also along one wall was a work bench with drawers and above it lines of hanging tools. Try as she might, she couldn't see O'Leary as some kind of DIY freak. And why had Cara said the garage was his private place that he spent a lot of time in, a place she was prohibited from entering? It look like a glorified tool shed to Pascal. Maybe he had moved stuff out and cleaned up before dropping the noose around his neck. Why the fuck didn't she try and question Cara before giving her the sleeping tablet? Too late now.

She got up and finally approached the hanging body and started to go through the pockets. The body was garbed in the same smart casual sports jacket, open neck shirt and slacks he had worn earlier in the day. She thought back carefully, going over the conversation, digging out the important bits. He'd said, "I'll give you what you want", and then later, "I need to get something for you from home - proof". But there was nothing in his pockets.

She reached up and studied the knotted rope, then his neck, then she felt around his scalp for any bumps or bruises, but there was nothing. She went over to the work bench and crouched down, studying all the surfaces, then went through the drawers - nothing. Now in the distance she could hear the sirens. She went over to the main garage door and pressed the button to the side, and it slowly slid up and over into the roof. She moved to the front of the house and then to the side, and looked through into the open back garden, and there over in the corner, completely hidden from the road, was a sawn off water butt with traces of smoke gently rising from it. She raced over and looked in at the embers and flickering flames. There was no way of telling what had been burned in there; it just looked like a pile of blackened smoking sludge.

She walked slowly out to the front as the first police car arrived, and then she saw Daly in a big smart looking black Lincoln drawing up and then climbing out onto the street. Then it hit her, the pent-up fatigue; she'd been out on her feet for hours, running on adrenaline, and now she was starting to pay the price. She felt shattered, as if she couldn't take another step. She wanted to curl up and go to sleep, but then Daly was approaching, grim smile on his face and she knew the evening wasn't over yet.

Chapter Twenty

Southern District Court

Day 7

I looked around the Southern District court. Today thankfully I was just an observer, a baby-sitter, and not a participant. I'd said I would accompany Hannah to court so Christoff could take the day off and see if he could run-down anything on John Fossey. I had wanted to speak to Pascal about what I could do to help during the break in my murder trial, but I couldn't get hold of her; her bed hadn't been slept in and she wasn't answering my calls, so now I was slumming it in the civil court.

I looked up and nodded as Morganna took her seat next to me, and then Hannah was making herself comfortable in the witness box. I glanced over at Browder, alone at the Defendant's table. He had studiously ignored me when I had earlier offered a curt 'good morning'. He looked bored, which wasn't exactly comforting in terms of how Morganna's trial strategy might be panning out. But Morganna looked great; there were no more nerves, and she looked smart and ready to roll. She stood and reminded Hannah where she had got to in her testimony and invited her to continue. I ran my eye down the jury box; they almost looked like young children waiting impatiently for the next chapter in a favourite fairytale.

Hannah coughed and then began to speak, her voice calm and measured, and as she spoke the jury seemed to lean forward in their chairs, but maybe that was just my mind playing tricks - hell, what did I know?

'Yes. I was talking about the months after my sister was born,' Hannah said. 'This was when we first started hearing stories about Jewish families being asked to go and work in the east, and that the Germans were asking for quotas or lists of names of people who would go.

'But over the months as these transports of jews to the east increased, rumours began to come back as to what was happening to these people. There were wild stories of shootings and so people began to go into hiding to avoid being taken in the quota's for the transports, so the Germans and Dutch auxiliary police began to engage in mass forcible round-ups.

'Then in August 1942 it happened. We received a deportation notice. I remember it quite clearly. We had all sat around the table and I read the document through aloud. It listed all of us, from Grandpa Isaac, all the way down to baby Helena. We were directed to assemble at the Dutch Theatre, within 24 hours with our possessions, ready for transport to the east.'

Hannah stopped there and looked at the jury. 'You really can't imagine how frightened we were. My mother did her best to be upbeat, to try and keep our spirits up, but I heard her crying at night and it broke my heart. But then Grandpa I think it was, practical as ever, said it was simple, we must go into hiding.

'Mother didn't think it was feasible for a family of five, and she didn't believe anyone would help us, but then Grandpa suggested we approach Mrs Van Der Valk, the mother of the boy whose life I had saved, and the person who had given me the Golden pendant and brooch.

'It was gone 7 pm that evening when we finally decided to ask Mrs Van Der Valk, and since we were due to assemble first thing next morning, I had to go out and see her that night. And of course there was a curfew in place for all Jews which you could be shot for breaching. So I remember that night very well, and also because it was the night that I ripped the hated yellow star we were all forced to wear, off my jacket and threw it away. Then I was gone into the night. I knew all the back ways and badly lit streets, and I knew the Germans could never touch me,' Hannah said, and for the first time there was the hint of a steely smile and her eyes were alive, almost like she was enjoying this part of her testimony.

I know I was, but then Judge Friedman was looking at the clock - hopefully thinking same as me, it was time for lunch, but he let Hannah's testimony run on until she had been going for around 2 hours straight without a break. Then he dutifully adjourned and we bundled our stuff up and made our way out of court and the first thing I saw was Pascal.

She was sitting on a bench in the waiting area, but the real shock was the strange looking little girl who was sitting calmly beside her. The girl had her arm around a moth-eaten teddybear and was holding tightly onto it, and onto Pascal's other hand, and she was watching everything -

lawyers, clients, witnesses - as they traipsed past her. As we approached, the child's eyes seemed huge, but also worryingly blank, and they didn't seemed to register us even when we were standing in front her. As I looked down at them I wondered what the hell Pascal had got herself into this time.

As Morganna stood before judge Friedman after the lunch break, I was still trying to process Pascal's story, especially O'Leary's death and the presence of the little girl. I watched a look of incredulity spread across Friedman's face as Morganna finished speaking.

'So what you're saying, in effect, if I am following you correctly, Miss Fedler, and I'm not at all sure that I am,' Friedman said, voice laced with sarcasm. 'Is that you want to go traipsing off to the Office of Children & Family Services so you can temporarily adopt, albeit on an emergency basis, an eight year old child, whilst you leave Mr Calver here, to run this case for you, a case for which you are the sole attorney of record? Do I have that about right, Miss Fedler?'

'Your honour, it will only be for the afternoon,' she said plaintively. 'You have seen that this witness is currently giving uninterrupted testimony that barely requires the presence of an attorney to elicit it. Mr Calver is actually far more knowledgable about this case than I am, and indeed, the plaintiff is in fact the client of his UK firm.'

I had to admire her chutzpah, and the way she came right back at Friedman, refusing to be cowed by him. So much for the rookie. But

Browder, unable to contain himself, was up again like a salmon going for fly. 'Your honour, I am sure it will not have escaped your attention that Mr Calver is currently on trial for murder. As well as that, he is precluded from acting anyway, as he is not licensed to practice as an attorney in the state of New York, or indeed, as far as I am aware, anywhere else in the US.'

'Your honour,' Morganna said, coming right back at Browder with the world weary air of a parent trying to explain something to a small child, 'I am surprised it should be necessary to remind Mr Browder that Mr Calver is innocent until proven guilty, and I might add that he vehemently denies the prosecutions case and will shortly be mounting a vigorous defense. Not only that, he has taken and passed the New York Bar exams last year.'

I was glad someone had such confidence in me. As I idly listened to the back and forth, another part of my mind was pondering Pascal's retelling of the events of the last 24 hours. From experience I knew it was foolhardy to accept everything she said at face value, so I wasn't going to.

I'd known there was some encrypted kiddie porn on O'Leary's laptop, but I hadn't known it was footage of him abusing his own 8 year old daughter. Pascal said she had gone to O'Leary and threatened him with exposure if he didn't tell us what really happened the night of the murder, and he had apparently just folded. Just like that. He'd given her the name John Fossey as a taster and promised more if she came to the house that night, and then he hangs himself. It made no sense to me.

It seemed more likely that he just went home and got rid of any incriminating evidence, and then hanged himself. It was clear to me that he'd lied throughout his testimony in my trial, and he was probably the only person who had evidence that could have got me an acquittal, and now he was gone, because of Pascal. And of course Pascal was also now a material witness to his death, and although it was clear they accepted, because of what Cara apparently told them and the estimated time of death, Pascal couldn't have been there when O'Leary dropped the noose around his neck, all it did was complicate things for me in my murder trial.

Great work Courtney - all she'd done was allow O'Leary to ditch vital evidence that I might have been able to use in my defense to prove my innocence. And now I was going to put on that defense when I had nothing to show the jury by way of evidence, other than me saying I didn't do it.

As all this roiled around in my overheated brain I tuned back in to the proceedings to hear Friedman saying, 'so I am afraid, Miss Fedler, I cannot accede to Mr Calver acting as an attorney here. He is not licensed, and none of— '

'Perhaps I could just act for myself this afternoon,' Hannah piped up from the witness box, all but forgotten by the jousting protagonists. For a second there was a startled silence. Then she added, 'I am simply telling my story and don't need counsel, and I'm sure I can handle anything that Mr Browder might throw at me in the meantime.'

There was some muffled laughter and I think I detected a faint ghost of a smile on Friedman's lips. Before anyone could answer I was on my feet. 'And I will stay and take notes, your honour and can report to Miss Fedler at the end of the day on any legal issues,' I said

Friedman mulled it for a moment. 'Mr Browder?'he said.

I watched Browder squirm; he knew the jury were with us on this and it would look churlish to object. Not only that, it really wasn't going to change anything other than make it easier for him if he did fancy making an objection during the afternoon.

As Browder stayed put in his chair, Friedman nodded. 'Miss Fedler you may go, and good luck with the child. Make sure you are back here tomorrow morning.' Then he turned to Hannah and said, 'please proceed.'

I nodded to Morganna and winked, and then she was racing for the door of the court where Pascal and Cara were waiting.

As the doors swung shut behind her, Hannah seemed to shake herself. She looked at Friedman and me once, then it was just her and the jury again, but this time with no Morganna to prompt her. But it didn't seem to phase her, and she got right back into it. I supposed she was anxious to get to the heart of the case.

'When I got to Mrs. Van Der Valk that night she immediately agreed to hide us so we could escape the deportation the next day. Remember,' Hannah said, looking up at the jury. 'I had saved her sons life and although she had given me the golden pendant and brooch, she was very glad to try and help us.

'When I got back to my family we packed that night and left by 4 am in the morning. Grandpa got the old coal cart out and we filled it with cases of clothing and other keepsakes, some food, pots and pans and what valuables we had, including the box with the treasured pendant and brooch.

'Funnily enough,' Hannah said smiling grimly, 'to start with it wasn't at all unpleasant living with the Van Der Valk's because we had the run of the house and garden, but within weeks we were hearing that the Germans were hunting for the people who were missing from the quotas, and people in hiding were being found or betrayed. The deportation notices were now coming out in the hundreds every week and the forced round-ups were becoming very frequent.

'As a result we had to move into the attic for fear of being discovered, and that was very grim. It was one room with a low roof, meaning you could never stand up straight, and there were no windows. It was cramped and stuffy and only one person could move at a time when we were all in there. We slept lined up on blankets on the floor, and when sealed in we had to use a bucket for a toilet. Access was via a ladder through a trapdoor and Grandpa had camouflaged it so it looked liked like part of the ceiling, although it would not survive a close examination.

'The first time the house was searched we were lucky— '

'Your honour,' Browder interjected lazily from his chair. 'Whilst we have great sympathy with the lady's sufferings seventy odd years ago, we have to ask, what exactly has any of this testimony got to do with the loss of the pendant and brooch?

I glanced at the jury and reckoned Browder might have badly miscalculated with his intervention. Legally of course he was on very firm ground as it was clear that Hannah's recent testimony had very little relevance to the issue before the court. But the jury quite clearly were interested, even engrossed, in her story.

I looked up at Friedman as he cogitated. 'Miss Palmer. Mr Browder does have a point, but I also believe,' he said, nodding over at them, 'the jury would like to hear the whole story of what happened.'

The jury clearly agreed with him as there was some generalised muttering and nodding of heads amongst them.

'But I have to be careful and fair to both sides whilst keeping in mind that evidence or testimony given here, must be relevant to be admissible in this court,' Friedman said.

It looked to me like Friedman was having trouble deciding, but I also thought he had warmed to Hannah as the trial had progressed and was probably genuinely interested in what had happened to her and her family.

'Just how much more testimony is there before you get to the important parts, if I can put it like that?' he asked Hannah.

'Oh, not much, your honour. Not much at all,' Hannah said, and I wondered whether she really knew that, or was just guessing.

'Mr. Browder,' Friedman said, nodding at him. 'I am going to allow some leeway, and in any event, from what plaintiff says, we are nearly there any way.'

'I understand, your honour,' Browder said, and for once he had the good sense not to argue the point.

Friedman looked over at Hannah. 'You said the first time the house was searched you were "lucky", so I am assuming that you were discovered in a later search, so perhaps,' he said looking up at the clock, 'when we come back, you can start your testimony from there, when you were discovered by the Germans?'

Hannah nodded and smiled gently. 'Yes, thank you honour,' she said.

'Good,' Friedman said. 'Court adjourned.'

239

Chapter Twenty One

Hannah, Christoff and I were sitting around the kitchen table chewing the fat when Pascal, Morganna and Cara arrived back from Children & Family Services looking like part of a carnival troupe. Morganna was carrying Cara, who was holding on tightly to her large moth-eaten teddybear. 'Meet the newest member of our commune,' Morganna said, doing a twirl. 'Miss Cara O'Leary. She's going to be staying a while until her Mom is better.'

Cara seemed bemused, holding on tightly to her teddybear. We all smiled back at her like idiots, and then Morganna said she and Hannah would go and settle our new guest in.

As they trooped out Pascal followed but returned moments later with a large bottle of Gin. Christoff ambled over to the side of the kitchen and rooted around in the fruit and vegetable trays until he found a lemon, then went to the fridge, cracked out a bucket of ice and brought it over with a large bottle of tonic water. No one spoke as Pascal mixed three large Gin & Tonics and passed them around. Then we each had a sip.

'John Fossey?' Pascal said, wiping her hand across her mouth.

'Christoff?' I said, turning to him.

'John Fossey,' he repeated slowly. 'You guys want to hazard a guess where he spent the night of the murder?' he asked.

'Somewhere in New York?' Pascal said.

'Yep, the Marriott. Five minute walk away.'

'Okay,' I said. 'But so what? My trial re-starts tomorrow, and I need something more than that. He was in New York. So what?'

I guess he detected the slightly desperate tone in my voice.

'Okay. Well have a look at this,' Christoff said, turning his laptop so that I could see the screen. It was a story in the Cincinnati Enquirer, from 9 years earlier with the headline, "*Conspiracy to Rob Trial Collapses.*"

I scanned the story. Seems that John Fossey along with two others was accused of conspiring to rob a large jewellery store. It was alleged that Fossey was the inside man for the heist, gave the other two the plan and then he got rid of the video surveillance tape. He had originally proffered a doctored tape to the prosecutor which then subsequently mysteriously disappeared when it was challenged. Seems the trial collapsed for other reasons, to do with legal technicalities, including chain of evidence and custody issues. The jewellery was never recovered and Fossey left the firm shortly afterwards.

I mulled over the little story. Back in the day 9 years ago the surveillance equipment was pretty primitive. Probably just a video tape; dead easy to doctor or lose. Nevertheless it showed Fossey had a predisposition towards that type of behaviour. Problem was, he was acquitted, and anyway, so far we couldn't link him to my case other than showing he stayed at a hotel nearby on the night of the murder. Back to square one, or maybe, just edging forward a bit. I turned to Pascal.

'Courtney?'

She drew breath as if she had been saving up to say something. 'Look, Calver, I know you think I'm getting too close to Daly, but I think you're wrong. The guy's stubborn as a mule, I know, but I think he's starting to take us seriously and ask some questions of his own about the murder, and I think he's a good detective. He's already suspicious about John Palmer's death and he's pulling the autopsy report for me. And he came straight down to O'Leary's when I called, which isn't his precinct, and without him there it would have gone pretty bad for me. The point is, he, just like us, keeps coming up against the CCTV, which so far seems irrefutable. Now this break, if it is a break, with Fossey, could be the thing that will convince him.'

'Okay,' I said, 'but what has Daly got to do with Fossey?'

'I think we need to enlist Daly to help us. We can't check Fossey's record or try and interview him, he'd see us coming a mile away and tell us to do one. I thought maybe we could try something, get in with Fossey somehow, but as you said, Calver, we, and especially you, don't have any more time. We need it now.'

'She's right, Jonas,' Christoff said.

'Wouldn't it mean him going off the plot with NYPD, freelancing? Aren't there rules about that, especially on a case where the investigations closed and he's a major prosecution witness?' I said, to test her, but already convinced that if she could get something out of him, it had to be worth a shot. What else did I have?

'Hey, trust me, Calver. That won't be a problem,' she said with a strange smile. 'I'm due to see him for a drink tonight, so are we all agreed? I'll give him what we've got, even though he's technically on the other side, and see if he'll help us out?'

I looked at Christoff who nodded, and then so did I, just as Pascal's smart phone started screeching out some awful thrash music. She checked the caller and answered immediately. 'Chantelle,' she said, smooth and friendly. 'How are you?'

She listened for a beat, then said, 'good, good. Look Chantelle, I'm with Jonas Calver and another friend, Christoff, whose helping us, and who I spoke to you about. Is it alright if I put you on speakerphone so we can all hear?'

'Sure honey,' she said, and I could hear her without the speakerphone, but then Pascal flicked it on and her voice boomed out. 'Not sure I've got anything that will help you all, but I did think of something about getting in the building,' she said.

We all looked at each other before Pascal said, 'go on.'

'Well back in the day, Angel just loved his German food. And we used to get a delivery from a Deli that also baked their own bread. Now these guys had special access if you like. Once a week the guy would bring this special bread that Angel loved but also other stuff like, what they call it, Wiener Schnitzel. I do remember the bread was called "Pumpernickel" and he told me the German bread is different to American Pumpernickel, so he ordered it in special.'

We looked at each other again, faces blank. Pascal, said, slowly, 'so how does this help us, Chantelle?'

There was a silence the other end, until Chantelle giggled. 'Well maybe I been watching too many Hollywood movies. Thought maybe you could impersonate the bread delivery guy, if they's still doing the deliveries……,' she said, her voice tailing off as she possibly realised just how far fetched it sounded.

I ran my hand across my eyes, ready to groan with frustration, but then I clocked how Pascal and Christoff were looking at each other. Surely they weren't taking it seriously?

'Did the bread delivery guy not pass through normal security, Chantelle? How did he get in?' Pascal asked.

'Oh no, he come up the service lift, then direct into the kitchen. Angel didn't want no one poking around in his food. He most particular about that. His son David and Schmidt didn't like it at all, but Angel refused to change, and end of the day, his word was law around there.'

'What was the name of the Deli, Chantelle?' Pascal asked.

'I think it was called "Oskars" , with a K.'

'Hi, Chantelle. Christoff here. Did the bread guy have any special ID he had to show, to get in? How did that work?'

'Hi, Christoff,' she said, her voice taking on a kind of flirtatiousness that hadn't been there when she was speaking to Pascal. 'Guy had a card. Think it was a blank one in my day, with maybe one of those magnetic strips on it. But I guess that's changed by now if they's still doing it.'

Pascal looked at me and Christoff to check if we had anymore to ask and we both shook our heads. 'One last question, Chantelle,' she said. 'D'you know when the K Building was actually built?'

'I'd guess the seventies,' she said.

Pascal thanked her and said we would probably have some more questions and maybe we'd come out there or arrange for her to come up to town so we could speak face to face. Chantelle said she'd like that and then Pascal finished the call.

Before anyone could say anything, Pascal looked at Christoff, and said, 'blueprints, building plans with service elevators, air condition ducts?'

'That's what I'm thinking,' he replied. 'I'll get on it.'

As Christoff departed I got ready to take issue with Pascal about what I thought was a pointless hair-brained scheme, and she adopted the resigned expression she put on when she knew exactly what I was going to say. But then I thought, what the hell, just let them get on with it. I had a speech to make in the morning and I didn't have time to argue with them. Pascal's face was a picture of surprise when I got up and left without saying a word.

Pascal sat across the table from Daly sipping a Coors beer and thinking about Calver's capitulation earlier in the evening. At the end of the day she guessed he had far too much on his plate to worry about what she and Christoff were getting up to. And he'd probably calculated, rightly, that their chances of surreptitiously gaining entry to the K tower penthouse and having a good look around were, lets say, pretty slim.

They were sat back in Daly's favourite sports bar in Chinatown, and tonight it was heaving with jocks and rednecks. She wondered whether Daly suggested the place just to wind her up, or to see whether she would chicken out and suggest somewhere else. If that was the case, he would have a long wait. She liked the place.

Daly was sipping a Bud and telling her selective information about the findings from the O'Leary enquiry, even though he wasn't officially involved.

'Rope was generic and untraceable; you can get it in any five and dime hardware store. They reckon he'd been dead at least three hours before we got there,' Daly said.

'That poor little girl, waiting in there for hours whilst her Daddy was swinging in the garage,' Pascal said.

'Yeah. What kind of a father does that?' Daly said, looking directly at Pascal with a speculative look in his eye.

She looked away and sipped her drink

'Look, why don't you just take me through it again,' he said, giving her the third degree with his eyes. 'The guys in the local precinct are buying your story and it'll go down as a slam dunk suicide, but I'm not buying it. You're not telling me everything. Maybe it was suicide, but what d'you know that you're not telling me? You said when you called, O'Leary had a reason for killing himself. So what was it?'

Pascal watched him over her bottle of Coors. He wasn't stupid. Okay, he presented a certain persona, partly to disguise what he was thinking, partly to catch people off guard, but underneath he was a careful and thoughtful detective. And he seemed to have that one essential ingredient you needed to do the job well, dogged determination. Thinking strategically, if she was going to try and enlist his help with Fossey, she was going to have to come clean about quite a lot of stuff she didn't want to tell him about. But then if she didn't let him in, at least some of the way, she could kiss goodbye to getting any help from him. She was going to have to walk a tightrope between truth and lies, something to be fair, she was pretty used to.

She took another sip of Coors. 'I got access, via an unknown third party, to a copy of O'Leary's laptop,' she said, tentatively, watching Daly's eyes widen imperceptibly as he took in the information. 'I'm guessing he destroyed the original just before he died. But on the copy, we discovered evidence that he had been systematically abusing Cara.'

'And you used that to put the squeeze on him, instead of coming to us and getting the guy arrested,' Daly said, and for the first time she sensed contempt in his voice. 'He'd probably still be alive and in custody if you'd come to us.'

'Bullshit,' she said before she could stop herself. 'You would never have taken that guy alive, believe me. He was a stoner pedophile, through and through, a believer - the very worst. He had genuinely convinced himself that his 8 year old daughter loved him in a sexual way - seriously. That was more important than all the other stuff. He was never going to see her again, so there was only one way out.'

Daly raised his hand and ordered another round of bottles. His eyes still looked hard and cold. After a while he said, 'I'm starting to get a handle on you, Pascal. It's too late to do anything about O'Leary now, so you didn't need to tell me about the laptop and the abuse. So, obviously, and forgive the cynicism, you want something.'

'You believe what you want, Daly. You don't know me. You

don—'

'I know you killed your stepfather, and that crooked lawyer, Calver, defended you. Knocked it down to second degree, manslaughter. Few years in the slammer and your back on the street working for him. Not bad going, and I hear you're ex- British intelligence. I'm guessing you'd sell your own grandmother if the price was right.'

'Fuck you, Daly. You know, I thought you were a good cop, a cop that always wanted to find out what really happened. Not just so you could put someone - anyone - away. But I guess I was wrong, huh? But forget all the bullshit for a minute. What do they tell every law enforcement officer on the planet when they're training them up? That's right: "Follow the evidence". Ring a bell, Daly? So why don't you start doing that, huh? Whether you like me or not.'

For moment they sat glaring at each other, then Daly started to smile, just at the edges of his mouth, and then he said, 'fuck you too, Pascal,' and clinked his bottle against hers. But behind the smile he was still watching her carefully, then he said, 'you know O'Leary's cellphone is missing? Its not at the house and its off the grid?'

That stopped Pascal in her tracks. She watched him to see if he was blowing smoke, but he looked solid. She hadn't seen a phone in the garage or the house although she hadn't really been looking. 'What about the stuff that was burning in the garden?'

'Nope,' Daly said, still watching her, eyes accusatory.

'I didn't find it, if that's what you're thinking - really,' she said, holding his gaze, until he nodded.

'But he did give you something before he died, didn't he?'

Yet again, he surprised her with his mental quickness, almost like there was a chess player hiding behind that hokey facade. Time to reveal her hand, if she wanted to get anything out of the clever detective. 'Yes. Look, I mentioned following the evidence just now, and believe me I'm not trying to tell you how to do your job, but tell me again. What stops you believing in the possibility that Calver might have been framed for Helena Palmer's murder?'

'The CCTV,' he replied instantly. 'And your guy couldn't shake the prosecutions expert. From 1 a m in the morning when Palmer returned to her room, until 9.40 a m when they went in with a master key, the only person. I repeat, the only person, who enters and leaves that room is Jonas Calver. And the CCTV proving that, is absolutely solid and unassailable.'

'O'Leary gave me a name,' she said.

'When you put the squeeze on him? What name?'

She ignored the dig. 'He gave us a guy called John Fossey. He's kind of head honcho at a CCTV security outfit called Protecta, based out in Cincinnati. K Corp hold around 19% of their stock. John Fossey was booked in at the Marriott five minutes walk from the murder scene, night of the killing. And check this out,' she said, handing him her smart phone with the story in the Cincinnati Enquirer about the collapse of Fossey's trial 9 years earlier.

As Daly read the story Pascal leant back on her stool, stretched, took a drag on her bottle and looked around the heaving bar. There were even some girls there tonight, making the place feel a little less like a male locker room. Daly leaned back as well and took a swig. She waited.

'You want me to pull Fossey's string, right, and check him out?' Daly said, not looking at her.

'You got it, detective,' she said.

People v Calver - Manhattan Supreme Court

Day 6

I was back at the defense table still trying to come up with an opening speech. My defense: I didn't do it, and they spiked the CCTV. Oh, but I can't prove it. How d'you say that to a jury and make it snappy? I didn't know.

I glanced up as judge Gonzalez breezed in and settled herself on the bench and nodded to the bailiff to get the jury in. My time was up but I still didn't know what I was going to say. Judge Gonzalez welcomed the jurors back and reminded them of some of the rules about procedure and conduct, and then she turned to me and said, 'Mr Calver, opening statement?'

I stayed seated for a long moment, finishing up a particularly complex doodle, and then I slowly rose to my feet, my mind a complete blank. I guess I'd have to wing it again.

'May it please the court,' I said as I ran my eye over the jury. They still looked reasonably alert and ready to listen, and that was something I guess.

'You know,' I said, starting off conversationally. 'I came over to this country to pursue a case for a client called Hannah Palmer. She's a little old lady and she is, as we speak, giving evidence in a civil trial taking place in your Southern district court, also in this city.

'Now *Helena* Palmer, the victim of this terrible murder that I am charged with, is the daughter of my client, Hannah. Complicated isn't it?' I said, with a whimsical smile. 'In that civil case currently taking place in the Southern district court, Hannah Palmer, the mother of our victim, is seeking recovery of jewellery that was taken from her during the second world war. The proceedings are against K Corporation, its CEO Angel Milken, his son, David, and his wife Kendra. All very prominent and powerful people in this city who I am sure you have heard of.

'Helena Palmer was over here to help me prosecute her mothers case, recover that jewellery and nail the people who slaughtered most of her family.' As I said the last words I checked Stahl and Gonzalez, expecting an objection, but it never came.

'Now, Mr Stahl here,' I said, nodding towards him. 'Alleges that my motive in killing the daughter of my client, is sexual, and I wont legitimise that with a response here and now. But what I will say, and what you may yourself have worked out from what I have told you about Hannah's claim, is that there are others out there - very powerful people - who have a far greater motive than I for silencing Helena Palmer.

'The evidence: no one witnessed me killing Helena Palmer, because I didn't kill her. The fundamental evidence against me is CCTV tape showing the entrance corridor leading to Helena Palmers room at the time of the killing. It purports to show only me entering and leaving her room at the material time. I intend to show that that CCTV evidence against me is fabricated. If I do that, Mr Stahl's case turns to smoke. Thank you ladies and gentlemen,' I said. Then I sat down.

Short and succinct it was, but it was also based on a wing and a prayer. I'd committed myself to showing the CCTV was a fraud, and if I couldn't do that, I would be smoke as well. It was stupid, but it was also just about the only thing I could do, and it was the truth. The only way to get out from under was to discredit the CCTV evidence, the rest of it was just hooey. So Pascal and her helpers better come up with something soon, or I could look forward to going back to Rikers, for good.

Chapter Twenty Two

As Pascal slid into the passenger seat of the nondescript black Hertz hire car parked at the curb, Christoff leaned over and took one of the styrofoam cups of coffee she had been carrying.

'Anything?' she asked, but then her cellphone was screaming, the caterwauling terminating abruptly as she held it to her ear and said, 'yes.' She listened for a minute or so, then said, 'okay, Daly. Thanks for trying. Now we'll do it my way.' She listened some more, then said, 'Will do. Call me and we'll get together.'

She turned to Christoff who was watching her. 'Fossey's blown Daly out,' she said. 'Won't talk without a lawyer, so Daly can't go any further. Thinks Fossey was scared, but will keep quiet about the approach unless he's pushed, so maybe no harm done. So we better have a go at him, and I've got an idea about how we can do that, but first things first. Anything doing over there?' she said, nodding her head at the building across the street from them.

Oskars, the delicatessens mentioned by Chantelle was on the ground floor of the large four storey block opposite them. The building seemed to house mostly apartments, but the ground floor was given over to commercial use, a mixture of offices, an Italian restaurant and then Oskars on the corner. The Deli was quite large and the trappings, the signage as well as the clientele they had seen going in and out for the last hour or so, suggested it was a pretty upmarket kind of a joint.

'Only thing I've seen so far is a little white delivery van that bowled up when you were getting our coffee,' Christoff said. 'Stopped for around five minutes while they loaded it up with some bread, looked like French sticks. Van was driven by a young guy, looked mid-twenties.'

Pascal ran a speculative eye over Christoff's attire. He was wearing a mustard yellow three piece suit with gold watch chain stretched across his waist and a bright green silk cravat at his neck. He caught her look and raised an eyebrow of enquiry.

'You look just perfect for the part, Christoff. A debonair, rich toff, ideal customer profile for an outfit like Oskars. If I go for Fossey now,' she said holding up her phone. 'You happy to take a run at Oskars?'

'You think I came out dressed like this for fun?' he said, raising his eyebrow again. He climbed out of the car and looked in at her with wolfish smile. 'Just like old times, eh, Courtney?'

'Just like old times,' she repeated, and then he was sauntering off towards the Deli.

As she watched him go she lifted her cellphone, located the number for Protecta in Cincinnati, and pressed the call button.

The interior of the deli was dark and cavernous, but in the half light

Christoff could make out glass topped counters stretching away. They seemed to contain an endless array of rich meats, game, hanging sausages, cheeses, pickles and sauces. He wandered down the aisle with a smile on his face, wallowing in the glorious food all around him. Then he caught the sweet smell of fresh baking bread, wafting and floating like a slipstream over all the other aromas.

Up ahead he could see a long white counter behind which stood a large round shaped man; from a distance he almost looked like a big rubber beach ball. As Christoff approached, he could see the man was swaddled in what looked like chef's whites, and he had a disposable blue coloured hairnet on his head. Christoff estimated the guy ran to at least 300 pounds, and he had that jolly look that a lot of fat men seemed to have, with a kind of perpetual friendly smile stamped on his fleshy face.

'Quite a place you got here,' Christoff said.

'Why, thank you, sir,' the big man responded immediately, enthusiasm vibrating through his chest, giving his voice a tone of eagerness. 'Can I help you? Are you looking for anything in particular? You're English, aren't you? A most discerning race when it comes to food, if I may say so.'

'Thank you. Yes, I am English born, but my forebears were German. Tell me, would you have such a thing as Pumpernickel bread here? I mean baked the German way like my grandmother used to make it? I just can't abide the American version,' Christoff said, trying to inject just the right tone of pedantic fastidiousness into his voice.

The mans smile almost disappeared into the folds of his face as he chortled away, his whole frame shaking with happiness, like a blancmange on a plate during a mild earthquake. 'Why, sir, you have come to exactly the right place. Wait here a moment, if you will,' he said,' skipping away down the counter at a surprising pace for such a large man.

Moments later Christoff was examining and smelling a variety of breads as the big man fussed around him pointing out the particularities of each one.

'What about delivery? I'm going to be here for 12 months and would like to maybe set something up, if that's a possibility.'

For the first time a hint of doubt crept into the big mans responses. 'Well we do a few special deliveries for our most favoured customers,' he said, looking more closely at Christoff for the first time. 'In fact we do do a weekly delivery for a very special customer, and for this very same bread,' he said nodding down at the tray. 'I believe he is Austrian or German.'

'I'll tell you what,' Christoff said. 'I just love this bread here. Why don't we start a trial run of weekly deliveries, and I'll pay up front for three months. How about that? And to make it easier, you can deliver to me on the same day as your special customer gets his. Say come to me first and then onto him, whatever time suits; save you time and trouble. Cause I gotta tell you, I can't live without this bread.'

When Christoff gave him the address of the loft apartments the big man nodded and seemed to relax, smiling, impressed at the upmarket location of the property. He checked delivery schedules on his computer screen. 'We do our deliveries on Wednesdays, noon at the K

Tower, so how about we come to you with delivery at 11. How would that suit?'

'That would be just fine and dandy. Credit card okay for payment?' Christoff asked.

The big man was smiling again as he dug out the card machine and worked out quantities and price.

'Just so I know who to expect, who does the deliveries for you?'

'Oh that will be Emilio. He's very good and reliable, been with us five years.'

'Great,' Christoff said, sliding his card into the machine.

'Hi, Mr Fossey, my name's Lucy Kellaway ,' Pascal said in her approximation of a New York accent. She was still sat in the car at the kerb watching Oskars as she spoke. Fossey had sounded guarded when he had answered the phone. She continued, in the same gushing tone. 'I'm an in house journo at the Hotel Business Review mag online and we're doing a piece on hotel security and CCTV. So we're casting around for industry pro's to talk to and be quoted in the piece. Your names come up a couple a times and I was wondering if you might have time to talk to me, give me an insight into your thinking about how you see the industry going forward. I understand you're regularly in New York on business and maybe you could fit me in for a chat next time you're up here. I know our readers would be fascinated to hear what you've got to say?'

'Well why didn't you say so,' he said, guarded tone instantly falling away. 'Forgive the caution, Lucy, but we've had some competitors snooping around. Dirty tricks - I'm sure you know the score if your in the industry, but to answer your question. You bet. I'd be delighted to talk to you guys at the review mag. We all read it here as do most folks in the industry.'

'That's great, John. Exactly what I wanted to hear, and thanks for the plug. We love to hear it when folks give us a vote of confidence. Look, John, we've got a deadline on this one, so how you fixed in terms of your diary?'

'Just let me put you on hold for a minute, Lucy. I'll check with my secretary, see if we can't juggle some appointments, bring my next New York trip forward.'

The phone went dead for a short while. Pascal watched the entrance to Oskars and finished the sugary dregs of her almost cold coffee, then Fossey was back on, full of enthusiasm. 'I could see you Wednesday, if that would suit? I'll be staying at the Marriott,' he said.

'That's great, John. How about the evening, unless you got a date,' she giggled coquettishly. 'I'm sure you'll want to keep your day free for scheduled appointments, and I wouldn't want to infringe on that.'

'How about 7 in the hotel bar, or,' he said, hesitating as if thinking about the propriety of it, 'you come up to my room? Be a bit cosier, and relaxed and I can talk more freely?'

'You got it, John. Looking forward to seeing you. Great to speak with you today,' she said, terminating the call. As she looked up

Christoff was just emerging from Oskars with a satisfied smile on his face.

Southern District Court

Day 8

'Now we are all back with miss Fedler in place,' Judge Friedman said, 'perhaps we can get this trial back on track.' He turned to Hannah. 'When we broke you indicated you would re-start your testimony with your discovery by the Germans in the attic. Please proceed.'

Hannah seemed fired up and ready to go. She nodded at the jury with a half smile. 'You may not believe it but it was almost a relief to get discovered in the attic. Life there was a terrible strain. Awful fear mixed in with stultifying boredom and the frustration of being locked away all day, stifling when it was hot and freezing when it was cold, tiptoeing around and whispering.

'In the end, like so many others, we were betrayed. The German's came at 3 am in the morning in a truck, lead by an SS officer. There were lots of soldiers this time with guns and dogs. They knew exactly where to go and no searching was necessary. When Mrs Van Der Valk answered the door, they pushed past her and made their way up the stairs to stand directly underneath the concealed attic trapdoor. Willem De Grout, the handyman, our betrayer was with them, translating for the SS officer. They said that unless we all came down within one minute, the soldiers would start shooting up through the ceiling and any survivors found would be shot immediately.

'I remember looking down from the attic trap-door. The SS officer was looking up at me, and he was tall and handsome. He said, in English, which I understood, and I remember his words to this day, "good morning, my fine Jewess. If there are more of your rabble up there, you must come down immediately or I will shoot all of you. You may bring a small bag of belongings each."

'Of course we climbed down. When I got onto the landing Willem De Grout was still there, with a smile on his face. I couldn't help it. I spat full in his face and the German officer laughed. De Grout started to tell the officer we had valuables. He'd obviously searched our belongings and found the Pendant, but the officer wasn't interested. In fact he dismissed De Grout with contempt.

'Then Mrs Van Der Valk ran up crying, and saying sorry. I begged the officer to spare her telling him that it wasn't her fault, and he surprised me by agreeing. He said the Van Der Valk's were important members of the community and it would not serve German interests to punish them.

'I asked him what was to happen to us. Maybe he was impressed by my lack of fear because he answered me seriously. He told us we would be taken to the Dutch Theatre for processing and then on by train to the transit camp at Westerbork. He said we had nothing to fear. That the facilities at the camp were good. From there, later on it was likely we would be sent on to work in the east.

It is funny because despite everything, I did believe him. Then they loaded us onto the trucks, and that was the last time I ever saw Mrs

Van Der Valk.

Chapter Twenty Three

People v Calver - Manhattan Supreme Court

Day 7

'Your honour,' I addressed judge Gonzalez. 'I intend to give evidence myself, and then of course Mr Stahl may cross examine me in the usual way.

Gonzalez nodded. 'Proceed,' she said.

I rose, walked over to the witness box and took my seat. In most major trials early evidence is usually elicited to build up an attractive portrait of the defendant by covering their background and explaining who they are. So that's what I did. I told the jury about myself, how I graduated in law, then qualified as a lawyer in the UK, my early years of practice and then my marriage. I then spent a little time dealing with the tape of Carmen's call to the police.

'Now, you heard my wife, Carmen, on the tape Mr Stahl played for you,' I said. 'On that night we had both consumed a significant amount of alcohol, but when we went to bed there was no animosity between us. I woke from a dream with my hands around her throat and it took me a few moments, given my intake of alcohol and the effects of just coming out of sleep, to realise what I was doing, and when I did, I immediately stopped.

'And for the record I am not into sadomasochistic sexual practices involving the infliction of pain, or strangling or any other type of perversion. And nor did I have any reason to want to try to strangle my wife,' I said, stopping for a moment to draw breath. 'In fact,' I added as an afterthought, 'although we're currently separated, I love her, and have every intention of trying to win her back, when I'm finished here.'

I took a sip of water from my glass and then moved on. 'So, the next question you may want answered is, why am I in the USA? Well, I did touch on that briefly in my opening. I came to America in July to deal with a case for my client, Hannah Palmer, who is the mother of the victim, Helena Palmer. Hannah is a UK citizen but her claim is against US citizens and so the proceedings are brought here in the USA. This case—'

'Your honour,' Stahl interrupted, rising to his feet. 'Relevance? I'm sure this civil case of Mr Calver's is fascinating, but what relevance does it have to these proceedings? He is merely attempting to muddy the waters, and should be asked to deal solely with the facts raised in this case.'

'Your honour,' I replied. 'With all due respect to Mr Stahl, Hannah Palmer's claim *is* highly relevant to these proceedings. Mr Stahl's case, if I have it right, is that my motive for killing Helena Palmer was sexual lust - I apparently get off on strangling women. Motive in a murder trial is central, especially this murder trial. He's raised it, and I am fully entitled to deal with it and point the jurors to others, who I say had a far better motive for killing Helena Palmer than I did.'

'I'll allow it,' Gonzalez said, grudgingly, 'but do move along please, Mr Calver.'

'Thank you, your honour. Hannah Palmer is currently giving evidence in your Southern District Court. She is 88 years old. On its face hers is a simple claim for return of some jewellery, taken from her in 1943. That jewellery, it is alleged, is now in the possession of K Corporation and its officers, Angel, David and Kendra Milken and the proceedings are against these individuals. It has to be said that their current legal stance is that the jewellery was acquired completely legitimately by purchase, and of course the purpose of those proceedings is to decide on just those issues. However in the investigation of the history of the events surrounding that case, some disturbing evidence is becoming apparent. Damaging and prejudicial evidence that some of New York's most powerful and prominent citizens will do whatever it takes to stop coming out.

'Helena Palmer came out here from UK to meet me and talk to the defendants about her mother's case. She came out because her brother John who was dealing with it here, died, some months ago in what can only be described as suspicious circumstances. He was found in his car in the river with excess alcohol in his blood even though he pathologically disliked alcohol.

'Hannah Palmer is Jewish. She grew up in Nazi occupied Holland, and although she is currently testifying, and I do not wish to pre-empt or interfere with those proceedings, it is clear that some violence was perpetrated on her. And her family's jewellery was not given up voluntarily. K Corporation and the Milken family, whether they have any involvement with what happened to Hannah or not - and I make no judgement about that, which is for others to decide - clearly do not want to be associated with such a story, and I say will go to some lengths, possibly extreme lengths, to kill the story Hannah is currently trying to tell.

'I say they calculated that a good way of doing that was to eliminate Helena, Hannah's daughter and spokesperson, and at the same time frame her lawyer - me - for the killing - two birds with one stone you might say. I believe they may have thought it would force Hannah to settle the claim on confidential terms with no publicity or admissions of guilt, but it hasn't; its just made her real mad,' I said with my first genuine grin of the day.

'Also,' I added almost as an afterthought, 'having a fortune of billions of dollars, as K Corp and Milken have, makes doing what I have just sketched out relatively easy and risk free.'

'Okay,' I said. 'Let's move on to the night of the murder.'

Southern District Court

'Now,' Morganna said, standing and addressing Hannah in the witness box, 'you left off testifying at the point where you and your family had been arrested at the Van Der Valk's house and loaded onto trucks. Please go on.'

Hannah nodded. 'The truck took us to the Dutch Theatre, a famous building in Amsterdam that the Nazi's were then using as a processing centre, and we spent the night there with hundreds of others. It was chaos. The next day they marched us around two miles in columns through the streets to *Muiderpoort* railway station where a train was waiting for us.'

Hannah paused there to take a sip of water. It was becoming noticeable that the gaps, pauses and silences, which had been so absent early on in her testimony, were now becoming more and more frequent as she struggled to recall events from so long ago. She sat now in the witness box, hunched over, seemingly deep in thought, her story temporarily suspended as her mind wandered back and forth, searching out the memories. It seemed to be getting harder and harder for her to tell her story the closer she got to whatever it was - what terrible revelation - that was so scaring her.

She sipped some more water, then looked down at her hands as she composed herself again, trying to remember, desperate to be truthful, so the jury would know what had happened. Then, as her mind picked up the thread again, she slowly began to speak.

'That train took us to the Westerbork transit camp in Northern Holland. It didn't take long to get to there, and when we arrived registration took place. Again,' she said, smiling grimly at the jury, 'I was strangely comforted by the fact that Westerbork was not a really terrible place, nothing like what I had been expecting anyway. To some extent the SS officer who had arrested us seemed to have told the truth about the place.

'What can I say?' Hannah said, a look of surprise on her face as she regarded the Jury. 'The place looked normal. People walked around freely, there didn't seem to be any work going on and there were many children running and playing. No one looked to be at the edge of starvation either. The camp was quite small, about 500 metres by 500 metres, surrounded by a moat and a single wire fence about six feet high, with a few watchtowers dotted around the perimeter. Barracks were single sex, so Mama, Helena and I were allocated to barracks 41 and Papa and Grandpa, barracks 68.

'At the end of the barracks were doors that led through to a bathing area with showers, and there was also an area with tables and chairs laid out for people to sit and talk, play cards, read and eat. Food, although simple and monotonous, was plentiful, provided from a fully functional kitchen. What made it easier I suppose was that there were many people there we knew from *Jodenhoek* and I know that helped my mother to relax a little.

'We soon settled into a calm and rather boring routine but I kept wondering what the catch was, what was the purpose of the Nazi's in having such a camp. I soon found out when I witnessed a train leaving the camp, packed full, on a Tuesday morning. When I asked about it, a man said simply, "train comes in empty Monday, train leaves full Tuesday morning. If you're on the list. You go."

'The following Monday all our names, Mama, Papa, Grandpa, Helena and mine were on the list for deportation the next day. We were told to assemble first thing Tuesday morning for roll call. It was April 5th 1943.'

People v Calver - Manhattan Supreme Court

I asked Judge Gonzalez if I might stand and move about the court, because sitting in the witness box was cramping my style. She looked at Stahl for comment, but he just shrugged his shoulders as if to say, "whatever". So I stood and walked around the court as I spoke, all the time focusing on the jury.

'On the day of the murder, Helena and I met with the defendants in Hannah Palmer's civil trial, at their registered offices in Manhattan. They were represented by their general counsel, Charles Browder, and later, David Milken, son of Angel, joined us. The meeting was stressful and quite difficult. No settlement was reached with them and we got a shock, not having realised the case was due to start the following Monday if no settlement was reached. So when we left we were feeling, shall we say, a might overwrought. I hardly knew Helena, had only just met her and we were both in a strange new country, so we decided to have dinner in my room and go on talking.

'We ordered up some steaks and wine and we relaxed and talked. I think its fair to say we got on very well and I ordered up some more wine from room service at about 9.35 pm, and you've heard from the waiter who brought that wine up to us.

'We were two people thrown together in a stressful situation a long way from home, in intimate circumstances with wine as well, and it is perhaps not so surprising that we ended up in bed. It was fully consensual and there was no element of strangulation or throttling or anything else.

'Later, at about 1 am, Helena awoke and said she would return to her room and she did so. I was restless after she had left; its a different time zone here and I am still not used to it. I got up and went down to the hotel bar at around 1.40 am. The CCTV shows, and I don't dispute it, that I was wearing my green silk tie when I went down to the bar. In the bar I had a few more drinks and spoke briefly to the head of security, John O'Leary. I was then told at around 2.15 am that there had been a phone call down from Helena asking me to go up to her room. I have seen no evidence, other than John O'Leary's testimony, that there was such a phone call and I believe it was fabricated to get me back up to her room.

'At the time I had no reason to doubt the phone call so I did go to Helena's room, arriving there at around 2.45 am, and I buzzed her. What corroborates my theory that there was no phone call is that it took Helena around 2 minutes to get out of bed and answer the door. If she had called down, I would have expected her to be waiting to answer as soon as I arrived. She also denied making the call when she let me in. We had both been drinking and were sleepy and just assumed there had been a mix up. We chatted for a while, I put on the TV and watched some news, and then I left her at 2.45 am. She was alive when I left the room and that was the last time I saw her. I went back to my room to sleep, until I was woken by Detective Daly knocking on my door sometime after 11 am, and shortly after he arrested me

'And there's one other thing that hasn't come out, and that's that I had all Hannah's case papers, depositions, tapes, witness statements and photographs in my room. These were brought over from the UK for her case against K Corp. When I was woken up by Daly that morning, all those case papers had gone - stolen,' I said.

I walked back to the defense table and checked my notes. Then I walked back towards the jury and stopped about six feet away from them. 'I didn't kill Helena Palmer,' I told them as strongly and firmly as I could. 'I had no reason to kill her, but someone else certainly did. Right now I am at a loss to explain the presence of my green silk tie or the CCTV, but I'm working on it. I believe my tie was planted and that the CCTV was fabricated in a very sophisticated way, and that could only have been done by persons with access to significant resources, financial and otherwise.'

I walked back to the defense table and told judge Gonzalez I had nothing further. She looked at the clock and then at the prosecutor. 'Cross examination, Mr Stahl, will have to wait for morning, as I propose to adjourn now. Thank you,' she said.

I felt relief that I wouldn't have to face Stahl straightaway. I thought I'd done alright with my testimony, but unless we could figure out the CCTV, I was just whistling in the wind. The other point was that as soon as Stahl finished cross examining me, which wouldn't take long, the case would essentially be over. I'd given up on calling any other witnesses, even the CCTV expert, as we still didn't know how they'd faked it. Fact is I'd just about run out of time.

Chapter Twenty Four

Pascal and Christoff sat in the kitchen poring over plans spread out across the table. It was around 10.30 am and they were drinking coffee.

'Courtesy of New York's Department of Buildings,' Christoff said, smoothing down a corner and placing a coffee cup on it to keep the paper flat. 'They've got blue-prints going back years for almost every structure in the city.'

'When was K Tower built?' Pascal asked.

'Opened by the Mayor in 1977. Full topping out ceremony with all the city's dignitaries.'

'So. What we got? Anything?'

Christoff paused, running his finger across the floor plan of the penthouse suite. 'Not really,' he said slowly.

'But?' Pascal said, glaring at him impatiently. 'Look, Christoff, Emilio will be here with the bread in a minute, so we need to get moving.'

'Keep your shorts on,' he quipped. 'The floor plans are not really detailed enough to draw firm conclusions from, but if you look here,' he said, placing his finger on one of the faint blue lines running across the plan. 'This is the rear boundary line of this room, which they've called "office/study". Now there are some faint dimensions shown here,' he said, pointing again. 'It says these plans are said to be not to scale, but I've been over them, and its clear that all the dimensions quoted, if you compare them to the length of the lines on the plan, are proportionate to each other and the dimensions quoted. That is, all except?'

'The office/study,' Pascal said.

'Give the lady a lollipop. You know who figured it out?' Christoff asked.

Pascal looked mystified. 'You?' she said

'Cara,' he said. 'She's one sharp cookie. I left her with the plans to have a look at and told her we were looking for a secret room, and she cracked it. The only room on the plan where the stated dimensions do not tally with the extent of the actual line on the plan, is that room. In English, the room as shown on the plan is actually a lot bigger than the measurement shown on the floor plan would suggest.'

Pascal sipped some coffee. 'Anything else?'

'Not really. Its a pretty bog standard skyscraper, and very much of its time. There's a service elevator to the rear of the building, and I'm guessing that's how Emilio delivers Angel's bread. But you should be able to check that shortly when you follow him. Speaking of which, he should be here any minute.'

'Right, I'll get ready,' she said, getting up from the table and leaving the room. Christoff put the empty cups in the sink, rolled up the plans and followed her out just as the security buzzer sounded from down in the ground floor porch.

He checked the security screen. It was the man he had seen with the delivery van outside Oskars. He pressed the intercom button, and said, 'Emilio?'

'Si, ' the man said, then, 'yes, I have your bread delivery sir.'

'Bring it on up,' Christoff said, pressing the door release control.

A short while later he lead Emilio into the kitchen. The young man seemed friendly, like he wanted to talk but was a little shy, perhaps embarrassed that his English wasn't quite up to scratch. As he removed the Pumpernickel loaves from his covered delivery basket, Christoff complimented him on the recipe and baking skills, trying to put Emilio at ease.

They chatted a bit, about where Emilio was from - Puerto Rico - and how long he had been in the city - 7 years - and how he liked the job - he loved it. Christoff asked if he would like a drink. 'Just a quick one, Emilio, to keep me company, yes?

Emilio looked conflicted, didn't want to appear rude, which was what Christoff was hoping. He needed to establish a routine of getting Emilio to accept a drink as that would be important if they were to perfect a plan for getting into K Tower.

'Okay, sir. I've time for a quick one. Orange juice, if you have it,'

'Coming up,' Christoff said, relieved, moving to the fridge.

People v Calver - Manhattan Supreme Court

Day 8

Stahl bounded out of his chair like a Doberman I'd just chucked a joint of lamb at. He wasn't quite foaming at the mouth, but you get the idea. He'd been waiting for this a while and now it was showtime. From the witness stand I glanced around the court. Judge Gonzalez had a tight little smile on her face, and the jury looked full of anticipation. With no preamble Stahl jumped right in. 'Let's face it, Calver, there's no cavalry coming to the rescue - no CCTV wizard waiting in the wings to waive a magic wand, and make it all go away.'

'Let me guess, Stahl,' I said from the stand. 'You used to mix drinks for your rich folks out in Martha's Vineyard, and now you just mix metaphors.'

There was some muffled laughs around the court at my lame banter, but it wasn't going to change anything. None of it really mattered. I still had nothing to discredit the CCTV showing me as the only person entering Helena's room at the time of the killing. That damning evidence stood like a mountain across my path, with no way round it.

From then on Stahl's cross examination was relentless and brutal, pounding away at me, leaving me nowhere to run except straight back to jail.

'And you like strangling women, don't you? You've got form for it. We all heard the tape of your petrified wife after you tried it on with her.'

'No. I don't like strangling women, Stahl. I was having a bad dream and I'd been drinking, and my wife knows that. Maybe that's why you didn't call her, because she'd say that and it would blow a hole in your case. And just to remind you, there's a world of difference between manual strangulation with bare hands and how Helena was killed, with a ligature. And what was my motive, Stahl? And why would an attorney with twenty years experience leave his own silk tie around the victims neck,' I said, turning to look at the jury. 'I was set up, Stahl, from start to finish.'

'So tell us about the CCTV, again, Mr Calver?' Stahl said, with that maddeningly knowing look.

And there he had me, of course. I looked down at my hands, cursing Pascal under my breath.

'Perhaps you'd like me to show it again? So we can all see you go in and come out, just at the time Helena was being murdered. No one else comes anywhere near that room from start to finish, other than you. Explain that to the jury?'

And of course I couldn't, and on it went.

Thirty minutes after Pascal left Christoff she sat in a hire car across the street from K Tower. She was wearing a blonde wig and dark glasses and she had a tourist map of New York in her hand. As Emilio drew up across the street in his delivery van, Pascal exited her vehicle and crossed the road, opening up her street map as she reached the sidewalk. Once there she slipped into character; confused and lost English tourist. She watched from the corner of her eye as Emilio took his delivery basket from the vehicle and made his way toward the entrance doors of K Tower. She followed him through, looking confused, studying her map.

When Emilio reached the reception desk there were only two guys manning it, one on the desk phone. Pascal sidled up next to Emilio, still looking closely at her street map. The guard nodded, ignoring Pascal, and said, 'how you doin', Emilio?

'Fine, fine. And you?' he asked, holding out some kind of plastic looking security pass. The security guy barely looked at it, then he scanned his eyes over the contents of Emilio's basket as he held the cover up. Then he was waving Emilio over to the service lift, which was directly next to the reception desk. Then he turned to Pascal, a resigned look on his face. 'Yes,' he said, unenthusiastically, but by then the other, younger security guy had finished his call and was looking Pascal over with a lot more enthusiasm. He said, 'how can I help you, ma'am?'

Pascal smiled at him and spread her street map out on the chest high counter, and then asked him about getting to the statue of Liberty. After five minutes or so, where the guy had started to try and chat her up, and his colleague was rolling his eyes, Pascal staggered slightly, and held her hand up to her forehead, as if about to faint. The young guy immediately grasped her shoulder, saying, 'are you okay, ma'am? Let me get you a chair. They got her sat down and got her a glass of water.

When Emilio finally emerged from the service lift, Pascal checked her watch. From getting into the lift, going up, and then coming back down and exiting, the time elapsed was 33 minutes. It was much longer than she had expected. It meant he must have engaged in conversation with whoever was up there, which was good news for them. She watched Emilio walk from the lifts; he didn't stop and there were no further checks. He just nodded to the security guys and then he was out the door.

Pascal lingered on for as long as she felt necessary to maintain the pretence of her cover. As she made her escape she was already thinking about the meeting that was due that evening with Fossey at the Marriott.

It was 7 pm on the dot when Pascal, still wearing her blonde wig, pressed the buzzer on the wall outside John Fossey's hotel room. The door was opened almost immediately by an average size guy with spiked up gelled brown hair. His Italian suit hung loosely on his thin frame and the tie was loosened around his neck. He held a glass in his hand, half full, and he looked like he'd already had a few.

' Lucy,' he said, smiling and proffering a limp sweaty hand for a quick shake. 'Come on over and sit,' he said, eyes appraising her. He led her over to a chair. 'How about a drink?' he offered. There was a bottle of vodka on the table.

'I'll take a vodka and orange,' she said, looking around the room. She noticed he had a laptop sitting open on the bed. She watched him, obliquely, out of the corner of her eye as he went to the door and locked it. Then he went to the table and mixed her a drink.

Pascal always did her homework. In this case it had involved wading through endless back issues of the Hotel Review and reading up on every aspect of the security and CCTV community. It had bored the hell out of her but was worth it because now she could bullshit outrageously on the subject, and this she proceeded to do for the next half hour, whilst also lightly flirting with Fossey.

He was starting to relax and lower his guard as she questioned him about his views on various CCTV systems, including Protecta's Cyclops. There was no discernible reaction at the mention of the system; he gave his views freely which Pascal recorded on her phone.

As they finished up and Pascal turned the recorder off, Fossey asked whether she might like some food sent up from room service. She smiled tentatively as if she was wavering, then said maybe she would. A burger with fries would do her fine.

Fossey got up and went to the phone. He sat on the bed with his back to her. She took out a capsule from her pocket. Christoff had prepared it earlier and it contained 4 mg/kg of powdered Sodium Thiopental, a good old fashioned truth drug. She finished Fossey's Vodka herself, and poured him a straight orange, then broke the capsule and sprinkled the powder into the drink.

There was nothing very scientific about it. The dose was low and not dangerous but it would loosen his lips if she could get him in the mood and ask the right questions. As he came back to his chair, face lit up like a Christmas tree, eyes bright, smile just starting to turn lecherous, Pascal raised her glass and said, 'drink up, John. You know, this bit of coverage in the trade mag could open a lot of doors for you. Take you to the next level. You ready to hang out with the big boys?'

Her last words were delivered with a kind of simper, as if she could see herself accompanying him as he broke into that august crowd.

Fossey's eyes had turned inward, glassy, as if he could see himself gliding through that rarified stratum of security dicks. Time to up it a notch.

'You know, John,' she said. 'We were talking in the office, other day, about vulnerabilities in the systems. Say like Cyclops. And the big question was: is it possible to dupe it, get around it, fool it maybe? We all agreed it was just about impossible?'

A shadow passed over Fossey's face, a guardedness, but when Pascal gave him her 1000 watt smile, that caution seemed to falter. 'Whew, its hot in her,' Pascal said, undoing the top button of her blouse and upping the wattage of her smile.

Fossey licked his lips, reached for the Vodka bottle and poured himself another shot. 'It could be done, if you got the right stuff,' he said, tapping the side of his head meaningfully and smiling mysteriously.

'Wow, that's awesome,' Pascal said. 'Lets play a game, John. A hypothetical.' She leaned forward and took his hand, studying his palm. 'You know, you're beginning to excite me. You're so knowledgeable,' she said, moving around in her chair as if she had ants in her pants. 'How would you do it?'

He turned Pascal's hand over in his and gripped it semi-hard, looking into her eyes. 'I'd do it with a slave,' he said.

'A slave?' Pascal said, thinking he had drifted into some kind of sexual fantasy.

She tried to pull her hand back, but he held on, and said, 'yeah. A computer slave. Cyclops has got a back door in. You can fool the system around the emergency power trip. You plug a laptop with a special programme into the system and you can fool it to make it think there's a power outage and go onto the emergency battery power, same time you can stop the camera whilst the clock keeps running. Bingo,' he said with a glassy smile.

Pascal felt a shiver of excitement; at last, something. But Fossey was now sweating profusely and starting to look confused. Pascal guessed the dosage was running down. She would need to get out pretty soon. 'Wow, that's cool,' she said, eating him up with her eyes. 'So you can stop the filming, and make the system think its still running, yeah? With the ticker tape clock and counter still running '

'Hey,' he said, suddenly. 'I was kidding, right?' And now he looked paranoid, looking around the room. His eyes coming back to rest on Pascal. He pulled her up roughly by her arm, into an embrace, trying to kiss her.

Time to get out. She pulled back. 'Whoa there, John,' she said, backing away, still smiling, but he wasn't.

He got up and started pacing about, running his hands through his hair and muttering to himself, almost as if he had forgotten her. She watched him, worrying that Christoff had got the dose wrong. He moved to the table and mixed himself another drink, heavy on the vodka. When he turned to her there was a calculating look in his eyes, and the smile was long gone. Looked like Christoff's little wonder drug had just worn off.

'You're not Lucy Kellaway, are you?' he said, calmly. 'And you don't work for the Hotel Review. So who the fuck are you?'

Pascal walked over to the table and mixed herself a screwdriver, heavy on the vodka. She sipped her drink, unperturbed. Calver was way out of time now so what did it matter? No time left for pussyfooting around. 'I work for Jonas Calver's defense team. We know you were at the murder scene, and we know you doctored the CCTV, and now we know how.'

Fossey didn't look shocked or scared or worried. He just watched her. 'You wearing a wire?' he asked.

She shook her and held her phone up. 'Nope. Just what you saw me record.'

'Well it doesn't matter, because I was just blowing smoke. I said nothing that would stand up in court, even if you could get me there. And of course I'll deny it all anyway.'

He was right. She changed directions. 'What happened to the jewels, John?' she said. 'You got away with that one, nine years ago. Pretty slick deal from what I hear. You doctored that tape as well?'

He smiled. 'Hey. I walked. They had nothing, just like you.'

'Really?' she said, leaving it hanging, watching his eyes.

He licked his lips again, and for a fraction of a second the mask seemed to slip and he looked scared, but then it was gone. 'Look, maybe you better leave now,' he said.

'Boy, you're more changeable than a prairie fire,' she said, rising to her feet. 'But yeah, maybe you're right, but I'll leave you with a thought. It's not beyond the realms of possibility that K Corp are watching you right now. They may even have seen me come in here. I guess you've met their security guy, Schmidt? You ever see a better candidate for psychopath of the year? I would not want to get on the wrong side of that guy,' she said, watching Fossey's face as he tried to keep it from showing anything.

'Not counting Helena Palmer, I think the body count currently stands at two. John Palmer, who didn't drink, apparently got drunk and drove his car into the harbour. And then there's John O'Leary, the main prosecution witness, hotel manager, and I'm sure the guy you met with the night of the murder. Well, he's dead as well. Apparently hanged himself, if you believe that?'

Fossey gulped his drink down and poured himself another. Pascal watched the slight tremor in his hand as he held the bottle. 'I want you to leave,' he said.

'Fine,' Pascal said, turning towards the door, and then turning back. 'You know, John, I'm guessing the only people in the world who can help you right now are the Justice Department. If you were to talk, they'd cut you a deal, like yesterday. Then they'd take the whole lot of these fuckers down or you'd go into witness protection. Think about it, but don't take too long. And John?'

'Yeah.'

'I'd seriously watch your back. Here's my number if you want to talk,' she said, scribbling it on a scrap of paper.

As she walked away, he said, quietly, 'I didn't know about the murder, you know. Until after....'

She whirled around. 'Who did it? Who was in that room that night after Calver?'

He shook his head, face closed and scared and she knew he

would never tell. He was more scared of K Corp than he would ever be of her. At the door she turned back, nodded and said, 'you enjoy the rest of your evening.'

She left him standing at the door, empty glass in his hand, looking scared.

As she went down in the lift she cursed. Fuck. Another blow-out. Now they knew how it had been done, but so what? Calver was going down. A dead end, everywhere they turned.

People v Calver - Manhattan Supreme Court

Day 9

I hadn't slept at all. I'd sat up with Pascal long into the night, talking about John Fossey and what he'd told her. I hadn't asked how she'd got him to talk. I no longer cared. But it didn't matter. What she'd got out of him merely confirmed what we already knew. They'd tampered with the CCTV, and even though Christoff had done his best to explain how they'd done it, it didn't matter. We couldn't use it. He wouldn't come to court, and even if we subpoenaed him, he wouldn't repeat it.

And what exactly did his words prove anyway? Nothing. I was still in Helena's room around the time of the murder. There was cast iron proof of that and I'd never disputed it. But, someone else was as well, but we couldn't prove it and nothing Fossey had said changed that. Even if we had evidence to suggest tampering with the CCTV, so what? They still had my presence, my DNA and my tie around Helena's neck.

Whichever way I turned, there was a hangman's noose waiting.

And now I had to make my closing speech, and frankly, if I was on that jury, I'd be convicting - logic dictated it. But I still had to say something, so I slowly rose to my feet and turned to face the jury.

I ran my eyes over them. They looked kind of tired of it all, and me, and I am sure they just wanted to get it over with and get on with their lives. It was almost as if my closing argument was a formality that needed to be got through, and then they could convict.

'You know,' I said, starting off slow, 'I told you about the claim against K Corp and you'll be pleased to know I'm not going to go over all that again. But I will just remind you of one part of what I told you. When Helena and I met with K Corp, to try and settle Hannah's claim, we suggested that if the case did not settle, it was likely some highly damaging allegations against them were likely to come out. What happened? That very same evening, Helena was murdered, and I was framed for it.

'I know, I know. You've heard it all before, but it is true. I just can't prove it,' I said.

'But one last thing. K Corp own 19% of a company called Protecta who specialise in CCTV and security. Their head of research is a guy called John Fossey. The night of Helena's murder he was booked into the Marriott Hotel, Manhattan, 5 minutes walk from the murder scene. If anyone could tamper with the CCTV, it would be him, but again, I can't prove anything. Whispers in the wind,' I said, pausing to draw breath and shoot a glance at Stahl. I had been expecting him to object like crazy to my last point as it was patently improper, having not featured at all in the evidence. But Stahl seemed oblivious, scribbling away on his yellow legal pad, barely listening to me. I guess he was so confident of a conviction, he'd already moved onto his next case.

'Oh, I said that was the last thing, but its not. In fact there are two more things. Firstly, I don't actually have to prove anything. That's for the prosecution. All I have to do is raise a reasonable doubt in your mind as to my guilt. Remember that.

'The final thing, is' I said, looking full on at the jury: 'I didn't kill Helena Palmer.'

I let that resonate a moment as I held my eyes on the jury.

'I would never kill another human except to defend myself. I had no motive, but someone else certainly did. I was framed. Thank you,' I said, and sat down.

Chapter Twenty Five

Southern District Court

Day 9

They were all back again, and now there were more watchers in the public gallery as people became increasingly bound up in Hannah's story, as it became darker and darker.

'You see,' Hannah said tiredly, looking intently at the jurors, anxious that they should understand. 'Almost everybody at Westerbork Transit camp believed that the transports that left on Tuesday mornings were taking people to the east for work. It made sense; the war was going badly for the Germans, and surely they needed an endless supply of workers for armaments, guns, tanks, planes, bombs and rifles. So when we assembled for roll call that Tuesday morning with our hand baggage, we were not especially frightened by the thought of the transport; after all, thousands had already gone before us.'

Hannah paused there, eyes closed now, head bowed, hands crossed in her lap. Her last session in the witness box had gone particularly slowly, with many stops and starts as she had tried to dig back in her memory. It was almost as if she was afraid to draw back the curtain veiling those memories, or couldn't draw it back, but now something seemed to driving her on, forcing her to confront the past and all its demons. And now she was back there again, and she could smell it, and feel it and see those sights again…….

………the train waited at the platform, smoke rising from its stack. It stood around 20 cattle wagons long, like some sinister mechanical snake waiting to devour them. There was an immediate change in atmosphere as the soldiers lost their smiles and began to harry and push people onto the wagons. When an old man fell trying to climb aboard, a giant soldier mercilessly clubbed the man with his rifle, then lifted him and bodily threw him into the wagon. Then it was just a mad scramble of pushing, shoving, screaming, rifles swinging and dogs barking until all the wagons were stuffed full of heaving, frightened humanity.

Each cramped wagon contained between 50 to 60 people stood squashed up together with barely room to move. At one end of the wagon there was a single pail of water for drinking, and at the other end an empty bucket for use as a toilet.

For the first few hours, people moved about as much as they could, trying to find a comfortable position. Embarrassment at using the bucket as a toilet soon abated as people became resigned to their fate. Hannah leant back against the side of the wagon and closed her eyes, the sound of the wheels on the track slowly, hypnotically drawing her into a dream. She was back in Papa's sunlit studio working on a beautiful painting and she was singing. Then she was walking with Mama across Dam square, and then down by the canals to go shopping, watching the people smiling and talking, moving, walking, living free.

After the first day as the sun began to go down and the train relentlessly moved across the European hinterland, sometimes crawling, sometimes at full steam, sometimes parked in a siding so a military train could pass, but always moving slowly east, Hannah knew that such a journey could not end well. By then the water had run out and children had begun to cry from thirst, and the other bucket was overflowing with excrement and the smell was indescribable. At around 10 pm they stopped in a siding for the night. To start with there were endless calls for water, food and to be let out onto the platform, but no one came. Just a solitary soldier walking down the side of the wagons, slamming his rifle butt into peoples faces if they dared to show them.

Eventually the cries subsided as the darkness enveloped the train. Hannah held Helena, gently rocking her as she slept. She looked out through a gap in the roof and could see the vast cloudless sky above, lit by an endless stream of stars stretching away to infinity. She thought of a book she had read the year before, The Time Machine, by H G Wells; her mind flitted into and out of dreams and visions of climbing into such a machine and leaving the world behind, journeying to a place where they could be free again. But then mama was coughing and retching, violently pulling Hannah out of her fantasy world back into the horror of the wagon. Hannah handed Helena to Papa and cradled Mama's head which was feverish, her brow beaded with sweat. Hannah could feel tremors running through her mothers thin frame.

In the end Hannah couldn't sleep so she stayed awake gently stroking mama's fevered brow as she slept. At 4 am hawkers and pedlars with carts of food and water appeared outside the train. Beseeching hands came out of the side of the wagons, begging for food and water, but the sellers wanted gold, diamonds or a fortune for a cup of water or a crust of bread. They jeered and cajoled, tipping water onto the ground and tossing scraps of bread into the wind. Hannah watched a well dressed woman hand her diamond ring over for a cup of water and a slice of bread.

When Mama suddenly woke with a start she seemed disoriented and unsure of where she was. Her face was pasty white, almost ethereal, and her huge dark eyes seemed blank and empty, bereft of the will to live. Hannah kissed Mama's brow and gently stroked her hair. As she did so the wagon gave a juddering lurch and began to move again, slowly edging out of the siding back onto the mainline track to the east.

People began to die on the third day, mostly the very old or people who were already sick before the journey began. One very old man died, standing up. When he toppled over, his body was already stiff with rigor mortis. Mama became worse during that day, calling out to Hannah and not recognising her when she spoke. Papa couldn't stop crying which seemed to make Mama worse, but then she drifted into sleep again around midday.

Hannah and Grandpa took turns to cradle Helena, quietly singing to her and playing with her. Grandpa talked to Hannah as he had never done before, about his youth, about his time fighting in the first world war, and about Mama when she was born and how joyful they had been, he and his long dead wife. He talked to her about Rudi as well, how he had heard that Rudi had died in one of the camps and he hadn't told Hannah because he knew it would upset her. He told her that he still had the painting Rudi had taken from the museum, rolled up in his rucksack.

Hannah asked to see it, but at that moment Mama had screamed in her sleep and woken, shaking and crying out for water. Mama died on the morning of the fourth day. Hannah was holding her and it was Grandpa who realised she had gone. Hannah thought she was just sleeping, but then she realised all the warmth had left Mama's body. Hannah couldn't seem to cry. Eventually Grandpa managed to pull her away and covered Mama's face with a cloth.

Papa died too, around the same time, but by his own hand. They found him later with a large piece of broken blood stained glass held tightly in his palm. He had slashed it across his neck, cutting the main artery and had quickly bled to death, and he wasn't alone. There were many suicides in the wagon that last day.

The train stopped mid-morning, but Hannah couldn't read the station sign. She saw a couple of men walking down the platform. They looked like the engine drivers. Then the train began to shunt slowly forward again, and Hannah idly wondered who was driving it. Grandpa and Hannah held Helena between them gently rocking her. Hannah felt lightheaded. She'd had little water and no food for days, and it was almost as if she were now a ghost. Her mind played tricks, awash with hot coloured dreams of the past, flickering in and out, tripping. Then the train stopped.

People v Calver - Manhattan Supreme Court
'Ladies and gentlemen of the jury, this is a very simple case,' Stahl said,

as he began his closing argument.

My eyes kept trying to close because I hadn't slept in a week, but the jury looked keen and alert again. They knew they would be going home soon.

'Thank you for all the time you've spent with us,' Stahl continued, looking at them with cod sincerity. 'Some of what you have had to see and hear in this trial has been rough, but we're nearly done. On that night we know the defendant and victim had dinner together in the defendants room. We know she went back to her room to sleep, and we know the time - 1 am - because we've seen the CCTV footage with its real-time clock showing on the ticker.

'We know the defendant later went down to the bar for a drink. We see him again on the CCTV in there. He gets a call from Helena Palmer. "Come up and see me", she says. He does. We watch him on the CCTV as he enters her room at 2.20 am. Then nothing until he leaves 25 minutes later at 2.45 am. No one else enters or leaves that room during that time or afterwards, until we see the busboy knocking at 9.30 am and getting no answer. Ten minutes later Mr O'Leary arrives with a master key and they enter and find Helena's dead body.

'Defendant says, "It wasn't me. It was someone else." Really? Who?' Stahl says, mock incredulous, really getting into it. 'Maybe it was the invisible man, because we know, don't we, members of the jury. No one else other than the defendant enters or leaves that room during the period when Helena Palmer died.

'So what happened in that room during those twenty five minutes? This defendant likes rough sex. We know that from hearing his wife's desperate call to emergency services after he tried to strangle her during sex. He's got form for it. Helena Palmer was anally raped whilst being garrotted with the defendants green silk tie. That tie was so deeply embedded in her neck that the first responders didn't even know it was there until they took a closer look. We don't know how it started. Perhaps the defendant broached the subject of rough sex. Maybe he suggested some form of role play, and maybe she didn't like it. See, the thing is, guys with hang-ups like Mr Calver here, they need the coercive element of the sex to get progressively harder, to satisfy their cravings. They become desensitised, so the sex must get rougher and rougher, harder and harder, in order to get them off. And we say that's what happened in this case. We say the deviant behaviour of such offenders escalates in form, until, as in this case, it ends in murder.

'You've seen the crime scene photographs and yes, they are horrible, but you needed to see them to get some idea of what Helena Palmer went through that night in order to satisfy this defendants sick cravings.

'Most cases are a deal more complicated than this one. This one is simple. Juries are often told to use their common sense in coming to a verdict, but I don't think you even need to do that. In this case all you need is logic. This defendant was the only other person in the room when Helena Palmer died.

'He can scream all he wants about some big corporate conspiracy, some phantom figure who really carried out the murder, and then had the expertise to tamper with the CCTV to frame the defendant. Really? Well, ask yourself one question: has this defendant, at any time during this trial, produced a single shred of evidence to support those contentions?'

Stahl paused, slowly running his eye along the jury box, letting that last question sink in and resonate. Then he added, 'I'll leave you to answer that yourselves, in your deliberations. Thank you.'

Pascal and Bob Jeffries sat at their usual table in Starbucks, sipping the same bland ersatz coffee as last time. Pascal had had to bring Cara along. The child was hugging her moth-eaten teddybear closely to her chest and warily eyeing Bob. He had tried smiling at her, but it hadn't seemed to work, but then another little girl had wandered over, staring at the teddybear with big round eyes and holding her hands out, and Cara had given it to her. And now the two girls were excitedly chattering away in the corner.

'You remember the rogues gallery you left me on the tablet, to have a look at? The London/New York Jihadi's?' Pascal said.

'Course I remember. I been waiting on you. I thought you were holding out on me,' Bob said.

'Not holding out, Bob, just taking my time, bearing in mind my original assessment that the job is bullshit. An ass covering exercise for your back office boys at Homeland Security, so yeah, I didn't take it too seriously. And anyway, what I've got is probably nothing,' she said turning her tablet around on the table so he could see the screen whilst she scrolled to a picture of the guy called Zaid Hamdani.

When she had first seen the mug-shot whilst idly panning through the rogues gallery down in the consulate basement, it had taken some time for the image to register, as it was a face from a while ago.

'I knew this guy in London for a very short period, way back in 2008, when I was running de-radicalisation workshops for the Met counter terrorism command. His name then was Yusuf Masri, and he was basically just a very bright and engaging seventeen year old refugee from Iraq. I didn't consider him to be at risk as he was far too bright to be taken in by any of that nihilistic Jihadi bullshit the local mullah's were peddling at the time. He was around for about six weeks and then he was gone. That was the way it was then, people constantly coming and going and moving on somewhere else, and we never kept tabs on them.'

Bob watched her, his eyes blank, thinking. She took a sip of the ultimate in homogenous blandness, a Starbucks Americano with whole milk and two sugars. Then as Bob sat quiet, checking out records on his hand-held, she glanced over at Cara and felt good for a beat because the little girl was smiling, and that was something solid and good, the awful past forgotten for a moment. Thank God children were so resilient she thought.

Then Bob was dragging her back to the world of Jihadi killers. 'Here's what we got,' he said looking at his phone screen. 'He's at an address in Brooklyn, a rooming house and he's single with no known family; seems to do freelance work related to the crypto digital currency world, and that's about it. Came to our attention because he was picked up by chance on a video surveillance camera at some demonstration against US involvement in Iraq, Afghanistan and Syria, just standing watching a speech, and that was it. He's on your list because his country of origin was shown as UK, when he first entered the US.'

Bob looked hard at the picture. 'So. I wonder what he's up to now?' he said.

'You know, Bob, if you'd asked me, where would Yusuf be in ten years, I would have said a dot-com millionaire. He was that sharp.'

'Well he sure aint no millionaire now, not living at that address. But we'll check him out, low priority,' Bob said, then looked pensive. Then he went on. 'You did good here, Courtney,' he said. 'And the US government, and me, are real grateful for the help.'

It was what she wanted to hear. 'How grateful, Bob?' she said, steeling a glance at him.

He glanced back at her, beginnings of a smile. 'You're some operator, Courtney. What d'you want this time? I take it, its not the British Government who want a favour, right?'

'It's Calver's trial, Bob,' she said.

He looked at her again, surprised at the edge of concern in her voice. 'Yeah, I been following it,' he muttered. Then, 'he doesn't seem to have a defense, so why doesn't he just cut a deal with the DA?'

'It's too late for that. He could have done a deal way back, but he said no and he even called for a quick trial. It was dumb and stupid but he can be like that sometimes. And with the DA now virtually guaranteed a conviction, why's he going to offer Calver anything?

'Calver always worked on the basis we'd crack the CCTV, and although we now think we know how it was done, we don't have any usable evidence. I reckon the judge is about to hand it off to the jury and I think Calver's just about given up. Essentially we've run out of time.'

'So what d'you want from me?'

'I'd like your world class tech guys to run the rule over trial exhibit JC4. That's the digital file of CCTV footage covering the hotel corridor outside the victims room on the night of murder,' she said.

She watched Bob ruminate, then she added, earnestly, trying to keep the desperation out of her voice, 'it's gotta be worth a punt, Bob. We've got nothing else. So how about it?'

He turned, studying her serious expression. 'I guess our cyber warrior tech boys might relish such a challenge,' he said with a chuckle. Then he looked serious again. 'I'm owed a favour, so maybe I'll call it in, see if my pal's might be up to some moonlighting. I'm not promising anything, Courtney, but if you want to email over the digital file I'll take a look.'

'Bob. Your a prince,' she said.

Chapter Twenty Six

It was early evening in the apartment and Christoff was looking for Hannah to see if she wanted a bite to eat. Everyone else seemed to be out. He found her sitting on her bed staring into space. It looked like she had been crying and there were moist tear tracks still evident on her face. He stood at the door feeling uncomfortable, not wishing to intrude, but she looked so inconsolable that he overcame his feelings. 'What is it, Hannah?' he asked gently.

She looked up at him, startled and confused, almost as if she didn't recognise him, but then her eyes cleared. Christoff moved over and sat on the bed next to her. He felt powerless to help, but then leaned forward tentatively and gently embraced her. For a while they just sat like that, then she pulled away slightly, and said, 'thank you,' quietly. He nodded. She looked down at her hands as if considering carefully what she was going to say. Christoff waited.

'You remember on the ship coming over, when you…' she stopped and laughed nervously. 'When you sort of, I don't know. Hypnotised me I suppose.'

'Of course I remember.'

'It frightened me, you know. That's why I didn't come back to you.'

'I know,' Christoff said. 'And now?'

'Tomorrow, I must start the hardest, darkest part of my testimony, and I can't remember anything, other than knowing its bad, very bad. But it's a black hole, a blank space. My mind has blocked it out for all these years, and I can't open it up.'

Christoff took her hands and looked into her eyes. 'You thought before you wouldn't be able to remember, but you have: you remembered that terrible train journey, the deaths of your mother and father, and you testified to it, clearly and the jury understood and followed it.'

'I know, but…' she said pulling her hands away, seeming frightened again. 'Christoff, I've tried, and it won't come. But, maybe… if we…' Her voice tailed off, and she seemed lost. But then her determination seemed to kick in again, and she continued, 'you know I have to do this. For John and for Helena, and all the others. I am old and won't be here much longer. It is time to confront the ghosts and lay them to rest. Will you help me?'

It was Christoff's turn to look down at his hands and think. Her reaction on the Atlantic crossing, when he had used the technique, had scared him, and he had only put her under for the briefest of moments. He hated to think how bad it might get if he were to try for any longer - an extended period. And it could be dangerous. He had heard of people suffering serious mental problems when they had used hypnosis to try and delve into blocked parts of their subconscious.

He turned and looked at Hannah, sitting there calmly waiting for his reply. It was hard to believe what this small humble woman had faced up to during her life. He knew he would never be able to get a handle on the suffering she had endured, but he also knew he had to try and help her face her demons, and tell her story, and finish that story - because now, at the end of her life, that was what she wanted to do - and who was he to gainsay that.

He took her hands in his again and looked deep into her eyes for a long moment. Then he nodded, and said, simply, 'lets do it.'

Southern District Court

Day 10

There was a buzz of anticipation in the Southern District Courtroom that morning. Perhaps they - the growing band of punters in the gallery, the jury, the court staff and other assorted watchers - knew that Hannah's testimony was about to come to the boil. But Morganna didn't feel like that. As she sat at the Plaintiff's table studying her notes she worried about Hannah's ability to hold up to what was to come. At breakfast that morning Hannah had seemed like a ghost, but a ghost wound up tight as a spring. Morganna was glad she had Christoff sitting next to her. He seemed to be the only one able to reach Hannah and keep her calm.

Christoff had told Morganna not to worry, Hannah would be fine, just get her through that mornings testimony. Now he sat, eyes glued to Hannah's, and it was as if there was some kind of strong invisible force passing between them, holding Hannah and giving her strength.

Judge Friedman nodded at Morganna. 'Miss Fedler, please proceed.'

Morganna rose to her feet. Hannah watched her apprehensively, then looked at Christoff. He smiled warmly at her with encouragement, and she seemed to relax slightly, the rigidity going out of her shoulders. Morganna addressed her. 'Hannah, you finished your testimony with your train coming to a halt. Please continue, and tell the jury what happened next?'

Hannah appeared calm, but inside she was in turmoil. The night before, Christoff had put her under for an extended period, gently tugging her down, deeper and deeper, and as she had descended it was as if there was a slow drawing back of a veil behind which lay horror. And now she was back again, and she smelled the smell of death and despair, and then the wagon door was sliding back.

'…..I can see a ramp,' Hannah said, her eyes tightly closed. 'It's like a train platform only shorter. I stand on that ramp, holding my baby sister in my arms. There are thunder clouds above, and dead bodies in the wagon behind me, including my parents. It's like I'm in a trance, not registering things, but I know I can't see grandpa anywhere, and I am worried about him.

Hannah opened her eyes and blinked. Then she began to speak again, talking directly to the jury. 'Then there was shouting, and soldiers with guns and dogs, and there were these other figures, like ghosts, wraiths, really,' she said with a kind of wonder in her voice. 'Skeletally thin shadowy people in striped clothing like dirty old pyjama's, running amongst us, always running, and driving us off the ramp.

'I could see we were in a kind of camp like Westerbork but with no barracks, just watchtowers and a square and some old buildings. Then grandpa appeared and I felt better, but then a soldier tried to take Helena off me. I screamed and he knocked me down with his rifle butt, and that's when he appeared, an officer. He reprimanded the soldier and then lead us over to one of the smaller buildings.

'It had a sign on it saying it was the infirmary, but it wasn't. The sign was fake. Inside it was bare apart from a vast burning pit that gave off an indescribably awful smell. I thought it was a rubbish pit but then I could see bodies in there burning,' she said, and her voice caught in her throat for the first time, and her breathing came quicker. She paused trying to calm herself. She took a sip of water and her hand shook a little as she raised the glass to her lips.

She swallowed, glancing quickly over at Christoff which seemed to calm her and then she was speaking again 'The tall soldier who led us into that hellish place was an SS officer with a peaked cap and black tinted aviator goggles. He took Grandpa's bundle and opened it. Inside was a rolled up painting, and I guessed it was the one Rudi had taken from the museum. The officer unfurled it and looked at the image, and I remember,' she said smiling grimly for the first time. 'It was of a painter walking down a road. The officer smiled and nodded, then opened the other item which was a small tin containing the gold and diamond pendant with matching brooch, given to me by Mrs Van Der Valk.

'The soldier straitened up, and he took his pistol out and……..and—'

'Mrs Palmer,' Judge Friedman cut in. 'Would you like a break, perhaps a glass of water?'

Hannah looked confused, as if woken from a deep sleep, then her face cleared as she remembered where she was . 'Thank you, no, Judge,' she said a little breathlessly. 'I must finish this now or I never will'.

'I understand,' Judge Friedman said gently. 'Please proceed when you are ready.'

'Thank you, Judge' she said with a tired sigh. 'The officer shot grandpa in the head and pushed him into the pit,' she said, eliciting at least one stifled gasp from the jury. 'I was so shocked I couldn't react. I stood rooted to the spot and all I could do was hold my sister tightly in my arms, and then I backed away towards the edge of the pit. I knew I was going to die, and I didn't really care. If it hadn't been for Helena in my arms, I would have just jumped into the pit and ended it there.

'I think now that that officer was enjoying his killing spree. He shot Grandpa like swatting a fly, without a thought, but then he stopped, because some blood had spattered onto his goggles. So he took them off and slowly cleaned them with a handkerchief. He knew I knew he was going to shoot me and my sister, and he took his time cleaning the glasses to increase the torture and enhance his pleasure. And all the time he smiled.

'It was almost a relief when he put his goggles back on, walked over and placed the barrel of the gun to Helena's head and fired. I felt the bullet go through her and then I was falling back into that stinking fiery pit.'

The courtroom was completely silent as Hannah finished

speaking. She looked calm, almost serene, but with a slightly puzzled expression on her face. At the Plaintiff's table Morganna waited a beat, letting Hannah's last words settle with the jury. Christoff put his hand on Morganna's and gave it a gentle squeeze.

'Did that bullet kill Helena?' Morganna asked gently

'Yes, instantly, but I survived,' she answered quietly, almost apologetically.

'Hannah. I'm going to come back to the man who took the jewellery and shot your sister and Grandfather. But for completeness and so the jury know, I'd like you to tell us how you got away from that awful place and how you came to be here with us today?'

Hannah was calm. The terrible revelation was out there now, and she seemed at peace. She spoke matter of factly. 'I lay for hours in that stinking pit full of dead bodies - women, children, old men, decomposing, rotting, some burning - and all the while I held my little sisters dead, bloodstained body. I wanted to die there with her, but I didn't. I lived on, completely unscathed, the flames never reaching us.

'Then what happened is that the officer who killed Helena must have remembered that our teeth hadn't been checked for gold fillings. So hours later he sent a work team back into the pit to check. The capo, that's like the leader of the work team - these were Jews saved from the transports to work in the camp - found me alive, and pulled me out. He almost had to kill me to get me to leave Helena's body, but I did in the end.

'It was quite simple then. A chance in a million. When they took me out, they were also at the time engaged in moving carts full of clothing taken from the people they had been murdering for months. They were moving these carts to the empty train that had brought us in earlier, and then loading the clothing onto the train for transport back to Germany for the war effort.

'That capo, I don't know why, bundled me under a huge mound of clothing in the train. I realised that because they had very strict roll calls there, and anyone missing would be immediately identified, I wouldn't be missed because I wasn't on any roll, because I was officially dead. He risked his life for me and I still don't even know his name, and I have forever felt ashamed that I never asked it.

'It didn't end there because before the train left, guards searched each wagon with bayonets, sticking them into the mounds of clothing. They found a young boy hiding in my wagon, and pulled him out and shot him there, on the spot. I was lucky, a bayonet missed my neck by about an inch. Then even when the search finished, the train sat there for hours. I thought it would never leave, but it did, eventually.

'I knew I couldn't go to Germany, so I jumped off the train in Poland. I waited until we were many hours away from the camp in thick forrest, and then I jumped when the train was going particularly slowly up an incline. Its a long, long whole other story, but to cut it short, eventually I was picked up by partisans and stayed with them until we were liberated by the Russians around two years later.'

Hannah paused there and took a sip of water. She seemed to have got her second wind now and was talking easily, relaxed and fluent. Morganna paused also, checking her notes. 'And so we come back to the whole crux of this case,' she said, turning from Hannah, to look at the jury. Browder finally seemed to stir for the first time, having stayed remarkably quiet throughout Hannah's testimony. Now he sat up and drew a yellow legal pad towards him and raised his pen.

Morganna directed her gaze at Hannah and asked her, 'so who was this man, Hannah? This man who took the pendant, the brooch, and the rolled up picture? This man who took your Grandfather's life and Helena's and almost took your life as well. Who was he?'

Hannah didn't hesitate. 'His name was August Matthes. Or to give him his official title: SS *Scharfuhrer* August Matthes.

'Although I didn't ask the capo who saved my life to give me his name, I did ask him the name of the officer who killed my family and tried to kill me, because I wanted to know.'

'Okay, Hannah. Now before moving on we need you to explain to the jury how you have come to remember these events, the killings of your grandfather and Helena. Because there is no mention of this incident in your statements and depositions prior to your testifying?'

Hannah sighed and looked down at her hands held lightly in her lap. 'Its difficult for me to explain in a way that you will understand,' she said, tentatively, feeling her way along. 'By August 1945 I was being held in a DP, or displaced persons camp in Seedorf. When I first got there I was suffering from terrible Typhus Fever. I was put in isolation and almost died. When I finally came out of it I had no memory of the final events, the arrival at the death camp, the killings and the escape. They had seemingly been wiped from my mind, maybe to protect my sanity, and to be honest, I didn't want to remember. I know it probably sounds callous, but I was young and I wanted to get on with my life, without reliving those awful events with every waking moment. And so it remained buried for over seventy years. In some ways, giving my testimony here has been cathartic, maybe even therapeutic,' she said with a quick smile. 'As each day has passed and I have given my testimony, the memory has slowly come back. I think the time is right, and I believe it is to do with age as well. I know I don't have much time left and there is a real urge within me to remember Mama, Papa, Grandpa and Helena, and to tell their story so the world will know.'

'Thank you, Hannah,' Morganna said, pausing again for a moment to let Hannah's simple and eloquent words sink in before moving on.

'After the killings and the theft of the jewellery, did you ever see August Matthes again?' Morganna asked.

'Yes. I saw him once in the DP camp in Seedorf in August 1945.'

'Do you know what happened to him?'

'I believe he took on the identity of another German soldier, a Major, or *Sturmbannfuhrer*, Franz Bauer of the Waffen SS. I saw—'

'Your honour,' Browder finally interrupted. 'I hope that the Plaintiff has some proof of these very serious allegations. It is well known and documented, and a matter of public record, that Angel Milken, CEO of the K Corporation, a defendant in this trial, was originally known as Franz Bauer.'

'Precisely,' Morganna said, then turning to Friedman and ignoring Browder's noisy harrumphing sounds, she added, ' we intend to prove to the satisfaction of this jury, exactly that. That Angel Milken and SS *Scharfuhrer* August Matthes, are one and the same person.'

'Well, with respect, Miss Fedler,' Browder said. 'Where is your evidence? If all you have is the word of a women who has just admitted she has only just remembered all this stuff, and after seventy plus years. Its hardly compelling, is it?'

'Well surely all Mr Angel Milken has to do,' Hannah interrupted from the witness box. 'Is come here and face me.'

There was murmuring from the jury box, and some vigorous nodding of heads, which was enough to stir judge Friedman to action. 'This is not a talking shop, it is a court of law, regulated by rules,' he said, sternly. 'Mr Browder, whether or not the Plaintiff has adduced sufficient evidence is a matter for the jury alone, and any comments you have on that issue you should save for your closing speech. And Miss Fedler, the Plaintiff should restrict herself to answering your questions, rather than offering her observations on who should be giving evidence here. Is that clear?' he said, glaring at both attorneys.

They both nodded. Friedman looked at the clock, tapped his pen on the lectern, thinking. 'We will adjourn now, until tomorrow,' he said, then turning to Browder, added, 'I'm guessing you may wish to take some instructions from your clients?'

'Indeed, your honour,' Browder said, his face drawn tight.

Chapter Twenty Seven

In the penthouse suite at the top of the K building, Angel Milken was holding what was effectively a board meeting, or what perhaps might better be described as a council of war. Such events were rare, not only because Angel held virtually all the voting stock in K Corp and made all major decisions himself, but also because he was becoming, with advancing age, increasingly paranoid.

He sat in his wheelchair at the head of the table in the large book-lined study. To his left was his son Michael, and opposite them on a lower level, perhaps indicative of a hierarchy of sorts, was Charles Browder IV and John Schmidt. Coffee had just been served. Alcohol was not permitted.

Angel turned his head and trained his one good grey eye on Browder. 'I have read the transcripts of today's proceedings in the Cohen civil claim. How would you characterise events?' he asked, voice quiet and precise.

Browder swallowed, intimidated by Angel, as he always was. 'Sir, the Cohen woman's evidence thus far is, at best, neutral. Uncorroborated fantasy. But, no matter. Tomorrow, when court resumes, I intend to eviscerate her with my cross examination. We can freely attack her strikingly sudden recollection of alleged events she had forgotten about for nigh on seventy years, and now suddenly and conveniently remembers just in time for trial.'

Angel smiled wolfishly, his one good eye boring in on Browder again. 'I am impressed by your confidence, Browder and I am sure you will be most effective in your destruction of the witnesses credibility,' he said. 'But, I intend to give evidence. I will not permit the Jewess to blacken my name and get away with it.'

'Sir. I really don't think—'

'That's right, Browder, you don't think, except in your own narrow and ploddingly legalistic way,' Angel said, cutting him off mid-stream. 'You may leave now, Browder. I have important matters to discuss with Michael and John.'

Browder nodded and departed, truth be known, highly relieved to get out.

Angel turned to Schmidt. 'Situation report?' he said. 'Particularly with regard to the killing of Helena Palmer and the trial of the lawyer, Calver.'

Schmidt allowed a rare smile to cross his face. Pride in reporting to the boss was the closest he got to a pleasurable experience outside of raping and killing. 'Games won, sir. Contained on all fronts,' he said, voice clipped and firm. He continued, 'I believe Fossey may have spoken to Calver's defense team, but it wont help them none. We could take Fossey out, but I don't think we need to. And another linked death is probably one too many, even for NYPD,' he said with a smile. 'Fossey's way too scared to cross us or even dream of testifying, whatever they could offer him, and what can he say anyway? He turned a camera off and turned it on again. Other than that, he saw nothing about which he could give evidence.'

'Good. I agree with your analysis, Schmidt. Go on.'

'So, sir, Calver's dead and buried. We can forget about him. He's going back to Jail for life, soon as the jury deliver our verdict. On the Cohen civil claim, I agree that Charlie should be able to rip her head off on the stand. But if not, if you are to give evidence, I don't see how she can win. And she loses the case, all her allegations go out the window.'

'Again, Schmidt, your analysis is faultless,' Angel said, watching Schmidt carefully, a questioning look in his eye. 'Something though still troubles you, Schmidt. What is it?'

The old man was still capable of surprising Schmidt. That he could still at such an advanced age pick up on something as subtle as Schmidt's faint feelings of unease at a potential threat out there was evidence of significant undimmed powers. 'Sir. O'Leary's cellphone is missing. It wasn't found at his home and my contacts in NYPD tell me it hasn't been recovered. Signals say it was last used at his home around an hour before he died, and then it disappears, and its been dead since.'

'You must find it, Schmidt,' Angel said, voice like a whip-crack

'I'm on it. We're regularly calling the number and have triangulation ready if anyone picks up. And I've got guys on the street. It'll turn up. And when it does, we'll be there.'

Angel sat back and closed his eye for a moment. The only sound that could be heard was of faint music seeping out of Michaels earbuds. 'You think, what, Schmidt? An insurance policy perhaps?' Angel said.

Schmidt nodded. 'Perhaps.'

'Find it.'

Schmidt nodded, got up and left. Michael hadn't said a word throughout and was still listening to his music.

Christoff smiled brightly at Hannah. 'Come on, you deserve a stiff Scotch after what you've been through today,' he said. They were sat in the cavernous living space in the loft apartment and it was around 7.30 pm. Hannah took a seat on the couch whilst Christoff dug out the Scotch and a couple of tumblers, and went out to the kitchen for some ice and soda. As he did so Hannah reached for one of the art books on the coffee table to leaf through the glossy photographs of missing and lost works.

Ever since the earlier testimony about Rudi's arrival from Germany with a mysterious painting, Christoff had started to look on the internet for missing works of art, but as Hannah didn't like looking at computer screens he had also gone to the local library and got out a handful of large art books for her to look at. They were hoping these might jog her memory if she saw something. The trouble had been that Hannah had no recollection of what the painting looked like, until that days shattering testimony when she had seen it for the first time in seventy years, albeit in her minds eye. It was the only time that Hannah had seen it, when it had been unfurled and studied by August Matthes just before the killings.

Christoff dropped ice cubes into the tumblers, poured in a liberal amount of scotch in each and then added a soupcon of soda. Then his phone rang and he ambled away, speaking, moving to stand at the huge windows to look out on the city. As the call finished a few minutes later, Christoff wandered back to the couch, and started when he saw Hannah's face. She seemed transfixed, looking down at something in the large art book that lay open on her lap.

'What is it, Hannah?' he asked.

She didn't answer, like she hadn't heard him.

Christoff got up and walked over behind the couch to look down over her shoulder at the large colour photograph of a painting. He felt the hairs on the back of his neck stand up. The image depicted was of an artist walking down a road, caught between two trees, with cornfields as a backdrop, all gold, yellows, blues and greens, and the identity of the artist was immediately obvious from the style. Christoff read the legend underneath the picture which ran, "Painter on the Road to Tarascon by Vincent Van Gogh 1888." Hannah slowly lifted her head, and turned to look back up at Christoff, and said, 'that's it. That's the picture grandpa had.'

'But that's impossible,' Christoff said. 'It must have been a print.'

Hannah shook her head slowly. 'I don't think so,' she said.

Christoff wandered back to his chair, deep in thought. He sat down and took a long sip of scotch. After a minute he seemed to rouse himself, muttering, 'well then. We better have a look see.' He turned to his laptop and began running a Google search.

Hannah sat quietly by his side and sipped her scotch.

Cara couldn't sleep. Her new pyjama's were stuck to her and the bed sheets seemed to be trying to act like a snake, twisting around her and trying to squeeze the life out of her, and now she could hardly breathe. She unravelled the sheets again and rolled over onto her other side to see if that would make sleeping any easier.

But she did like her new bedroom, even if she had to share it with a load of new soft toys, now staring back at her from the edge of the bed. And she didn't think Rupert was too keen on them either. The moth-eaten teddy had always been there for her, ever since she could first remember anything. Now she cuddled him tightly, singing softly to him as her mind wandered. She knew her father was gone, but she still felt uneasy, as if she were somehow to blame for everything that had happened.

'Why can't I sleep?' she wondered, rolling Rupert over and trying to use him as a pillow. A moment later she felt something hard, sticking out of Rupert into the side of her head. 'What could it be?' she wondered, lifting up the dog-eared teddy and feeling around his fur. There was definitely something there. She got out of bed and tiptoed over to the light switch, flicked it on and scampered back to bed, jumping under the covers.

She slid the short zipper down the side of Rupert and felt around inside his tummy. Her eyes widened when her hand felt the shape of something large and rectangular. She pulled it out and held it up. It was

Daddy's smart phone.

As she studied it she heard footsteps outside her door. For some reason she didn't understand, she quickly hid the phone under her pillow. Then Morganna was poking her head around the edge of the door. 'Lights out, young lady. It's gone nine,' she said, mock severe.

Cara smiled. 'Okay,' she said. 'Night, night.'

'Night,' Morganna said, flicking off the light and closing the door.

As the room descended into darkness Cara finally drifted into a deep sleep, forgetting all about the phone hidden under her pillow.

Southern District Court

Day 11

Browder looked back over his shoulder from his seat at the defendants table and frowned as David Milken and John Schmidt entered the courtroom. They hadn't told him they were coming, probably guessing he'd have tried to blow them off. They really didn't seem to get it, or they did, and they just didn't give a fuck. Was the presence of a certifiable psychopath like Schmidt glaring at the jury really likely to help Angel's case? Or maybe they were just so confident, it didn't matter.

Milken junior nodded and moved into the public gallery, but Schmidt made his way over and took the seat next to Browder, handing him a couple of sheets of folded paper from his jacket. 'This should help,' he said. 'Its a rundown on the Plaintiff's sidekick, Christoff Wisliceny.'

Schmidt stood up to leave and Browder let out a sigh of relief, but then the fat, squat gargoyle turned back, leaned down and fixed Browder with a chilling smile. He said, 'make sure you do your job, Charlie. Cause I'd hate to have to come back and straighten you out. You wouldn't like it.'

Then he walked away. Browder's heart was beating loud and his hand shook as he turned the papers over and scanned them. But then his spirits rose a jot as he took in the contents; there might be something there he could use. Then the judge was edging his way along the bench to his seat and the court was being called to attention. Friedman nodded at Browder, and said, 'cross examination, Mr Browder?'

'Yes indeed, your honour,' Browder replied, rising to his feet and turning to face a calm and relaxed looking Hannah. 'Good morning, Miss Cohen,' he said, friendly conversational tone. Hannah nodded back.

'Could you identify the gentlemen who has been accompanying you to court each day, and is currently sitting beside Miss Fedler at the Plaintiff's table?' Browder asked, gesturing over at Christoff, who looked surprised and uncomfortable at being singled out.

Hannah looked nonplussed by the question for a second, but then replied, 'his name is Christoff Wisliceny, and he's a friend who is supporting me.'

'And when you say supporting you, does this extend to helping you with your memory?' Browder asked, all wide-eyed innocence.

'Yes. I mean, no,' Hannah struggled. 'He helps me to relax when I'm away from here, calms me so the memory comes easier.'

'I see,' Browder said, his look suggesting he didn't see at all. 'And so tell me, Miss Cohen, just how does Mr Wisliceny relax and calm you, as you put it, so the memory comes?'

'Well,' Hannah said, looking over at Morganna and Christoff helplessly, and then looking down in her lap. 'He. He is a calm person. He talks to me, and this helps me…' she said, her voice tailing off uncertainly.

At the Plaintiff's table, Morganna turned to look at Christoff. He shrugged and looked away uncomfortably. Morganna knew now something had been going on between Hannah and Christoff to do with Hannah's memory. But how the hell had Browder picked up on it, and she hadn't? Maybe Browder wasn't such a klutz after all, and maybe her inexperience was starting to tell. She should have queried Hannah's sudden flood of memory.

But she had another problem, an odd problem, and that was that Hannah was way too honest. And that was likely now going to cost them, if Browder could tease something out and then go in for the kill. Morganna knew she would have to try and help Hannah, but her inexperience meant that she didn't really know how.

Browder smiled a thin smile as he regarded Hannah. 'And what does he say to you, when he talks to you, that is so helpful in terms of your memory?' Browder asked, skilfully honing in on the nub of the issue.

'Your honour,' Morganna said, finally realising she needed to do something to try and protect Hannah. 'Counsel is browbeating the witness. She's answered the question, and he should move along,' she said feebly, wishing she could think of something better to say.

'On the contrary, Miss Fedler,' judge Friedman said. 'You opened the door when you asked Miss Cohen about how she had suddenly remembered these events, and Mr Browder is perfectly entitled to pursue it. And of course, the witness has not answered the question.'

Morganna sank back into her chair, stung.

'Miss Cohen?' Browder prompted Hannah.

'He would just talk, Mr Browder, gently, taking me back, asking questions,' she answered with a slight edge to her voice.

'You mean he coached you?' Browder said, subtly upping the ante, and the pressure on the witness.

'No. He didn't coach—'

'You know, don't you,' Browder broke in on Hannah, 'Mr Wisliceny worked for British Intelligence, MI5 I believe, an organisation well versed in techniques of auto-suggestion, interrogation —'

'Your honour,' Morganna was on her feet again. 'I really must —'

'*Sit down*, Miss Fedler,' Friedman roared. 'Counsel will approach,' he added, quieter, as he switched his mike off, and leant down to speak to the approaching attorneys. He said, 'I will not have you turn my court into a circus, Miss Fedler. If you wish to make an objection then I would expect it to be properly founded. Mr Browder's line of questioning is perfectly proper and within the rules. And I'll say it again. You opened the door, Miss Fedler, and Mr Browder has walked through it. If you come into my court and don't have the requisite experience to prosecute your case, you will be found out. Now, proceed with your questioning Mr Browder.'

As Morganna desultorily walked back to her table she knew she'd blown it. Browder had engineered a situation where he'd get a free run at Hannah, with Morganna effectively blocked off from objecting, and protecting Hannah, unless she could come up with perfectly reasoned objections. And there was fat chance of that with her lack of courtroom experience. So now it was down to Hannah.

'Yes, Mr Browder,' Hannah said, pre-empting the next question on Browder's lips. 'I did know that Mr Wisliceny had previously worked for British Intelligence. What of it?'

'Well, you see, I'm interested, Miss Cohen, as I am sure the jury are,' Browder said, silkily. 'In just what occurred during these gentle talks you had with Mr Wisliceny. Take us through an example, if you will, say from the night before your final testimony. What happened?'

For a long moment Hannah looked down in her lap, her brow furrowed in concentration, then she looked up and over at Christoff, a faint apologetic smile on her face. Then she said, 'Christoff - Mr Wisliceny, briefly used some light hypnosis techniques on me to help me remember those events.'

Her words seemed to release pent-up tension in the courtroom, a rising hubbub of noisy chatter. Browder smiled as the jury moved around and murmured to each other in a questioning tone, until Friedman called the court to order. Morganna seemed frozen rigid, staring down at her yellow legal pad, wishing she were somewhere else.

Friedman fixed Morganna with a baleful stare. 'Did you know about this, Miss Fedler?' he asked.

'Absolutely not, your honour,' Morganna answered reflexively, realising as the words left her mouth that it was absolutely the wrong thing to say, even if it was true. Another demonstration of her woeful lack of experience she thought bitterly. She should never have agreed to take the case. It was fine taking days and days of unobjectionable unopposed testimony, but as soon as she met any kind of challenge, she was exposed. She felt like a fraud and wished she could crawl away into a dark corner and hide.

'Your honour,' Browder said, rising to his feet again, triumphant look on his face. 'I would like you to strike all the Plaintiff's hypnosis induced testimony from the record as being inadmissible. In particular, that testimony running from the opening of the cattle wagon doors, up to the time of the witnesses arrival in the UK.'

Friedman considered Morganna. 'Miss Fedler?' he asked her, aware she was now completely at sea.

Morganna turned and looked over at Hannah, now sitting with her head bowed, eyes hooded. She suddenly looked very old and small, this extraordinary woman who at every turn in her life seemed to have stood up and fought, whatever the odds. And now because of her own attorneys deluded arrogance and inexperience, she was going to lose again. Beaten by the man who in all likelihood had murdered her entire family and stolen all they had. Morganna felt a ripple of shame that she was even thinking of cutting and running at the first sign of trouble, just as so many others had done in the early part of Hannah's life when the Nazi's had come. She knew one thing for sure though: if Hannah were the attorney, she would *never* give in. Then Morganna thought about Calver, a street fighting lawyer who knew a trick or two. And then she thought about her father, and her brother, all lawyers who said it wasn't always what you knew; sometimes you just had to fight and trust in the stars.

Morganna rose to her feet. 'Your honour. I don't agree with Mr Browder's analysis. Perhaps I might argue the point in chambers, in the absence of the jury?'

Friedman studied her, weighing it, and the thought of being appealed if he acted too hastily. Browder looked on, still supremely confident. 'By all means, Miss Fedler,' Friedman said. Then turning to the jury he added, 'I'm going to hear some *very* brief legal argument, that shouldn't take more than ten minutes. Don't go away.'

'Such testimony is inherently unreliable, Miss Fedler, and has repeatedly been excluded as being inadmissible,' Judge Friedman said. 'Why should I make an exception in this case?'
They were in Friedman's book lined chambers. He sat at his desk in shirtsleeves having discarded his black gown. Browder stood apart,

leaning back against the door jamb nonchalantly studying his finger nails. Morganna sat across from Friedman, scrolling through some case law on her tablet. They had been arguing the point back and forth for nearly ten minutes, and it was clear Friedman was going to exclude the hypnosis induced testimony, the effect of which would be catastrophic for Hannah's case. It would take out Hannah's identification of August Matthes and her eye witness testimony of his taking of the pendant and the brooch, not to mention the murder of Helena and Hannah's grandfather. That is, it would take out the absolute heart of her case, leaving them with nothing.

'Your honour,' Morganna said, whilst speed reading some case law. 'My understanding of the law on this complex subject, whilst far from expert, is that many cases turn on what the witness testified to prior to hypnosis. That testimony is not tainted by hypnotherapy, it pre-existed hypnosis and should stand in the normal way. I appreciate that it appears you are going to throw out the ID of August Matthes from the death camp and the actual taking of the jewellery. However, it is clear that Hannah Cohen recognised and identified August Matthes, later at the displaced persons camp in Seedorf. Now that ID, your honour, is independent of any hypnosis. That memory pre-existed, although Hannah may not have appreciated its significance prior to these latest developments. When you combine this with the corroborative fact that Angel Milken currently has custody of the jewellery in issue in this case, and was previously known as Franz Bauer, who my client alleges is in fact August Matthes, that part of her testimony - the ID of Matthes at the DP camp - must stand.'

'So you keep Angel Milken in the frame, eh, Miss Fedler?' Friedman said, a faint gleam of admiration flickering in his eye at her hastily discovered powers of persuasion. 'Mr Browder?' he said, turning to look at defense counsel.

'Absolute poppycock, judge,' Browder said, contemptuously. 'Plaintiff only gets the significance of the later DP camp ID because of what she gleans from the hypnosis session, so it all has to go.'

Friedman held his hand up as Morganna was about to come back at him. 'I've heard enough,' he said. 'If you don't agree my ruling, Mr Browder, appeal. You've cut a huge swathe of their case away, and if you can't win it now, you need to think about another career.

'So, I'm not going to chuck it all out. The later DP camp ID stays in, because I believe what Miss Fedler says is right.' He looked at both attorneys, neither of whom were happy, but Morganna couldn't resist a quick smile. She'd fought, instead of run, and she'd got something. The game was still on - just. And if she could get Milken in the box, even for just one minute, then she'd try a few tricks of her own.

Chapter Twenty Eight

Browder was feeling particularly pleased with himself as he entered the penthouse suite at the top of K Tower. He'd stopped off earlier at a bar where lawyers congregated at the end of each day, and he'd got to regale a couple of them with his exploits in the Southern District Court that day, and now he felt a warm pleasant alcoholic glow around him.

As he came into the study Angel Milken was sat at his desk reading, his face illuminated by light from a single lamp. Browder came to a halt in front of the desk and waited, the alcohol he had imbibed earlier giving him a measure of calmness he didn't usually feel in the presence of the great man.

Milken looked up, a thin dry smile on his face. Browder could see he had been reading a transcript of the days hearing, in both English and German. 'And so, Charles, you have been celebrating, Schmidt tells me, yes?' Milken said with a dry laugh.

Browder shivered, realising Schmidt must have been watching him in the bar earlier, and Angel was letting him know he knew about it. 'Yes, sir. I'm sorry, I should have come here straight away,' Browder said.

'No, no, Browder,' Angel said, waiving him into the chair opposite. 'You certainly did very well in getting the main testimony excluded, it was masterful, and I am most grateful for your endeavours.'

'Thank you, sir,' Browder said, preening with pride.

'But, Charles, we are still left with the Bauer allegation. What is your advice?' he asked.

Although slightly drunk, Browder was ready for the question. 'Sir, I don't believe its necessary for you to testify,' he said.

'How so?'

'They will have nothing left, sir. Because I will dismiss the central part of the Cohen woman's testimony in my closing speech. I will say her words are simply the rantings of a severely disturbed individual who has tried to use dubious hypnosis methods to conjure up a story for the jury,' Browder said, watching the boss, eager for approval.

'I disagree,' Angel said slowly, leaning back in his chair. Because the day in court had gone well, Angel was feeling expansive and a little more talkative than usual. 'I did study law you know, Charles, many years ago, in Germany, before the war. The receipt for the jewellery I purchased in Munich needs to be personally validated by me with testimony. As does my refutation of the Jewesses allegation regarding what occurred at the DP camp. The jury need to see me. I have no fear of what these swindling Jews can do, and I will face them down tomorrow. Arrange it,' he said dismissively, indicating the meeting was over.

As Christoff, Hannah and Pascal piled into the kitchen chattering away about Van Gogh and his lost painting, they found Calver there hunched over the table hugging a half empty bottle of Scotch. Pascal rolled her eyes and made sign language behind Calver's back that Christoff and Hannah should leave, which they did, silently.

Pascal went and got a tumbler and then sat down opposite him. She noticed his eyes were very bloodshot and didn't seem to be focusing. She held out her hand for the bottle and said, 'gimme.'

He looked up, and it was clear he hadn't realised she was there. His eyes slowly cleared. He looked down at the bottle with surprise, and then handed it to her. He rubbed his hands across his eyes. 'Jury's out and I'm going down, Courtney. Thanks a bunch, mate,' he said

She poured some scotch into a tumbler. 'What d'you want me to do, Calver?' she asked, wearied by his self-pitying whining. 'We know they looped the tape. We even half know how they did it, and who got that for you?' she asked. 'That's right, me. But we can't prove it. And the people with the proof will never talk. They're more scared of Schmidt and his crew than they'll ever be of us. Again, Calver. What d'you want me to do about it?'

I got up from the table, unsteady on my feet, the room spinning. I knew she was right. She couldn't do any more. That afternoon, the judge had summed up and sent the jury out, so come morning I'd get a verdict. And then I'd be going back to jail, probably for life without parole. I picked up the bottle from the table and staggered out, and then weaved my way towards the bedroom, determined to obliterate the fear with drink.

As Calver staggered out of the kitchen, Pascal raised her cell-phone and tried Bob Jeffries again, but he still wasn't picking up. She knew it was too late for Calver, but if she could get something, if Bob's world class tech boys had found anything in the CCTV digital file, it might give Calver some hope. And it would be there for an appeal. She sent a text chasing Bob. To it she attached a picture of a naked woman, hating herself but knowing it was more likely to get Bob's attention than anything else.

Cara was in bed again. She was looking at the smartphone but she was frightened to touch it. As soon as her hand had slipped under the pillow and felt it she had remembered everything. But she also remembered other things, like when Daddy had hurt her, he had always had the phone with him. As she studied the dead black screen she began to cry. Then, after a moment, she looked up and caught Rupert staring at her sternly from the edge of the bed. His one glass eye looked so real, and he seemed to be saying, 'stop crying, you silly little fool. Only little girls cry.'

She sniffed and rubbed her nose. 'You're right, Rupert,' she muttered, and reached down and powered up the phone. After about 5 seconds it began to ring. She immediately jumped back, frightened, and then quickly switched it off.

Schmidt sat with Wilkins in the bar where Pascal had seen them before. They were in a booth and Schmidt was listening to Wilkins and sipping scotch.

'So, boss, I told you before, the crew, when they were in O'Leary's house, they ripped it apart. Nothing. No phone. And now the guys on the street. Same. Nothing.'

Schmidt didn't seem to be listening. He'd known they wouldn't find anything. O'Leary had been cleverer than he looked. Kiddie fiddlers usually were. A life spent hoodwinking the world usually taught a guy how to deceive. Schmidt toyed with the burner in his left hand. It was programmed with just one number: O'Leary's, and it was set to phone that number every 5 minutes. It was on speakerphone.

As Wilkins signalled the waiter for another round, the burner suddenly vibrated in Schmidt's hand and started emitting a live dial tone. Schmidt smiled and slowly placed the vibrating phone on the table. Then it stopped.

'So,' Schmidt said. 'Its out there.'

'How you going to get them to answer, boss?' Wilkins said.

'Oh, they'll answer all right,' Schmidt said. 'They'll just have to know who's calling them. Curiosity trumps caution every time, and we know what curiosity did, don't we? Kitty, Kitty. We just gotta wait, and then kill ourselves a cat.'

Southern District Court

Day 12

As Michael Milken wheeled his father into the Southern District Courtroom a distinct hush fell on the place. This was despite the fact that the public and press areas were now stuffed to the gills with assorted media, including foreign outlets, punters, lawyer groupies and the usual courtroom nut-jobs. It was a strange turnaround; for weeks of testimony the court had essentially been empty apart from judge, clerk, stenographer, lawyers and the parties themselves. But now look at it?

Morganna turned from the onlookers to study Angel Milken as Michael manoeuvred the old man into place at the defendant's table. The wheelchair was an old battered manual job, no doubt chosen for effect, and Angel had a ratty green tartan blanket spread over his knees, making him look distinctly old and infirm. But the face itself didn't look old at all, it was still finely sculpted and distinguished by dramatic planes underneath a large cerebral looking forehead. Then you had that single fierce, almost eagle like grey eye, staring out indomitably at the world, offset dramatically by the contrasting black patch covering the other eye. Interestingly there were virtually no modern photograph's of Angel Milken anywhere, so this was the first real opportunity Morganna had had to get a look at him.

She cast a sidelong glance at Hannah and stiffened, shocked by what she saw. Hannah's face was white as snow as she watched Milken, her eyes crawling over his face, registering every crag and line. It really did look like she was seeing a ghost.

Then Browder was rising to his feet and formally calling Angel Milken to the stand. There was a slight delay as Milken was helped into the witness box and settled down, and then Browder was away with the basics of name, address and similar as he sketched out the witnesses background. Milken's voice in answering was loud, firm and authoritative and he seemed to be completely relaxed.

'Now your original name was not Angel Milken, correct?' Browder said, quickly getting into it.

'My original name was Franz Bauer, which I changed to Angel Milken soon after I arrived in this great country back in 1947. I was born in Cologne, Germany on 3rd May 1923.

Browder studied his notes. 'Now you know that there have been allegations against you suggesting you are not who you say you are, and there is also an inference that you were present when some very valuable jewellery went missing in April 1943. To start with can you tell us what you were doing and where you were around this time?'

'Certainly,' Milken said. I was a *Sturmbannfuhrer*, or major, in your parlance, in the Waffen SS. Panzergrenadier division, Leibstandarte SS Adolf Hitler. In August 1942 we were pulled out of the line from Rostov where there had been a massive soviet counter-attack, and we were sent back to France for re-fitting. In February 1943 we were put back into the line at Kharkov to try and hold the city, which then changed hands a couple of times following vicious fighting and huge casualties. After that we were in almost continuous combat, fighting the red army. Then on 5th July 1943 our division spearheaded the southern pincer movement in the greatest tank battle in history at Kursk, and this lasted way into August of that year. After that we were in a state of almost constant retreat under fire.

'So to answer your questions specifically, I was in combat in southern Russia in April 1943.'

'Thank you, Mr Milken,' Browder said, voice dripping with servility. 'Now, again you will have heard that it is alleged that this jewellery appears to have originally gone missing at one of the camps, and we have heard testimony that Dutch Jews were sent to places the names of which are now burned into the psyche of peoples all around the world. Places such as Auschwitz- Birkenau and Sobibor. Were you ever present or did you ever visit any of these places during April 1943, or indeed at any time?'

Again, without hesitation Milken responded. 'Absolutely not. We were a combat unit. As I've said, in April 1943 I was fighting for my life deep in Southern Russia. Despite being an SS man, I did not agree with the extermination of the Jews. Indeed my view was that far too many resources were diverted to this dubious end, when they should have been used to help our brave and courageous fighting troops. I'll admit I, like many Germans of my generation, did hate the Jews. I considered them to be an existential threat living amongst us, but my remedy would have been just to cast them out of our territories.'

'Thank you again, Mr Milken. Moving on, following the end of the war, I understand that you were interned in a displaced persons, or DP camp, in Seedorf?'

'That is correct.'

'Tell us about that?'

'As our world collapsed around us, a major concern for those of us who wanted to go on living, and many didn't, was not to fall into the hands of the red army. Or be identified as being a member of the Waffen SS - revenge, as we observed on many occasions, would be swift and brutal. So I discarded my uniform in the ruins of Berlin in April 1945 and was soon after taken prisoner by the Americans who after a short period transferred me to Seedorf.

'After becoming aware that I spoke perfect English they employed me to do translation work and as they got to trust me, they involved me in helping track down wanted Nazi's. In order to get to that level of trust, I had concluded that I would have to come clean about my identity, which I quickly did, and which ironically I believe actually enhanced their trust in me.'

'Now, perhaps the most outlandish allegation levelled against you in this case,' Browder said, pausing for a beat to turn and look wide-eyed at the jury, 'is that whilst in the DP camp you took on the identity of Franz Bauer. That in fact you were someone else, and that you did away with the real Franz Bauer, and then became him?'

For the first time Milken smiled thinly, his bloodless lips creasing slightly at the edges, whilst his single eye remained trained directly on the centre of the jury box. 'Hah,' he said, impatiently. 'Is that really a serious question for me?'

'I am afraid it is, however absurd, Mr Milken.'

'Of course that did not happen. How could it? I was surrounded by soldiers and military police, as well as Jews eager for retribution, and other inmates, all with their own agenda. How would I have achieved it? It is fantastical and a nonsense. Indeed you have my original identification documents there,' he said pointing at the bundle of dog-eared papers sitting on Browder's table. 'It would simply not have been possible to do what you suggest.'

Browder nodded, then turned to glance at Hannah sitting quietly at the plaintiff's table, her eyes locked onto Milken's. 'Do you know, or have you ever met the plaintiff in this case, Miss Hannah Cohen?' Browder said, holding out his hand in Hannah's direction.

Milken didn't really look at Hannah. He said, 'Never. I have never met this person, on my honour.'

Hannah snorted, unable to keep quiet any longer. 'On your *honour,'* she muttered loudly enough for the judge and jury to hear, prompting Friedman to intervene. 'We are all getting a might emotional, and I want everybody to calm down, especially the Plaintiff,' he said, looking directly at Hannah, not unkindly.

Hannah slowly regained her composure and then nodded.

'Good. Proceed, Mr Browder.'

'Thank you your honour,' Browder said, turning back to Milken, who appeared completely unmoved by Hannah's outburst. 'I am now handing you, Mr Milken, Exhibit "HC6" being a receipt for the purchase of a pendant and brooch,' he said, passing to Milken a single yellowing sheet of paper.

Milken took the paper and placed it down in front of him and then looked up, along with the jury, at a blown up photograph of it on a large screen, which also contained an image of a certified English translation alongside it. It showed a simple and brief receipt, although the description of the jewellery was very detailed. It confirmed the sale of a jewell encrusted antique pendant and matching brooch, by Pieter Kopp, licensed jewellers and antique dealers of Schlossstrasse 26, Munich to a Mr Angel Milken of New York City. The receipt showed a date of 7th June 1953.

'Please explain what this is, Mr Milken?'

'Its the original receipt for my legitimate purchase of the jewellery that the plaintiff alleges I somehow obtained illegally,' Milken said.

'And it's been validated?'

'Yes it has,' Milken said. 'I believe you have an exchange of correspondence with Pieter Kopp's heirs, who incidentally still run the dealership, comprehensively confirming the position. And I also understand you have an experts opinion that the jewellery in the TV clip seen by the plaintiff that started this whole farce, is the same jewellery referred to in the invoice.'

'Thank you, Mr Milken,' Browder said. 'I have nothing further for you, but please wait there as I anticipate that the plaintiff's may want to question you also.'

But before any cross examination could start, Friedman adjourned.

People v Calver - Manhattan Central Criminal Court

Day 10

As the jury filed back into court I wanted to crawl away and die. My head throbbed as if someone were using it as a drumhead, and I could still taste the stale whiskey in the back of my throat. I hadn't really slept at all, just endured a kind of tortured, fearful, drunken slumber. And this morning I hadn't had time to shave, or find a clean shirt, so I guess I looked like any street guy coming out of a week long drunk. My eyes kept trying to close as I tried to concentrate on what the clerk was saying as she asked everyone to stand.

'Ladies and gentlemen of the jury, have you reached a verdict,' she asked them.

'Yes,' the foreman replied.

'As to count one, the murder of Helena Palmer?'

'Guilty.'

It was still a shock, even though I knew it was coming. I didn't bother asking for a poll of the jury, I knew what it would tell me. Stahl was happy though. Hollywood smile and then some, but when I looked over at Daly, who'd turned up for the verdict, there was a kind of speculative look in his eyes, maybe a question mark there. But who was I kidding? It was over for me now.

I didn't want to cry, not with everyone there watching me, so I just about kept myself together. Then Pascal was there, next to me, as

Gonzalez addressed me, and again I knew what was coming.

'Mr Calver you will be remanded back to custody on Rikers Island pending sentencing.'

As they led me away, Pascal grabbed my arm and said, 'I'm gonna get you out, Calver.'

I wrenched my arm away and didn't bother looking back. What was the point. As they took me down I was thinking: rope or knife.

Chapter Twenty Nine

Cara wasn't going to school that day because she'd decided to throw a sickie. Only Christoff was in that morning and he was a soft touch; plus he seemed to be very busy in the kitchen with a load of make-up and photographs. What was all that about she wondered? Anyway, when she'd told him she didn't feel well and better stay off school, he hadn't put up much of a fight.

She made sure the bedroom door was firmly closed and then she carefully pulled the smart phone out from under the pillow. She looked over at Rupert sitting at the end of the bed. He seemed to be giving her his nod of approval. She flicked the phone on and watched it light up, then load whatever it was it had to load, and then settle down with its familiar colourful ikons strung out across the screen.

She looked up at Rupert again, biting her lip with indecision, then the phone buzzed into life, ring tone sounding very loud in the quietness of the bedroom. She jumped back startled. The screen flashed "unknown caller" and the phone moved about on the surface of the bed as it vibrated. Who could still be calling Daddy? Rupert seemed to be urging her to answer it but she was scared. Her finger hovered over the answer button. She looked at Rupert again, gulped, and pressed the button.

Then she leaned down and said a meek and tentative, 'hello.'

There was a brief pause as the caller processed the fact it was a child answering the phone, and then a voice came back on the speakerphone loud and friendly. 'Hi. You must be Cara. This is John. Big friend of your Daddy's and I have something for you, sweetheart. A present your Daddy left with me to give you. Would you like it?'

Cara looked at Rupert and smiled. She always liked presents and John sounded so friendly. She said, 'yes. What is it?'

'Its a surprise, honey, and you only get it if you keep this a secret. Our secret. You mustn't tell anyone.'

'But can't I tell Rupert?' she said before she could stop herself.

'Rupert?'

'My bear, Rupert. Mayn't I tell him?'

'Oh yes. You can tell Rupert, but no one else. Deal?'

'Deal. When can I see it? My present?'

'I have it right here with me, sweetheart. Are you in the apartment now?'

'Yes.'

'Say. How about I take you to the zoo, and I'll give you your present there. How does that sound?'

'Cool. May I bring Rupert?'

'Of course, and make sure you bring the phone with you. But we need to hurry. And its very secret, so you will have to sneak out. Can you do that sweetheart?'

She thought for a moment, then smiled. 'Yes,' she said, excitedly. 'I told Christoff I was sick and couldn't go to school. I'll tell him I'm feeling better and am going to go in.'

'Good. You're a clever girl, Cara. Come now, and I will be waiting outside, across the road in the big black car. I'm really looking forward to meeting you. See you in a minute, and remember: not a word to anyone; its to be our secret,' Schmidt said, chilling grin, dead eyes oscillating in his face. It had been a while since he'd killed a child, but it wasn't something you forgot how to do in hurry he thought with a smirk. He was already sat across from the loft apartments in the big black car, waiting patiently, watching the entrance way like a cat watching a mouse-hole.

When she climbed into the big black car, John was funny and made her laugh and he gave her some sweets. He told her they just had to stop off at the magic tower to get her present before they went on to the zoo. The car was bigger than any she had ever been in before and very comfortable. She sat up front, hardly able to see over the dashboard, and Rupert was excited too.

Then the car was nosing into the underground car park. John took her hand and led her into the penthouse private entry area and into the lift. Cara shyly watched him from the corner of her eye. He looked familiar somehow; not his face which was very strange, like one of the orcs in the fantasy books she read, but his shape. She was sure she had seen it before, not his face, just that strange shape, like a kind of big beach ball with lumps.

John seemed to smile a lot and didn't say much which was fine. But his eyes looked false to Cara, cold, almost like the eyes of the snake she had seen in the reptile house on a school trip. She cuddled Rupert. She just wanted her present, then she could go back and see Courtney and Morganna, and maybe they'd play together.

John led her out of the lift, through an entrance door, down a corridor and into a small bedroom that looked unused, like a spare room. 'Wait here,' John said, and now his smile was gone and his voice sounded different. Harsh and demanding.

As John turned and walked away towards the door, she recognised the shape of his receding back and where she had seen it before. As she heard the lock click, it all came back. The night that Daddy had died in the garage, that was the shape she had seen, through the curtain, under the street lamp, leaving the outside entrance of the garage, about two hours before Courtney had rung their bell. And now she remembered even more; he had got into the same big black car. It had been sitting at the kerb, and then he'd driven away. At the time she had thought nothing of it, and then with all the shock she had forgotten and hadn't mentioned it to the police when they questioned her. They had seemed very sorry and kept repeating the word 'suicide'. She knew what that meant but didn't believe Daddy would ever have actually killed himself. She was glad he had though, if he had, because he had been a bad man, and he had hurt her so many times, and now that was finished. But maybe John was bad as well and he was going to hurt her too.

She cuddled Rupert. Why had John locked the door she

wondered.

'How long we got?' Pascal asked Christoff as she dumped her jacket and looked around the stuff he had set up in the kitchen. 'And where is everyone?'

Christoff checked his watch. 'Everyone's out, and we got about an hour before Emilio gets here,' he said. He had been busy in the kitchen. There were big blow-up photographs of Emilio pinned up around the room, and on the table was a large screen laptop running a filmed clip of Christoff's meeting with Emilio when he had first come to the apartment to deliver the bread. Christoff said, 'its on a loop, and I've loudened his voice so listen carefully, and get the inflection right. You should only have to say a few words.'

Pascal nodded and glanced at the other stuff on the table. It looked like some very expensive make-up products and there was also a prosthetic chin and a nose. Christoff eyed Pascal up and down critically. 'Luckily you're just the right size, but we may have to put some padding around your midriff. Now if you want to strip off and lie back in the chair I can get to work,'

'You really think you can make me look like Emilio?' she asked.

'Enough to get you past those dummies on the desk at K Tower, yeah.'

'Good enough,' she said as she stripped down to her underwear and lay back. As Christoff got to work her mind was back on Calver.

Okay, she'd known the guilty verdict was a nailed down certainty, but when it came it had still been a shock, and now she was worried. He'd looked so broken, completely defeated, like she'd never seen him before. If she couldn't find something quick and get him out , she' didn't think he'd last long. Soon as you gave up hope in there things went down hill quick, the US penal system being one of the most brutal and unforgiving in the world. So finding something now, maybe in K tower or from Bob Jeffries tech boys , if he'd ever wake up and get back to her, had to be the way. Either could throw up a lead that might crack the case wide open, and all she could do was keep her foot on the gas and keep pushing and praying that something would turn up.

Southern District Court

Day 13

Morganna sat in her chair at the plaintiff's table and watched Angel Milken in the witness box as they waited for the judge to appear. This was to be her first real test as an attorney; cross examination - the hardest of all the legal arts. And this guy had shown he was no doozy; he was a formidable witness, and very, very sharp, even with his advanced years. She would have to be careful, but she would also have to attack. With the throwing out of the testimony of the killings and taking of the jewellery, she had no choice. If they couldn't shake him, they were done, and he would win, and Hannah would lose, again - and there would be no second chances for her.

'All rise,' the bailiff intoned as Judge Friedman entered court and made his way along the bench to his seat.

Pascal stared at her image in the mirror Christoff held out for her, and she couldn't quite believe it was her face staring back. 'How the fuck did you do it, Christoff?' she said, marvelling at his skill.

'Encapsulated Pro Gel pieces for the nose and chin, manufactured to the contours of your face from the molds I took. Add in some Screenface eye shadow, M.A.C. black eye liner pencil and some Lancome colour for the skin, dab of pitch black hair dye, and *voila*,' he said with a flourish.

'I have your bread delivery here, sir,' Pascal said, mimicking the voice she had been listening to on the loop as Christoff had worked on her face.

'Good. Little bit deeper though,' Christoff said.

She tried it again. 'That's it. Good enough to get you in,' he said.

Pascal checked her watch. 'You got the drug ready?'

'Check.'

Then the buzzer went. They both froze for a second then they were moving, Christoff to the door entry system, and Pascal out of the way, and to pick up some stuff for the operation.

Christoff checked the screen, leaned in, and said, 'come on up, Emilio. Got some ice cold orange juice waiting for you.' Then he pressed the entry door release button.

A minute later, Christoff lead Emilio into the living space where the delivery man put his bread basket down and took the proffered large glass of orange juice. 'Thanks, man,' he said, taking a long drag on the juice, and looking around the large space.

Christoff picked the basket up and lifted the cover. 'Hot damn, that smells good,' he said.

'Glad you like it, Mr Wisliceny,' Emilio said. Then he blinked his eyes a couple of times as he felt the first effects of the drug. He finished the orange juice and handed the glass back to Christoff, swaying slightly on his feet. 'Wow, man, I suddenly feel sleepy,' he said, involuntarily plumping himself down on the couch.

'Are you okay, Emilio? Just sit back and take a moment,' Christoff said, watching as the man slowly sank under, his eyelids fluttering and then finally closing. Christoff let out a piercing whistle, and Pascal was there in seconds. They quickly undressed Emilio and Pascal donned the uniform. She put the distinctive "Oskars" red liveried cap on which did quite a good job of hiding her face, and then an added bonus; in the top breast pocket of the uniform he had some shades; she put them on as well.

Christoff studied her critically. 'Hot damn, you look good to go, even if I say so myself.'

She smiled and picked up the bread basket. Christoff dug through Emilio's wallet and handed her the ID card, and then he tossed her the van keys. 'Be careful,' he said.

'Always,' she answered as she turned to go, adrenaline starting to surge.

Southern District Court

Morganna rose from her seat, watching Milken all the while. 'Good morning, Mr Milken,' she said with a wide smile. Then, 'I am a Jew. How d'you like that?'

Browder was up in an instant. 'Really, your honour. This is a courtroom, not a playground. Could Miss Fedler be enjoined to move along and deal with the facts?'

Friedman nodded. 'Quite. Miss Fedler, in case its escaped your attention, this is a case about some missing jewellery, nothing else. So can we stick to that?'

'Certainly your honour,' Morganna said, miffed that her carefully crafted quip had backfired. She had hoped it might provoke Milken in some way, give her an opening, but Browder had protected his client like a good attorney and taken the wind right out of her sails. She studied her notes and turned back to Milken. 'Just remind us, please. You were born when and where?'

'I was born in Cologne on 3rd May 1923, as I have already told the court,' Milken said. He smiled, almost playfully, whilst adding, 'and by the way, Miss Fedler, I have absolutely no problem with you being a Jew. Some of my best friends here in the city are Jewish.'

Morganna ignored the jibe. 'Are you sure it wasn't Dusseldorf, 3rd March 1923?'

'Absolutely. And to save you a lot of tiresome and repetitive questions, I'll say it again, Miss Fedler, for the court: I was born Franz Bauer in Cologne, not August Matthes, in Dusseldorf.'

'Now you joined the Hitler Youth—'

'Your honour,' Browder broke in, but Friedman stilled him with a wave.

'Is this going somewhere, Miss Fedler? Because it looks to me like you're floundering around, wasting court time with a load of superfluous and irrelevant questions, because you can't think of anything better to ask. And another thing, which I'm sure they're still teaching in law school but you may've forgotten; when a witness has answered a question, he's answered the question. So move along.'

As Morganna took her dressing down, Browder and Milken looked on, enjoying her discomfort. She cast a quick glance at the jury and her heart sank. They looked in the main disaffected and bored. It was pretty obvious they wanted her to stop wasting their time and get on with it as well - the judge was right.

If she'd lost them already, and she'd barely even started, where the hell did she go from here? She looked down at her sparse notes, desperate for some inspiration, but nothing was coming.

The only phone number Cara knew was Courtney's. Courtney had made her memorise it. She liked Courtney because Courtney was so different from everyone else; such a strange person. Courtney had promised to take her to the Dojo, whatever that was, and teach her Judo. She unzipped Rupert and pulled out Daddy's smartphone and slowly typed in Courtney's number, but then she heard the lock clicking and the door was opening. She pressed call and slipped the phone back inside Rupert, pulling the zip back.

'Where's the phone, sweetheart?' John said, coming into the room, watching her carefully. 'You were holding it earlier. Where is it?'

She cuddled Rupert and looked down.

Schmidt slapped her hard across the face, knocking her back onto the bed and sending Rupert flying through the air into the corner of the room. Cara's huge eyes registered no real shock. Daddy had sometimes hurt her far worse. She wiped a hand across her mouth, watching Schmidt. Then she slowly got up off the bed and went over to collect Rupert. At the window she looked out over the city. She noticed the window was open at the bottom, and she moved up and looked down over the small ledge at the street so far below that the people looked like ants. For a moment she thought about flying with Rupert, just jumping out and leaving the world, like Daddy had.

'I said, where's the—' Schmidt started, but was interrupted by his own phone ringing. He immediately turned away from Cara, pulling the cellphone out of his pocket and answering, voice curt.

As Schmidt spoke on the phone, his back turned, Cara pushed the window open and slowly crawled out onto the ledge, which was about six inches wide. She dragged Rupert out behind her, and then slowly began to edge along the ledge on her bottom, towards the corner of the building.

Chapter Thirty

As Pascal approached the K Tower security desk, she kept her head down but her step jaunty, bread basket held high. She flipped the plastic pass out in her other hand. It was just the older janitor guy on his own today, reading his paper.

'*Hey, Que pasa, Emilio,*' he said, barely looking up at Pascal, and not looking at all at the proffered card, waving her through to the lifts all in one motion. Then he leaned over and pressed a buzzer on his desk and lazily drawled into the mike, 'bread delivery coming up'. Then he went back to reading his paper.

As Pascal entered the lift, her phone buzzed. She hesitated for a second, but then habit kicked in and she snapped it to her ear as the lift doors closed. All she could hear initially was an indistinct, muffled voice, then as she focused, straining her ears, her eyes narrowed as she suddenly recognised it and realised where she had heard it before, way back in England, at Hannah's care Home. It was John Schmidt, saying, "Where's the phone, sweetheart?" Then, "You were holding it earlier. Where is it?"

She looked at the phone, puzzled, then heard the unmistakeable sound of a slap or punch, hand or fist against flesh, and a gasp. Then, "I said, where's the—', and then, just as abruptly, nothing, just dead sound.

Then a blip as if the phone battery might have died or the connection had been terminated. There was only one person who might have her number and would call like that.

Christoff was running back-up and answered instantly. 'Where's Cara?' she asked without preamble. He recognised the urgency in her voice and explained the mornings events of Cara crying off School, then changing her mind. He added, 'I did happen to look out when she left and saw her get into a black car, and I just thought it was parents of school friends giving her a lift. What with Emilio arriving I didn't think,' he said, but he was talking to a dead phone.

As the lift came to a halt, Pascal's mind was in turmoil, and she was scared. Scared for Cara and what could happen, knowing what Schmidt was. She tried to calm herself as she knew losing it wasn't going to help. First principles; if Schmidt had Cara, and that now seemed a racing certainty, in terms of probabilities, the most likely place he would take her would be the tower. Sooner or later, he'd have to take her there, and probably sooner, so she was in the right place, but that didn't make it any easier to bear. But where else could they look anyway? She had no location, just a muffled voice, overheard on a phone. There was no time to triangulate, so they had jackshit. In the end she had to believe they'd turn up there. All she could do was get on with the plan and watch out for the little girl.

Pascal steeled herself as the lift doors slid apart. Standing there to meet her was a Hispanic maid in black and white livery who smiled gently at her and then gestured that she should follow. As they walked Pascal had the floor plan spread out in her head, so she knew they were headed for the kitchen. The place seemed to have cameras everywhere, and she'd bet there were plenty more concealed.

The kitchen when they reached it was vast, with no windows and illuminated entirely by artificial lighting. It didn't look as if anyone ever ate there, but there was a long table in the centre of the room obviously used as a work surface to prepare meals. Pascal placed her basket down on the table, and the maid said, 'you want your usual, Emilio?

'Sure,' Pascal said. 'You join me?'

'I have my coffee,' she said.

As the maid went to the fridge Pascal looked around and saw the cup of coffee on the table. She had no set plan, essentially making it up as she went along, but she had brought along a few things that might help. She moved to the table quickly, two tabs of gamma-hydroxybutyric acid, or GHB, held between her fingers. As the maid reached into the fridge to get the orange juice, Pascal crumbled the tablets into the coffee, her actions shielded from the camera, which was behind her.

The maid brought over the orange juice, handed it to Pascal and went over to retrieve her coffee. They both drank together as Pascal continued to look around, now worrying about the maid simply collapsing if they stayed there too long. At the side of the kitchen was a walk in pantry. As Pascal sipped her orange she walked over and casually opened it and looked into the dark interior

'You seem very strange today, Emilio,' the maid said absently. Then she sat down abruptly at the table.

'You okay?' Pascal asked, going over to her. The maid looked okay, if a bit drowsy, eyes drooping, ready to close. 'Look, I better leave the bread and go,' Pascal added, lifting the bread out and placing it on the table and moving to the door. She opened it, went out, but then leaned back in and switched the light off plunging the room into complete darkness. She quickly retraced her steps to the table where the maid was now gently snoring, lifted her up and manoeuvred her into the pantry. She would be okay there for a while, as it was not airtight. She closed the pantry door and then she was moving again, quickly retracing her steps to the door, going out, reaching in again and switching on the light. She knew it wouldn't take Sherlock Holmes to work out what was going on, if anyone happened to be watching the security camera's in real-time. But it would have to do for now.

She made her way down the corridor. Then she turned sharp left and made for Angel's study.

Southern District Court

'Mr Milken,' Morganna asked, still doggedly pursuing her quarry, but with the hope of landing a punch receding fast. 'Do you accept that Hannah Palmer's family did originally own the Pendant and Brooch that are the subject matter of these proceedings?'

'Simple answer, Miss Fedler. I don't know. I've seen Hannah Cohen's testimony and depositions. I Don't believe she's lying to the extent that *she* believes that what she is telling us is the truth, but most of it of course isn't. But then again the Jews have always owned and dealt in jewellery, diamonds and gold,' he said, with another playful smile. 'But the rest of what she said was pure fantasy. And of course even if her family did own these items, who's to say they didn't sell them legitimately, as many Jews did during that awful time. The fact is, as I have already testified, I purchased the pendant and brooch perfectly legitimately in 1953.'

'Yes, so you've said, and we'll get to that in a minute,' Morganna said. She was starting to feel now, with things going so badly, that she didn't have much to lose, so worrying so much about what questions to ask was pretty pointless. She needed to just kind of hunker down and grind out the questions, try and find a rhythm and a way forward. Maybe something would come up and she'd get to pick him open. She had to believe that. From hereon in she would just trust to intuition and follow her gut. 'Tell us about the displaced persons camp at Seedorf.'

'Gladly, but I have already testified about it. What in particular would you like to know, Miss Fedler?' he asked, enjoying himself. It seemed like it was a game to Milken now, a type of sport.

Morganna steeled a concerned glance at Hannah sitting next to her, because for the last few moments she had felt the old lady becoming restless, fidgeting, and moving around in her seat. It was clear she was becoming upset and angry at Milken's evasive answers. Morganna lightly squeezed Hannah's arm as she asked her next question

'Well, for example, did you meet August Matthes there?' she said

Milken turned to the jury and raised his arms slightly in a kind of shrug. 'Who was August Matthes?' he asked of no one in particular. Then, 'was there ever such a person? Or,' he said, turning to face Hannah, voice rising, 'is he the creation of a dishonest and vengeful mind, intent on blackening my name, calling me a monster, a murderer even, and a thief?'

'*Nehmen Sie Ihre Augenklappe weg*,' Hannah said calmly, eyes riveted on Milken's face.

Morganna whipped around to look at Hannah, whose gaze remained locked on Milken, and then she looked at Milken too, and just for a second it was like a net curtain twitching and she saw something, a glimpse of what looked like naked fear. But then it was gone, replaced by an unconvincing smile. What the hell had Hannah just asked him, Morganna wondered, but she didn't have time to stop and ask. She scribbled a note and slid it across the table to Hannah as she asked her next question. 'So that's a no is it, Mr Milken? You didn't meet August Matthes at the DP camp. Could that be because you are in fact August Matthes?'

Milken laughed, but it seemed to Morganna to be a little less confident, but maybe that was just wishful thinking?

'*Nien*,' he said. Then, 'No, that's not true, and I've answered that question more than once,' he added, looking to Friedman for support.

The judge nodded, looking pensive, but then said, 'a few moments ago, Miss Fedler, your client addressed the witness in German. Now, maybe it was just an insult,' he said with a smile, 'but I can see that the jury want to know what was said. No doubt because of the quite obvious reaction your clients words seemed to engender in the witness.'

Morganna watched the jury as they nodded their heads acknowledging the truth of what the judge had said, then she looked down at the scribbled note Hannah had slid back across the desk to her. But as she read the words, Hannah was already addressing the judge herself. She said, 'I asked Mr Milken to remove his eye patch.'

'And why is that, Miss Palmer?

'Because it will identify him,' she said, calmly pointing at Milken, 'as August Matthes, the man who murdered my sister and grandfather and stole our jewellery.'

An eruption of noise rolled across the courtroom and it took a good minute before Friedman was able to restore the court to order. 'I will not tolerate these outbursts,' he said, looking sternly around the court. Then he turned to Morganna and said, 'I know its a little unorthodox, Ms Fedler, but might it be worth you having your client sworn again? Mr Milken can remain where he is, as there will be more questions for him.

'Certainly, your honour,' Morganna said, watching as Hannah was sworn again, in her chair at the plaintiff's table.

The judge turned to her. 'Remember, Mrs Palmer, I have thrown out all your testimony derived from your hypnosis sessions with Mr Wisliceny and—'

'That's just it, your honour,' Hannah said, breaking in on him. 'My memory of this aspect has nothing to do with hypnosis, it comes directly from simply seeing this witness again, after more than 70 years.'

The judge watched her for a moment, then as Browder rose from his seat full of bluster, he turned to him and said with a noticeable edge to his voice, '*sit down*, Mr Browder.'

Friedman looked back at Hannah, ruminating. What was now taking place in his courtroom was pretty much unprecedented. It was almost a casual two way conversation between two witnesses, both sworn, and in front of the jury. But Friedman, some of whose distant family had died in the Holocaust, was getting old and wasn't scared of the appeals process anymore. Maybe he wanted to see justice done for a change, rather than just seeing lip service being paid to the principle. As Browder subsided into his seat in sulky silence, Friedman said to Hannah, 'go on.'

Hannah swallowed, then began to speak slowly. 'Your honour, seeing Mr Milken again, has… How can I put it? Restored my memory, and its crystal clear.' She closed her eyes and began to speak again, eyes still closed. 'You see, when we were in the Lazarett. That's what they called the fake infirmary where they murdered the old, the sick and the very young - they were shot there and thrown into the pit just as we were. When we were there - and I can see it now, in my mind, clear as day - after he had shot grandpa, Matthes had to remove his black aviator goggles, because they had been sprayed with grandpa's blood when he shot him at close range.' Hannah swallowed again. 'You see, when he took his goggles off, I saw his eyes. And I will never forget that because they were so beautiful. Such a contrast to all that death, murder and horror all around us.'

'What do you mean, so beautiful?' Friedman asked, puzzled.

'You see they were, how can I put it. They were a different

colour. You see,' she said, looking over at Milken. 'His visible eye is grey. But I can tell you, if you were to order him to remove his eye patch, you won't see an empty socket. You will see a bright blue Aryan eye.'

This time the court really did erupt.

Chapter Thirty One

In Angel's study Pascal made straight for the bookcase at the rear of the room. That's where Chantelle had said the secret space was located. She ran her hands over the spines of the books on the shelves, feeling for anything that didn't belong there, but she couldn't concentrate, couldn't get the thought of Cara out of her head, and what Schmidt might be doing to her - it made her blood run cold.

But she had to keep going, doing something, anything to keep her mind running, occupied, praying Schmidt would bring Cara there. She checked her watch, sweat starting to stand out on her forehead. She looked back at the door to the study and then up at the camera looking down at her with its dark, black, searching eye. She turned back to the bookcase.

She needed to calm down. She started again over the book covers, taking a bit more time, feeling more carefully, and then she felt the surface of one of the books that didn't feel right. It was hard and shiny, like plastic, and then she could see a join. She worked her finger nail into it and prized the back cover out, until it opened on a hinge. Underneath there was just a small panel containing a red and a black button. She pressed the red button. Nothing happened for perhaps 5 seconds, during which Pascal worried it might be a secret alarm, but then there was a satisfyingly loud thunking sound, as if gears were engaging, and then the whole panel of the bookcase began to move sideways. She was in.

It was a large space, like four ordinary sized rooms joined together. There was art on the walls. Looked like old masters and some modern stuff, all lit with their own lights as if in a museum. But there were also large blow-up photographs, intermingled on the walls between the glorious art, but these photo's weren't artistic, they were in the most part graphic depictions of shootings. Mostly groups of naked children, shivering over freshly dug pits, but there were also pictures of multiple hangings, gallows with eight or nine bodies hanging down from the ropes; groups of laughing SS men in the background.

There were also glass cabinets scattered around the room containing gold, silver and platinum pendants, rings, brooches and other types of jewellery

Pascal took it all in, in the space of a few seconds as she moved through the room. Set up at the end of the space was a large screen with some chairs, set up like a private auditorium. Then there was a larger leather recliner chair set out on its own directly in front of the screen, positioned to provide the maximum viewing experience. On the arm of the chair was a control panel. Pascal looked back at the door; nothing so far, and there didn't appear to be any cameras inside the room. Maybe no one was about; perhaps they were all at court with Angel.

Pascal slumped into the recliner chair, pressed what looked like the power-up switch. The screen lit up with a kind of low glimmer fader effect. Pascal looked down the control panel and pressed "play".

Cara hadn't been scared when she had climbed out on the ledge, but now she could feel the fear climbing up inside her. She had reached the corner, and couldn't get around it. Then she looked down and froze, petrified; stuck. She looked to her left at the open window which now seemed a long way off.

Then she remembered the phone. Rupert was held tightly in her lap and it was easy to unzip him and pull the phone out without moving her bottom on the ledge. But when she got the phone out it was dead, just a black, blank screen.

As she looked back at the window John's head appeared, poking out, looking huge like a giants. For a second she saw screaming rage on his face, almost instantly replaced by that phoney smile, but there was also something else showing. Then she realised he was scared. His eyes were locked onto the smartphone she still held in her hand.

He smiled. 'You want Rupert to die, sweetheart? You're both going to fall, you don't crawl back in here.'

'You killed Daddy, didn't you?' she said matter of factly. She looked back at him and now he was leaning out and he had a large gun in his hand. He was looking carefully at the ledge, calculating whether he could crawl out.

Then he levelled the gun at her; at the last moment she realised he was aiming at the smartphone she was holding out face on to him, so she snatched it back as he fired. The bullet went through her sleeve, grazing along her arm and pulling her around sharply, then off the ledge. A world of skyscraper towers seemed to rear up around her head as she swung out into the void, just one small hand holding onto the edge. She desperately, with the last of her strength, scrabbled around, pulling herself back, grabbing the ledge with her free hand also, then pulling herself up so that now she was facing the wall, resting just on her elbows on the ledge, body dangling down. She turned back and watched over her shoulder as Rupert fell, tumbling head over heels downwards. The smartphone now lay just in front of her, also on the ledge.

After five minutes or so of watching clips, Pascal's eyes looked dead and empty, bled out by sorrow. She dug out her cell phone and began a text message for Morganna, but then she heard the unmistakeable sound of a gunshot, very close, and then she was sprinting towards the sound. It had to be related to Cara she thought desperately as she careened down the corridor, and then she was at the open bedroom door going into the room.

She took in the scene in an instant; Schmidt had his back to her and was leaning out of the window, head turned to the right. But as she came hurtling in, he must have heard her or sensed her approach, because he was instantly pulling back, whirling around at the same time as he levelled the gun at her.

'Whoa there. Slow down,' he said with a grin. 'Just in time for the show. Your little friend's about to take a dive. One perfect pavement

Pizza, coming up.'

Pascal froze, not understanding what he was saying, then it dawned on her and she was brushing past Schmidt, not caring about the gun. She leaned out of the window. Cara was now just clinging on, face to the wall. She was about nine feet away, head down on her elbows, which were what was holding her in place.

Behind her Pascal heard Schmidt say, 'you get her back in here with the cellphone, you get to live a bit longer.'

She ignored Schmidt and, so as not to scare Cara who hadn't seen her yet, said, calmly, 'Cara. I'm here and I'm going to help you in. Don't move.'

Cara whimpered, turning her head, the last of her strength almost gone, 'I'm sorry, Courtney. I *can't* hold on any longer. I want to go with Rupert,' she said, looking over her shoulder again.

'Yes you can hold on. Rupert will be fine,' Pascal said, and then she was moving into the window, up and out onto the ledge, standing now, heels hanging over the edge, palms gripping the wall; then she was moving along the ledge. Then Cara was looking up at her, smiling through her tears. 'I knew you'd come,' she said.

As she reached her, Pascal said, 'Hey, we're not out of this yet. Hold on.' She gravely studied the situation. It looked very bad, but she kept a calm smile on her face. 'You see how I am standing, Cara? I am going to take hold of your right wrist, and I am going to lift you up, so you are standing like me. There is plenty of room here on the ledge, especially for a small person like you.'

Cara looked up at her, unsure. Then she nodded, trusting.

'Okay,' she said.

'Good.' Pascal reached down and grasped Cara's wrist firmly, moving her fingers around it, getting purchase. Then she said, 'after three. One, two, three.' And she hoisted her up, but as she was level, Cara's foot scuffed the ledge, and she swung back, out into the void again. Pascal winced, praying, ready to go as well, but just managing to hold, right hand fingers desperately splayed flat, trying to grip on the wall, praying that Cara's momentum would swing her back in. It seemed like forever, but then Cara was swinging back, her light weight saving her. Then she was standing next to Pascal, both of them pressed against the wall, faces turned to the right.

Pascal looked down at the smartphone, and started to move down again to pick it up, but Cara beat her to it. 'Let me, Courtney. I'm smaller,' she said, suddenly full of confidence. Pascal laughed as all the tension seeped out of her, then she made the mistake of looking down at the street. She shivered. They needed to get the fuck off the ledge.

'We're going back in now, Cara. So follow me, nice and slow.'

Then they were both moving slowly, edging along the wall.

Southern District Court

Very slowly, as the noise around the courtroom abated, all eyes turned to Angel Milken. Now he was the one who looked all alone, almost as if he had taken over Hannah's erstwhile role. He sat there in the witness box, his back still ramrod straight, face rigid and defiant, the playful smile long gone. 'I have no intention of engaging in these, these theatrics,' he said indignantly

'Well, Mr Milken,' Judge Friedman said, 'the jury will be entitled to draw certain inferences from your refusal to remove your eye-patch. I'm sure you understand that, and Mr Browder will so advise you.'

As Milken sat there, Hannah spoke up loudly. 'You've heard my story,' she said, turning to the jury. 'You must judge.' Then she turned back to Milken and began to speak again, matter of factly, as if she might have been discussing a school day trip from long ago. 'We were happy in *Jodenhoek*, until you came. I had a wonderful mother and father, full of life and love; a cousin, Rudi, Grandpa Isaac, and my beautiful, beautiful, little sister, Helena. You murdered them all, and for what? A sick, racial, genocidal ideology promulgated by a lunatic, but I guess you were only following orders.'

Hannah looked down in her lap again; a single tear ran down her cheek. The court was absolutely, eerily, silent. 'Just tell me, now,' she said, wearily, 'because it doesn't really matter anymore. We are both old and our time is gone. So tell me, why? Why did my whole family have to die? Are you brave enough to face me, now, without your guns and your dogs, when you're all alone, like I was. If you believe in what you did, and you have any strength of character, then tell me. Tell us all?'

Hannah held his gaze, both of them unblinking, then she shrugged dismissively and turned away, but as she did so, he calmly raised his hand and pulled the eye-patch off.

As Pascal clambered back into the room, Schmidt was there waiting with the gun. She ignored him to reach back out and help Cara back in and down onto the floor. Then she turned back and faced him. She said, 'Now what?'

'Now we go back to where I guess you've been sniffing around. Where you had no right to be,' he said. 'Bring the brat and the phone,' he added gesturing with the gun. She took Cara's hand and began to move, Schmidt following.

As they arrived back in the hidden room Schmidt said, 'I see you've been admiring my work,' nodding up at the screen on which Pascal had left the frozen image of Helena, green silk tie pulled tight around her neck, her face caught in a rictus of pain and terror.

'Who took the video, Schmidt? Was it O'Leary? Pascal asked, standing in front of the screen so Cara wouldn't see it. She watched the squat killer with the dead eyes staring back at her. He seemed completely relaxed now; and he had put the gun away in his underarm holster, almost like an invitation to her to try something, like he wanted some kind of contest with her, and there was something else there in his look; anticipation.

'That Mick schmuck? Are you kidding me? Kiddie fiddler with a habit? No, the man who took that amazing footage for the boss was Mayberry Wilkins,' he said, moving into the room.

'That the clown who scoped me at the airport? The one been hanging around outside the apartment?' she said, sitting down in a chair to bolster Schmidt's sense of security, working on getting an angle, anyway to make him feel comfortable, that she was no threat.

Schmidt ignored her and turned to Cara. 'Give me the cell phone, honey,' he said.

She handed it to him and he plugged it into mains power and a connection to the large screen, then scrolled and pressed. 'Lets just see what your Daddy thought he was doing, before I stretched his neck.'

There was a crackling sound, then John O'Leary's face appeared smiling, filling up the entire screen. Cara started when she saw it and Schmidt laughed. Then O'Leary was holding up his wrist watch to the camera showing the time and date: it showed 3.15 am on the morning of the murder. Then the camera turns and shows the corridor outside Helena Palmers room, the room number, then John Schmidt and Mayberry Wilkins approaching and entering the room. As the door closes behind them O'Leary can be heard whispering, 'just in case.' Then the screen goes blank.

'So you killed Helena. What about John with the car in the harbour?'

Schmidt just carried on smiling, which was answer enough for Pascal. She looked around at the art and the other treasures in the room. 'So he kept all the looted stuff hidden away here, along with the atrocity porn, in his own little secret cave. How fucked up and sad is that?'

'Keep on talking, bitch, cause I'm going fuck you every which way, just like Helena, and then I'm going to cap you, along with your little friend here.'

'Are you sure about that?' Pascal said, playful.

For a second something moved in his eyes. She guessed he wasn't used to people being unafraid; a new experience for him.

She stood up abruptly. Schmidt stepped back apace, surprised at her sudden movement, his eyes watchful and wary. She knew now he wasn't going to slip up and their time had just about run out. If she was going to save Cara, she was going to have to take him head on.

She suddenly shoved Cara hard away towards the wall and flipped back towards Schmidt. She watched him a moment and then smiled. 'Come on then you chicken shit motherfucker,' she said, still smiling, goading. 'You like raping and killing submissive women, yeah? So how about you give me a try?'

As he reached into his jacket for the gun she was airborne, launching herself at him so that her body was horizontal as she hit him across the chest. He went over backwards with his hand still inside his jacket. But he was up again like a jack-in-a-box. As he brought the gun out, straightening his arm to fire, Cara, who had been watching spellbound, lifted a large priceless Ming vase off a pedestal and threw it underarm in a shot she had been practicing in netball classes, all in one smooth motion. It was a lucky shot, the vase disintegrating against the gun, knocking it from Schmidt's grasp, sending it skittering across the parquet floor. Schmidt went down into a crouch, and began to walk slowly towards Pascal, stamping each foot, almost as if he were a Sumo wrestler.

Pascal watched as he approached, knowing she'd have to try and use his mass against him, but he was formidably well built. His legs were like tree trunks, and she knew a foot sweep to try and unbalance him would be hopeless. The gun looked out of reach for both of them, unless she just turned and ran for it. He saw her eyes darting towards it, and then it was a race.

She got there first, just; it was an old style .357 magnum and she grasped it as she went into her roll, her fingers desperately feeling the contours, safety off, finger on trigger. Then she was coming out of the roll, onto her stomach, gun held two-handed, out in front of her, pointed directly at him as he came on, almost on top of her, as she pulled hard on the trigger. The sound was deafening, and the blood spurted out of him as he kept on coming, three, four, five bullets hitting him like giant punches, riddling his guts, making him almost dance on the spot as they ripped into him. Then he was toppling onto her in a crumpled bloody heap, smoke rising off him, the sound of the gunfire echoing away into an eerie crypt like silence, broken only by the sound of Cara softly moaning in the background.

Pascal must have lain there for a minute, drawing in huge lung-full's of air, unaware of the weight on her and the blood dripping onto her face. Then she slowly began to move around tentatively, and then she gave a determined heave, and Schmidt's body rolled off her. And then Cara was on her, hugging her tightly, trying to wipe Schmidt's blood from her face. Pascal dug out her cell and speed dialled detective Daly, still hugging Cara. He answered almost instantly, saying,' kinda busy now, Pascal—'

'Schmidt's dead. I'm in K Tower with all the evidence you'll need to indict Angel Milken et al with conspiracy to murder multiple times. Interested?' she said.

'How the hell..? Never mind,' he said. 'I'll be there, and don't screw up my crime scene.'

Southern District Court

The eye revealed was indeed bright blue. And even with Angel Milken's advanced age it seemed to glitter, an extraordinary counterpoint to his other familiar grey eye. The effect was eerie and, when combined with his other features, gave him a kind of ethereal, otherworldly appearance.

He had risen to his feet, a look of contempt on his face as he surveyed the watching crowd. His eyes moved to Hannah. 'I should have shot you when I shot your sister,' he said, calmly. Then he looked up at the judge, the authority in the court, and continued. 'Hitler was very clear,' he said, voice strong and full of zeal. 'You are, you Jews, and you were, an existential threat that required a radical solution, and that solution was National Socialism. You, Miss Cohen,' he said, looking back at Hannah, 'ironically, have proved Hitler right. He said we must kill *all* the Jews, especially the children, or they will come back and avenge their dead. You have done that, and I salute you for it. You are far far braver than all the others here today.'

As Milken looked around the courtroom, a kind of mad expression on his face, Hannah slid another note across the table to Morganna. It read, "tell security to check his mouth for a cyanide capsule." Morganna looked up at her, expecting a joking smile, and then realised from her face that she was serious. She beckoned a guard over and passed him the note, getting the same initial reaction, before he too got it and started to move slowly over towards the witness box, where he whispered to a couple of security guys.

They grabbed Milken from behind, one of them managing to wedge a ruler into his mouth, preventing him from biting down on anything, as Morganna rose to her feet. 'Sorry, your honour, for that, but my client apprehends that Mr Milken may have a suicide pill in his mouth,' she said.

Speechless, Friedman's incredulous look faded as the security guy held up a round blue shaped pill, covered in Milken's saliva. Then Milken was shouting in a mixture of English and German, calling for his son, Michael, to bring the wheelchair, so he could leave. As this was taking place two official looking men in suits approached the bench and one leant up and whispered to the judge who nodded a couple of times. Then Friedman was addressing Milken. 'Mr Milken, these gentlemen are from the Justice department war crimes unit, and they would like to speak with you about certain matters. And I am sure there will be many other government agencies who will wish to speak to you also.'

Epilogue

The farewell celebratory dinner was held early, 7.30 pm sharp, so Cara could attend before her bedtime. It was a little sad because we were saying goodbye to Hannah and to Cara. Hannah was flying home in the morning, and Cara was going back to her mother, just out of rehab, but apparently doing very well.

'A toast,' Hannah said, raising her glass of red wine and touching it against Cara's tall glass of cola. Around the table were sat Pascal, Detective Daly, Morganna, Christoff, Hannah and Cara. The centrepiece of our gathering sat on a little plinth in the middle of the table, the golden diamond encrusted pendant that had brought us all together and caused, it had to be said, so much mayhem and misery. But that was the past, and now it was time for the future, and so we raised our glasses to Hannah as she made the toast. '*L'chaim*. To life.'

'To life,' we all repeated, then Hannah said, 'in fact I'll go further. '*l'chaim tovim ul'shalom*; for good life, and for peace.'

We all echoed that as well, and as I leaned back, sipping wine, my mind wandered, reliving the last frenetic week.

After viewing O'Leary and Schmidt's phone footage, Stahl had confirmed the DA's office would not oppose an appeal if I were minded to make one. It was a done deal, just a paper exercise, and so judge

Gonzalez had immediately released me on bail pending that appeal. So, having just arrived back at Rikers, I left almost immediately on a cloud of euphoria. I was also told by Pascal that it wasn't just the O'Leary footage that convinced Stahl. He had also spoken with Bob Jeffries at Homeland Security about the CCTV digital file, but what was said between them was all a bit hush-hush, Pascal had said mysteriously.

Angel Milken was unlikely to ever see the light of day again, but I doubted he would endure for long; guys like that never seemed to do much penance. Suicide or an early death were likely. The hidden room in K Tower had thrown up a host of long lost treasures, including Rudi's famous Van Gogh, the Road to Tarascon, missing since the 1940's, that he'd forged and replaced and taken out of Germany all those years ago, a tribute to his courage and bravery. Efforts were being made to find the original owner, pending that it was going to the Dutch government.

And Michael Milken, anxious to avoid even more bad publicity made a big payout to Chantelle Latifah, although in the end it probably wasn't going to help him much. But so far Charles Browder was still free and would probably be able to slime his way out; typical lawyer really.

I looked over at Detective Daly, canoodling with Pascal, and now a friend since he'd come over to my side. He'd cleared up the deaths of John Palmer and O'Leary, based upon film clips found in Milken's private cinema. Seemed Schmidt had been under standing orders to film any killings for Milken's enjoyment; stupid and arrogant. Still it had allowed Daly to arrest and indict Mayberry Wilkins, Schmidt's sidekick, for murder, and Fossey had agreed to testify against him for a lesser sentence.

As I looked around the table a momentous decision I had been wrestling with for a while suddenly seemed to resolve itself. As a gap in the conversation opened up I looked over at Morganna and said, 'how does Calver & Fedler LLP, New York Attorneys at Law sound?'

'I thought you'd never ask, Calver,' she said with a twinkle in her eye. 'But maybe Fedler & Calver sounds better,' she added with an impish grin, then, 'and with our own in house investigator, Ms Courtney Pascal, and her little helper, Miss Cara O'Leary, but only in the school holidays?'

THE END

About the Author

Mark Young practiced as a lawyer and ran his own law firm before starting to write. This is his second novel after his first, Explosive Verdict, was published in 2016. He lives in Suffolk.

www.mark-young.com